A Lesson Unlearned

Sha Rhonda Dukes

Published by Sha Rhonda Dukes
in association with
In Him Alone Enterprises

For information, please contact:
In Him Alone Enterprises
P.O. Box 90151
Atlanta, Georgia 30364

First published by Dog Ear Publishing
4010 W. 86th Street, Ste H
Indianapolis, IN 46268
www.dogearpublishing.net

ISBN: 1-59858-165-1

This book is printed on acid-free paper.
This book is a work of Fiction. Places, events, and situations in this book are purely Fictional and any resemblance to actual persons, living or dead, is coincidental.

Printed in the United States of America

Dedication

I dedicate this book to mom and dad, Willie and Jannie Dukes. I thank God for blessing me with the both of you.

Dad, I thank God for allowing you to share this experience with me. Although mom wasn't able to see the finished product, I'm sure she's looking down from heaven and is as proud of me up there as she would've been if she were still here in the flesh. I thank both of you for the lessons I have learned from you. Thank you for instilling the word of God in me...now look at your harvest.

Acknowledgements

Sincere thanks to Tyler Perry, who is the inspiration of my career in writing and performing. May God bless you to continue entertaining the world.

Mae, Larry and Magnus, thanks for all the support and encouraging words you've given me when times got hard and I wanted to give up.

Prologue

*D*ifferent ranges of sirens are blaring in the air. Red, white and blue lights are flashing all around her. The streets are busy. Buses, trains and taxis are colliding. Accidents are everywhere.

A charter bus slams into the rear of her car. She crawls out of the burning car, hearing a constant baritone voice calling her, "Ronnie, don't leave me! I love you!"

Skyscraper buildings began to crumble and fall to the ground.

Ronnie starts to run. The faster she runs, safety appears to be moving farther away. Her feet start sticking to the pavement as the buildings collapse onto the streets and on the sidewalks behind her. She is buried alive by the rubble.

Breathing very intensely, Ronnie awakes in a cold sweat. She looks around to see if she can find the owner of the baritone voice, but sees no one. As soon as she attempts to lie back down, the alarm clock goes off and nearly scares her to death.

It's time to get up and hit the road. Ronnie insists on lying there for a brief moment to catch her breath. She snaps back to reality and scurries to get her robe and slippers on so that she can beat her sister to the bathroom.

Ronnie Williams, a twenty three year old with lots of aspirations about life, is about to face a major transition when she awakes in the morning. She and her family of three; two sisters, Renae and Monica; and her mother, Veronica Williams, are moving from a small rural area in New Jersey to the hectic and busy suburbs of Atlanta, Georgia. As Ronnie sleeps restlessly, she begins to have a reoccurring nightmare of how she perceives Atlanta.

Renae, better known as Nae, stands to her feet quite discombobulated. Her eyes remain partially closed as she begins stumbling around in her room trying to gather her under garments. When she reaches for her robe at the foot of her air mattress, a small envelope falls from her robe onto the floor. She picks up the envelope and opens it. A small note inside says:

"Dear Renae, It took me so long to find you. Now that I have you, it seems impossible to keep you. I will find you again, if it's the last thing I do." Nae sits down on the air mattress for a moment. She thinks, "It sounds like Darryl is threatening me."

When Monica's clock goes off, she reluctantly gets up and into the shower. While showering, she begins to think of how different Atlanta was going to be, compared to New Jersey. "I only have one more year of school left. Hopefully I can get through it without being sidetracked by all of those fine, educated men Georgia has to offer."

Monica, also known as Monie, was pretty popular in college, and befriended many of her peers who were already in sororities and fraternities. She wanted to pledge to become a Greek Soror, however, decided to put that thought on the back-burner until she was settled in Atlanta. Her fellow classmates had thrown her a going away party the previous night. Although she was extremely exhausted, Monie knew her mother would become a very furious 'drill sergeant' if she didn't move abruptly.

While Monie was attending one party, her ex-boyfriend, Damon, and his family were across town throwing her another party. Of course, she failed to show at Damon's party.

All throughout the night Monie's cell phone silently rang and vibrated all over the floor with invitations to attend her friends' gatherings and parties.

Veronica hollered up the stairs, "Come on ladies, it's time to hit the road!"

Nae leaned over the banister and hollered back, "We're coming, as soon as Ronnie comes out of the bathroom".

By the time the girls came downstairs Veronica was indeed furious. They had fallen an hour behind before they had even gotten started. The remainders of their small belongings, that weren't packed away in the U-Haul, were grabbed and stuffed in the car.

Monie and Veronica loaded their things in the U-Haul while Ronnie and Nae loaded up in their mother's car. The family headed to McDonald's for breakfast, before hitting the interstate.

After ordering their food and finding a nice cozy booth in the corner, Veronica thought a pleasant family discussion would be appropriate at this time. This may have been just what the family needed to get their day started off on the right track. At least it would help from this point forward.

"So girls, how do you think you're going to like Atlanta?"

"Mom, it's too early to think about Atlanta right now," replied Ronnie who was very much disoriented.

She fumbled trying to open her steamy, mouth-watering sausage and cheese biscuit. The aroma was making her even hungrier. With Ronnie being disoriented, hungry, and unwilling to participate in Veronica's initiated family discussion so early in the morning, this was beginning to be an ensemble of bad combinations.

"Did anyone leave an envelope in my room last night?" Nae asked.

She was still puzzled as to how Darryl's note got in her room. She figured he couldn't have snuck in through the window. He would have fallen and broke his neck. He dare not have a key. Nae didn't think she was careless enough to have left her keys unattended long enough for him to get it and duplicate it. Although he was extremely close to the family, things could've gotten really ugly between Darryl and Veronica if that were the case.

Darryl was the kind of guy who could manipulate anyone—especially women, and have them at his mercy. He was very close to the Williams family. It was not unusual for him to be in the kitchen cooking dinner while everyone else was doing chores, running errands, sleeping, or just watching TV. He considered himself to be the son that Veronica never had. He didn't necessarily have to get Nae's keys to make a copy. He was confident and brave enough to get Veronica's key to accomplish his deviant acts.

Monie quickly looked up at Nae as if she was the guilty one. "I saw him come down the stairs last night. I thought you might've told him to see his way out".

Nae squinted at Monie, "Monie, what did he say?"

"He said have a good trip and I'll see you soon."

"Why didn't you question him about what he was doing?"

Monie shrugged her shoulders, rolled her eyes at her sister and checked her phone to see who was calling her that early in the morning, all while trying to get another mouth full of pancakes before answering it.

"Hello."

On the other end was Monie's ex boyfriend Damon.

Nae was still asking Monie about the previous night. Monie waved her hand at Nae and tuned her out to resume her phone conversation.

" Monie, What happened to you last night? Are you still in Jersey?" Damon asked in distress.

"Yeah. As a matter of fact, my family and I are having breakfast at McDonalds. We're going to be leaving shortly."

"Can I see you before you leave? I can be there in twenty minutes."

"We'll be gone in twenty minutes. You know how Veronica can be. I'll give you a call when we touch down in Atlanta."

"Monie, I don't want you to leave without me seeing you," Damon replied, sounding extremely disappointed and desperate.

"Damon, I just can't right now. I'll come back to see you the first chance I get, okay."

Monie hung up the phone with a guilty conscious and tears in her eyes. She regrouped quickly, but nothing could get past Veronica.

"What's wrong sweetie?" Veronica asked.

"Oh nothing. I missed a party last night and a few friends were just a little worried because I didn't show."

Nae insisted on getting as much information out of Monie as she could.

"Monie, did he walk out of the door after you saw him?"

"Nae, I don't know. I was running around getting ready for a party."

"You just said that you missed the party."

Nae tried to catch Monie in a lie. Monie angrily stuck her fork down in the top of her pancakes and pointed at Nae. "You need to mind your own damn business."

Monie was ready to drop the conversation and finish her breakfast. Nae insisted on getting the last word. "You should've at least stopped him and asked him what he was doing!"

"Where were you?" Monie asked.

"I had to run to the store. Next time try not to be so friendly," Nae added.

"Next time, stay home and monitor your own damn company!"

Ronnie was fed up with the back and forth bickering between her sisters.

"Alright, already…its spilt milk at this point so would both of ya'll shut up and eat!" Ronnie exclaimed.

Veronica recognized the bickering as a part of the girls' usual morning behavior and ignored it. She still attempted to make an honest effort to figure out how Darryl gained access to her house—full of women, and no one seemed to know exactly how he got in. "Just as he got in, someone else could've gotten in as well," Veronica said under her breath. She at least wanted to know how he got in, and everything would have been all right. Silence overtook the family as they finished their meals.

Just as Nae stood up to go empty her trash she saw Darryl pull up at the drive through window. Nae jumped behind the wall by the exit doors and pulled Ronnie behind the wall with her. Ronnie was wondering what was going on.

"What is with you? Why are you so jumpy?"

Nae peaked around the corner and pointed out Darryl's car to Ronnie. Veronica and Monie were busy emptying their trash into the garbage cans. Behind their mother's back, Nae whispered to Ronnie, "I'll tell you in the car."

Everyone boarded their designated vehicles and proceeded to Interstate 95 South. Nae finally explained to Ronnie that Darryl had proposed to her a month ago and tried to get her pregnant, thinking that a baby would make her stay with him. He didn't know that she had started on birth control. She dodged him, never giving him an answer, since she knew that she'd be moving. She figured she'd be able to leave peacefully, not knowing that Darryl had been stalking her.

Ronnie exclaimed, "Oh, so that's why he's been questioning Monie and me every time we saw him".

Nae continued driving in silence trying to put one and one together, growing frustrated at the fact that neither of her sisters told her about the frequent conversations they'd had with Darryl.

Nae was puzzled, "I'm still wondering how Darryl got in the house last night."

Nae had broken things off with Darryl at least twelve times in the past year. Every time she found a way out, he'd make twenty excuses justifying his immortal stupidity. Darryl was deeply in love with Nae, but because of his immortal behavior, Nae lost interest in the relationship a long time ago. For whatever reasons, she found herself just going through the motions.

Darryl burdened Nae more than he uplifted her. She'd be better off alone. The problem was, this left Darryl hopeless and lonely.

"Nae, let it go, you don't have to worry about him anymore," Ronnie suggested. Veronica, as she always did, drilled Monie about which school she was planning to attend in Atlanta. Monie was always pretty much on top of things.

She had already submitted her transcripts to Spelman College. During her follow up call, she gladly learned that everything had gone smoothly. She was starting school three weeks after the move to Atlanta was complete. All Monie could think about at the time was pledging with her favorite sorority and the fine, educated men she'd been hearing so much about. Monie wanted nothing more than to be a Delta so she could perform at step shows and have a close relationship with the Q-dogs.

Veronica was so busy making sure things were situated before they moved. She had totally forgotten about one of her closest girlfriends, who had moved to Atlanta about five years ago, due to the same working situations.

"Mom, does your friend still live in Atlanta?" Monie asked.

"Which friend might that be, sweetie?"

"The lady who used to work with you. She had two 'fine' sons around the same ages as Ronnie and me."

"Oh yeah. Juanita Robinson is her name. I need to contact her. I hadn't talked to her in about six months. As a matter of fact, we'll be working together again in Atlanta.

"Are her sons in college down there?" Monie asked with excitement and a conception of a plan.

Monie's phone rang again. She discreetly turned the phone on a lower ring tone while she and her mother finished their conversation. Monie remembered that Ms. Robinson had a couple of handsome sons around her age. Her interest was already sparked in hopes that her mother would have some information about the young Robinson guys.

Veronica's train of thought was interrupted by her daughter's ringing phone again. Her curiosity began to rise.

"Sweetie you must be really popular in school because your phone hasn't stopped ringing all morning—and it's only six o'clock," Veronica commented.

"It's just a couple of my friends who wanted to see me before I left."

"Guys or girls?" Veronica asked, pleased to see her little girl was transforming into a lady right before her eyes.

Monie started to blush "Guys," she whispered.

"Are you screwin' 'em or owe 'em money or somethin'? What's the deal?" Veronica asked jokingly, enjoying her and her baby's first official conversation about guys.

"No! We're just friends. Now back to what you were saying."

Monie's heart was nearly pumping cool-aid to hear her mother speak like that. She and her mother never talked about guys or sex before—especially being so blunt like such. Monie felt a little uncomfortable and embarrassed at first, but she eventually felt good to know that she could talk freely and joke with her mother about guys and sex if she wanted to or needed to.

Veronica explained that Jason, Ms. Robinson's son around Monie's age, was in the music industry. He had written a few songs for Usher and Genuine, and collaborated on a few projects with Babyface.

Ms. Robinson's other son Josh, who was Ronnie's age, went into the Air Force. However, he was currently stationed in Atlanta. He's been all around the world with the military. Veronica stated that he was an aircraft engineer and didn't have much of a social life.

The more Veronica described Josh to Monie, the more she started having blissful thoughts about Josh and Ronnie sharing mutual interests. Ronnie was a good girl, but often fell for the 'bad boy' kind of guys. Veronica figured this could be a necessary transformation for her daughter as well as a positive influence on her life.

Veronica suggested, "Maybe you all should hook up and go out or something. I'm sure one of those boys could find a friend for Nae".

Unless the young Robinson men were in school, or already had an established career making plenty of money, Monie was not interested in them like that. She was thinking more along the lines of a few free meals or a couple of dollars to buy a few schoolbooks here or there. Veronica was glad to see that at least one of her girls was very disciplined, focused, and wouldn't settle for less than the best. Veronica just hoped she'd stay that way and not be influenced by her sisters or peers once they got to the big city.

Chapter 1

*R*ock, a bald but well groomed, solid, chocolate, muscular, two hundred forty-five pound, six foot five inch frame, kingpin, made all the women in the club do a double-take and practically drool at the mouth. Most of the women had already bumped pelvises with Rock, so they knew what he was capable of. Rock could barely remember half their names. Four and five women at a time would approach him.

"Hey Rock, why haven't you called me back"?

"Oh hey beautiful. I haven't forgotten about you. I'll get back with you," was Rock's usual reply.

Rock was quite a lady's man. He knew all the right places to lick and nibble on to make any woman drop her panties at the drop of a dime. He knew the right words to say, how to say them, and when to say them.

He was just tired of changing women as much as he changed his underwear. Having all the women was good for a while, but he had just gotten to a point where he wanted one woman to settle down with. He had lots of love to give, but found it difficult finding the right one to give it to.

He had been playing this game for so long, and with so many different women, that he had forgotten how to be faithful to just one.

It would definitely take a while for the right woman, who was a strong sista, to put the funk down. One who would let him know that it was going to be the right way or no way.

Rock parked his truck and sat in the parking lot of his brother's club. He reminisced about how his father lived his life, before being killed in a drug operation that went bad. He remembered answering his mother's phone so many times while she was away on business, only to hear the voices of other women on the other end. He loved his father dearly and often referred to him as his hero. However, he hated how his father cheated on his mother with so many different women. He found himself in a state of depression because his life was now a replica of his father's.

Rock entered the club giving dap to his right hand man and closest cousin, Trey and Mike. He greeted his brother, Rome, and then his boys, Tony and Rick. Rick took the last sip of his Heineken and hesitated before he initiated a conversation with Rock. He studied Rock for a moment, knowing that something was unusually wrong.

"What's up Rock?" Trey said, greeting Rock.

Rock sat down at the end of the bar and beckoned for the bartender to bring over his favorite drink, Tanguray.

Rock wondered why Trey was so apprehensive to talk to him, "What's goin' on?" Rock asked. Trey gathered his thoughts and explained that Rock's ex, Ashanti (Tee), had been looking for him all day. Rock automatically knew that Tee wanted money for her child.

Rock had been there for Tee ever since she got pregnant and had the child. Because Rock was so powerful, she wanted everyone to think that her son, Shaun, was his baby. Rock knew deep down inside that he hadn't fathered this child.

Rock quickly scanned the club looking for her.

"Trey, is she in here?" Rock asked.

"No. The last time I spoke with her she said she'd be here around ten."

It was already nine thirty. Rock knew then that he needed to leave before she came with a whole lot of unnecessary drama. Rock told Trey and Tony that if they saw her, to tell her that they hadn't seen him.

As Rock exited the club he ran into Tee in the parking lot.

"Why are you leaving so soon Rock?" she asked

Rock tried to make up a quick lie and brush her off. Tee used to sell drugs for Rock when he was still considered a small timer, so she knew the game. She knew that if something was going down, Rock could easily send one of his boys to handle it.

Tee started to feel neglected by Rock.

"Rock, why are you always trying to avoid me?" she asked.

Rock started to walk faster toward his new Cadillac truck. Tee followed him to the truck and exclaimed emotionally, "Rock, stop ignoring me!"

Rock turned around and told her, "I'm not ignoring you, but I have some important stuff to do".

As Rock got in the truck, Tee jumped in on the passenger side, crying.

"Shaun and I aren't important enough for you to listen to what I have to say?"

"Tee. You and Shaun aren't my responsibility," Rock replied heartlessly. That hit Tee like a ton of bricks. She got out of the truck and yelled, "Is that the way you feel about us?"

Rock felt bad because he knew that even though he wasn't Shaun's biological father, he was the only father figure Shaun ever had. Rock got out of the truck, walked over to Tee and hugged her trying to comfort her. She then tried to kiss him and lick on his neck, thinking that she maybe able to get him in bed by the end of the night.

Rock gently pushed her away by the waist, enough to back her off of him, and looked into her eyes. Tee wondered what Rock was thinking at this point.

"What's wrong Rock?"

Rock didn't know what to say. He just knew that he owed her for all the times she had taken the wrap for him so he wouldn't have to go to jail. He remembered the times she slept with other men for months at a time for him to find out their secrets and how they ran their operations. He didn't know how to repay her for the calls that she answered at two and three in the morning for her to come over, after he and his boys finished an operation, and count five and six hundred thousand dollars at a time.

Rock told Tee, "We had our time. Unfortunately, it didn't work out. I'll still be there for when you need me, but I'm not interested in you like that anymore". Tee felt rejected and betrayed, which would eventually lead her to bitterness.

"Rock, we have history and we have a child together," Tee stated.

Rock agreed they had history, but not a child.

"No! You have a child, and I'd appreciate it if you'd stop telling everyone that we have a child.

Rock pulled out three, one hundred dollar bills to give Tee. She looked at the money and then looked at Rock, "Are you trying to disown your child all of a sudden?"

Rock had an evil expression on his face.

"Tee, I don't know what you're trying to pull, but you know as well as I do that Shaun is not mine. We hadn't had sex in four months when you came to me, three months pregnant, saying you were having my baby. Now, you do the math."

Rock threw the money at Tee, jumped in his truck and sped off. Just as he sped off Trey, Tony and Rick came outside and saw Tee picking up the money in the parking lot. Tee got in her car and sat there for a minute trying to stop crying and regain her composure. The guys walked over to Tee's car to see what happened.

With hopes of getting some compassion, Tee told them that Rock said he wanted nothing more to do with her or Shaun. The guys all looked at each other and then at her, knowing that she was lying. Rock truly cared about Shaun, and to say something like that just wasn't his style. They still insisted on giving her some sympathetic words to help her get through her moment.

Trey told her, "We'll talk to Rock to see what's going on with him, but in the mean time, keep your head up and give lil' man some dap for me".

Tee started her car and slowly drove off, looking in her rear mirrors to see which direction the guys were heading. They knew she was watching them. They walked to Trey's Chevy SUV, got in and headed to Rick's house. They knew that Tee would have followed them straight to Rock's house to stir up more drama.

On the way to Rick's house, the guys spotted a carload of beautiful young women at a traffic light. The young, flirtatious female driver waved and smiled at Trey. It made him feel quite extraordinary, so he decided to follow her lead.

She pointed and pulled into a nearby sports bar dance hall, where she and her girlfriends were heading. Since the guys didn't have any other plans, they decided to spend the remainder of the evening with these lovely ladies.

The three guys and five girls all got out of their vehicles in the parking lot of the bar, which appeared to be nearly neglected, and introduced themselves.

Tony got out of the truck walking up between two of the girls, putting each of his arms around their necks.

"I'm Tony." He turned to the girl to the right of him and said, "Let me guess, you're beautiful" then turned to the girl to the left of him and said, "And you're sexy, right?"

That instantly broke the ice for the whole group. They tagged Tony as being the funny man. The guys and their newly found friends headed towards the entrance of the building. They were faced with about ten stairs before actually getting to the door.

One of the girls said, "I'm Vonnie, and this is Mia."

Mia was a bit quiet, but Vonnie took up the slack. There was one Hawaiian descendant girl named Poulania, who was automatically turned on by Trey's big beautiful, innocent looking hazel eyes. The other two girls, Rhonda and Leah fell back and were accompanied by Rick.

The assembly of eight walked along side the dance floor, where everyone scuffled trying to keep up with Missy Elliot's fast tempo dance track. The bass was banging through the speakers. Rick danced as they continued out onto the bar's deck to find a table large enough to accommodate their groups' size. He was feelin' that spot. He hadn't been there in months, but his goal for the night was to impress the ladies. The girls were astounded when Rick made it known to the waitress that the first two rounds of drinks were on him.

Meanwhile, by the time Rock made it home, he had received twenty-eight calls on his cell phone, which he had been ignoring as he drove. He thought that if he refused to answer the phone, maybe it would soon stop ringing. He figured it was Tee calling to apologize for the scene she'd just made at the club. He then went in the house to relax and wind down from all of the excitement that she had just caused.

Rock started to retrieve all of his intentionally missed messages and found that there were many more on his home telephone. Tee called at least five of the twenty eight times, to indeed ask for forgiveness and another chance to make things right with him, at least for Shaun's sake she explained.

Another call came from another one of his dramatic ex's, Shonte. She was a straight up drama queen.

"Hey Rock, it's me, Shonte. Just sitting home alone bored, thinking about you and all the things we used to do on Friday nights. If you're out and want to stop by, you're more than welcome. Hope to see you in a few."

He erased the message and moved on to the next one.

"This is Trina. Just wanted to know if you wanted to hang out if you weren't too busy tonight. Call me later, love you."

One of Rock's Latino lovers called. "Hey Pa'pe, Heidi. I'm headed back home to Cali for a few days. I could use some company. Just wanted to know if you would join me if your schedule permits it. I've been celibate for a while and I'm tired of waiting for you to get back with me. Call me ASAP. Adios"

Rock thought he must have been extremely intoxicated to deal with some of the nymphomaniacs and drama queens he'd been dealing with. He laughed at some of the messages. Others, he couldn't withstand hearing the hurt and rejection in their voices that he'd caused by having sexual relations with them and subsequently disappearing.

He had made it clear to all of them that he was dealing with at least five other women at a time.

He couldn't understand why they would still have a desire to be involved with him, even after being told that there were other females who he was romantically involved with.

Before Rock finished checking the messages on his cell phone, another call was coming through on his home telephone. He looked at the caller ID and realized someone was at his front gate. He reluctantly answered it knowing it could have been one of the countless drama queens who had just left so many annoying messages.

"Hello?" Rock answered.

"Hi, Rock?"

"Yeah"

"It's Shonte. I was just driving by and decided to stop. Is it alright if I come up for just a minute?"

"For what? I'm about to walk out the door."

Rock knew he had to be creative with his thoughts and answers, dealing with Shonte. He tried to think of a smooth, yet believable way to get out of being with her.

Shonte replied, "That's okay. Since you're headed out, I'll just wait for you here at the gate".

Rock slammed the phone down on its' base with frustration. He stood in the middle of the floor briefly, racking his brain as to what he was going to say to her once he was face to face with her.

Rock picked up the remote control to his sixty-two inch television and turned it on to one of the premium channels. He grabbed a cold Heineken out of the refrigerator, kicked off his shoes, and laid back in his black, soft leather, lazy boy recliner.

Rock decided he would have a relaxing and peaceful night alone. He was becoming fed up with the club scene, hanging out with the fella's, hosting cookouts, and being with women that he really didn't desire anymore.

Twenty minutes later, Shonte called back from the speaker box at the front gate. By that time she was horny and quite upset that Rock would totally disregard her presence for that length of time. She figured if she could convince Rick or Trey to contact him for her, they could persuade him to leave the house and she could trap him at the gate.

Shonte eagerly called Rick's cell phone hoping he'd be able to lure Rock to the gate. When Rick finally answered the phone after six rings, Shonte heard nothing but laughter and overbearingly loud club music in Rick's background.

"Hello Rick...Rick...can you hear me? Rick where are you! I can hardly hear you!" Shonte shouted.

Rick knew it was Shonte from the caller ID of his bright, blue lit, flip phone. He, Trey, Tony and their new female friends were all on the dance floor trying to dance without falling down or stepping on each other. Rick made gestures to Trey and Tony to ignore their phones if Shonte attempted to call them. She angrily ended the worthless call.

She then attempted to call Trey's cell phone. She knew that if Rick were at a club Trey would be there as well. She hoped Trey would have enough common sense to go to the restroom long enough to talk on the phone if he answered. Trey's phone went directly into his voice-mail. She tried extremely hard to remember Tony's number, but always had a problem with transposing his phone number.

Shonte was furious and became more desperate to get to Rock. She contemplated jumping the fence to gain access to his home. She realized the fence was too high and the motion detectors would sound the alarm.

She thought about staging an accident, but if he ever found out that it was a fake, he'd probably beat her into a coma. She finally accepted the fact that all of her brilliant ideas were useless. She then gave up all hope of being with Rock on that particular night, and left his estate feeling very lonely and rejected, worse than she felt before she'd arrived there.

The time was approaching 3 a.m. and everyone was leaving the bar. Rick's intentions were to eventually have sexual relations with at least two of the girls and nothing more.

Tony didn't care one way or the other if he ever saw the girls again or not. He just had fun with them that night.

Trey liked his new found friends, but he really wasn't interested enough to date any of them. If they were to cross paths again to have casual sex, that would've been fine by him, but he didn't feel like this was something to pursue. They all exchanged phone numbers and departed in their own separate ways.

Chapter 2

*F*or at least a week now Ronnie, Nae and Monie were job hunting. Monie only wanted something part-time to accommodate her school schedule. The girls went out almost daily looking for work.

Late evenings they would go to the malls, downtown Atlanta, and shopping strips searching for recreation. One night Ronnie and Nae were out joy riding. They drove past a club. There were a lot of luxurious and expensive cars in the parking lot, so they decided to stop and see what the atmosphere was like. They'd never seen such automotive beauty before. It was as if they were touring a car dealership.

On that particular night, a fight broke out at Club Passion. The bouncers tried to stop the fight, but matters seemed to get worse, and eventually things got out of hand. One of the dancers was giving a lap dance to one of her regulars, when her fiancé came out of nowhere with a small handgun.

Ronnie and Nae hesitantly walked towards the club, but were approached by Mike.

"Good evening ladies. You both are looking very lovely tonight." Ronnie and Nae glanced at each other, looked at their attire, and knew instantaneously that Mike was full of crap. The girls had on stretchy denim Capri's, iridescent fitted v-neck shirts and high-heel sandals. It was nothing fancy. Very nonchalantly, Ronnie said, "Thanks".

Facetiously Mike asked, "Are you ladies here for a good time or a job?"

Nae asked, "A job? What kind of jobs do you have here to offer?" Nae knew right then that he was either talking about waiting tables, strip dancing or prostitution.

Mike replied, "You have a great physique, I was just wondering if you be interested in dancing?"

Nae paused for a moment, "I'll think about it".

"Yes, please do that and get back with me. My name is Mike. Here's my card. If you'll please excuse me, I have a mess to attend to inside. You ladies have a good night." It was apparent Ronnie was more 'excited' than Nae was.

"Pervert," Nae muttered, as she twisted her face and frowned as Mike walked away. She then turned her attention back to Ronnie.

"Girl, look at all of these Lexus', Beemers, Benzes and Hummers. It looks like you may come out of here with some pretty big tips every night" Ronnie commented. She nodded as her facial expressions concurred, appearing to have big plans for her sister. Besides the eerie feeling she had already gotten from Mike's lame lines, Nae started getting butterflies in the pit of her stomach.

Things were getting awfully bad inside. The girls heard the entire tumult from several feet away before they'd opened the door. One of the bouncers had to come outside and shoot his handgun twice in the air just to get everyone's attention. He then ran back inside to ensure everyone's safety while expeditiously exiting the club.

The girls saw everyone running toward, and decided it would probably be best to have a few drinks at one of the sport's bars they'd passed on the way there, and call it a night. As the girls were getting back in the car, Nae spotted Rock staring at Ronnie.

Nae continued looking in the rear view mirror as she drove away. Rock was still staring at the car hoping to see the reverse lights pop on.

Nae told Ronnie in a jealous tone, "I see you have an admirer all ready."

Ronnie was very nervous, and felt as if a drink was just what she needed—especially after hearing gunshots about five feet away from her. She paid no attention to what Nae was saying.

"Ronnie, did you see that guy staring at you?"

Ronnie gave Nae a blank stare, and asked "What guy?"

"The biggest guy out there. The guy that got in that brand new Escalade!"

Ronnie wished she'd seen the guy, but after all, she was frantic. "Was he fine?" Her curiosity wouldn't let that inquiry go unanswered.

Nae laughed and looked at Ronnie "Hell yeah!"

While Nae was joking with Ronnie, she thought long and hard about taking the dancing job. She also thought about what her mother would think if she took the job. Veronica would probably damn near treat her like the prodigal child.

Throughout the night Nae pondered about whether or not she would accept Mike's proposition. She needed the money, in the worst way, to get another car. After all, there were a lot of luxurious rides in the parking lot at the club. She figured she could be a valuable asset to the club and maybe one-day couple up with one of those big ballers that she'd seen there.

Ronnie went on mumbling about how they should go back to the club during the weekend to see if she could find this big handsome guy that Nae talked her to death about.

"Do you think I should take the job?" asked Nae.

Ronnie had a puzzled look on her face because Nae's response had absolutely nothing to do with what she was talking about.

The girls finally arrived at the sport's bar. Ronnie asked the waiter to bring her a Pena Colada. Nae was indecisive, as usual.

"Could you bring me a Strawberry Daiquiri please?" Nae asked.

Ronnie noticed her sister was disturbed by something. She just couldn't put her finger on it. "What is wrong with you Nae? You've been acting strange off and on since the situation with Darryl."

Nae was hesitant to tell her sister about her decision to take the job, "Ronnie, I'm going to dance. Just until I get enough money to buy a car." Ronnie held up her glass and proposed a toast. "To your new job", the girls tapped their glasses together.

Monie spent most of her time home on the phone with Damon and her best girlfriend Chenille. Damon wanted to continue the unfinished conversation they'd started on the phone when Monie was at McDonalds. He was more interested in when Monie was going to make it back to Jersey. Damon heard the commotion that was going on between Monie and Nae at McDonalds. This made him very curious.

Chenille was having trouble with men and always looked to Monie for advice. A few months ago Monie had just taken Chenille to have an abortion in Philly. A week ago, Chenille found that the same guy that she was pregnant by had given her herpes. To make matters worse, he had another baby on the way by someone else.

Monie's heart went out to her friend for being so stupid and irresponsible. She had told Chenille to leave the guy alone when she first started dealing with him. Chenille wanted to relocate to Atlanta to be closer to Monie. Monie wasn't quite cool with that idea because she disliked the impractical lifestyle her friend was living.

However, she promised Chenille that she would talk to her mother and get back with her. She also thought that this may be a chance for Chenille to escape her old and tainted lifestyle and start fresh.

Monie knew what the conversation would be like with her mother about having Chenille come to stay with them. Veronica really wasn't thrilled about Nae and Ronnie living with her, but since they are her daughters, she had no choice but to allow them to stay. Monie understood that her mothers' perception on life was that everyone needs their own space once they've reached a certain age. Ronnie and Nae were at that age, and if they weren't in school, Veronica would be pushing for them to get a place of their own.

Monie thought long and hard about the approach she would use to talk to Veronica about Chenille coming to stay with them. She practiced her conversation over and over until she came up with something feasible. After a couple of hours, Monie finally built up the nerve to go downstairs and talk to her mother.

Monie went into the kitchen where her mother was. Veronica had just begun cooking.

"You need some help?" Monie asked.

"No sweetie. I think I can manage. What's on your mind?"

"Nothing…I just talked to Damon and Chenille."

Veronica knew something was bothering Monie, but she didn't want to pressure her into talking. She figured she may have been homesick. Veronica was silent until Monie started to open up to her. At that particular moment their relationship was taken to a level it had never gone before.

"Mom, how would you feel about me getting an apartment?"

"By yourself?"

"Well, Chenille was talking about moving down here, and we might get an apartment together."

"You and Chenille? That's a joke, right?" Veronica asked in amusement.

"What's wrong with that?"

"Sweetie, Chenille is not at all responsible and she seems a bit promiscuous."

Monie wondered how her mother knew this type of information about Chenille.

"What makes you say that?"

Veronica gave Monie a piercing stare as if she was able see right through her soul and find the untold truth about Chenille, bottled up inside of her. Monie began to wonder if her mother had telepathic intuition.

"What gives you the impression that she's like that? She doesn't dress like a prostitute or anything. You've never seen her with anyone."

Veronica explained that she went to school with Chenille's parents, and all of the doctors and lawyers, who all lived in the small town in which they had just moved from.

"Everybody knows everybody and everything that goes on there." Veronica explained to her naïve daughter.

"What do you know about Chenille that makes you so uneasy about us getting a place together?" Monie asked.

"Well, I know that she contracted herpes from the boy who she just had an abortion by. She's now pregnant by someone else."

Monie was stunned that her mother knew this kind of information about her friend. Her mother had just given her some news that she didn't even know. She didn't know about the pregnancy by someone else. Monie was turned off by the news and suddenly didn't want to even be affiliated with Chenille.

Monie still didn't know that Chenille's mother was the custodian and Damon's father was the supervisor at General Motors. Veronica talked to Chenille's mother on a daily basis while working at the New Jersey plant. Monie was hurt to find out that her best friend would withhold such information from her.

Monie was amazed by her mothers' knowledge of her friend. She slowly went upstairs to call Chenille to let her know her mothers final answer. Monie dialed the numbers in disbelief of what Veronica had just told her.

"Chenille. It's Monie. My mom is not havin' it."

"Did she say why?"

"No. I'll just give you a call later," Monie said in a depressed tone.

"Don't sound so depressed because I can't come right now. I'll be there soon."

"Oh that's not it by far," Monie said with an attitude.

"What's wrong Monie. You don't sound like yourself?"

"Nothing. I'll call you later!" Monie exclaimed.

"Monie please talk to me. You're all I've got" Chenille begged.

Monie blared out, "It's obvious I'm not all you've got. You've got another baby on the way. How could you not tell me something like that?"

"Monie, I was trying to find a way to tell you. I was scared of what you may have said or thought of me."

Chenille started crying. She thought Damon may have told her about the pregnancy, but she wasn't sure. She questioned Monie about how she acquired the information. Monie did everything to avoid answering her. She didn't want Chenille to know that her mother knew how much of a whore she was.

"Chenille, are you going to keep this one?"

Monie asked in concern for her friend's health.

"Monie, I can't afford to have a baby," Chenille replied in fear of what Monie might say.

"Chenille, this is your fourth one. You're gonna kill your dumb self."

Chenille was still crying, not only because she was dealing with an unwanted pregnancy, but she was also losing her best friend. Chenille finally got herself under control enough to resume their conversation.

"Monie, I'm not ready to have a baby yet."

To hear the nonsense that her friend was carelessly saying made Monie snap.

"Well stop screwin' around!" Monie shouted and slammed the phone down on its base.

Monie was upset that her friend was so stupid and selfish. She didn't even bother to ask who the father was. She felt like he probably was a loser that she met at a club or at the gas station. She figured her mother probably knew, but at that time, she was so frustrated until she didn't even care who he was.

Veronica heard all of the anger and frustration her daughter was releasing in her room. She knew that she was deeply hurt, especially if she found out that Chenille was pregnant by Damon. Monie still had strong feelings for Damon, and it would destroy her to find out that her best friend was screwing her ex, whom she was still very close with.

After a strenuous move and a week's vacation, Veronica had to finally return to work.

The day before she was due to report in for duty, she took a trial run to learn the exact location of her new work site. Veronica met her new manager and supervisors and received a full tour of the facility.

She was nearly intimidated by the size of the plant. She knew the staff was massive, which would bring on more drama than she needed at the time. She began to think that there was no hope of reuniting with her soon to be considered, long lost friend.

The very next morning, Veronica went to work and trained with some of the nicest people. She tends to build a wall from time to time, preventing people from getting close to her. Starting fresh in a new environment took her back down memory lane of when she first began work at the New Jersey plant—almost sixteen years ago.

Veronica was very popular back in the day and turned heads everyday. She was borderline- what many consider a 'red bone'. She was a size six and had long wavy hair, mid-way down the length of her back. In most cases, she'd turn the heads of married men. Veronica stayed focused and maintained plutonic relationships with her male friends. That was, of course, until Mr. Williams came along and stole her heart.

Veronica asked around to see if anyone knew her friend or which department she worked in. Everyone either knew her personally or knew of Juanita Robinson. She was an all around team player and was loved by everyone.

This information let her know that Juanita hadn't changed a bit since they worked together in the extremely small plant in New Jersey. Veronica always envied Juanita for having such an outgoing personality, and for having the ability to capture the hearts of everyone around her.

Veronica could hardly wait to be back in the presence of Juanita. For all of the positive things she'd instilled in her girls over the years, she felt as if she now needed some optimism in her life. She thought Juanita was just the person to get her back on track.

Chapter 3

*I*t's Friday morning. Rock and Trey are headed for downtown Atlanta to pick up some new gear and music for the small cookout they were having that night.

"Man, who's gonna be on your arm tonight?" Trey inquired.

This was the first time Trey had ever seen Rock without a date. Rock didn't care who came as long as long as it wasn't Tee or his other crazy ex girlfriend, Shonte.

Ronnie and Nae woke up to find that Veronica and Monie were already gone. The girls decided to skip breakfast and catch the train downtown to see what the big deal was at Underground Atlanta. Before they left, Monie had called to let them know that she was downtown on a few job interviews. Nae told Monie to hang out down there for a minute because she and Ronnie were on their way to meet up with her.

By the time the girls caught up with Monie, it was lunchtime. Nae began to complain about hunger pains and spotted a hot wings place. She refused to go any further without stopping there for lunch. Monie wanted the new Usher CD. She begged Ronnie to go next door with her to get it.

As Ronnie and Monie walked next door to the music store, Rock and Trey drove by. Rock realized who Ronnie was. He slowed down and blew the horn to get their attention. The girls looked around but didn't recognize the vehicle. So, they continued walking.

Rock parked the truck in a nearby lot. He and Trey walked up to the music store where the girls were. Rock stopped Trey at the door before they entered so he could get a good look at Ronnie.

"Trey, that's the chick I seen at the club the other night."

Trey had no clue as to what Rock was talking about.

"She and another female were riding in a black car with New Jersey plates."

Rock and Trey finally walked into the music store. Rock walked past Ronnie at least three times. Once Ronnie realized he was checking her out, she looked up and into Rock's chest, and then slowly looked up directly into his eyes. Ronnie took two steps back and said, "Do you mind?"

She tried to keep her cool, but this guy was making her weak at the knees. She felt bubbly and tingly inside.

The same baritone voice she'd heard in her dreams said, "Excuse me ma'am. I believe I've seen you somewhere before?"

Ronnie started to get nervous. "I don't think so," Ronnie replied.

Ronnie continued scrutinizing the Jadakiss CD that was in her hands, thinking that Rock would leave her alone and walk away.

"Are you from here?"

Ronnie tried to play hard to get. "No."

"By chance, are you from New Jersey?"

Ronnie's eyes got as big as quarters.

"I think I saw you the other night with another female, riding in a black car with Jersey plates."

Ronnie automatically knew he must have been the guy that was staring at her and Nae at the club. She started checking him out on the sly as she slowly walked down the aisle, pretending she was interested in other CD's.

"By the way, my name is Rakeem. People call me Rock." Ronnie was flabbergasted. She finally had a name to go with this incredible body.

"I'm Ronnie…"

Trey saw Monie for the first time and found her to be very attractive. Her babyish face and petit body reminded him of Aaliyah. He walked over to her and just started talking as if they had come to the store together.

"I see you like Usher. Have you heard the new Mary J? It's banging."

She ignored Trey and kept walking down the aisle looking for more music. By this time she had picked up four CD's. Trey walked up to her again,

"Won't you let me buy those for you, beautiful?"

That got Monie's attention.

"Sure" she said.

She looked into Trey's big, pretty, hazel eyes and thought he is such a gentleman.

The both of them walked up to the cashier. Trey pulled out a wad of fifty and hundred dollar bills. Monie glanced at the wad of money. She didn't want to stare or give the impression that she was materialistic, but the wad looked very enticing.

The cashier seemed a bit timid, yet was flirtatious, and obviously high maintenance. She looked at Trey and slightly above a sexy whisper, said "That'll be forty four twenty eight."

Trey pulled out a fifty-dollar bill and handed it to the cashier. He then looked at Monie and said, "I didn't catch your name."

"I didn't throw it," Monie replied sincerely.

She looked at the cashier and smiled.

"Excuse me ma'am. Are you currently hiring?" Monie inquired.

From the conversation Trey and Monie were having, the cashier knew that this couple in front of her was strangers. Since Monie didn't seem interested, the cashier didn't want to seem obvious, but she had developed a slight interest in Trey. The cashier told Monie that they were in fact hiring.

She just needed to fill out an application and come back in an hour or two to interview. Trey didn't want Monie to feel smothered by him, especially since she was conducting business. So, he began to wander around the store, mainly toward the exit, so he wouldn't miss her when she left.

As Monie filled out the application, the cashier introduced herself as Senoya, the store manager, and she would be the one doing the interview.

"It's very nice to meet you, Senoya. I'm Monica."

"Are you new to Atlanta?" Senoya asked. "How long have you been here?"

"About two weeks," replied Monica.

"I see that you're getting a taste of how the men are down here."

Senoya tried to pick Monie for information as to whether or not she was going to pursue anything with Trey. Senoya wanted to hire Monie instantly just to see if she would eventually date Trey. Monie sensed a deviant vibe from Senoya and hurried to complete the application.

"He's a handsome little guy. Won't you give him a chance?"

Monie had a hunch that the conversation would turn in that direction. Monie shrugged her shoulders, tooted up her nose, and shook her head, "I don't know. I'll think about it."

"Don't think too long sweetie. Somebody might scoop him up."

"Yeah, he's kind of cute," Monie replied and handed the completed application to Senoya and thanked her.

"You know Monie, I like you. Will you be able to report to work on Thursday? That'll give your paperwork and background check enough time to go through."

Monie replied without even thinking, "Sure. What time?"

"Come in at nine a.m. I'll train you and get you situated, then you'll be on your way."

"Okay. I'll see you Thursday. Thank you."

In about twenty minutes Monie had finished with Senoya. She found that Trey was still waiting patiently for her at the door. She looked at Trey and laughed. "My name is Monica. Everyone calls me Monie."

"It's good to finally formally meet you. I'm Treyvon—you can call me Trey."

Trey and Monie walked outside to find Ronnie blushing and full of giggles as she conversed with Rock.

The girls tried to dismiss themselves so they could go meet Nae next door for lunch. Rock kept starting up new conversations every time Ronnie attempted to walk away. Ronnie would've loved to chat with Rock all day, but she couldn't leave her sisters to run off with this stranger. Besides, she'd already heard myths about Atlanta being over-populated with weirdo's.

Rock was determined to spend as much time as possible with this beautiful young lady that he'd been trying to track down for weeks. "So, what are you ladies getting into now?" Ronnie replied. "We're about to meet our sister next door for lunch."

That was right up Trey's alley. His stomach roared extremely loud like the thunder from a hurricane. He hoped no one heard it. He was so embarrassed.

Rock hoped the girls would ask if he and Trey would join them. The invitation was coming too slow for Rock, so he offered to buy them all lunch. That was an offer he knew they wouldn't refuse.

As they stood on the sidewalk discussing lunch, an accident occurred at the intersection right before Ronnie's eyes. As she took a couple of steps towards the accident, she panicked and panted. Feeling like she was having an outer body experience, she stared at the accident, while Monie continued talking to Trey and Rock. As they approached, she saw the fire trucks, police, and the ambulance. It took her back to her dream, making her feel like she'd been there before. In a mysterious way, she felt like her perception of Atlanta was on point.

Everyone walked in the restaurant and greeted Nae. She immediately knew that Rock was the guy from the club. She wondered how Ronnie ended up with him, though. Monie approached Nae first. "Trey, this is my other sister Renae." Nae shook Trey's hand.

"It's nice to meet you." She still had her wondering eye on Rock. Ronnie lingered behind, clinging to Rock. "Rock, this is my sister Nae— the driver of the black car." Ronnie figured Nae would've caught on if she said that. "Nice to meet you too. You're the driver of the Escalade, right?" Rock nodded and wondered why she was so anxious to meet him.

The five of them sat in a booth. Nae felt like a fifth leg, everyone else was coupled up. Nae tried to make small talk, but quickly ran out of appropriate things to say. Nae watched Rock as he looked at the menu long and hard. She felt a little jealous because Rock was interested in Ronnie instead of her. All Nae saw was dollar signs.

Rock felt a materialistic kind of vibe coming from Nae and was quickly turned off. "So what are you ladies having?" Nae told him that she'd already placed an order of wings.

Rock snapped his fingers twice in the air and beckoned for the waitress to come over. The frenzied looking waitress anxiously came over to see what Rock wanted.

"Yes sir. Can I start you all off with something to drink?"

"Yes ma'am. I'm ready to order."

The waitress looked at Rock over the top of her glasses and smiled.

"Let me get a fifty piece order of wings, two large orders of onion rings, two Heineken's, bottled, and whatever the ladies want."

Rock's loud baritone and aggressive voice intimidated the little lady. "Get whatever you want," he said. It's on me."

Rock excused himself to go to the restroom. The waitress stepped aside so Rock could get out. "Could I get you anything else?" The girls were unsure if they should order something else or see if Rock was going to share the fifty pieces that he'd ordered. "We'll have two virgin Daiquiris."

Ronnie asked Trey, "Is he always that demanding?" he laughed. Trey knew that's what the girls were thinking. "He doesn't mean any harm. That's just the way he is."

Trey asked the girls to come to their cookout later on that night.

He knew Rock wanted them to come, but if he waited for Rock to ask them, the girls may have felt like Rock was demanding them to be there and their chances of getting a no would be greater.

Rock returned from the restroom and sat directly across from Ronnie. "So how long have ya'll been in Atlanta?" Ronnie felt a little uneasy about Rock sitting across from her. She knew that he'd stare at her during their whole meal. Ronnie timidly said, "About three weeks."

Trey exclaimed, "Three weeks and ya'll are already out job hunting?" Nae looked at Trey with an attitude, "Yes. Sista's can't survive by sitting at home watching soaps and Oprah all day." Trey gave Rock a look of astonishment and said "Feisty." Ronnie looked at Nae and discreetly motioned her to calm down. "Some guy name Mike offered Nae a job— dancing at the club." Rock didn't see Mike outside that night. He wondered how Mike got a chance to talk to the ladies before he did. "So you met Mike already. That's my cousin. Him and my brother Rome own that club."

Trey told Rock that the girls were going to go to the cookout later. Rock was ecstatic, but he couldn't let it show. "Word! I'll send a car to pick ya'll up around nine."

Monie was overtaken by curiosity as to what type of careers they had. Their mannerisms showed that they were classy. They seemed to be professionals, well dressed, groomed, and manicured. "You'll send a car to pick us up? What type of work do you do?" Before Rock got a chance to come up with a justifiable answer, the food came.

Silence fell over the table. Everyone said their individual blessing and began eating like they hadn't eaten in weeks. Smacking and clanging of the silverware was all you heard. The girls weren't at all worried about being cute or getting their hands messy while eating.

Once lunch was over, Ronnie told Rock that she was appreciative for everything. She gave him her address and phone number so he could call before he sent the car to pick them up. She also apologized for giving him such a hard time in the music store.

Rock was pleased to finally meet a woman who was confident of herself. Ronnie was pretty much a plain Jane, who required very little maintenance, but yet impressed him.

Although he had only known her for a few hours, to him, she seemed to be the kind of person who really wanted to get to know him.

Somebody who wanted to be with him for who was and not what she could get out of him. She was genuine, and Rock appreciated and respected that in a woman.

The girls returned home around six o'clock Friday evening. Although they used Veronica's car often, they were getting very familiar with the public transportation system. Nae was determined to save up another fifteen hundred dollars and get a car of her own.

They were anxious to hear about their mothers first day of work at the new site. Since Veronica's workday ended at four, they thought she should've been home from work by now. The girls started to get a little worried, because this wasn't normal behavior for their mother. It was not usual for her to be away from home and not phone or leave a note if she wasn't coming directly home from work.

The girls started ironing clothes, washing hair, and taking showers to prepare for their big dates later than night. By seven o'clock the girls became more worried and started to realize how and why Veronica always worried about them when they showed up late or sometimes did-n't show up at all.

Veronica found Juanita at work almost at quitting time. The two decided to go out for drinks after work to catch up on all of their lost years. Juanita explained that just two years ago, she'd been in an abusive relationship for a whole year, which nearly cost her life.

Juanita was just getting back in the swing of things. She'd recently started dealing with a guy name Tyrone, whom she met at IHOP one day while eating breakfast. Juanita mentioned that Tyrone had a twin brother name Jerome, who just needed a plutonic friend since he had been widowed for about nine months. Veronica understood Jerome's situation very well, but showed no interest in it when Juanita presented it to her.

Juanita asked, "Veronica, when was the last time you were involved?"

It had been so long, Veronica couldn't give her an honest answer.

"Girl, you need to get out more and stop worrying about your grown daughters."

Veronica took a slight offence to that comment. Juanita could tell that Veronica was offended by the expression on her face.

"Look Veronica, I know that your girls are all you've got, but you have to let them go. Live your own life and let them live theirs. I guar-antee that they're out getting their groove on, and if you want to continue to stay young like me, you better do likewise."

Veronica sat back and thought about what Juanita was saying, as she slowly sipped on her Fuzzy Navel. Veronica thought, with a self-centered attitude like that and not knowing what your children are doing, she wondered if Juanita had any grand children.

"Juanita, do you have any grand kids."

"Not that I know of," Juanita replied.

Veronica began to wonder how her friend could be so carefree about life. Both women were tipsy at this point, although not enough to alter their thoughts, but just enough for them to freely voice their opinions.

Veronica wasn't used to hanging out and drinking. The alcohol started to make her extremely sluggish and sleepy. She was also eager to get home to share her first experience at work with her girls. It was going on eight o'clock, and her bedtime was approaching quickly.

"Well Juanita, it's been real but I truly have to go. We must do this again soon."

Juanita replied "Yeah like tomorrow. It's the weekend. Relax a bit." Juanita shook her head at her friend, noticing she lacked any kind of a social life. "I gotta get you out more."

"Okay, tomorrow it is." Veronica didn't know that Juanita was talking about going out again that soon.

The ladies paid their bills, got up, and slowly headed toward the door, slightly staggering to their vehicles.

Veronica made it home by eight thirty. Ronnie was at the window when her mother pulled up. As Veronica walked in the house, Nae was coming down the stairs. The girls hit their mother with a ton of questions and a lecture as if she was the child coming home past curfew.

The girls chimed together in harmony "Where were you?"

Nae took the role as the responsible adult. "You had us worried, and why didn't you call to let us know you weren't coming straight home after work?"

Veronica immediately caught an attitude and exclaimed, "I pay the mortgage here, and I am not a child. So, if I choose not to come home at all, that's my prerogative!"

The girls knew that their mother had a buzz. They were quite stunned because they hadn't ever seen her like that. Nae and Ronnie were a little relieved to see her in this state. That made them realize that she wasn't perfect, and whatever had gotten into her they wished it would come about more often.

Veronica went over to the kitchen sink to get a cold glass of water when she realized that she may have been a bit harsh. She would've had the same reaction if they had come in four hours late. She apologized to her girls and stared out of the kitchen window. She noticed a limo had stopped in front of the house.

"This limo must be at the wrong address." Veronica thought aloud.

Nae ran up to the window and looked out to see this long, black, shiny stretch limo. "It's not at the wrong address, that's Ronnie's friend."

Still not in her right mind, Veronica replied "Oh really? Ronnie who?"

"Your daughter, Ronnie."

"My daughter, Ronnie, has friends with limos?"

"She and Monie met some guys today who obviously have plenty of money."

"Monie?"

The chauffer rang the doorbell. Veronica looked at Nae in disbelief as she walked over to answer the door. "If Monie has a date I'm sure there's someone in the mix for you."

Monie was in the dining room listening to the whole conversation between her mother and Nae, scared to come out, thinking she'd be faced with a non-stop interrogation. When Monie heard the doorbell she appeared at the door the same time as Veronica. Veronica wanted so badly to curse at Monie. However, she just bit her bottom lip and opened the door. Monie grabbed the door to open it wider so she could see the chauffer and squeeze by Veronica to get to the limo.

Monie and Veronica greeted the chauffer.

"Hello sir, how are you?" They both asked mannerly.

The chauffer replied, "Good evening madams. I'm looking for Ms. Ronnie, Ms. Monica and Ms. Renae."

Monie looked her mother in the face, smiled and swiftly walked past her. The chauffer tilted his hat, wished Veronica a great evening, and turned to escort Monie to the car.

Ronnie heard the conversation and ran down the stairs and interrupted them, "She knows somebody is going to be there for her to talk to."

Ronnie stopped running briefly enough to look Nae in the eyes, "Shut up and come on."

Ronnie grabbed Nae by the hand and drugged her outside as she started running again.

Ronnie yelled back at her mom, "Don't wait up," while she and Nae jumped in the car. Monie was already in the car waiting patiently.

Veronica was concerned about what her daughters had gotten into. Who do they know with a limo? How did they meet these guys? Where did they meet them and where are they going? She had to take a deep breath and think about what Juanita told her about letting go.

She leaned on the counter top, putting her upper weight on her elbows as she watched the limo drive away with all three of her babies in it. She was almost in tears thinking about the direction in which her life was going and trying to figure out where she'd made a wrong turn. She stayed there for a while, in deep thought, before she headed upstairs to watch TV in bed.

As the girls rode in the back of the amber and purple-lit limo, Monie started opening different compartments of the car. She first found ammunition, and showed it to her sisters. The further she dug, she found several 9mm handguns, a couple of sawed off shotguns and an oozy. Monie began to wonder what kind of people she and her sisters were trying to befriend.

Nae was having second thoughts about attending the cookout. She was tempted to ask the driver to take her back home. Nae became hysterical, "What did these guys tell ya'll they did? Bounty hunting?"

Ronnie responded, "They didn't say, but I will find out tonight."

"If we make it out of here alive," Nae said as she threw her leg over the other and turned away to stare out of the window.

Monie tried to put a semi positive twist on things, "Maybe it's not what we think. They could possibly be in the military or doing some kind of classified undercover work for the government."

Nae disputed Monie's honest efforts to justify the weaponry. Regardless of what was found, Ronnie was still eager to be in Rock's presents. Silence fell upon the car as each of the girls had their own personal views of what their newfound friends were all about. Ronnie broke the silence.

"Look Nae, nobody put a gun to your head and made you come.

But since you're already here, let's just take it easy and gradually feel our way through the night."

Nae let out a long sigh and quickly put an end to her ungratefulness. She thought about it. She could've been at home watching syndicated TV sitcoms all night. Nae and Monie both agreed to be inquisitive, but not too knowledgeable of the artillery that they'd found.

They approached Rock's mini mansion and went through the well-designed, steel privacy gate at the end of the driveway. The girls looked with amazement at the three-foot high angel fountain that stood in the center of the brick driveway. Four acres of well-manicured lawn and colorful landscaping were on both sides of the driveway. When the car stopped, all of the girls instantly felt tensed.

After the girls stepped out of the limo, like celebrities, Rock greeted them at the front door of his estate.

"Welcome to my home ladies."

Monie replied, "Do you need an assistant at your office, or where ever you conduct business?"

Rock laughed as if he found Monie to be quite amusing. Trey came out of the front door extending his arms toward Monie for a hug before escorting her inside. Monie looked at Rock and wondered why he laughed at her sincerity.

"I failed to see the humor in that. I'm in school and I truly need a reliable source of income."

Ronnie looked at Monie with frustration and rolled her eyes indicating that she needed to stop meddling and being so direct.

Trey instantly gained more interest in Monie knowing that she was in school. He threw a peace sign in the air, nodded at Rock, then took Monie by the hand and led her to a secluded corner in the house to acquire some quality and bonding time together. He beckoned for the server to bring over a few drinks.

"So Ms. Jersey girl, tell me a little about you. What are you in school for?"

"I'm studying law at Spelman."

"A lawyer. Maybe I need to leave you alone now. All of the dirt I've been in, I don't want to be your first case."

"What kind of dirt are you into?"

"You really don't want to know."

"I really do want to know. I've been wondering what you do for a living since I met you. How do ya'll make so much money?"

Trey hesitated for a while before he said anything. He tried going around the question several times and asking if she wanted something to eat or some more to drink. Monie continued with her persistence. Trey excused himself to go refresh their drinks, thinking that when he returned, she would have forgotten where they left off in the conversation.

Once Trey returned, Monie picked up where they left off.

"You're gonna be a damn good lawyer because you don't forget anything." Trey stated.

"That's my goal," Monie replied and calmly laughed.

Trey finally admitted to Monie that Rock was a kingpin and he was his right hand man. Trey couldn't stress how bad he wanted to give up that lifestyle. He confessed that he had gotten so used to the fast and easy money. He had no concept on how to make an honest living. He wanted a wife and children to come home to at the end of the day after working on a legit job.

Monie asked, "Exactly how much money do you see in a week?"

At this time, Trey was comfortable enough with Monie to tell her that he made about ten thousand dollars a week.

Monie developed a liking to Trey even before finances became a part of the conversation. She found herself creating a space in her heart for him. She knew that this man would make her break her own rules. Although she was not out for his money, it did however, put icing on the cake.

She usually wouldn't give a brother like him a chance, but this situation was all together different. She felt something within his spirit that quickly changed her perspectives.

Rock introduced Nae to his other right hand man, Tony. Tony was a bright-skinned, muscular, curly haired, pretty boy. He was very down to earth, but Nae normally wasn't attracted to bright-skinned men. She figured they all had a certain arrogance that she didn't care to be around.

Tony had been cooking on the grill, so when he met Nae, he was shirtless. Nae was instantly attracted to Tony's 'buns of steel' and his greatly sculptured chest and six-pack abs. Tony extended his hand to Nae to receive hers, and placed a small friendly kiss upon it.

"My name is Tony. I'm very pleased to meet you Ms. Renae."

Nae was flattered by all of the hospitality she had been shown since she'd been in their presence. She was also shocked to learn that Tony had a mutual attraction for her. He was the type of gentleman to let his actions speak for him. Nae noticed that his actions were saying quite a bit, like the fact that he wanted to spend the rest of his evening in her presence.

Every time Nae tried to slip off to mingle with other guests, she realized Tony wasn't extremely far away. When Tony introduced Nae to Rick, he made it a known fact that Rick was already married. Nae sensed this protective shield that Tony had placed around her.

Rock's brother, Rome, was also well known to everyone due to his partial ownership of Club Passion. Rome walked around the party loosely; drinking and have a great time flirting with the few women that were there without a mate.

He introduced himself to Nae and hoped to have a pleasant conversation. Rome was just as attractive as Rock. Rome was a bit more muscular and taller than Rock, which made him stand at six foot six inches tall, with a very small gap in his top front teeth.

Nae thought Rome was cool, but more along the lines of being the brother she'd never had. She found herself wondering where Tony had run off to, hoping he'd come rescue her from this big brotherly figure she'd run into, and felt slightly intimidated by.

Tony watched Nae and Rome converse from a hidden corner of the loft upstairs. Tony took notice of Nae gestures and assumed she may have been uncomfortable. After about twenty minutes had gone by, he finally went over to end Nae's obvious misery. "Hey Rome, I'm gonna take this gorgeous lady to meet a couple more people that just came in."

Rome was confident that Nae would eventually come back to finish their conversation. He found her to be pretty interesting and planned to ask her on a date once she returned. He had no idea that his partner and cousin, Mike, asked her to be a dancer at their club.

Nae walked with Tony upstairs to Rock's huge bonus room, which contained a large pool table, an air hockey table, a digital surround sound for the stereo system, and a sixty-two inch screen TV.

Nae felt a bit nervous being isolated from everyone else. Tony, as well as Rock, knew the tricks of the trade of seducing women. But Nae was different; Tony thought of her as being a precious and delicate gift that he was trying to gently open.

Tony put on the smooth sounds of Sade, and dimmed the lights. This put Nae at ease.

"Do you know how to shoot pool?" Tony asked.

Nae replied, "No, but I'm sure you can teach me."

Nae felt like there was no one else in the house but the two of them. She learned a lot about pool, different perspectives on life, and the drug game. After shooting pool and talking to Tony, Nae felt like she could relax and let her hair down, so to speak.

Tony often complimented her, calling her gorgeous and beautiful every time he spoke to her. Although Nae was on the tipsy side, she knew that what she was hearing made her feel very confident and loved.

The alcohol made Nae do things she wouldn't ordinarily do. She unbuttoned her shirt past her breast and started dancing exotically. Although Tony enjoyed every moment of it, he didn't take advantage of her because he knew that she was under the influence. She danced very closely in front of Tony, making him aroused. Tony passionately kissed her as they danced to 'The Sweetest Taboo'.

Rock walked around inside and outside of his lavish home mingling with guests.

He held Ronnie's hand all night long. Rock made sure that his lovely companion always had a drink in her hand and wherever they went, he made sure she was at his side. He introduced Ronnie as his woman to all of his closest friends and associates.

As the time grew closer to midnight the crowd diminished to a very few friends of Rock's, who primarily stayed to help tidy up the house, so the cleaning crew would have very little to do the next morning.

Rock's cell phone was constantly ringing. He put it on vibrate, but the vibration gave off a loud disturbing noise, which distracted him from focusing on Ronnie. He answered the phone once, only to hear Tees' voice on the other end. Ronnie heard a woman's loud and angry voice blaring through the phone just before Rock hung up and turned it completely off. Ronnie was unsure of what had just happened.

"If you need to talk to your friend, I'll let you talk to her."

Ronnie stood up as if she was going to walk away. Rock pulled her back down onto the bench.

"You are my friend, and I'm going to stay here and talk to you."

Ronnie felt privileged. She knew she was at the top of the totem pole. She felt like the queen.

Rock was excited to finally have a chance to spend some quiet quality time with his new companion. The two sat in the back yard, in the gazebo, enjoying this beautiful summer night.

They discussed everything from birth to that particular moment. They talked about music, videos, movies, politics and sex.

Rock explained that he had been in the drug game so long, that he'd have to move away from Georgia to get out of it. He asked Ronnie if she'd be willing to relocate again.

She thought about it for a moment and shrugged her shoulders, unsure of how to answer him.

"So why did you get into drugs?" Ronnie asked.

Rock explained that he used to do small drops for his father, who was a big time drug dealer. After he saw that he could make as much money in one night as his mother made in two weeks, he became eager to learn the ropes.

"I've been addicted to money ever since," Rock commented.

Ronnie was brave enough to ask Rock of an estimate on how much money he had in the bank. Rock didn't want to reveal exactly how deep his pockets were, but he didn't want to start this new relationship feeling like he had to hide things—at least not everything.

Rock tried to go around the subject, reverse it and sugarcoat things, to prevent giving an answer. Ronnie gave an inquisitive stare. Rock finally stated that he'd reached the million-dollar mark a few years ago, and left it at that. Ronnie began to have hot flashes, but quickly recovered, and resumed focusing on him and not what he had or how much of it.

Ronnie attentively listened to what Rock was saying. She decided that whatever happened between them from that point on, she would not be in opposition to it. Ronnie figured a relationship with Rock would be nothing less than marvelous. All the money she needed would be at her fingertips. She could stay in this enormous mansion and be the envy of all of her friends; have an incredible man to adore her, all at once.

The time was rapidly approaching two a.m. and everyone started yawning and getting restless. Although Rock didn't want to see the girls leave, he decided that it would be appropriate for his guests to head home, out of respect for them living at home with their mother.

The three couples loaded up in the back of the limo and were chauffeured to the Williams' home. The conversation was very little because the girls kept falling asleep. To be on the safe side, Rock thought it would behoove them all if the chauffeur escorted the girls to the door. Veronica heard the girls coming in, laughing aloud, bumping into walls and furniture, as well as each other. She came out of her room and stopped at the top of the stairs, furious, and flipped the light switch on.

"What the hell is going on down there?"

"We're okay!" Nae yelled.

Veronica walked down the first two stairs in slow motion, fussing and cursing.

"Where have you been, and with whom," Veronica shouted!

A drunken Monie replied "We went with Rock nem."

Ronnie nudged Monie nearly knocking her down, and then tried to clean up her drunken sister's version of the story.

"We went to a friend's cook-out. It lasted longer than we thought, but since we weren't driving, we couldn't come home until they decided when they wanted to bring us.

Veronica added, "Ya'll don't even know those men. If you hadn't come home at all I would've had a clue as to where to begin looking for you. Ya'll are some dizzy ass broads!"

Monie started snickering, which made Veronica even madder. "You girls think this is a fucking game?"

The girls looked at Veronica with amazement and an expression of sorrow. Veronica went back in her room, slammed the door, and got back in the bed.

Chapter 4

*V*eronica got up and cooked herself breakfast. She made fluffy, golden brown pancakes, sausage patties, and cheese eggs like the color of the sun, with a tall glass of apple juice on the side.

Still thinking and very frustrated, agitated and disappointed about last night, she didn't cook anything for her daughters. She thought that since they figured they were grown and could run the streets all night long, they could get off of their lazy and drunken asses and cook their own breakfast.

Monie was the first one down the stairs and at the table.

"Good morning mommy. Is this my plate on the table?"

Monie sat down at Veronica's plate.

Veronica was very abrupt with a harsh tone. Veronica walked over to the table and moved her meal to the next empty space on the table.

"No!"

"Where's mine?"

"It's raw and in the refrigerator," Veronica answered.

As she washed the dishes, Veronica called Juanita to ask if she wanted to spend the day hanging out together. She was so angry with her daughters she didn't want to be around them at all for a while. She figured if she had her car with her, they would be stuck at home—unless they got those rich men from the previous night to pick them up.

Juanita agreed to hang out with Veronica, only if Veronica agreed to meet Jerome. Veronica sat down to her breakfast and ate in content. Monie tried to talk to her mother and convince her that she and her sisters did nothing wrong. Veronica continued ignoring her. Monie got up from the table, looked at Veronica and said, "You did the same thing by coming in drunk without us knowing where you were."

Veronica added nonchalantly "During the daytime."

Monie rolled her eyes and ran upstairs. By that time her sisters were awake wondering why Monie was trying to reason with their mother.

Veronica finished her meal and headed over to Juanita's house. As Veronica pulled up in Juanita's yard, she passed a forest green Land Rover parking next to a cherry red Lexus Land Cruiser. She noticed a brand new charcoal gray, big body Mercedes Benz was backed in the other side of Juanita's two-car garage next to her car. Juanita greeted Veronica at the door with open arms. Veronica detected her friend's strange behavior and thought that there may have been a hidden agenda behind all of the hugs and jittery gestures.

"Veronica, you remember my boys—Josh and Jason?"

"Yes. They're all grown up. They've grown into six-foot men. How are you boys doing? Excuse me, men." Veronica said correcting herself.

The young Robinson men gave Veronica hugs.

"You don't remember me, do you?"

Josh replied, "Yes ma'am. I remember you. How's your daughter Ronnie doing?"

"You remember Ronnie? She just fine. As a matter of fact she still may be at the house. Here's the number. Give her a call this evening if you get a chance."

Veronica wrote her home number on the back of an old receipt she'd found in her purse. Veronica was thrilled that these handsome men remembered her and her daughters. She asked Jason if he remembered Monica. He vaguely remembered her, but she didn't give up hope. She told him to call Monica. It brightened up Veronica's day to know that she had directed this abundance of potential to her daughter's paths.

Veronica took a seat in Juanita's living room, as she scrounged to find two matching shoes. Juanita came out of her room, gave each of her boys a kiss on the check and beckoned for Veronica to follow her outside.

"Boys, make sure you lock up when you leave." Juanita added.

The two women got into the Mercedes to leave. Veronica was curious as to whose car she was riding in.

"Is this your 'going to church' car or for Sunday cruising?" Veronica asked.

"No girl, this is Tyrone's car."

"What does he do for a living?" Veronica's curiosity was at an all time high.

"He's a real estate broker, an author of two novels, and a self help book. He does a lot of traveling. He mostly goes to Chicago, sometimes L.A., and parts of Florida. When he's on travel he leaves me the car." Juanita bragged.

"Where is he now?" Veronica asked.

"He's at the movies waiting for me. I hope you don't mind. I set up a date for him and his brother Jerome to meet us at the movies and we'll all go out for dinner afterwards."

"Juanita!" Veronica exclaimed. "It would've been nice of you to let me know I was going on a date."

"Relax. You agreed to meet him. I figured it would be cool if we went to a public place so you'd be comfortable."

"Yeah, but at least I would've known how to dress. I look like somebody's grandmother."

"No you don't. Please believe I would not be dragging someone's grandmother out with me—especially to go meet a man."

The women pulled into the parking lot of the theater. While looking for a near parking space, Veronica saw two handsome identical men, who appeared to be in their early to mid forties, standing next to the entrance.

Veronica and Juanita got out of the car and strutted up to the two men who were standing there waiting for them with the movie tickets in their hands.

"Hey love, how are you?" Juanita said as she gave Tyrone a big hug and kiss.

"This is my girlfriend, Veronica, from Jersey. The one I told you who works with me."

"Veronica, this is the love of my life, Tyrone Ellis, and his twin brother, Jerome."

Jerome extended his hand and gave Veronica a delicate handshake, then extended his elbow to escort her in the theater. Veronica was still content from the late breakfast she'd had before going to Juanita's house. Jerome insisted she at least had a drink. She finally accepted the offer, got her drink, and they all proceeded into the theater.

Ronnie and her sisters cleaned the house from top to bottom, and then lounged for the most part of the day. Rock called Ronnie to see if she wanted to go out looking for cell phones so he could be in touch with her at all times. Ronnie wanted to build up the nerve to ask him to buy her a small car so she and her sisters wouldn't have to bother their mother for hers.

Once Rock made it over to the Williams', he came to the door with a dozen of beautiful, long stemmed red roses. Ronnie opened the door and greeted him with a hug, a long juicy kiss, and then offered him a seat in the dining room where Nae was enjoying one of her favorite movies. Ronnie put the roses in a vase of warm water and rushed upstairs to put on her shoes and her most seductive fragrance.

Nae was used to being the center of attention and having men at her beckoning call. All the attention was now focused on Ronnie, who made Nae very jealous and filled with animosity toward her sister. Nae tried her best to be cordial, but her inner feelings got the best of her.

"So what made you want to date my sister?" she asked Rock.

"Her inner and outer beauty and her personality. She's just a genuine and fun loving person. Do you have a problem with that?"

"No. I was just wondering. So where's your friend?"

"I'm not sure. I figured he'd be somewhere trying to touch base with you."

Rock's phone rang. Rock looked at Nae. She looked back over at him as if he was up to something. Rock answered the phone.

"Hello?"

His ex girlfriend Shonte was on the other end.

"What cha doin'?"

Rock tried to play it off in front of Nae. She sensed that he was talking to another female and figured he was up to no good. She also knew that if she tried to tell her sister that she had just witnessed him talking to someone else, it would only turn into a fight. Nae decided to stand clear of the situation and let Ronnie find out what was going on. She then could determine on her own if she wanted to stay with Rock or not.

Rock explained to Shonte that he was in the middle of something important. She heard the sound of the TV in the background. Shonte wasn't the kind of person to fall for anything that easily. She was still bitter about the way things happened when he left her outside of the gate of his home.

"I'm not buyin' that Rock. Where are you and who are you with!?" Shonte exclaimed.

Rock tried to answer her as calmly as he could without actually giving Nae conformation that he was talking to another female.

He tried to whisper into the phone, "I'm not with anyone. I'll call you later."

Shonte knew he was lying from the way he was replying to her.

Ronnie finally came downstairs hollering out,

"I'm ready."

She made it to the bottom of the stairs and looked at Rock. She threw her hand up over her mouth, acknowledging that he was on the phone. She walked up close to him and softly whispered, "Sorry."

Nae continued to act as if she was watching TV. She saw what was going on with Rock. He noticed she knew what had just happened. Rock rudely ended his call with Shonte by hanging up on her and stood up to greet Ronnie. Rock kissed her on the cheek then looked at Nae, putting his hands up as if he was going to give an explanation, but said I'll tell Tony to give you a call."

Rock was almost sure that Nae was going to pull Ronnie aside before they left and tell her what happened. He was relieved that she didn't. This enabled him to conjure up a story to enlighten Ronnie about his phone conversation that her sister may have overheard.

As Ronnie and Rock walked out the door, the phone rang. It was Josh calling for Ronnie. Nae answered the phone, "Hello."

"Yes, may I speak to Ronnie please?"

Nae didn't catch the voice. She wondered if Ronnie had met someone without her knowing. The caller ID read an Atlanta number. She figured if she kept talking she'd be able to recognize this voice that nearly sent chills down her spine.

"Nae just stepped out. May I take a message or is there something I can help you with?"

"No. I'll just give her a call back later. Is this her sister Renae or Monie?"

Nae wondered which one of Ronnie's friends was here in Atlanta, with a voice sounding that good referring to her as Renae, and knew Monie.

"This is Nae, who am I speaking with?"

"This is Josh. Do you remember Juanita Williams? She used to work with your mom at the G.M. plant in Jersey. We left Jersey about five years ago. My cousins and I had gotten new cars for graduation and we always tried to take ya'll to the movies and the clubs in Philly, but we were too young to get in," Josh reminisced, trying to jog Nae's memory.

Nae remember exactly who he was, so she wanted the conversation to last as long as it could.

"Yeah, you have a cousin or a brother named Jason?"

"Yes, Jason is my brother. Jeff is my cousin. Jeff wanted to talk to you in the worst way."

"I remember you. How are you doing?" Nae said, as she got a visual of them in her mind.

"I'm good. How are you?"

Nae was ready to rekindle an old friendship. She was ready to do anything except stay in the house. She started thinking of ways to try to get Josh to ask her to go out. Anywhere with him would be fine. She didn't want to make it seem like she was trying to deter his attention from Ronnie, but besides, she was already gone out with someone else.

"So where's Jeff these days?" Nae asked anxiously.

"He's in the Air Force as well as I, but he's stationed in California."

Nae's hopes for a date fell once again.

"I would like to see all of you. It's been a really long time since we've gone out."

"What are you doing now?" Josh asked.

"Nothing! I'm just sitting here watching Lifetime."

Nae was sure Josh heard the anxiety in her voice. She'd accomplished her goal to get him to ask her to go out and do something.

"You and I could go out to get drinks if you'd like. We could catch up on the past five years."

"I'd like that," Nae replied with a smile from ear to ear.

Nae explained to Josh how to get to her house. She got off the phone and figured she needed to get 'dolled' up in case he was a knight in shining armor, or knew someone who might be interested in a smart, young, single female like herself.

As soon as Nae stepped out of the shower, Tony called. Her heart fell to her toes. She thought if she'd been more patient, she would've been going on a date with him. She explained that she was going out with Josh, and how their families connected and had history together. She made a later date with Tony for that night.

Veronica and Jerome decided to go to nice cozy Mexican restaurant for Margaritas. She didn't know how to act around this guy. He was extremely nice and handsome. It was well over due for Veronica to get her groove on. She just wanted to take it easy and not jump into anything she couldn't quite handle. She couldn't allow herself to venture with anymore-emotional roller coasters.

Jerome was very warm and compassionate. He was caring, charming, and successful, which turned Veronica on. He explained about his wife passing from breast cancer nearly a year ago. He told Veronica that he was scarred for life, but he knows his wife would've wanted him to continue his life and be happy. His children are grown and he just wanted to settle down with someone who will live life to the fullest and not take it for granted.

Veronica believed in her heart that she could honestly do that. She didn't think that was asking for too much. She needed someone in her life to get her out more and away from her daughters so much. She was ready to take Juanita's advice and get her life back on track.

The couple laughed, talked, drank and enjoyed each other's company for the most part of the night. Veronica hadn't had that much fun in years. Jerome made her feel special, the way her husband used to many years ago. They both knew that this was the beginning of something extraordinary.

Rock explained to Ronnie that he'd had some really strange relationships with strange women. He mentioned how Tee was delusional and how deranged Shonte was. He made it known that both women are crazy about him, and will manipulate anyone who'll give them the slightest opportunity. Ronnie really didn't care about Rock's past with women. She was trying to be a part of his future.

While shopping, Ronnie came out of the mall with five new outfits with matching shoes and accessories, new sneakers and a cell phone. She didn't know how she was going to get all of her new stuff in the house without Veronica noticing and saying something negative about it.

She explained to Rock that she really needed a job to get all of the things she needed and wanted. Rock couldn't let his newfound love get a job because it would take away from the time he wanted to spend with her. He asked what all did she need.

"Rock, I have to get a car," she said pitifully.

"You can keep my Benz for as long as you need it."

Ronnie didn't think he was serious.

"I can't keep your Mercedes. My mom would trip out on the both of us."

"You ever thought about getting your own place so your mom won't trip on everything you and your sisters do?"

"Obviously you don't comprehend what I'm saying. I don't have a job or money."

"Sweetheart, as long as you're with me, you don't have to worry about money, cars, jewels or anything. I got your back."

"Who's to say I'm gonna to be with you forever?"

"Ronnie, I'm not letting you go for anyone, and don't you ever forget that."

What Rock was saying frightened Ronnie more than it gave her a sense of security. Rock gave Ronnie the keys to his Benz and told her that she could get it whenever she wanted to. Ronnie never had anyone to give her anything. She didn't know how to accept it.

When they returned to Rock's house, Ronnie jumped out of the truck and threw her arms around his neck and started passionately kissing him.

Since Ronnie was comfortable with kissing him the way she was, Rock was ready to take the relationship to the next level.

Rock took Ronnie up to his bedroom. He turned out the lights and lit about fifteen candles. He put on the sweet sounds of 'Moments in Love' by The Art of Noise. He left her in the room alone as he went downstairs to the kitchen to get some strawberries, glaze, and Champagne.

When he returned to the room, Ronnie had on nothing but her red satin Victoria Secret's undergarments. Rock took off his shirt and stared at her, lying on the bed with her long hair flowing across his satin pillow, enjoying the easy listening music.

Rock sat on the foot of the bed and put Ronnie's feet on his lap. He picked her right foot and caressed it until it was very warm. He got on the floor on his knees at the foot of the bed. He dipped the strawberry in the glaze, swiped the bottom of her foot with the glazed strawberry, and licked it back off. He began to suck on her toes one by one.

Ronnie enjoyed every moment of it. Rock got on top of the bed and straddled her, nibbling on her neck and earlobes. He slid his hands underneath her to unlatch her bra. Ronnie carefully wiggled her way out of the bra trying not to make any sudden moves so Rock wouldn't have to stop kissing her. He dipped another strawberry into the glaze and dabbed it on her nipples, all the way down her stomach to her panty line.

He carefully pulled her panties down until they were completely off. He licked on her navel and ate the glaze off her naked body. He laid on top of her for a moment, long enough to make her wonder what was going to happen next. She turned her head away from him and took a long deep breath and wondered if that was all she was going to get that night.

She felt Rock aggressively pull her legs apart. It happened so quickly, that by the time she turned her head to see what he was doing, she saw his head between her legs and felt his tongue inside of her. Rock went down on her for at least a half hour, counting how many times she had orgasms. He then got on top of her and made passionate love to her.

When he was finished, Ronnie rolled onto her side and fell asleep as he lay behind her hugging her tightly. He drifted off to sleep as well.

Ronnie woke up at 4 a.m., scared to wake Rock up so he could take her home.

She decided to leave him a note saying that she enjoyed her night, but unfortunately she had to leave. Ronnie scrambled through her purse in the dark to find the Mercedes key that he had given her, so she could drive herself home. She found her shoes and tipped to the door trying not to disturb her sleeping mate. By the time she made it half way to the bedroom door; Rock woke up and felt that her side of the bed was empty.

He lifted his head and asked her, "Where you goin' baby?"

She stopped in her tracks, and went back over to the bed and sat on the edge.

"Rock I've got to go home. I'll call you later." She gave Rock a quick, soft and gentle kiss and stood up.

"1 5 9 7#, " Rock recited.

Ronnie looked at him wondering what he was talking about. He told her that it was the code to his front gate in case she ever wanted to come in without him. She felt privileged to get that type of information from him without asking for it. She was the only female he'd ever given the code to.

Rock got up and put on his robe and slippers. He escorted her to the car, carrying all of her shopping bags. He informed her about the hundred dollars he kept in the ashtray. He told her to use it for gas and any other expenses she may need it for. He also promised her that he would keep that money in there for her at all times.

By the time Ronnie made it home everyone was asleep. She crept up the stairs as quietly as she could, trying not to wake anyone. Veronica awoke when she heard the stairs squeak. She automatically knew it was Ronnie because she was the only one who wasn't home when she went to sleep around midnight.

Veronica decided she was going to let the girls do what they wanted to do. She was ready to begin living her life to the fullest with Jerome.

She figured fussing at Ronnie would only add fuel to the fire, so she laid there in bed and drifted back off to sleep.

Chapter 5

*V*eronica woke up around 6:30 Sunday morning, feeling very refreshed from the previous night. All she could think about was spending her day with Jerome. She lay there in bed for another half hour imagining what it would be like having a man around the house with her girls still living there. She then imagined what it would be like having a man around without her girls. She tended to like the idea of her and Jerome being able to spend their time together alone.

Jerome's children were grown, like Veronica's. He was a Vice-Admiral in the U.S. Navy and only had one more year to work before he was eligible for retirement. For Veronica, this was possibly a match made in heaven.

Veronica went downstairs to get a glass and her bottle of wine that Jerome purchased for her the night before. She went over to the kitchen sink to rinse out her glass, and noticed out of the kitchen window, that a black Mercedes was parked in front of her house.

Veronica went back upstairs and sat on the side of her garden tub as the water ran for her bubble bath. She pinned her hair up, lit some aromatherapy candles, then took off her robe and stepped into the warm, silky textured water.

Once she finished her bath, she went back into her room with her wine and laid down across the bed. Jerome called her at around eight to see if she wanted to go out for breakfast. She immediately accepted his invitation and put on her best fragrance and her most 'comfortable' outfit.

After she got dressed she rushed downstairs to find her basket to set up for a picnic later in the day. She made cold cut sandwiches, cut in fours; then she cut up some bananas and strawberries to make small fruit cups. She found some of Monie's individual snack size bags of potato chips and threw them in her basket. She figured this picnic would be well appreciated by Jerome. She scribbled a quick note and left it on the refrigerator door for the girls to not touch her basket, which was inside.

By the time Jerome arrived, Nae was up and wandering around downstairs in her sleep attire. Nae ran to the window when Jerome rang the doorbell.

"Mom, are you expecting company?" she asked.

"Yes I am. So, could take your half naked buttocks upstairs please?"

Veronica tapped Nae on the behind rushing her, as Nae ran up the stairs. "Ronnie, Monie. Mom has a date!"

Nae screamed out as she ran upstairs. When Nae was out of sight, Veronica opened the door to a dozen bright, fresh, red, white and yellow roses already in a beautiful purplish vase. Jerome handed Veronica the vase and placed a soft friendly kiss upon her cheek.

Veronica placed the vase on the counter top near the kitchen sink. She hurried back to the door where Jerome stood, so they could get their fun-filled day started. Nae and Ronnie stood, peaking out of Ronnie's bedroom window, watching as Jerome escorted their mother to his two-year old gold Lexus.

Nae jumped on Ronnie's bed, eager to hear about how her night went with Rock, especially since she'd seen all of the shopping bags.

Ronnie explained how romantic Rock was and how fragile he treated her as they made love. Nae told Ronnie about her experience reuniting with Josh.

"Who's Josh," Ronnie asked.

Nae explained that he was Ms. Robinson's son. Ronnie remembered exactly who he was because he constantly followed her around when they were in junior high school together, trying to talk to her. Nae told her sister that he called for her, but she had just left with Rock. Josh extended an invitation for her to go have drinks with him, and she gladly accepted since she was sitting home bored, with nothing but time on her hands.

Nae convinced Ronnie that she wouldn't be interested in Josh, because he was nowhere near as exciting as Rock. She mentioned that Josh was more like a brother that they never had rather than someone any of them would consider dating.

Ronnie was exceptionally understanding of why her sister went out with Josh. Besides, they were all childhood friends and nothing more.

Rock had Ronnie's full attention, so she could care less about anyone else who may have tried to date her.

Monie came in Ronnie's room to join her sisters and to find out what all the commotion was about. She sat down in Ronnie's computer chair across from the bed, looking very unenthusiastic and depressed.

Nae told Monie that Jason would probably give her a call before the day was over, thinking that would've cheered her up. Monie was partially interested in Jason already because of what Veronica told her. She was still curious to find out what Trey had on his agenda. Rock's whole entourage overwhelmed all three of the girls.

"What's wrong Monie?" Nae asked with profound concern.

Monie was still in shock about Chenille.

"Chenille is pregnant again," Monie replied.

"Your girlfriend back home? Isn't this like the sixth time?" Ronnie asked with no remorse.

"It's the fourth time," Monie murmured.

"She's never heard of birth control or abstinence?" Ronnie added.

Nae raised her eyebrows and sighed. "Anyway," Nae mumbled, clearly showing disinterest in Chenille's issues.

Ronnie dangled the Mercedes key showing that she had Rock's car, making herself the envy of her sisters.

"You got the Benz!" Nae screamed.

Nae danced around in her t-shirt and her panties, screaming. "It's time to ride out!"

Monie hadn't thought about Trey in a few days. Since her sisters were planning to hook up with Rock and Tony, she figured she'd hang out too, to be sociable.

"So what's the plan?" Monie asked.

No one had taken the time to come up with a plan. It was obvious that the money and glamour had taken over and changed the girls quite rapidly. Nae called Tony to find out what the guys had going on that day.

Tony informed her that they wouldn't be able to hook up with them because of a big business deal they had going on in the Carolina's. Nae was already disappointed because Tony never called her back about their date the night before. Tony sincerely apologized and promised to make it up to her.

Nae then called Mike to see if she could start work that night.

Mike was extremely obliged to know that she was still interested in dancing for him. Ronnie was again more excited than Nae was about the job. She agreed to take her sister to work that night.

The girls finally got dressed and headed to IHOP for breakfast. As they pulled in the parking lot, Nae spotted and recognized Jerome's car leaving the parking lot. The girls thought nothing of it. They figured it could've been an innocent relationship formed at their mother's job.

Rock, Trey, Tony and Rick headed toward South Carolina for a big drug deal. As Rick drove Rock's shinny black Hummer, the other guys loaded their artillery with ammunition in case the amateur buyers didn't want to cooperate or go by Rock's rules.

Not often, but on some occasions the guys would get into nasty brawls with new and unprofessional business partners.

Rock was curious to know how Trey felt about Monie, since he hadn't saw her in several days. Trey told Rock that he liked her, but there was something different about her, so he was going to take his time with her. He thought it would be better if he waited until she was out of school before he pursued something serious with her. She was a young lady trying to do something positive with her life, and he felt it would be wrong to get her caught up in their world and deter her from her goals and dreams.

Rock thought that was fair enough. He told Trey about the sexual experience he'd had with Ronnie. He sincerely felt like she would be the one he married, if he ever got married. Rock was starting to fall in love all ready. The feelings he had for Ronnie were feelings he'd never had for a woman before.

Veronica and Jerome went to Blockbuster to rent several movies. They decided to go over to his house and watch them. This would be more convenient and romantic since he didn't have any of his four grown children living with him. Veronica and Jerome just wanted to spend the entire day together just getting to know each other better.

Veronica found Jerome to be quite a comedian. He told so many stories about his childhood, to a point that by the time they'd left Blockbuster and made it closer to his house, Veronica had stomach pains from laughing so hard.

Jerome made a right turn on a street very unfamiliar to Veronica. The community in which they were riding through was absolutely breathtaking. When he turned into his driveway, Veronica was truly impressed with his two-story, full-sided brick home.

He pulled into his spacious three-car garage located on the backside of the house. Veronica began to wonder how one man could afford all of this, and why he needed so much room for just himself.

Jerome took Veronica on a full tour of his five bedroom, four bath, lavish home. She instantly fell in love with the plush, emerald green carpet that ran throughout most of the house.

The kitchen was huge, filled with all stainless steel appliances. The large island and cabinets were cherry oak wood with white marble counter tops. The floor tile was white with black hashes cut into them. Jerome wrapped his arms around Veronica's waist and said, "This is where most of our meals will be made."

Veronica turned to face Jerome with a big smile.

"This home is immaculate, but why do you need so much space?" Veronica asked.

He explained that his wife was a real estate attorney. While she was in college, she worked at a nursing home part time. One of the old, rich patients didn't have any next of kin and took a liking to her. The old lady died right before his wife graduated law school. Later she found out that the old lady had put her in her will before she died, and fortunately she inherited everything the lady had, which was the house and a half million dollars.

Jerome mentioned that the house had more space than he needed, but he was going to keep it due to its sentimental values. He also explained that before his wife died, she made him promise that he would go on with his life, find another wife, and be happy.

The new couple watched their movies and played Scrabble for most of the evening. Veronica told Jerome to take her home to get something that she'd forgotten. When she arrived at her house she noticed that the black Mercedes was still in front of the house. Since her mind was on Jerome, she didn't bother to ask her daughters if they had any knowledge of it. She was so wrapped up in her day, she really wasn't too concerned about who the car belonged to. She just never imagined one of her daughters having it in their possession.

When Veronica came out of the house, Jerome saw that she had a picnic basket. He knew the perfect place to take her where she would be happy and able to follow through with her plans. He took her to a park with a beautiful lawn, a shaded walking trail and a pond full of swimming swans.

Veronica found an old Frisbee in the bottom of her picnic basket. After she and Jerome finished their snack, they played Frisbee. They both felt young and alive again in each other's presence. She knew that he would eventually be her husband.

Meanwhile, the girls decided to go to the park where all the guys hang out and ride their motorcycles. They knew they would be the center of attention while riding around in a Mercedes with twenty-inch rims. Ronnie was fascinated with motorcycles. She hoped she'd be able to sweet talk one of the guys into taking her for a ride while she was out there.

Monie warned her that she was playing with fire. Most of the guys out there knew Rock's vehicles and knew that she had to be his woman in order for her to be in his car. Ronnie figured she wasn't going to cross any boundaries with any of the guys, but since Rock was out of town, he wouldn't know anything once he returned.

Nae spotted Josh sitting on the curb near his motorcycle, bobbing his head to some music that was playing from a truck parked in front of him. She and her sisters walked over to him.

"Hey Josh, what's goin' on? I didn't know you had a bike." Nae said.

Josh instantly recognized Ronnie. He stood up and gave Ronnie and Monie big long hugs. He was still attracted to Ronnie as he was nearly ten years ago when they were relatively young back in junior high school. Even though Josh was attracted to Ronnie years ago, she never considered dating him. They just remained close and hung out like they were family.

"You remember us?" Monie asked.

"Yeah, I do. How can I forget you? Ya'll are like the sisters I never had," Josh replied.

"So, what are you doing down here?" Monie asked.

"I'm waiting for my brother, Jason, and my cousins, Chris and Corey. They went to get some gas so we can go riding."

"When are you going to take me for a ride?" Ronnie asked seductively.

"I didn't know you liked to ride. I can take you now if you're ready to go," Josh happily replied.

Ronnie was ready to jump on the back of Josh's shinny red and black Ninja Kawasaki. They heard the idling engines of a couple of motorcycles approaching. Ronnie put her leg back down to wait and see if her sisters were planning to ride as well.

Jason and his cousins drove up and parked next to the girls and his brother. Jason didn't bother to take his helmet off. He jumped off his bike and ran over to Monie, picked her up, and spent her around. He was overly anxious to see her. He'd heard she was in Atlanta, but he never received the number from his brother to call her.

He finally took his helmet off, and Monie had to do a double take. She'd never seen a man so handsome, who was overwhelmed by her presence the way Jason was. She knew she would have to think long and hard about if she would pass on an opportunity of possibly dating him, or should she pursue something serious with Trey. At that point, dating anyone was pushed on the back burner. She was only worried about jumping on the back of someone's bike.

Nae thought it would be a good idea to take Rock's car home. They didn't know if he had enemies or ex-girlfriends, who would come and do something to the car, while they were gone riding. She wanted to say something, but she didn't want to put Ronnie on the spot in front of Josh.

Josh interrupted all of the small conversations that were going on amongst them to introduce everyone.

"Excuse me. I'm sorry for being so rude. Corey and Chris, these lovely ladies are our childhood friends from Jersey. This is Ronnie, this is Monie, and this is Renae."

Corey and Chris chimed in together, "It's nice to finally meet you."

"I thought they forgot about an introduction. We weren't gonna try to take ya'll away from them or nothin'," said Chris.

Nae thought Chris and Corey looked okay. They weren't drop dead gorgeous or anything, but they were comical. Nae suggested that the guys follow them back to the house so they could drop off the car and then go riding. The guys agreed. Ronnie was so eager to get on the bike that she made Nae and Monie take the car, while she, Josh and everyone else trailed them on the bikes.

Shonte drove up just as Nae and Monie were about to get in the Benz. Shonte realized that it was Rock's car and stopped next to them.

Nae noticed Shonte was giving her a long continuous stare. Before Nae got in the drivers door, she stopped, rolled her neck to one side and asked Shonte, "Can I help you with something?"

Shonte rolled her eyes and sped off. She immediately called Rock to inform him of what was going on. Rock saw Shonte's number on his cell phone's caller ID and refused to answer it the first few times it rang.

Shonte knew that one of the girls had to either be Rock's new girlfriend or someone he had doing drops for him. She was ready to stir up some drama. She couldn't wait to tell Rock about what she'd just witnessed. She'd seen the girls conversing with Josh, but she wasn't sure of what kind of relationship they had with Rock or how they managed to get his car.

Shonte attempted to call Rock a fourth time. He was tired of her calling his phone, so he decided to answer.

"Hey Rock, where are you?" Shonte asked with devious intentions.

"Why? What do you want?" Rock asked furiously.

"I just wanted to know if you knew where your black Benz was."

"Thanks for your concern, but as a matter of fact, I do know where it is."

"You already know about the three girls doggin' your ride?"

Rock listened for a moment because he knew Shonte didn't know about Ronnie and her sisters, so there could've been a slight bit truth in what she was saying.

"The girls who have your car were hugging and kissing all over some guys on motorcycles down here at the park," Shonte emphasized.

"I'll handle it. Again, I appreciate your concern," Rock replied.

Rock ended the call as he heard Shonte about speak, ready to add more lies onto the truth in which she'd already stretched.

Rock had already called Ronnie several times before Shonte called him. He just wanted to hear her sweet voice as he journeyed to the Carolina's. He continued calling her, unable to succeed in getting an answer. His mind began wandering due to his unsuccessful attempts in reaching her on her new cell phone and the story he'd just heard from Shonte.

Nae got in the car and began to drive off when she heard a phone ring. She and Monie both were unaware that Ronnie had a phone. Monie picked up Ronnie's purse from underneath the front passenger seat and found a new cell phone inside. She figured Rock had bought it for her, so it may have been him calling. She didn't answer it because she didn't know how to explain why she was in a car with Ronnie's phone, and Ronnie couldn't answer the call. The same caller called the phone at least six times by the time they reached their house.

Nae parked the Benz and got out, ready to get on Chris's bike. Monie handed Ronnie her phone to show her all of her missed calls. Ronnie got off the bike and walked toward the house to call Rock back. When he answered, he sounded furious.

"I've been trying to call you for the past hour. Where were you?" Rock asked calmly.

"I was at the park."

"With who?"

"I'm with Monie and Nae. Why? What's wrong?"

"Nothing. I was just missing you."

The guys were in the background revving up their engines and showing off for the girls; unaware that Ronnie was on the phone. Rock was starting to wonder how much of Shonte's story was factual. Rock was picking Ronnie for the truth. She was unaware that someone had already given him their perspective of what happened at the park.

"Are you riding on motorcycles or something?"

Rock asked, hoping to get a feasible story.

Ronnie explained that she and her sisters went to the park and ran into Josh and Jason, who were their childhood friends, and in many cases, they considered themselves to be cousins since their mother's were so close. Since the guys were on their motorcycles and offered to take the girls out for a ride, they took his car home so it would be safe.

Rock gave off a sigh of relief, knowing that Ronnie could be trusted and be courteous while handling his personal belongings. Rock believed that Ronnie had no reason to lie, and the story was now on track and made sense.

"Can I call you later?" Ronnie asked with innocence.

"Sure," Rock replied.

"Okay. I'll talk to you then."

Ronnie ended the call and ran back down to where everyone was waiting for her. She grabbed her purse from the front seat of the car, stuffed her phone in it, and ran back up to the house to leave her purse there. As Ronnie walked back down the hill to get on Josh's bike, she noticed a car turning around in the cul-de-sac. She didn't think twice about the car's normal activity.

Nae and Corey were on his bike, waiting for the car to pass so Corey could pull off. As the car passed, Nae looked in it and recognized the driver of the car from the park. She knew it was the girl who was staring at her as she got in Rock's car. Nae knew the girl probably followed them home, but she didn't know why the girl was trying to give her such a hard time. Nae was going to mention it to Ronnie the first chance she got.

The guys pulled off and took the girls downtown on North Ave. and Peachtree Street to where the rest of the bikers hung out. The guys wanted to show off their bikes and the girls. The girls were ecstatic just to be there.

After being there mingling and checking out other bikes for a few hours, Nae asked Corey to take her home so she could get ready for work. Corey asked her where she worked. He wanted to drive her to work if she didn't mind. Nae was embarrassed to inform him that it was her first night as a dancer at Club Passion.

Nae told Corey that it would be her first night working at Club Passion; however, she lied about her job description. She told him that she would be waiting tables. After she let the lie roll off of her tongue, she regretted saying it, because she didn't know if he would probably think less of her by thinking she was just a waitress.

Corey saw the humility in her eyes and in her facial expressions. He comforted her by telling her about how beautiful she was and that she would still be beautiful if she scrubbed toilets and floors.

Nae appreciated his generous comments, but then she thought if she'd told him the truth, he might not have been as generous. She just hoped he never came to the club when it was her turn to perform.

The guys felt it would be better if all of the girls stayed together, so Josh and Jason took Ronnie and Monie home as well. Ronnie had the urge to hang out all night, but she was a bit uncomfortable hanging out with four guys and being the only female. Monie would've stayed out with her, but she had class the next morning and felt that it would be in her best interest to wrap things up early.

The time was approaching nine thirty. Nae and Ronnie were on their way to the club since Nae had to be there by ten o'clock. Ronnie constantly talked to Nae trying to ease her mind and calm her nerves so her night would go smoothly.

After Ronnie dropped her sister off and headed home, Nae was overcome by fear. She felt like she was all alone in a whole new world.

She knew she wouldn't be working there long.

When Nae reached the dressing room, some of the girls looked at her as if they were wishing she would fail and never return. Some of the girls greeted her with open arms, giving words of encouragement and motivation. Nae was simply ready for the night to end. She didn't like to be looked at by a bunch of females like she was a piece of meat.

A fairly pretty, young lady named Sondra approached her. Sondra had danced at another club for a few months, but she was new to Passions also.

"Hey newbie," Sondra whispered.

Nae looked around to see who was calling her a newbie. Sondra extended her hand to shake Nae's hand.

"I'm Sondra."

Nae shook Sondra's hand and gave her a nervous smile.

"I'm Nae."

"Girl, you look horrified. Don't feel bad. I'm new too," Sondra said.

"Is this your first time dancing?"

Nae nodded her head. She didn't want to seem obvious, but it came naturally. Sondra gave Nae a few tips about being on stage. She told her to find the ugliest guy in the audience and give him direct eye contact. Nae started laughing, thinking Sondra was trying to be funny. It broke the ice between the two girls, but Sondra explained that she was dead serious. She told Nae to make this ugly man feel like he was the most important guy in the club. In return she would get good tips from him and his buddies. At the same time, he would make her feel like she was the best dancer the club had to offer.

Sondra heard her name as the next performer up. She gently slapped Nae on the on her hip and said, "Good luck Newbie."

Nae looked at how thin and curvaceous Sondra was and started feeling discouraged. Nae was kind of thick, but her butt wasn't as round as she would've liked it to have been. She knew she would have to join a gym soon. She started feeling a bit self-conscious from wearing such a skimpy costume. She meditated on what Sondra told her to do in order to overcome her fear.

Nae heard her name as the next performer up. She stood by to step onto the stage after Sondra was finished with her performance and made it back to the dressing room. She wiggled her shoulders and hips and whirled her head around in a circular motion to pop her neck and loosen up.

When Nae walked out on stage, she'd forgotten everything that she and Ronnie practiced for that particular night. She scanned the room for an ugly man to focus her attention on. Luckily she found an older, drunk, ugly man at the edge of the stage waving five and ten dollar bills at her.

She was unsure of what she should do, so she danced over to the man, collected the money and started mimicking sexy moves from music videos that she'd seen by J-Lo and Janet Jackson. She tried to search the club for more unattractive men. She started collecting so many tips. By the time she positioned herself to scan the club, the music was going off and her time was up.

Nae returned to the dressing room to put on her street clothes and count up her tips. She was surprised that she'd made nearly fifty dollars on her first night. She was now a little more comfortable being in that kind of atmosphere, but she was desperately hoping that Ronnie would be outside to pick her up.

When Nae got outside, she saw no signs of her sister. Nae thought the first thing she was going to do was buy a cell phone to prevent that type of situation from occurring again.

Sondra walked passed Nae in the parking lot. Sondra guessed that Nae may have been stranded. She offered to take her home, but Nae was a bit skeptical at first. Then she realized that this was the same female whose advice helped her make it through the night. She finally accepted the offer.

Nae felt a little uneasy about being around Sondra, but she couldn't put her finger on what type of vibe she was getting from her.

On the way to Nae's house, Sondra told Nae that her performance was great. Nae thanked her and continued giving Sondra directions, looking around nervously, as if she was enjoying the imaginary scenery.

Sondra asked Nae if she liked to go out to sports bars. Nae told her that she and her sisters go out for drinks sometimes. She mentioned that she didn't have a lot of girl friends and offered to take Nae out to have a good time. Nae accepted thinking that everything was cool.

When they arrived at Nae's house, Sondra asked if she could use the restroom.

Nae didn't think anything of it, so she invited Sondra in to use the restroom and to get a cold drink. When Nae walked Sondra outside of the front door, Sondra quickly turned around startling Nae. She asked Nae if Thursday would be a good night for them to go out. Nae shook her head and smiled. Sondra tried to give Nae a good night kiss. Nae quickly jerked her head back.

"What the...girl, you must be outta your damn mind! You've got me mixed up with somebody else. I don't play that!" Nae exclaimed.

"I'm sorry if I offended you," said Sondra.

Nae felt violated and was almost ready to fight. The Jersey in her was finally about to show itself strong.

"I just wanted to show you my true feelings," Sondra pleaded.

"Thanks for the ride, but I don't get down like that," Nae replied.

She then realized why she was having such weird vibes about Sondra. She wondered what kind of psychotic nut she was about to befriend. At that point she knew that she and her sisters needed to be extremely careful at choosing their company.

Chapter 6

*T*wo weeks later, the girls were very eager to meet their mothers' new love interest. They noticed a drastic change in her behavior. She hadn't been drilling them about their lives the way she used to. They were beginning to worry about her. Besides, Veronica always worried about them and their affairs. It seems her concern was slowly coming to an end.

For a whole week Veronica had been helping Juanita prepare for Tyrone's birthday party she was going to have on Saturday. Veronica suggested that it would only be fair for them to throw a party for both of the guys. Juanita welcomed the idea of having a double party. She joked around, telling Veronica that they'd probably have a double wedding too.

"Maybe," Veronica said cheerfully.

Juanita was curious to find out what had been going on the past few weeks, to get such a response from her friend. She noticed she'd been seeing a lot less of Veronica since Jerome came into the picture. Veronica gave Juanita the abbreviated version of how Jerome wined and dined her, made her feel special, and channeled her attention from her girls' drama to something more fulfilling to her.

"Romance must be in their blood," Juanita added.

The women gave each other a high five and laughed it off.

When Veronica came home from work on Thursday, she was exhausted from all the running around she had been doing all week. Since it was partially for Jerome, she felt as though it was well worth it.

Veronica felt as though she could talk to Monie and catch up on things that were happening with all of the girls. As Veronica started a simple dinner after a tiring days' work, Monie noticed that Veronica looked tired. She felt sorry for her and told her mother to sit down while she finished preparing dinner.

"So, when is your new man coming over?" Monie asked.

"Soon. He comes over quite often. Ya'll just aren't ever here to meet him. So, when is your new man coming over?" Veronica replied sarcastically.

"Soon, I guess."

"So, what does he do for a living?"

Monie had to think quickly to come up with something that sounded legit.

"He does pharmaceutical transporting."

"Is that the fancy way of saying he's a drug dealer?"

"Anyway," Monie replied.

"Anyway my foot. You wanted to talk, so let's talk."

Monie knew that she was fighting a losing battle. There was no easy way for her to clean up or sugar coat things to explain Trey's lifestyle. Monie started explaining that he indeed was into drugs, but he was trying to find a way out of it. Veronica listened but she wasn't buying it.

Monie pulled two thousand dollars out of her purse and tried to give it Veronica to convince her that Trey was trying to do some type of mortal deeds, even though he lived a treacherous life.

"Trey said to give this to you to put towards my tuition. He'll give you some more next semester."

Veronica was in a state of shock. She didn't know if Monie was playing a game on her; or whether she should take the money, or just throw it in the trash. Whatever was going on, she knew her daughter had two thousand dollars in cash that she didn't work for or save up over a period of time.

Veronica told Monie to use the money for books and clothes. Monie informed her that Trey had already bought her books and took her shopping for clothes. Veronica had more questions than answers and knew that Monie couldn't formulate the kind of answers she needed to put the pieces of her confusing puzzle together.

As Veronica sat at the kitchen table in a daze trying to gather her thoughts, Ronnie walked through the front door with a few shopping bags. Veronica glimpsed at Ronnie long enough to speak and went directly back into her zone.

Ronnie went upstairs to put her new merchandise in her room, and then went back downstairs to sit and chat with her mother.

"What's wrong ma?" Ronnie asked.

"Nothing baby. Just thinking about a few things."

Veronica gave Monie a look and discreetly shook her head so she wouldn't say anything about the money.

"So, tell me something juicy about you and your new man." Ronnie said with a huge grin on her face.

"Baby, at my age all the juice is gone. My life is dry. Tell me something juicy about you and your new man. What's his name?"

"His name is Rock. He's tall, handsome and charming."

"Rock, as in a pebble?" Veronica asked.

Ronnie laughed, thinking Veronica was just making jokes and having fun.

"Is he a…" Veronica paused trying to think of Monie's fancy terminology, "…Monie, what's that new term you used for a drug dealer?" Veronica asked Monie nonchalantly.

"Pharmaceutical transporter," Monie mumbled.

"Is he into that also?" Veronica asked.

Veronica already knew the answers to her own questions. She just wanted to see what kind of brilliant answers her daughters would come up with to tell her.

"So what kind of retirement plan does dude have set aside for the future? What is he going to do when he gets too old to sell drugs anymore? I'd hate to see a fifty year old trying to sell drugs to get a tube of Fixodent."

Veronica was being very facetious and knew that the girls hadn't thought that far ahead. She was merely looking out for their futures because she knew that they had failed to do so. She wanted to see if they knew anything about these guys. Veronica was ready to put them to the test.

"Where are these guys from?" Veronica asked.

"Atlanta," Monie replied.

"Were they born and raised here? Where are their parents?"

There was nothing but silence in the kitchen, except for the slight sound of Monie's boiling pot.

"Ronnie, how many children does your friend have?"

"None," Ronnie said with uncertainty.

"You don't sound so sure about that. Has he done time in jail or prison? If so, for what and for how long was he incarcerated?"

Ronnie and Monie both looked at Veronica with gloom in their eyes. Ronnie thought she'd be smart and ask Veronica some of the same questions about her new man to see if she had all the answers.

"So what is your man all about?"

"He's all about business, but he does it legally. He's forty-six and makes about seventy grand a year as a Vice Admiral in the U.S. Navy. And, he is about to retire next year. His four children are grown and have moved out of his house. His wife and mother are deceased, and his father is a retired Marine who resides here in Atlanta."

"You wanna know anything else Ms. Thang?"

"Does he make you laugh?" Monie asked.

"All the time and I'm pretty sure he wouldn't do anything to make me cry."

"I just want to ensure that you're happy," Monie said.

"Well, thank you sweetie."

Veronica scooted her chair from under the table and excused herself to go upstairs to take a shower. Monie told Ronnie, "If she's happy, it'll make our lives a hell of a lot easier."

Ronnie's phone rang. She didn't think it would be Rock, because she had just spent the day with him. She answered the phone, and it was Rock. He was extending an invitation for her and her sisters to go to Miami, Florida with him, Trey, Tony and Rick.

"The three of us going to Miami? My mom would kill us all."

Monie turned her attention her to Ronnie's conversation.

He told her to tell her mother that they were going out of town with a few of their girlfriends.

"She's not quite that dumb Rock. She knows that we don't have any girlfriends down here."

Rock was sitting outside of Ronnie's house in his truck. He told her to come outside. Ronnie looked out of the kitchen window to see if he was actually out there.

"Okay," she replied.

She ended the call and was skeptical about going outside to talk to him. She started to think he was crazy and deranged. She wondered why he didn't talk to her about the trip at all during the time they were together earlier that day.

When Ronnie got in the truck, he had a dozen red roses. She knew red roses stood for love. She had mixed feelings about how she should've been feeling at that time. She was very excited, but still a bit scared that this big hardcore man had fallen in love with her in a month and a half.

Rock asked Ronnie to move in with him so she wouldn't have to be treated like a child by her mother. She thought it would be a good idea for the reasons that he had given, but she had a few doubts in her mind. She was wondering if the relationship would last a long period of time.

"Let me think about it," Ronnie said.

"Ronnie, I love you and I want to be with you—without you needing your mom's permission to live freely. I want to take exotic trips and explore the world with you."

Ronnie had never been in a relationship with anyone who was willing to do so many things and had the means to do it. She thought that if things didn't work out that she could always move back home with Veronica; or she and Nae could get the apartment they'd talked about getting together.

Ronnie saw all of the advantages of the arrangement. But where there were advantages, there would also be disadvantages. With Rock's lifestyle she was scared to see what the disadvantages could be like.

"Let me sleep on it," Ronnie said with more skepticism.

Ronnie thanked Rock for the roses, gave him a good night kiss, and got out of the truck to go in the house. Veronica was back at the table talking to Monie when Ronnie went back inside.

Veronica complimented the flowers and started to ask more questions about Rock.

"Sweetheart, do you think a man of Rock's stature would take you seriously? He must have tons of other women. Women are crazy about money, especially if it comes to them fast and easy," Veronica stated, trying to get her daughter to really think about what she was doing.

Ronnie explained to her mother that Rock told her about his ex's, and that she hadn't been faced with any drama since they've been together. Ronnie was getting frustrated because Veronica hadn't said anything to Monie about dealing with Trey.

"Honey, trust me. Those ex's will come back to haunt you," Veronica added.

"Well, why haven't you said anything to Monie and Nae! They deal with Rock's right hand men."

Veronica explained that she hadn't seen Nae long enough to talk to her about anything. She questioned Ronnie and Monie of Nae's whereabouts.'

Both of the girls acted as if they had no knowledge of where their sister was, but they knew she was at the club working.

Ronnie wanted to tell her mother that Rock asked her to move in with him, but she was terrified of what Veronica might've said.

"You might want to give this relationship a little more thought," Veronica said.

"I think I can handle it," Ronnie replied.

With the negative responses Ronnie received from her mother, she felt like she wanted to rebel against everything her mother had said. She was beginning to feel bitter towards her mother for judging Rock before she'd even met him. Ronnie felt as if she was grown and that Veronica should stay out of her business and concentrate on her own relationship.

"How can you tell me what to do about my relationship and you're just starting a new one too?"

Veronica was stunned to hear that her daughter had such an attitude and would let those kinds of words roll off of her tongue, and directed to her.

"You must be talking to Monie," Veronica replied with a major attitude.

"No, I'm talking to you. How can you give me such critical advice, when you're starting a brand new relationship too?"

Veronica looked at Ronnie as if she had just lost her mind. She put the backside of her hand against Ronnie's forehead to feel if her temperature was normal. Ronnie wondered what her mother was doing.

"Are you feeling alright?" Veronica asked.

"Yes, I'm okay."

"It's obvious that you're not okay. I'm gonna let that last comment slide."

Monie turned her pot off and went upstairs to put her shoes on in case she had to break up a fight that she saw coming. She knew things were about to get extremely ugly.

Veronica was fed up with Ronnie's disruptive behavior and smart remarks. She was tired of arguing trying to make her daughters see that they were heading down the wrong path. Veronica got up from the table and walked towards the stairs.

As Veronica made it to the staircase, Nae walked in the front door and greeted her mother and sister. Veronica turned and looked at Ronnie sitting at the kitchen table.

"If you want to screw up your life, go ahead. Just don't call me when you need help," Veronica said calmly. She walked up the stairs into her bedroom and gently closed and locked the door behind her.

"What was that all about?" Nae asked.

"Mom's trying to give me a lesson on love." Ronnie replied.

Nae got a cold glass of water and sat down at the table with Ronnie. Ronnie was so mad she was almost in tears. Nae tried to comfort her sister by rubbing and patting her on the back, telling her it was going to be okay.

Nae tried to make her sister smile by telling her that their mother either needed to get her groove on or she may have been in the need of some hormone pills. She then started telling Ronnie about the wild experience she'd had with Sondra.

Veronica sat on her bed thinking about the direction in which her family's life was going. She wasn't happy with the thoughts that went through her mind.

Veronica fell to her knees on the side of her bed and cried out in prayer, which was something she hadn't done in a long time.

She asked the Lord to forgive her for the way she talked to her daughters. She never used to curse at them and tell them how dumb or stupid she thought their mistakes were. She always uplifted them, and told them in a rational way that their mistakes were merely learning experiences. She realized that her own behavior was changing just as theirs was.

Ronnie listened to her sister's story about being hit on by a dike, but inside, she was still bitter from the things her mother said to her. Ronnie wanted to talk and express her feelings, but she didn't feel like Nae would be the best person to talk to—especially since she was dealing with her own issues.

Monie would only give out educated advice and answers about how she would deal with their mother. Plus, if she told Monie anything, she knew that Veronica would eventually hear about it and would probably start World War III.

Ronnie didn't want to call Rock because he'd only be harping all night about her moving in with him. The only person she knew to call who might actually listen to her, without passing judgment on anyone, was Josh. She called and asked if he would come over because she needed a shoulder to cry on.

Rock sat at home thinking of ways to convince Ronnie that it would be more beneficial for her to stay with him. As he reclined in his recliner chair with a Heineken in hand, Shonte called from the security box at the front gate. As usual, she was giving him another sob story. Rock really wasn't in the mood for Shonte or her need for sympathy. However, for whatever reason, he let her in anyway.

When Rock opened the door, she came in with a skimpy spaghetti strapped shirt and a too small mini skirt, no panties, and some slip on shoes. She smelled good, but Rock knew that behind the sweet Victoria Secret's fragrance, there was still a trifling and devious woman.

Rock walked back to his recliner. Before he sat down, Shonte ran up in front of him, unzipped his pants and pushed him down into the chair. She got down on her knees in front of the chair and started talking about her issues, with the intent to eventually perform oral sex. He laid back, sipped on his beer and tuned her out, still concentrating on Ronnie. He wanted to spend the night just holding her and cuddling. In his mind, he had to go back to her house and pick her up, regardless of what her mother thought. He just couldn't be without her.

Rock tried to get Ronnie off of his mind. He heard his father's voice in his head telling him to go get Ronnie, and express to her how much he loves her. He continued to sit there and ignore the internal voice. He then saw an image of his father's face. His father demanded him to not make the same mistakes he made when it came to the woman he truly loves.

After about twenty minutes he couldn't take anymore of Shonte's sobbing. He pushed her head back and told her that they had to leave. She got up calmly thinking they were about to go somewhere together.

Once they got outside Rock told Shonte he'd call her later and expeditiously jumped in his truck and started the engine. Rock made sure Shonte left his estate by driving down the long driveway behind her allowing the gate to close behind him.

When Rock made it back to Ronnie's subdivision, he stopped four houses up from Veronica's house, turned off his headlights. He then noticed Josh's truck was backed up in the driveway. He didn't know which of the women may've had company, but he was going to proceed with caution.

He saw two people on the porch, but couldn't quite make out if it was Ronnie or one of her sisters. He did realize that the female appeared to be crying. He discreetly walked down the street pass a few other houses to see if he could make out which sister it was.

Josh stood to his feet in preparation to leave, failing to notice Rock was approaching the house.

After Ronnie blew her nose she lifted her head, removing her hands from her red and partially swollen eyes. She was surprised to see Rock standing directly in front of the house staring at her. She saw Rock moving toward Josh and hurried to introduce them before Rock attempted to hurt Josh.

"Rock, this is Josh, my friend who I went motorcycle riding with."

"Josh this is Rock," Ronnie said without tagging Rock with a title.

When Rock found out who Josh was, he immediately backed off and shook his hand. He grabbed Ronnie and began hugging her, stroking the back her head, as she cried on his shoulder. Josh didn't know who Rock was, but he was glad to see that his demeanor suddenly changed upon their introduction. Josh was ready to tussle when he saw Rock coming toward him in a rage.

Josh walked down the stairs towards his truck with an uneasy feeling. He had high hopes of eventually dating Ronnie, but saw that this guy was obviously her man. All of a sudden it all came together. The Mercedes that was parked in front of the house was the one Ronnie was driving when they'd met at the park. *This has to be his car,* Josh thought. He still wanted to befriend Ronnie, as long as she could contain her outrageous boyfriend.

Josh pulled out of the driveway and headed down the street. As he passed Rock's Cadillac SUV, he knew it must have belonged to Rock too. He wondered what Rock did for a living. He wasn't going to start snooping in Ronnie's affairs. He figured he had her trust and she'd tell him what she wanted him to know in her own time.

"I know ya'll go way back, but I don't like you hanging with him," Rock told Ronnie. "Did he make you cry?"

"Do you know how ridiculous you sound?"

"You're so beautiful and loving. I just don't trust other men around you."

"You don't trust other men or you don't trust me?"

Rock heard the hostility in her voice. She was becoming defensive on her friends behalf.

"How are you going to just pop up without calling?" Ronnie asked angrily.

This was the second time Rock had come over unannounced in one day.

"I couldn't stop thinking about you. Ronnie, would you please stay with me tonight? If your mom starts trippin' I'll take the blame."

Ronnie was already stressing because Veronica didn't want her to be with Rock at all. She wasn't ready to deal with him being all mushy. Plus, she didn't appreciate how he intimidated Josh.

"No Rock. I'm staying here tonight."

Rock grabbed Ronnie by the arm unaware that he was hurting her.

"Ouch," Ronnie moaned.

She snatched her arm away from him and started walking toward the door.

"Baby I'm sorry. I didn't mean to hurt you."

Ronnie was startled and felt like she was in danger. She'd never seen Rock in such a state before. It was like he was paranoid about something.

"Ronnie I need you. Please come and stay with me tonight."

"Okay. Let me grab a change of clothes."

Ronnie wasn't feeling it. She walked in the house to get her clothes. On her way back outside she stopped and gave Nae her cell phone, the code to Rock's gate and the Benz key. She told Nae, "If I call you on my cell phone, it's an emergency so come and get me from Rock's house."

"What's going on? Should I call the police?"

"No and don't tell mom, but I'm staying over Rock's tonight. He seems a little strange, so if I call you on my cell phone you know what to do," Ronnie said, giving Nae precise instructions.

While Ronnie was getting her clothes, Rock brought the truck down the street and parked in the driveway. Ronnie reluctantly walked out the door to get in the truck and head home with Rock. As soon as she got in the truck he pulled off slowly. She looked at him as if she was going to blow a fuse.

"Let's get one thing straight," as she pointed her short and slightly crooked finger in his face. "You're not going to start telling me who I can and can't hang with. I knew Josh long before you ever came into the picture," Ronnie said firmly.

Rock drove with one hand and threw his other hand up, blocking Ronnie's finger from hitting him on the side of his face. He forced her pointing finger down with the rest of them forming her hand into a fist, and palmed her small fist in his giant hand. He slightly squeezed her fist, enough to get her attention to let her know that he was the boss.

"No, you get one thing straight. As long as I'm your man and I'm winin' and dinin' you and providing for you, you're not gonna be hangin' out with those other nigga's."

"Let's nip this in the bud right now. Let me out of this truck and I'll walk back home from here. You can come get your phone, your Mercedes and your keys, and you won't have to worry about me anymore." Ronnie replied angrily, hoping he wouldn't call her bluff.

While they were stopped, sitting at a traffic light, Ronnie flung the truck door open as if she was going to get out. Rock grabbed her by the arm to stop her from getting out on the side of the street.

"If that's what I wanted to do, I would've done it! I wanted you to be with me tonight. I didn't come over here to argue with you. I love you girl." Rock confessed.

Ronnie became extremely frightened and remained silent for duration of the trip. Rock tried to hold Ronnie's hand. She quickly removed her arm from the armrest and crossed her arms across her breast. She had never seen Rock go from one extreme to the total opposite in a matter of seconds.

"Baby, don't be mad at me," Rock pleaded.

Ronnie ignored him and continued looking out of the window.

"A lot of women would pay to be in your shoes right about now," Rock commented arrogantly.

Ronnie snapped her head to the left side to look at Rock.

"Is that supposed to be a compliment? If this is what it's like, they could have these damn shoes!"

Ronnie crossed her arms across her breast and continued looking out of the window again. Rock gave up on trying to converse with her until they arrived at his house. Ronnie jumped out of the truck, slammed the door as hard as she could, and sashayed into the house. She plopped down on the sofa and picked up the remote control. Before she was able to turn the TV on, Rock snatched the remote out of her hand

and put it on the coffee table.

Rock scooped Ronnie up off of the sofa and carried her up the spiral staircase into his bedroom. She tried to be as stubborn as she could, but he finally succeeded in making her laugh by tickling her under her armpits as he tossed her onto his fluffy king size bed.

Ronnie picked up one of Rock's king size pillows and hit him in the stomach with it, starting a pillow fight. They chased each other around the room beating each other with the pillows. Then they started wrestling until they were out of breath and energy.

Ronnie laid on her side on the edge of the bed, with her back towards Rock. He laid behind her gently kissing her on her shoulders and arms. He treated her as delicate as a fresh egg.

Chapter 7

*V*eronica woke up at 9 a.m. Saturday morning and called Juanita to find out what time they were going to start cooking and decorating for the guys' party. Juanita told her to come over as soon as she got dressed.

To help her wake up, Veronica went downstairs to get a glass of orange juice. She noticed Ronnie and Monie in the living room watching TV. She told them to get up and get dressed. She wanted them to go over Juanita's house with her to help prepare for the party.

Ronnie was sure that Josh would show up at his mother's house at some point during the day. She was unsure about going over there to face him after the incident that had gone down with him and Rock. She knew she would have to face him one day, but she didn't want that day to be today. Ronnie finally forced herself to get up and go with her mother.

When Veronica pulled up in Juanita's yard, the first vehicle Ronnie spotted was Josh's. Her first instinct was to tell her mother that she'd forgotten something at home so she could leave without having to face him. She wasn't sure why fear had overcome her so heavily. After all, Rock didn't punch Josh or call him out of his name or anything. Ronnie was just more humiliated than anything else.

Juanita's front door was open. Veronica tapped on the screen door and let herself and her daughters in. Juanita hugged Monie and Ronnie with excitement. It had been five years since she had seen them.

"You girls have grown into such beautiful young ladies," Juanita commented.

Josh had his arms folded across his chest, while leaning against the wall that connected the kitchen and the dining room. He was staring at Ronnie from the time she walked in the door and hugged his mother until she looked him dead in his eyes. At first Ronnie was hesitant to say anything to him. She walked over to him and gave him a big hug.

"I'm sorry about how things went down the other night. Rock is just…"

Josh cut her off as she was in the middle of her explanation.

"That's okay. You don't have to explain. If you were mine I'd defend you too. I can't fault that man for protecting what's his."

Josh held her hands and placed a soft, but quick kiss on her lips so no one would notice. He then glided away to see if his mother needed him to do anything for her. Monie saw what had just happened and walked over to Ronnie smiling.

"Somebody likes you," Monie teased.

Monie had no idea about what happened with Josh and Rock. She just knew that Ronnie was feeling Josh at the park and he was definitely feeling her at that very moment.

Jason snuck up behind Monie and startled her. She turned around and gave Jason a hug.

"Where you been hiding?" Jason asked.

"I've been in school, doing homework, working, studying for tests…you know how it goes," Monie explained.

"You're always so busy. That's why I can never catch up with you," Jason replied.

"I'm just trying to get out of school so I can get the career thing going."

"Well, let's go out for drinks tonight or whenever we leave here." Jason suggested.

Monie blushed and nodded her head, "Okay".

Nae finally woke up and took her shower. She went downstairs to see if anyone was home. She couldn't find a trace of anyone or not even a note indicating their whereabouts'. She looked out the kitchen window to see if Rock's Mercedes was out there. She saw his Mercedes and his Escalade parked in the driveway. Then she saw Rock walking up the front steps.

As Nae headed to the dining room to get the cordless phone, Rock rang the doorbell. When she answered the door she saw Rock standing there like he was in a zone.

"Hey Nae, is Ronnie here?"

"No, I'm looking for everyone myself. I just woke up. What's wrong?"

"Nothing," Rock said as if he had a lot on his mind.

"You ever heard of calling first before you just pop up over somebody's house?"

"I wanted to surprise her."

"You're gonna get enough of surprises."

"What is that suppose to mean?" Rock asked with suspicion.

"Nothing," Nae said with connivance.

Nae's comment made Rock feel like Ronnie may have been doing something she had no business doing. He already had an eerie feeling about her and Josh.

"Nae, if Ronnie was seeing someone else, would you tell me?"

"Hell no! Would you tell me if Tony was seeing someone else? Besides, I know you were talking to some female when you were sittin' down here waiting to take her shopping that day," Nae responded with a major attitude. "She'd be too scared to cheat on your crazy ass anyway."

Everything Nae was saying made him think about why Ronnie was acting like she didn't want to spend an abundance of time with him like she once did.

"Did she tell you she thought I was crazy?"

"No, but she did tell me about when you spent the whole day with her, and then popped up out of the blue, begging her to spend the night with you."

"Nae, do you ever just feel like you're in this world all alone?"

From that question alone, Nae knew that Rock had some unresolved issues within, that he needed to take care of before he drug her sister into his whirlwind of trouble with him.

"Did you all have a chance to bond with your father?" Rock asked.

"No, my dad left when Monie was three."

"If my dad would've treated my mom differently and left the drug game and all of his other women alone, I wouldn't be the way I am today," Rock confessed.

"You're blaming your father for all of your issues?"

"I realize I'm a replica of my father. I don't want to be the way I am, but it's the only way I know how to be."

Nae was starting to sympathize with Rock. She now understood the cause of his anger.

She called Ronnie on her cell phone to find out where she was.

Ronnie informed her that everyone was over Ms. Robinson's house.

"What are you doing over there?" Nae asked through clenched teeth.

"Mom and Ms. Robinson are having a party for their boyfriends. Did you know that their boyfriends are twins?" Ronnie asked cheerfully.

"Did you know that your crazy boyfriend is over here looking for you?" Nae whispered as she walked away from Rock.

"What is he doing over there?"

"Looking for you," Nae blurted out in a loud whisper.

"Tell him I'm out with mom."

"I'm not telling this crazy nigga anything. You tell him. Hold on."

"Rock. Ronnie's on the phone."

Nae handed the phone to Rock. She wanted to go upstairs but she was scared to leave him downstairs unattended. She sat down on the sofa trying to expect the unexpected from him. She didn't know what Ronnie had done to this huge, hardcore gangsta to make him act like he was literally crazy.

"Baby, where are you?" Rock asked with concern.

"I'm with mom and Monie over mom's friend's house."

"How long are you going to be over there?"

"I don't know Rock. Why? What's wrong with you, and why are you at my house?"

"I wanna talk to you. I wanted to take you up to the mountains today. Can I come pick you up? We could go up there now."

"No we can't. I will call you when I get home. Let me speak to Nae."

"Okay, don't forget to call me. I love you."

Rock gave the phone back to Nae.

"Thanks Nae. I'll see you later."

Rock walked out the door closing it behind him.

"Girl, what did you do to that fool?" Nae asked her sister.

"Nothing, he's naturally crazy. Anyway, I left the Benz key under my pillow for you to drive in case you wanted to come over here."

"Okay, thanks." Nae said, happy to have a car in her possession.

Nae quickly hung the phone up and called Tony. She was curious to find out if Rock had ever experienced any mental problems. She honestly believed he needed psychiatric treatment. As Tony's phone rang, she wondered how she would initiate such conversation.

"Hello?"

"Hey boo, what are you doing?" Nae asked Tony.

"Actually I was on my way to come pick you up for lunch."

"It would've been nice of you to call to find out if I was here, or if I was busy or hungry."

"I was going to surprise you. I have something for you."

"You and your buddy Rock are going to get enough of surprising people."

"Yeah, we're full of surprises. Listen baby, I'll see you in a minute."

Tony just let it go and ended the call. He wasn't in the mood for arguing with her. He had intentions of buying her a car after they ate lunch. He wanted to have a really enjoyable day with her.

In twenty minutes Tony was at Nae's house ringing the doorbell. When she opened the door, he 'bo-guarded' his way in, kissing and hugging her. He walked behind her, following her into her bedroom. He pushed her across her bed and laid down beside her so that both of their legs could hang off the edge of the bed.

"What are you doing? What if my mom was here?" Nae asked.

"I would've simply told her that I'm in love with her daughter."

The couple laughed it off. Nae swung her leg across Tony straddling him, starring in his eyes. He slid his hands under her shirt to unsnap her bra. When her bra was loose enough to slightly slide down off of her shoulders, he caressed her breast. Tony pulled her shirt up and off over her head. Nae snatched her unsnapped bra off of her arms and dropped it on the pillow beside them.

For about ten minutes Nae moaned with complete satisfaction moving her hips to Tony's rhythm. They had passionate sex, and then realized they both were on a tight schedule-especially by not knowing when Veronica was going to return home. Tony quickly pulled himself away from Nae and released his organic fluids in his hands. Nae sat up and looked at Tony in disbelief.

She scooted to the edge of the bed and rushed to the bathroom with her under garments in her hand. She ran back to her bedroom door and threw Tony a warm, damp washcloth for him to get himself together while she washed up at the basin. After she was all cleaned up, she ran back into her room rushing frantically to find a different outfit to put on so she could get out of the house before anyone came home and found out what she'd done.

Tony went in the bathroom after Nae came out. He had to finish getting his clothes together to make it appear like he was only using the bathroom in case anyone came home and caught him in the act. He splashed cold water on his face and patted it dry with the hand towel that was hanging above the sink. He looked in the mirror and silently asked himself, "What are you doing dummy? This girl means more to you than any earthly possessions you could ever possibly own. The first time you had sex with her shouldn't have been a quickie. Somehow you've got to let her know that she means a hell of a lot more to you than that."

Tony couldn't believe what he had just done. He was acting like a boy who had just gotten a taste of his first sexual experience. He hadn't done that since high school. He felt the need to apologize to Nae for treating her like a schoolgirl.

He went back in her room and sat on the edge of her bed and waited for her to finish getting dressed. Nae entered in her walk-in closet searching for the matching shoes to her outfit.

"Baby I'm sorry," Tony sobbed.

"Can you apologize when we get in the truck? Nae panted.

She was out of breath from searching for her lost shoe.

"I can't find my damn shoe," she panted with frustration.

Tony saw a lonely shoe in the corner behind her stereo. He walked over to get it for her as she fell to her knees with one shoe in her hand, looking under the bed for the other one.

"Is this the one you're looking for?"

"Yeah," she said with embarrassment.

She grabbed the shoe from Tony and carried the pair of shoes in her hand. As she exited her bedroom door, she grabbed her purse and headed down the stairs. Tony followed her closely down the stairs. She opened the front door and let Tony out first. Then she locked the door and slammed it shut behind her. Once they got outside they both let out a sigh of relief and thanked God for not letting them get caught.

On the way to Piccadilly, Tony wanted to complete his apology to Nae. He was still a bit panic-stricken, so he remained quiet during the whole ride. Nae wanted to ask Tony about Rock's psychiatric state, but she was still unsure about how she should initiate the conversation. So, she remained quiet as well.

When Tyrone and Jerome arrived at Juanita's house, Ronnie and Monie were more excited to see them than their own women were.

Jerome walked in first and saw all of the blue and white balloons taped to the wall. He hugged Juanita first, politely spoke to everyone else, then walked over to Veronica and gave her a big hug and plastered her lips with a long intimate kiss.

Tyrone came in the house dancing to the music. He grabbed every female's hand and placed a delicate kiss on it. He gave Josh and Jason some dap. When he got to Juanita, he picked her up in the air, spinning her around, letting her slide down slowly against his body, in his arms, until her feet anchored on the floor.

Jerome stood behind Veronica with his arm around her neck, hugging her and kissing her on her cheek. Veronica broke out of Jerome's embrace to change the music from the hip hop station, to something the birthday men could better relate to.

"Baby turn on some Al Green," Jerome shouted.

Veronica went through all of Juanita's old music until she found an old Al Green record. She put the record on and danced her way back over to Jerome and replaced herself back into his arms in the position in which she had just broken out of.

"Girls, this is Jerome. Jerome this is my middle daughter Ronnie and my baby Monica. We call her Monie."

"So, you're the one who has my mom all bubbly these days. It is so wonderful to finally meet you." Monie said sincerely.

"Don't be so quick to push your mother off on me," Jerome said jovially.

"Huh, if you only knew…" Ronnie murmured under her breath then showed her mother a fake smile.

Jerome picked up on Ronnie's slightly negative attitude towards her mother, but he didn't say a word. He just kept smiling and admiring his new woman.

"So, are your children coming over to celebrate your birthday with you?" Monie asked.

She only wanted to find out if he had any sons. Then she thought about it. If he and her mother got married, his sons would become her stepbrothers. Monie lost interest in that conversation before he could give her a response.

"One of my sons said that he would try to make it. One of my daughters is away in college."

"Damn, how many kids do you have?" Monie blurted out loud before she realized it.

"I have four children; two boys and two girls."

"Why won't the other son and the other daughter come?" Monie asked without remorse.

"They have issues," Jerome replied in a short tone.

Jerome noticed that the girls didn't withhold their opinions or bite their tongues. He found them to be very open and honest. He could appreciate that more rather than hearing them snickering and talking behind his back.

Ronnie was a bit embarrassed because Monie always blurt things out before she thought about whether or not it would upset or hurt someone's feelings. She was going to start telling people that her sister had Tourette's syndrome.

Ronnie politely excused herself, and went outside onto the deck to sit with Josh and Jason. They were cooking chicken, pork chops and hamburgers on the grill. Josh got a wine cooler out of the beverage cooler and popped the top off for her. Ronnie laughed at Josh's too big chef's hat, drooping down in his face. Josh continued to make Ronnie laugh as he emulated Al Green by doing old dances and singing into the spatula.

Making Ronnie laugh was the best feeling imaginable to Josh. That was something he'd tried to do since their days at junior high school. Monie heard all of the loud laughter coming from the deck and decided to join the younger group of adults. Besides, she was tired of watching her mother and Juanita smooched up under those guys like they were teenage girls.

Jason got Monie a wine cooler too so she wouldn't feel left out. Jason and Josh started cracking jokes about their mother and her boyfriend. They never said anything belittling them; they just told how their mother always blushed at the slightest thing he said.

"Do ya'll get along with dude?" Monie asked.

"I don't have a problem with him. That's her life. If he makes her happy that's cool 'cause I'm gonna be with whoever makes me happy, and I know it would be cool with her," Jason replied truthfully.

"Why. Are ya'll not feeling your mom's friend?" Josh asked.

"I don't know. This is our first time meeting him," Ronnie replied.

Ronnie was starting to develop a certain kind of indescribable feeling about Josh. She felt like he was rational and compassionate. He was mindful of how the females around him were feeling, unlike Rock.

It was as if Josh wanted to shower his woman with love, whereas Rock would only smother her with gifts and forget about love and the small things, which is what really counted. She wasn't trying, but she couldn't help but to compare the two men. From the way she saw it, Rock's end of the scale was falling lower and lower.

The time was approaching 3:00 and no one had heard anything from Nae. Ronnie tried calling the house from her cell phone but didn't get an answer. She didn't want to be bothered with Rock, so she told Monie to call Trey for Tony's cell phone number to see if they were together.

Monie finally reached Tony, but Nae answered the phone.

"Hello," Nae answered.

"What are you doing answering that man's phone?" Monie asked.

"Who is this?" Nae asked feeling a slight attitude building up inside of her.

"This is your sister, where are you?"

"I'm at the car dealership. Tony just bought me a car," trying to whisper to Monie.

"He bought you a car!" Monie exclaimed without noticing that Veronica and Jerome were standing in the patio doorway with the door wide open. They were looking directly at her, listening to her phone conversation.

Monie held her head down with infamy, realizing she'd blurted out something else that would probably incriminate one of her sisters. She slowly passed the phone to Ronnie, hoping she could clean up another one of her messes.

"Who has a new car?" Veronica asked.

Monie put her wine cooler up to her mouth trying to slowly drink every drop of it. She was hoping Ronnie would get off the phone and answer Veronica before she finished her drink. Veronica pulled the bottle down and away from Monie's mouth and asked her again.

"Who has a new car? Nae?"

"Yeah, I guess her job pays pretty well," Monie added franticly.

"Nae has a job?"

Veronica already knew that Nae was working somewhere. The late hours of the night she'd come in on a regular basis was the biggest clue. She figured since she was on a roll, she may have been able to pull that information out of Monie too. Veronica thought it may have been at a club, but she wanted Jerome to see that this aspiring lawyer was always at her best when it came to talking her way out of jams.

Monie started wiggling but the music had stopped.

"So, where does Nae work, Monie?"

"I don't know," Monie replied.

"Monie," Veronica stressed as if she was lying to her.

"I heard she worked at some restaurant, but I really don't know how true that may be. Right now, all I know is that I need to go to the restroom in the worst way."

Monie handed Veronica the nearly empty bottle and squeezed passed her and Jerome, heading toward the restroom. Ronnie crept down the back stairs, perpetrating like she needed privacy to talk on the phone. No one knew that Nae hung up a long time ago. Ronnie was just trying to evade answering Veronica's questions. Josh and Jason snickered to themselves over in an isolated corner because they knew all the answers to Veronica's questions, but pretended to be in their own little conversation.

"You see what I have to go through to get some information from my family," Veronica asked rhetorically. She, Jerome, Josh and Jason busted out in laughter.

Jason saw Monie peeking around the side of the house. When Veronica and Jerome got their food off the grill and went back inside, Monie crept around the back of the house. She and Ronnie discreetly walked back up the deck's stairs to avoid their mother.

Juanita called everyone in the house to sing happy birthday. Everyone went inside, gathering around the dinning room table to sing, and pictures being snapped of the guys cutting their double layer, strawberry center-filled cake. The cake had the number 46 on each end of it. When it was time to make a wish and blow out the candles, Jerome said out loud…

"I wish this beautiful lady would be my wife—soon!" he then let out a sigh of relief, and blew out the fire on his candle. Letting her know how he felt about her in front of everyone was no easy task for him.

He didn't want anyone to think he was soft or that he was in a vulnerable state. He had a burning sensation within that wanted to get mushy with her. He wanted to pour out his heart and share his innermost feelings with Veronica, but he knew this was neither the appropriate time nor place.

Meanwhile back at the Honda dealership, Nae picked out a fairly new maroon and gold Honda Accord. She wasn't able to drive a stick shift, so she drove Tony's truck home and let him follow her in the car. She was overwhelmed by the fact that she had a new car and was about to learn how to drive a stick shift.

When Nae and Tony arrived at Veronica's house, Tony began to teach Nae how to drive a stick shift. She knew the concept of shifting gears and that it was maneuvered in the shape of the letter H, but she had problems operating the clutch.

Once she mastered the combination of shifting gears and operating the clutch, she took a chance in her new car to go pick up Ronnie from Juanita's house. From the itinerary she and Tony formed that day, she felt a higher level of comfort with him.

On the way there, Nae finally built up enough courage to ask about Rock's mental state. She told Tony about his fanatical acts and behavior towards her sister, and she was afraid that he might become outraged at some point. Tony told Nae to call him if Rock's behavior ever became too irrational.

Tony's comfort zone with Nae was heightened as well. He suddenly was ready to pour out his heart to her with confessions. He told her that his entourage had been in many drug wars, and that they'd killed and done some unimaginable things to a lot of people. He stated that Rock may have been paranoid, thinking that maybe his time was coming soon.

He mentioned that Rock was deeply in love with Ronnie and just wanted to ensure her safety. He also explained that in the drug game, your enemies may not necessarily come after the one they have issues with, but they may go after their loved ones.

Nae started evaluating her situation and questioning her own decisions of whether or not she wanted to be with Tony if she was going to have to live her life looking over her shoulder.

Nae parked her car at the end of Juanita's driveway and walked up to the front door. Veronica saw her before she made it there. Veronica opened the door for her and immediately introduced her to Jerome.

"Jerome, this is my oldest daughter Renae."

"Hello," Nae said to Jerome without further conversation to him. Jerome sensed that Nae wasn't interested in meeting him or participating in his celebration.

"Ma, is Ronnie still here?" Nae asked.

"No sweetie. I think she left with Josh. Why?"

Veronica walked Nae outside to get away from all the noise of the party. Veronica saw the car and someone inside of it waiting for Nae.

"Who's that?" Veronica asked while peeping around the parked vehicles in the driveway, trying to see if she could recognize the face.

While still conversing with Nae, Veronica started walking toward the car. Veronica was going to make it known that she was Nae's mother to whom ever was in the passenger seat.

"Whose car?" Veronica asked.

Nae hesitated for a while trying to think of something. She wanted to tell her it was Tony's, but she knew she would have to park the car at home, which meant Veronica would see it there and make a big fuss. Veronica already knew it was her car. She wanted to see if Nae was as clever as Monie was with coming up with a feasible answer.

"That's Tony's. He's letting me use the car to get back and forth to work until I can get one of my own."

Although it sounded good, she saw the paper tag in the window and knew Nae wasn't telling the truth.

"He bought a new car for you to borrow?" Veronica asked sarcastically.

Tony got out of the car to shake Veronica's hand.

"Hello, I'm Veronica, Nae's mother. You must be…"

"I'm Tony."

"Tony, it's nice to finally meet you. I've heard absolutely nothing about you. I've heard of Rock. Are you his…cousin?" Veronica guessed.

"No ma'am. Rock and I are just close friends."

"Oh, okay," Veronica turned to Nae. "Ronnie left with Josh. I'm not sure where they may have gone. Call her on her cell."

Nae looked at her mother with her eyes stretched nearly big as quarters.

"Sorry," Veronica lip-synced.

Nae thought, *Mom is going to get Ronnie killed. I hope Tony doesn't go back and tell Rock that she left with another guy.*

"Monie and Jason are still here. I think they're around back," Veronica added.

Nae ran to the driver's side of the car.

"I'll give Ronnie a call on her cell. I'll see you tonight," Nae hollered across the car.

Josh and Ronnie stopped at a nearby coffee shop to get iced Latté's before Josh dropped Ronnie at home. Ronnie wanted to continue having an enjoyable evening with Josh. She suggested stopping to rent movies or riding his motorcycle. Unfortunately Josh had to take a rain check. He had obligations to fulfill with his mother and brother by helping them clean the house after the party was over. He promised to make it up to her the following day.

Once Josh dropped Ronnie off at home and left, Ronnie called Rock to see why he needed to see her earlier that day. He answered the phone right before she was about to hang up.

"Hello," Rock said, sounding like he'd had one too many beers.

"Rock, I just got home. Did you need to speak to me?"

"I tried calling you at least twenty times today and you never answered any of my calls," Rock exclaimed with a slurred speech.

"I went to my mother's boyfriend's birthday party," Ronnie explained.

"And it was an all day affair? Was it really mom's boyfriend or yours?"

Ronnie snatched the receiver from her ear and looked at it in disbelief of she was hearing.

"I'll talk to you when you're sober," Ronnie exclaimed with an attitude and ended the call.

Rock attempted to call her back at least fifteen times, but she refused to answer the calls knowing that she'd only be accused and insulted.

She figured if she was going to be accused, she should at least make it worth her while. Just by being with Josh all day, the idea of dating him was becoming very tempting.

Ronnie laid across her bed attempting to watch TV. She smiled at the blissful thoughts she had about being with Josh. When she thought of Rock, Ronnie frowned and felt a bit melancholy. She knew it was backwards thinking. She'd catch hell trying to get rid of Rock. She felt like she'd only put Josh in harms way if Rock ever found out that she'd dump him for Josh.

Chapter 8

*T*he blue flashes of lightning flickering through the bedroom window and the loud roars of thunder woke Ronnie up around 7a.m. Sunday morning. She looked around hoping that nothing was about to collapse on her head, thinking she was having her reoccurring dream again. She felt at ease when she saw that it was only a storm, realizing she'd never taken her clothes off and officially gone to bed.

She was so exhausted from Jerome's party, which turned into a cookout. She spent the night lying across the bed with the TV on.

Ronnie got up and took a long, hot shower trying to get rid of the old smoky scent out of clothes, from Jerome's cookout, in which she'd worn all night. She put on her loungewear and went downstairs to watch TV. She'd planned to spend the entire day at home watching movies. She fixed a bowl of cereal and cuddled up on the sofa surrounding herself with all of the pillows.

The rest of the family slowly came down to join Ronnie in her movie marathon. By 9 a.m., all four women were on the sofa watching TV. Veronica asked the girls their true feelings about Jerome and what kind of affect it would have on them if she ever decided to marry him.

"Are you that serious about this guy?" Nae asked.

The girls felt like Jerome was eventually going break up their close-knit family by taking their mother away from them.

"So when are you getting married?" Ronnie asked.

"It's not definite that we are getting married. I haven't known him that long," Veronica replied.

Veronica suggested that they should all invite their male friends over for an extended family day. To Ronnie it sounded like a great idea, but she wasn't ready quite for Veronica to meet Rock. She figured Josh would be the male friend she invited over.

"We've all met Jerome. You've met Tony. So I assume Tony could be excused from the meet and greet," Nae added.

"When did you meet Tony?" Ronnie asked nervously.

"I met him yesterday. He seemed to be very polite," Veronica replied in a calm manner.

Ronnie thought that if Tony came, word would definitely get back to Rock that she dealing with someone else.

"I'll help prepare for it, but I don't think I want to have any friends over," said Ronnie.

"Sweetie that would defeat the purpose of the function. We all should equally participate," Veronica added, with a curious idea of why Ronnie was so skeptical.

"When is this function supposed to happen?" Monie asked.

"Today," Veronica announced.

"Today?" the girls chimed in together.

"I'm not feeling it today. I want a stress free day to myself to just hibernate," Ronnie said with frustrated emotions as if she'd recently been stressed out. The girls were more interested in the movie that was playing on TV, than what Veronica was saying. They had already labeled Veronica's conversation and suggestions as 'non-sense'.

Veronica was persistent with trying to initiate a gathering among all of their significant others. She finally realized her girls had absolutely no more interest in what she was saying and plus, they didn't respond with any feedback or further suggestions.

Ronnie heard her cell phone ringing upstairs. She ignored it because she knew it probably was Rock. She ignored it several other times but noticed how agitated her family was getting by the ringing phone. Ronnie finally ran upstairs to answer it.

"Hello," Ronnie answered nearly out of breath.

"Is this Ronnie?" The girl on the other end of the phone asked.

"This is Rock's girlfriend, Shonte. I found your number in his phone and I was calling to let you know that he is still very much involved with me."

Ronnie was stunned by the absurd news she was hearing. In a way she was pleased, but she wasn't at all content with the way this information was being presented to her.

"Well if you're his 'other' girlfriend, I wish you the best of luck. Now maybe he'll leave me the hell alone, and I suggest you do the same. Oh by the way, tell him to come get his Benz," Ronnie replied arrogantly.

"What are you doin' with his Benz?" Shonte asked angrily.

"I have it because I was truly his woman," Ronnie said and ended the call. She turned the phone off and resumed her position on the sofa downstairs lounging with her family.

Ronnie remembered that Rock told her that Shonte was deranged and manipulative. She was aware that this was probably one of Shonte's sickening attempts to try to make her leave Rock alone so she could torment him again.

Twenty minutes later Rock called on the house phone, desperately wanting to speak with Ronnie. Ronnie picked up the phone and saw Rakeem Wilcox's name on the caller ID. She told her mother to answer the phone so she wouldn't have to deal with him.

"Hello?" Veronica answered.

"Hello Ms. Williams. This is Rock. How are you?"

"I'm fine for now, and you?"

"Fine thanks. May I speak to Ronnie please?" Rock asked politely.

Ronnie was sitting across from Veronica shaking her head "no". Veronica knew this was going to be the start of a dramatic day.

"I'm sorry, but Ronnie's not available to come to the phone right now. Can I take a message?" Of course, Veronica was lying for her daughter.

"No ma'am, I'll just call her back," Rock replied.

Veronica hung up the phone and asked Ronnie, "What did you do to him?"

"I didn't do anything to him. He's just ordinarily crazy."

Nae cosigned Ronnie's factual comments.

"Ma, he's the type of guy that you don't have to do anything to. He has unresolved issues he needs to take care of," Nae stressed.

"He sounds like he's a deranged lunatic. Ronnie, you might want to leave this guy alone. I'm not telling you what to do, but as your mother, it's my duty to suggest certain things like this to you."

Ronnie wanted to take heed to what her mother was telling her, but she still had a burning flame in her soul that urged her to rebel. The demonic spirit within Ronnie was telling her, that Veronica had no right to tell her that she should disassociate herself with her man, while at the same time, she was stuck to Jerome like glue.

Ronnie knew her relationship with Rock was an unhealthy one, but she had gotten used to being treated like a queen when they were together. She knew Josh would treat her well, but he didn't quite have the funds like Rock. Besides, her mother always taught her and her sisters to never except anything less than being treated like a queen.

She figured if she gave Rock a fair chance, their awkward situation could be reconciled and possibly, gain the potential of a normal relationship. She just had to make it clear to him that she wasn't going to take anymore of his crap.

Fifteen minutes later the phone rang again. Veronica snatched the phone off of the coffee table, frustrated because it deterred her attention from her Lifetime movie.

She looked at the caller ID and saw that it was Rock again. She pointed the phone in Ronnie's direction and said, "You need to go out on the porch and set dude straight. If you don't, I will. I guarantee he won't like it if I did it."

Ronnie grabbed the phone and went out on the porch.

"Hello?" Ronnie answered.

"Ronnie, I need to talk to you, but I need you to come pick me up."

"Rock I don't know what the hell you and your girlfriend have goin' on, but I'm too old for games."

"Ronnie I'm at the hospital all bandaged and stitched up. Shonte stabbed me and tried to run me over with her car. Baby I promise I'll explain everything to you when you get here."

Ronnie didn't know what to think. She didn't know what Rock may or may not have done to Shonte to make her go haywire. She didn't know if she was next on Shonte's list. Whatever the case may've been, she knew that Rock would have to do something with Shonte for this erratic behavior to end.

Ronnie ran upstairs to throw on some clothes. On her way out the front door she notified everyone that she was going to pick Rock up from the hospital. Veronica felt bad because she'd lied to Rock and advised Ronnie to tell him off before she understood the circumstances.

Ronnie rushed in the hospital to the information desk and asked the receptionist where she might find her boyfriend who'd been stabbed. The receptionist pointed her in the direction of the emergency room. Once she made it to the emergency room, she saw Rock sitting in a wheelchair with his arm bandaged up, waiting for her to show up so he could be discharged.

The nurse told Ronnie to sign the discharge papers and bring her vehicle around to the emergency room's exit doors.

When Ronnie brought the Benz around to the exit, the nurse helped Rock get into the car. She told Ronnie that she would need to be responsible for him for the next week.

Ronnie didn't want to take on that type of responsibility. She felt as though she had nothing to do with him and Shonte's altercation. Ronnie was bitter about the whole situation. She had to have a moment to reflect.

For one, he took her away from her drama free day and put her in the middle of this unnecessary chaos. And what the hell was he doing with Shonte anyway. Where are his boys and why couldn't one of them come pick him up?

"Rock, what happened? And dam' it, you better tell me the truth!"

"That psychotic nut Shonte. She stabbed me and took my phone, and then she tried to run me over with her car."

"I wouldn't have sex with her or give her any money or attention. She threatened to call you and tell you a bunch of lies so you'd stop messing with me. The next time I see her I swear I'm gonna…"

Rock had to take a minute to breathe. His ribs were beginning to hurt worse as he raised his voice in anger. He remembered as a child he watched his father beat one of his girlfriends until she was nearly dead. It scared Rock to death. He said that he would never beat anyone that bad, especially a woman he once loved.

Rock pulled his shirt up and showed Ronnie that his torso around his rib cage area was all bandaged up.

"Rock, I've never heard of a woman cutting a man up like a steak because he wouldn't have sex with her. How did she get close enough to you to cut you up and take your phone? Since you're such a big timer don't you have the power to make her stop doing this crazy crap to you?"

"Ronnie, I watched my father do a lot of foul stuff to people. He talked to them like they were the scum of the earth. I never want to get that bad. I don't want to draw more attention to myself than I already have. What goes around comes around. I don't wanna be found somewhere dead like my dad. I have a strong feeling that my day is coming soon. That's why I control my temper in a lot of cases."

Ronnie admired his will to be different from his father. She still had so many questions and didn't give Rock a chance to answer any of them. Rock couldn't keep up with all of her questions to give her answers to any of them. He had a headache and was delirious from all of the painkillers the hospital had given him.

Rock was tired of hearing Ronnie's mouth, but he knew she was right. He also knew that she was fed up with his and Shonte's drama, and wasn't going to tolerate it much longer. He knew that if he didn't do something fast, he was definitely going to loose her. He wouldn't know how to cope with that because she was the most valued gift he'd ever had. He assured her that Rick would take care of Shonte once and for all.

It finally hit Ronnie as to what it sounded like Rock was talking about. "You're talking about taking care of her once and for all. Are you talking about killing her?" Ronnie exclaimed with extreme emotions.

Rock remained silent and looked at Ronnie out of the corner of his eye. Rock went into deep thought, trying to come up with ways to make Shonte's disappearance appear to be a suicide or an accident. He thought that a traffic accident might not get the job done. Suicide was the only option left. He had enough confidence in his buddy Rick to know that whatever avenue they decided to take would be a success.

He saw Ronnie's hands flying in the air in slow motion as if she was trying to explain something. Her mouth was moving but nothing was coming out as she focused her attention on Rock more than she focused on the road. Her mouth even appeared to be moving in slow motion. Rock knew it was time for him to lye down.

When Ronnie drove up to the front door of Rock's estate, she noticed glass and skid marks on the brick driveway. When she got out of the car to help Rock up the stairs, she then noticed blood in the driveway as well.

She replayed the story in her head the way Rock told it to her. She tried to get a visual of how things might have gone down, but a few things were still unclear to her. She wondered why Rock let her in the gate in the first place.

As soon as Rock walked in the door he turned on the TV just loud enough to override a low-toned phone conversation. He then grabbed the phone to call Rick. He sat on the edge of the sofa and slowly dialed Rick's number. You could tell that Rock was suffering with the obvious pain that Shonte caused. She had crossed the line and Rock was out to get her. He had to make sure that he was the last person she hurt.

"Hey man what's up? Ronnie picked me up from the hospital and brought me home.

"Yeah, she's all yours," Rock said in code trying not to reveal any names or anything around Ronnie, but Rick knew he was referring to Shonte.

"I wasn't trying to give her a black eye, but I had to get her off me," Rock replied.

Ronnie had no idea what Rick may have been saying on the other end of the phone. Her curiosity was eating her up. Whatever it was, it couldn't have been good. Ronnie was trying to make sense of what Rock was saying, but to her he was talking in circles.

Rock was silent until he struggled to stand up and stabilize himself. His pride wouldn't allow him to let his woman see that her muscular hunk wasn't physically strong enough to maneuver on his own. He grunted and moaned as the excruciating pain shot through his arms and rib cage. However, he was determined to make and expedite a plan to get Shonte off his back forever.

He turned his back towards Ronnie and limped into the kitchen, getting away from her, so she wouldn't hear anymore of his conversation. Ronnie turned down the volume on the TV trying to decipher what Rock was telling Rick. She tried to discreetly go in the kitchen-mostly to hear more of the conversation that Rock tried desperately to keep her from overhearing.

"A traffic accident or suicide," Rock whispered.

As soon as he looked up, he saw Ronnie standing in the doorway of the kitchen and the dining area. She acted like she didn't hear what he'd just said. Her heart raced uncontrollably as she walked over to him and kissed him.

"Sweetie, you need to lye down. I'll get whatever you need," Ronnie said calmly and with sincerity.

"I got it baby. Just go sit down and relax," Rock replied with gratitude.

Ronnie made an honest effort to stick around the kitchen to hear as much of the conversation as she could. Rock was on to her game. He swiftly changed the conversation to something he knew she had absolutely no interest in. When she realized he was on to her, she went back into the den and sat down.

Ronnie suddenly felt uncomfortable being in Rock's presence. She knew he'd killed people before in drug wars, but she didn't think he'd go as far as killing an ex-girlfriend. She realized that she needed to really stand clear and remain in good standings with him. However, Ronnie was also afraid to try and end things with him while he was in that state of mind.

"What exactly do you want me to do?" Rick asked.

"Dam'it you're the hit man. I don't give a damn what you do, just make it happen!" Rock exclaimed.

That was the last thing Ronnie heard because it was in the loudest tone that Rock was able to use at that time. Shortly afterwards, she saw him limping back in the den with ham, turkey and cheese sandwiches for the both of them.

Ronnie was scared to eat, thinking that he may have marinated the meat in bleach or slipped some rat poison or something lethal in it. She examined the sandwich thoroughly, but still had a bit of skepticism. Her once hearty appetite had dwindled drastically.

"Rock, please understand that you've drug me into this uncomfortable situation, and I just need to go home and get my head together," Ronnie pleaded.

"That's okay baby. I totally understand," Rock murmured. "Go home and get yourself together. Take your time. I'll be alright."

When Ronnie made it home, she walked through the door to find Monie sitting on the sofa next to Veronica, crying. Veronica stroked Monie's hair and gently rubbed her head, trying to comfort her.

"What's wrong with Monie!" Ronnie screamed. "Sweetie you okay?" Ronnie asked as if she was Monie's concerned mother.

"She'll explain everything to you when she's ready to talk," Veronica informed Ronnie.

Monie tried to open her mouth to explain, but nothing came out but gibberish. More tears and mucus rushed down Monie's face as she tried to get herself together. Monie got up and went in the powder room to rinse her face with cold water.

Veronica explained to Ronnie that Monie and her ex boyfriend,

Damon, had planned to eventually work things out once he finished college. He was supposed to finish college before Monie, with plans of moving to Atlanta to be with her. Unfortunately Monie had just found out that Damon had gotten her so-called best friend, Chenille pregnant.

Monie was experiencing hurt like she'd never imagined. She felt betrayed by her first love and her best friend. The pain she endured was like someone ripping pieces of her heart out with a jagged dagger. Veronica hated to see her daughter caught up in this triangular warfare that stemmed from what was a peaceful first time love affair.

Veronica asked Ronnie about Rock's situation and what caused him to end up in the hospital. Ronnie explained that he and his ex had gotten into an altercation. Veronica sarcastically threw Ronnie's words back in her face.

"I thought you were the only one he was dealing with," Veronica said with a look on her face that boldly screamed, "I told you so".

At that moment, Veronica felt like all hope was gone in trying to get her daughters to wake up and realize what was actually going on in the big picture. A word of advice was all she had left to give at that point. She'd noticed the girls obviously weren't taking *that* for what it was worth.

"Ronnie, one day you'll understand that there are two kinds of lessons everyone is faced with at some point. They are the lessons that are learned…and there are those that are unlearned."

Veronica shook her head and went into the kitchen to get a glass of juice. She really couldn't be upset with any of her daughters. They needed to go through different experiences with men to learn how to overcome obstacles and hardships on their own. She had to overcome way too many obstacles with their father.

Veronica went upstairs and locked herself in her bedroom. She kneeled down at the edge of her bed and said a long prayer for her daughters. Her prayer was for them to overcome their present trials with a better understanding of life.

When Veronica was finished praying, she laid on the bed feeling refreshed. She began to think about Jerome. She thought about how Jerome may have handled the situation and what kind of advice would he have given to his daughters if they were presented with similar issues.

Veronica picked up the phone to call Jerome. She didn't get an answer at his home. She called his cell phone and didn't get an answer. This is strange. She hadn't heard from him all day. First inquisition sat in, then anxiety began to rise. Veronica wondered where he could've been, or if he'd thought about her at all. She looked at her watch; it was only 2:00.

She figured he may have been getting out of a late church service and would probably call once he got home.

Monie's phone was ringing in her bedroom. She found enough energy to make it upstairs and answer it before it stopped. Damon was on the other end. As soon as she caught the voice, her first words were, "You have the audacity…"

"Monie. Monie. Would you please just calm down?" Damon pleaded.

"I can't believe you have balls big enough to call me?"

Damon had no idea how Monie knew about him and Chenille because he'd just got off the phone with Chenille. He knew she hadn't told her anything. Little did he know Chenille's cousin, Charmaine, called Monie earlier that day to chat, and of course, to fill her in on all of the latest news that was going on in Jersey.

"Monie I don't know what to say," Damon replied sadly.

"You don't have anything else to say to me!"

"Monie, please understand you and I were already broken up. She and I ended up at a party together. Both of us were drunk and it just happened."

"Nothing just happens, Damon! Apparently you weren't drunk enough to…"

Veronica busted in Monie's room, startling her.

"Are you okay sweetie?" Veronica asked.

"Yeah ma, I'm fine," Monie replied while crying and gesturing frustration.

Veronica just shook her head, closed Monie's bedroom door, and went back downstairs. Monie resumed her interrupted conversation.

"I can guarantee one thing. There will never be anything else between us," Monie replied and slammed the phone down on its base. She rolled over on her bed and continued crying uncontrollably. She knew she was a total mess. As hard as she tried, she couldn't regain her composure.

She felt like someone had been stabbing her in the heart, while twisting the knife, so it would go deeper and deeper, trying to kill her.

She had no energy left in her body to do anything so she cried herself to sleep.

Veronica, Ronnie and Nae continued to watch TV downstairs. The phone rang and broke the silence. Veronica received a devastating call from Juanita stating that she was at the hospital with Jason, Chris and Corey.

"Oh my god! What happened? Is everyone okay?" Veronica asked hysterically.

Juanita informed Veronica that Corey had been shot.

"He's been shot! I'm on my way," Veronica responded to the news. The girls saw their mother running around in frenzy, trying to gather her purse and shoes.

"Ma, what's wrong? Who's been shot?" Nae screamed with fear. It felt like her heart had fallen to her feet and started pumping cool aid.

"Juanita's nephew Corey has been shot!"

"Corey!" the girls screamed. Ronnie and Nae grabbed their shoes so they could go to the hospital with their mother.

On the way to the hospital, the girls questioned Veronica about how, when and where the incident occurred. Veronica didn't have any information to pass on to the girls. She figured she'd inquire about what happened once she saw Juanita.

When Veronica and the girls arrived at the hospital the only person they saw Jason.

"Sweetie, where's your mom?" Veronica asked.

Jason was discreetly crying and pacing the floor. He was still in a state of shock and could barely answer Veronica's questions. He confusingly pointed towards the nurse's station. Veronica saw that Jason was incapable of giving her any accurate information.

Veronica asked Jason where Josh was. All he could do was shrug his shoulders.

Nae unattached Jason's cell phone from his belt. She scrolled through his numbers to find Josh's cell phone number. When she successfully found Josh's number she called it to find out exactly what was going on.

"Josh? This is Nae. What is going on? Where are you? Your brother is in a state of shock and he can't accurately respond to anything."

"He went out with Chris and Corey last night. They got carjacked and when one of the jackers saw Corey trying to ID him, he shot him. My mom is in ICU with him."

"Where are you and Chris?" Nae inquired hysterically.

"We're headed to the airport to pick up my aunt Jackie. She's flying in from Jersey. We should be back in the next thirty minutes."

Veronica embraced Jason trying to comfort him and reminded him to stay prayerful. Veronica realized that she had been relying on prayer a lot lately. She was starting to get back in tune with her spirituality that she once had strongly.

Ronnie's phone rang while she sat in the waiting area, waiting to hear any type of progress report. She excused herself and went outside to talk to Rock.

"Baby, where are you?" Rock asked. "I've been trying to call you at the house for at least an hour."

"I'm at the hospital," Ronnie replied.

"Again? What happened this time? Are your mom and sisters okay?"

"Yeah we're fine. A close friend of the family was shot. I'm here with Nae and my mom."

"You're not up there with that guy who I told you to stay away from, are you?"

"Yeah, Rock his cousin was carjacked and shot last night."

"Yeah, and I was stabbed this morning, but you're not over here nurturing me back to health."

"Rock, please. Understand that this is not the time to act like this."

"Understand? I understand that my woman dropped me like I was a plague to run to the rescue of some other nigga."

Josh drove up while she was still on the phone. He helped his Aunt Jackie get out of the truck and escorted her to the hospital door where Ronnie was standing.

"Aunt Jackie, this is Ronnie, a close friend of the family from Jersey." Josh attempted to give a formal introduction.

"Hi sweetie." Jackie threw her hand up greeting Ronnie without breaking her stride, proceeding into the hospital. Jackie had no other concerns except getting to Corey, and being by his side in his time of need.

"That's Chris and Corey's mother- Aunt Jackie," Josh explained.

Chris pointed to the lobby and whispered, "I'll see you when you come in," and followed his mother and Josh into the hospital.

Jackie was classy and quite wealthy. She worked as a part-time manager at an embroidery shop in South Jersey. She contracted herself out to major corporate companies and exquisite hotels for Pennsylvania and parts of New York, making banners and personalized linen. She owned and operated an interior home décor gallery.

Jackie was a bit hippy, yet curvaceous, with a semi thin physique. She strode with confidence with her fitted pink and black Gucci pantsuit, placing her matching Gucci handbag on her wrist.

Jackie was very conservative and never let things get the best of her. Although she may have had a lot on her mind, she never appeared to be in distress, not until she heard the news of her baby being shot.

Ronnie took a double take of Jackie and resumed her meaningless conversation with Rock. He heard Chris whisper something to Ronnie, but he couldn't make out what was said.

"He can't even respect the fact that you're on the phone!" Rock exclaimed.

"When you get finished playing nurse to him, could you come and play nurse to me since I am the one who takes care of you."

"You know what Rock, since you don't know what's going on, you need to shut the hell up!" Ronnie exclaimed and abruptly ended the call.

He didn't appreciate being hung up on. He called her right back but was sent directly to her voice mail. He left her a message.

"Ronnie, I totally understand what you may be going through right now. Just do me one favor? The next time you need something, run to that nigga and tell him about it. I'm through with your trifling ass!"

Rock was amazed that Ronnie would still stand up to him, even after hearing the bits and pieces of what he and Rick were planning against Shonte. Rock realized he'd met his match. He wasn't used to a female standing up to him the way Ronnie did. He was used to a female jumping when he gave the command. He noticed that Ronnie was a different breed of female.

Ronnie returned inside of the hospital to see if the doctors had given a progress report. Jason had come out of his state of shock when he saw his aunt Jackie. By the time Ronnie made it to the waiting area to be with the rest of the family, the doctors had already escorted Jackie up to the ICU.

While the two close-knit families waited patiently in the waiting area, Veronica spotted Jerome walking down the hall past the waiting area. She jumped to her feet and rushed into the hall to get his attention before he'd gotten out of sight.

"Jerome!" Veronica yelled.

Jerome was a bit teary-eyed, with a lot on his mind. He turned around and to his surprise, he saw Veronica standing in the middle of the hallway. Obviously, she looked bothered by something he had no knowledge of. She thought he may have been there to show support to Juanita or to drop Tyrone off to be with her.

"I tried to call you earlier, but I guess you were up here. Did you see Corey already?"

"Who's Corey?" Jerome asked.

"Corey's Juanita's nephew. I'm sorry I thought you were here to see him."

"No baby. I wanted to call you. Unfortunately I was here visiting my son."

"I'm sorry. I didn't know your son was sick."

"Yeah, he's pretty sick," Jerome replied with dismay. "Give me a call when you get home."

"Okay, if it's not too late," Veronica added.

"I don't care what time it is. Just call me." Jerome kissed her on the cheek and swiftly walked away.

Jerome had been at the hospital all day, going back and forth between his son and daughter's rooms. Jerome had never mentioned to Veronica that his son was gay, and that he was dying of AIDS. His daughter was suffering with breast cancer.

It wasn't easy for Jerome to talk about it. He didn't want Veronica to feel uneasy around him, knowing that his son was an AIDS patient.

Sometimes Jerome questioned himself about if he had gone wrong in raising his son. No one ever wants to admit that their child is gay. He was somewhat embarrassed of his son's, Kevin, lifestyle.

Jerome knew in his heart that he was wrong, but he was more sympathetic towards his daughter's, Cynthia, situation. Kevin led a normal life in the public eye, but on the down low, he had some very surprising skeletons in his closet.

Jerome had only known about Kevin's illness for about four months. He was shocked, hurt and disappointed when he heard the news of his son having full blown AIDS, because of a secret lifestyle on the side. For six years Kevin had been cheating on his wife and children, with a close male friend of the family.

Jerome wondered if his wife, Kathy, knew about Kevin's secret life before she died. He wondered how she would've reacted if she would had known. He had thought about calling Kevin once he got home. He just wanted to ask him if he'd told his mother about his issues before she was laid to rest.

Jerome was so disoriented. It was a major struggle for him to maintain focus to drive home safely. His eyes continuously overflowed with tears. He truly loved his son, but since he was so hurt, he could hardly find the appropriate words in his vocabulary to describe it to Veronica. He'd tried hard in the past to talk to her about it, but shame and disgrace overtook him, and he immediately changed the direction of their conversations.

Jerome could have dealt with his son's situation better if it had been overcoming alcoholism, drug abuse, or even engaging in sexual activities with prostitutes. He just had a major issue knowing that his son was battling AIDS because of his engagements in homosexual activities. He asked God to take away the hostility he held in his heart towards his son, but his faith wasn't quite strong enough to make him believe that this particular prayer would be answered.

Veronica and her girls, along with Josh and Jason, left Jackie and Juanita at the hospital at Corey's bedside in ICU. Veronica headed straight home to call Jerome to find out the severity of his son's illness.

When Veronica made it home, she went directly to her room and prepared herself for bed. Then she called Jerome. She noticed he still had a distraught tone of voice and an unusually low-key demeanor.

He finally told her the news about Cynthia's battle with breast cancer. Veronica knew that must be a hard pill to swallow. However, she knew something else was bothering him, but he just refused to say what it was. She remembered he said earlier that his son was sick too. Since he didn't mention it, she figured it may have been a sensitive matter that would come out at a later date.

Veronica knew his son's situation was serious because whenever she'd mention anything about his son, Jerome remained quiet for a while. After a moment of silence, he would then resume speaking, but with a scratchy and hoarse voice as if he'd been crying. She no longer thought he had a nearly perfect life.

"Veronica, I really do love you, but I've been going through a lot lately. I don't want to overburden you with all of my baggage."

Veronica totally understood that he needed his time to reflect on the things happening in his life. She thought her daughters had serious issues until she put things in perspective. Realization that everyone around her had an overabundance of detrimental issues, more than she could ever imagine herself going through, finally hit her.

Juanita's nephew was in ICU hanging on to life by a thread. Jason continuously blamed and beat himself up for not helping his cousin, a situation in which he had no control over. Jerome had two ill children in the hospital, both on their deathbeds.

How can I sit complaining about my daughter's relationships? How unbalanced is that? She thought. Veronica knew then that she needed to stop complaining and start thanking God and counting her blessings.

Chapter 9

*E*arly Monday morning, just before the sun rose, Veronica woke up and decided to call off from work. She used a personal day so she could sit with Corey at the hospital in case he came out of ICU. Juanita and Jackie went home to get some rest. Veronica was sure that they had stayed at the hospital all night.

After speaking with the personnel department, Veronica went into Monie's room to check on her. No one had heard anything from Monie all night long. Veronica wasn't sure if Ronnie or Nae had informed her of Corey's condition. As she sat on the edge of Monie's bed, Veronica started telling her about the incident; including Jerome's son and daughters' illnesses. Veronica let her know that she would be at the hospital all day checking in on the three victims.

"Everything that's going on is too much for one family to handle," Monie commented as if she was still in an unidentifiable zone.

"Sweetie, just stay here in bed today and relax," Veronica replied to her devastated daughter. She felt bad for Monie who suffered with such pain. This was only the beginning of many heartaches she would have to conquer in her lifetime.

Monie grabbed her mother, embracing her with a long hug as tightly as she could. Monie felt like Veronica was the only person who wouldn't let her down. She was still very angry and hurt from the news she'd received about Damon and Chenille.

For a brief moment, she cried on her mother's shoulder, and then rolled back over onto her side in the fetal position, with her back toward Veronica.

Before she left, Veronica checked on Ronnie and Nae to ensure that they were okay. Life was a great deal more valuable, more than it was in the past. No longer did she want to feel as if she was taking life for granted. People in her life would know how much she loved and appreciated them, starting with Jerome.

Veronica gathered the belongings she would need for the entire day and began loading them in her car. The phone rang as soon as she pulled out of the garage. It was Jerome. He thought she would be up eating breakfast before heading off to work. Jerome didn't know Veronica was planning to call him as soon as she got situated at the hospital.

Jerome had taken a leave of absence from his job for two weeks to prepare for Kevin and Cynthia's heartbreaking departures. Finishing his morning cup of coffee, just before he left home to start his hectic day, Jerome called Veronica's house again.

As she came out of the bathroom, Monie heard the phone ringing. She debated whether she should answer it or just curl back up in the bed.

While walking into the bedroom, closing the door behind her, Monie was thinking that the caller could have been her mother trying to notify someone of an emergency. Who else would've been calling at 6:30 a.m.? She quickly slung her door open, dashed into Veronica's room, leaped onto the bed and answered the phone before it stopped ringing.

"Good morning. Is Veronica in?" Jerome asked politely.

"She's not here. Is this Mr. Jerome," Monie asked.

"Yes it is. I'm awfully sorry if I woke you. Which one of her daughters is this?"

"This is Monie. Mom took the day off of work to spend at the hospital with Ms. Juanita's nephew, Corey. I don't know if you heard about it, but he was shot the other night. He's in intensive care."

"Yes, I was told. My sympathy goes out to Juanita and her family."

Monie was hesitant and a bit unsure about how to express her sympathies to him for his ill children.

"I'm sorry if I was at all rude at your party. I didn't mean any harm," Monie confessed.

At that moment, Jerome knew that Veronica had told Monie about his children's illnesses. He accepted Monie's apology. They both made peace with each other, both verbally and in their hearts.

Jerome released a long relieving sigh; "I'm going to get that woman a cell phone today. I can never get in touch with her."

He and Monie laughed in agreement.

"Thanks for all of your help Monie. I hope you have a pleasant day, despite the early wake up call."

"You're welcome." Monie laid the phone down on the base and decided to go downstairs to watch TV. This was the first time in two days she felt like she had a peace of mind.

Jerome left his house and headed to his lawyers office. He hated to deal with paperwork, but he needed to get Cynthia's funeral arrangements together and her college papers in order. He was just trying to prepare himself for the inevitable. His lawyer told him that he couldn't ever prepare himself enough to lose one of his children. He expressed his sympathy to Jerome as well.

He still had high hopes for Cynthia to go into remission, but for Kevin, there was no hope. He and Kevin's wife needed to sign a legal document stating that Kevin's wishes were to be cremated.

As Veronica rode up to the third floor in the hospital's elevator, her stomach began to growl as if an angry beast was trying to escape from her belly. There was a young man in the elevator with her. He appeared to be in his early to mid twenties. He looked at her and smiled. Veronica was hoping he hadn't heard the emulation of a beast coming from her stomach.

Veronica looked at the young man and smiled as well. He had strong features like Jerome, but she figured it may have been far fetched to meet his son in an elevator. What were the odds of that she thought? Since he didn't look gay, nor did he have any flowers, so he couldn't have been coming to see a female. Veronica decided to start a friendly conversation, mainly to suppress the loud noises divulging from her stomach.

"Sweetie you look sleepy," Veronica said sincerely, feeling like she had a connection with the young man.

"Yes ma'am. I'm tired and sleepy. I had to get up early to come here to see my cousin before I leave on a 12:00 flight today, to go see my sister next, in Chicago."

"Well, you have an awfully busy day ahead of you," Veronica replied.

Once the elevator came to a complete stop, she said, smiling at the young man "I hope you have a nice trip."

"Thanks ma'am. You have a nice day," the young man replied.

"Oh my god" she thought, "He sounds exactly like Jerome. He even wears similar cologne. That had to be his other son".

By the time she came to that conclusion, the elevator was long gone and she was half way to the ICU area, where Juanita and Jackie sat with Corey.

Veronica spotted Juanita asleep with her head slumped over to the side, with an afghan thrown over her shoulders. Juanita had a cup of cappuccino in her hand that was about to fall onto the floor. There were four empty cappuccino cups sitting on the floor beside her foot.

Veronica stooped down in front of her sleepy friend and tried to pry the empty cup of cappuccino residue out of her hand. Juanita frantically jumped and tried to secure her cup, jerking her body into attention as if she was a military soldier. She wiped the morning moisture from the side of her face and mouth and focused her half dilated pupils on Veronica, and surrendered her cup.

"Where's Jackie," Veronica asked.

"I don't know," Juanita responded as she yawned and stretched trying to wake up.

"I came here to sit with Corey so you and Jackie could go home and get some sleep."

Juanita informed Veronica that she stayed at home all night. However, she and Tyrone had just returned to the hospital, in exchange for Jackie, so she could go to her house and get some rest.

"Where's Tyrone now?" Veronica inquired.

Juanita explained that he and his son were meeting each other so they could visit one of Tyrone's nephews. Veronica started putting the pieces of the puzzle together.

"So that was Tyrone's son in the elevator?" Veronica asked as if Juanita saw the guy as well.

"Oh, so you met T.J.—Tyrone junior?" Juanita asked.

"Not exactly. I knew he had to be a part of the family because he looked so much like Jerome. I thought it was Jerome's other son coming to visit his brother."

Juanita had to think about that for a minute. Tyrone told her that one of his nephew's was sick, but she never thought it was one of Jerome's children since he was so upbeat at the party.

"Jerome has a son in this hospital?" Juanita asked surprisingly.

"Yeah, Kevin."

"Oh yeah. Tyrone told me all about Kevin and his battle with cancer."

"Cancer? No, Cynthia has cancer. Kevin has AIDS," Veronica

responded with confusion.

"Tyrone specifically told me that Kevin had cancer. Who is Cynthia?"

"Cynthia is Jerome's daughter. She's suffering with breast cancer," Veronica added.

"He never mentioned that Jerome had a sick daughter."

"Well maybe we should go up to the sixth floor to see what's going on before he leaves," Veronica suggested.

"He's not leaving any time soon," Juanita assured Veronica.

"Oh, I thought he may have been leaving to take his son to the airport."

"To the airport? I wonder where T.J. is going now. He's always going somewhere."

Veronica really didn't know too much about Tyrone, except for the bits and pieces Jerome had told her. The little information that she knew didn't amount to much. She mentioned that the young man said he was going to Chicago to see his sister.

"His sister!" Juanita exclaimed. "Tyrone said he and his ex wife only had three sons."

The two women started walking towards the elevator trying to make it to Kevin's room before Tyrone left. They wanted to get a clear explanation of all the mixed stories they had been hearing. One of the nurses was coming out Kevin's room as they arrived there. The nurse stopped the women and told them that family members were the only people allowed in the room. Juanita peeked over the nurse's shoulder to see if Tyrone was still in there.

"I am family. That's my husband sitting in that chair right there." Juanita fiercely pointed at Tyrone with her long, red fingernails, as she tried to forcefully enter the room between the nurse and the doorframe.

Leaping out of the chair, Tyrone dashed toward the door and stood there looking out of the window wondering why Juanita was so wound up. T.J peeked over his dad's shoulder and saw Veronica again, this time with Juanita.

"I just met that lady in the elevator. I didn't know you and Ms. Juanita knew her." T.J said, trying to figure out how all of them were so ironically connected.

"That's Veronica, Juanita's best friend. Let me go handle this. I'll be right back." Tyrone told his son as he went out into the hallway. He closed the door behind him as if he was hiding something.

"Tyrone, you're gonna talk to me right now, and you're gonna tell me the truth about everything that's goin' on!"

"Could you lower you're voice please? We are in a hospital." Tyrone asked calmly.

"Could you tell me what I need to know?" Juanita asked with a major attitude.

"Juanita, I'm going back downstairs to find out where Corey is. I'll see you in a few," Veronica stated trying to get away from her rowdy friend.

"What do you want to know Juanita?" Tyrone asked.

"I wanna know everything. Who is this sister T.J. is talking about? Does the poor child in there have cancer or AIDS? Why haven't you ever mentioned Cynthia?"

"Juanita, this is not the time. We'll go to lunch and we'll talk about everything, okay?" Tyrone tried to whisper to contain the situation.

"No it's not okay. Your stories are not adding up!" Juanita was making a huge scene in the middle of the hallway.

Tyrone stuck his head in the room and told his son "If I'm not back in time to take you to the airport, ask Ms. Veronica if she could do it. If she can't do it, she has three beautiful daughters who might be interested," he hinted. He was good at redirecting the heat off of himself and onto something more appealing. He didn't think his son would recognize that he was deserting him once again. "I have to go take care of some business real quick."

T.J. waved his dad off and redirected his attention to someone who well deserved and needed it.

Tyrone went back in the hallway, where Juanita was standing waiting for him. It was apparent that Tyrone was upset and his demeanor was entirely different than what Juanita was used to.

"Where do you suggest we go and talk?" Tyrone asked with hatred in his eyes.

Juanita took a long deep breath to regain her composure. "Baby, let's have a rational conversation over breakfast at Cracker Barrel." Juanita suggested.

Jerome figured Veronica didn't have time to eat. After he left the lawyer's office, he went to buy Veronica a cell phone so he could contact her anytime. On his way to the hospital, he stopped at IHOP. He got her a carry out order of scrambled eggs with cheese, hot cakes, and sausage.

Once he arrived at the hospital, Jerome stopped at the information desk near the main entrance to acquire Corey's room number. He wasn't sure of Corey's last name so he asked for directions to the ICU. Once Jerome made it to the third floor and exited the elevator, he immediately saw Veronica sitting in the ICU's waiting area massaging her temples with her eyes closed. She had a distressed look on her face. He walked over to where she was and sat next to her.

"Hey honey, I thought you could use this."

He opened the bag so she could see that he had brought her some breakfast. Grabbing her by the hands, they walked through the halls surrounding the waiting lobby. He was looking for an area where she could sit at a table comfortably to eat her breakfast.

Once they found a small break room and sat down, Jerome asked Veronica, "So what's the game plan?"

Jerome knew something out of the ordinary was bothering Veronica. She was acting a bit unusual towards him.

"What's wrong honey?" Jerome asked sincerely.

"What's right Jerome?" Veronica asked sarcastically. "Juanita's up at your sons' room questioning Tyrone, trying to make sense of the nonsense he's been feeding her."

"What are they doing in Kevin's room?" Jerome asked as he began to get furious.

"She's trying to figure out why she's never heard of the sister T.J. was talking about in Chicago. She also wanted to know why she's never heard of Cynthia and her illness, and why Ty proclaimed Kevin as having cancer instead of AIDS. She had a lot of questions and no sensible answers." Veronica explained in defense of her friend.

Although he knew that if Veronica went back and told Juanita the truth about Ty, Tyrone and Juanita's relationship would end abruptly. His brother would blame him for the breakup. Jerome still tried to carefully explain his brother's complicated life to Veronica, hoping she'd keep it confidential.

Jerome began by telling her that Tyrone does have a daughter and a wife in Chicago. He mentioned that both he and his brother had issues with their children being homosexuals.

When Tyrone found out that his daughter Serita, was a lesbian at age fifteen, he tried to kick her out of the house. His wife wouldn't let him put their daughter on the street at such a young age, so Tyrone decided that his daughter and wife both needed to leave.

Tyrone's wife, Sonya, decided to go back to Chicago where she was born, and get a place for her and her daughter to live. He mentioned that Tyrone never divorced his wife, and he still disowns his daughter.

Veronica was starting to perfectly understand everything except for why Tyrone never mentioned Cynthia to Juanita. She asked Jerome about that situation.

"Tyrone was convinced that my wife was cheating on me when Cynthia was conceived," Jerome explained. He also informed her that Tyrone never claimed Cynthia as his niece from the time she was born.

Veronica felt more at ease from listening to Jerome's sensible version of the mangled stories. His story sounded much more believable than the patched up stories Juanita had been hearing from Tyrone.

"Why didn't you tell me all of this before now?" Veronica asked with an attitude.

Jerome was wondering where this sudden attitude came from so quickly. He had to set her straight.

"Listen. First of all, I don't know what my brother may have told Juanita. Secondly, it's none of our business what they do or say in their relationship. Besides, it may not be apparent to you yet, but I have two children on their death beds and Tyrone's inadmissible behavior is the least of my worries."

Veronica was appalled to hear Jerome use such an aggressive and angry tone with her.

"Baby I'm so sorry. I had no right to snap at you. We're all under an enormous amount of stress. It was starting to get the best of me," she said apologizing.

Jerome stood up and took Veronica by the hands, helping her to her feet. He embraced her, giving her a long passionate kiss, to assure her that everything was all right. He discarded the IHOP trash and escorted her back to ICU to check on Corey. She asked the nurse about Corey's condition.

The nurse enlightened Veronica by telling her that Corey's condition was stabilized. He had been released to a regular recovery room on the second floor. It felt to Veronica like a vast burden had been lifted off of her shoulders.

She felt like it was her duty to get the word to Juanita as quickly as possible. The drama with Tyrone should've now become secondary. She and Jerome rushed up to Kevin's room to tell Juanita the good news about Corey. When they arrived at Kevin's room, Juanita and Tyrone were gone. T.J. was sitting at his cousins' bedside, holding his hand, crying, as Kevin lies there dead.

Jerome walked into the room, staring at his sons' lifeless body. He sat in the chair at the foot of the bed and hugged Veronica tightly. He endured the pain like a man. He didn't shed a tear. Jerome stood up slowly, walked down to the end of the hallway to the nurses' station. He advised them to begin making calls to notify the rest of the family that they needed to come to the hospital.

Veronica thought Jerome may have needed some time to himself to get things in order. She suggested that she go downstairs and see Corey, to let him know that someone was there to support him.

However, Jerome refused to let her out of his sight. He figured she was trying to bail out on him at one of the most critical times of his life.

He didn't believe he was emotionally strong enough to handle this loss. It would be even harder going to the fourth floor to tell Cynthia about her brother. Veronica was now realizing that Jerome really needed her support more than anything.

Veronica started to have a bad feeling in the pit of her stomach because of not knowing where Juanita and Tyrone had disappeared. If she could get in touch with her girls, this would help put her at ease. At least she'd know that someone was at Corey's bedside, just in case he awakened completely.

Veronica scrounged for an available phone at the nurse's station so she could call home. Jerome had forgotten to give her the new cell phone, until he saw her attempting to use one of the raggedy switchboard phones at the nurses' desk.

As he talked on his phone, Jerome grabbed Veronica's arm, getting her attention while handing her the new phone. He didn't have time to explain the technicalities of the phone. He put his call on hold.

"Just dial the number and talk. I'll explain the mechanics later," Jerome whispered, trying to quickly get back to his call.

Veronica was able to get in touch with Ronnie. "Ronnie, I need you to come to the hospital to sit with Corey. He's in a recovery room in stable condition."

"Where are you?" Ronnie asked.

"I'm at the hospital, but Jerome's son just died, so I'm trying to help him handle a few things. I'll explain everything to you later."

"Oh my God! I'm on my way," Ronnie replied.

While Veronica had the phone in her possession, she tried calling Juanita to find out where she was. She didn't want to call Jackie. She knew she'd be resting, and questioning Juanita's whereabouts' would only frighten her.

Jerome had called his other son and daughter, his father, and Kevin's wife for them all to meet him at his house instead of the hospital. He took Veronica by the hand, leading her to the elevator. They went to Cynthia's room to give her the bad news. Cynthia hadn't walked in almost two months, but when they arrived at her room, the nurse was helping her walk out of the restroom on a walker.

Jerome was instantly overjoyed to see that she had made such progress. As soon as Cynthia saw her father she hollered out "Daddy, I'm so glad you're here. You must be Ms. Veronica. I'm glad to finally meet you."

Cynthia extended her arm to shake Veronica's hand. Veronica noticed Cynthia had a grip of a very healthy person. Jerome hadn't seen Cynthia in high spirits like this in several months. He didn't know how to break the new to his ailing daughter. The disgruntled look on his face told everything before he opened his mouth.

Cynthia already knew her brother was very sick and was going to pass away at any moment. By the look on her father's face, she knew Kevin had already expired.

"What's wrong daddy? It's Kevin, isn't it? When did he die?"

"About a half hour ago."

Jerome maintained his composure. Cynthia knew she needed to be strong for her father. She was extremely happy that Veronica was in his life to help him through this hard time. T.J. walked in Cynthia's room and sat on the foot of her bed.

"What's up cuz?" asked Cynthia.

"Not much. It's good to see that you're feeling alright," T.J. replied.

"If I continually feel as good as I am now, I'll be able to attend Kevin's funeral."

T.J. couldn't understand how everyone could feel okay and quickly accept the fact that their loved one had just passed.

"T.J. Do you know where your dad and Ms. Juanita went?" Veronica asked.

"No, I'm not sure where they are. He told me to ask if you could take me to the airport if he wasn't back by the time I needed to leave."

Veronica looked at Jerome with confusion. Jerome stood up and explained to Cynthia that he called a family meeting at his house, so he had to leave. Since Jerome had to take T.J. to the airport, he was pressed for time. He promised her that he would return later when things calmed down. He kissed his daughter on the forehead and he, Veronica, and T.J. walked out of the room to head to the airport.

As Ronnie and Monie headed to the hospital, Rock called Ronnie on her cell phone. Ronnie struggled to get her earpiece out of the car's console to lessen the havoc of driving while on the phone.

"Hey baby, let's go to lunch," Rock proposed cheerfully.

"Rock, I have a lot of drama going on right now. I can't do breakfast right now."

Rock exploded like a stick of dynamite.

"You always have drama going on and never have time for me!" he exclaimed.

Ronnie explained that Jerome's son had just passed, and his daughter wasn't doing too well with her battle with cancer. She failed to mention anything about Corey, knowing that it would only lead to a fight.

Rock apologized for blowing up at her without knowing the circumstances. He felt bad because she hadn't spent any time with him in several days. He was glad to know that he had such a compassionate young lady in his life.

Monie felt bad because she hadn't talked to Trey in nearly a week. She knew he was beginning to worry about her. With all the drama going on with her mother, Corey, Damon and Chenille, she wasn't in the mood to face anyone. She decided to call him anyway. After all, he was paying her way through school. She was suddenly hit with a reality check.

"This man is paying my tuition and never asked for anything in return. I'm sitting at home crying my eyes out over a two timing, good for nothing bastard who's never done anything except break my heart. I've gotta make some major changes," she thought to herself.

Monie used Ronnie's cell phone to call Trey. Just as she thought, he had begun to worry about her. She explained that she'd been going through tons of drama, and that she was on her way to the hospital to help tend to a friend who had been shot.

Trey told Monie that Rock had mentioned it to him. He informed her to warn Ronnie to watch her back because Rock was jealous of the guy. He had already threatened Ronnie if she didn't stay away from him.

Monie ended the call with Trey and tried to convince Ronnie to go spend time with Rock. From the way Trey made things sound to Monie, Rock was on the verge of hurting her if she continued hanging with other male friends, refusing to put forth any effort to be with him.

Ronnie took Monie's advice. She dropped Monie off at the hospital and headed over to Rock's house to spend some quality time with him. When Ronnie walked through Rock's front door, unexpectedly, his first reaction was to grab his gun and point it at whom he thought may have been a burglary suspect. When Rock saw that it was Ronnie, he limped up to her, ramming her against the door, embracing her tightly. Ronnie frantically tried to beat the gun out of Rock's hand. He didn't know that she had a phobia of guns.

Ronnie still had a strange look in her eyes when she looked at Rock. "I don't know why I'm here. I guess I should be somewhere else with my other nigga huh?" Ronnie said in response to Rock's message.

"Baby, I'm…"

"Sorry…You damn right!" Ronnie chimed in anticipating that to be his next word. She had gotten used to his apologies.

A part of him wanted to punch her in the face. However, the loving and more sensitive part of him was ecstatic. It was the fact of knowing that she thought enough about him to take time out of her busy schedule to spend some quality time with him. He wanted to do something special with his Nubian queen. He suggested that they go away to an island where there was no drama. Ronnie took his suggestion as a joke. Rock just wanted to show her that he honestly loved her and wanted to feel loved by her.

After about an hour of convincing Ronnie that he was serious about his proposal to get away, she finally agreed to it. The couple packed their bags and hit the road. Ronnie called Nae to inform her of her disappearing act that would last for a few days.

Nae was scared for her sister, but if that's what it took to keep Rock happy and to prevent him from going postal on everybody, she knew her sister had to do what she had to do.

Jerome and Veronica dropped T.J. off at the airport and headed to Jerome's house to meet with his family.

Veronica was there for Jerome physically, but emotionally, she was challenged. She wasn't able to think clearly from wondering what Tyrone may have done to Juanita. Veronica called Juanita's cell phone continuously, but never received an answer. She finally called her house.

Jackie answered the phone in a distressed tone of voice.

"Is everything okay?" Veronica asked with a small bit of relief, mixed with anger.

"No, everything isn't okay. Tyrone just brought Juanita home all beat and banged up. They both were bloody and bruised. I'm trying to get a sensible story out of her," Jackie muttered along with some other incomprehensible babble.

"Where's Tyrone?" Veronica asked with apprehension.

"After he brought Nita in the house, he staggered out of here as if he was high on something. He mumbled something about his son needed him. Do you know if he has a drug problem?" Jackie panted as she tried to explain to Veronica and get Juanita situated in bed at the same time.

Veronica enlightened Jackie that Corey had been released from ICU and placed in a regular recovery room. Jackie was elated to hear the good news. She felt like she was in a whirlwind of chaos. Her state of mind was distraught. When she hung up after talking to Veronica, she realized that instead of Juanita being in bed, she needed to go to the hospital to be examined, just in case Tyrone had given her some drugs.

Jackie, struggling to get her sister in the car, rushed Juanita to the emergency room. A few of the doctors on duty in the emergency room remembered seeing the sisters there waiting for Corey. Once Jackie explained Juanita's incoherence and lack of response to the doctors, they checked her vital signs. They knew exactly what had happened to her.

Just as Jackie suspected, Tyrone had given Juanita an overdose of drugs. The doctor also informed Jackie that they would have to pump her sister's stomach to prevent further poisoning of her internal system. As soon as Jackie received all of the information, she immediately called

Veronica, giving her an update on what the doctor's had just advised her of.

While Jerome conducted a family meeting in the den, Veronica sat at his kitchen table as she received the terrible news from Jackie. She got Jerome's attention and beckoned for him to come in the kitchen where she was, being conscience of not baring any slanderous rumors about Tyrone in front of their family.

"Baby, I think your brother may be on drugs," Veronica cried discreetly to Jerome.

"What makes you say that?" Jerome asked with a look of frustration.

"Juanita's sister just took her to the hospital. The doctors diagnosed that she had a drug overdose and they have to pump her stomach. Juanita's not a drug user. Jackie mentioned earlier that Tyrone looked like he was high or something," Veronica explained.

Jerome explained to Veronica that his brother once had a drug addiction. Once he gets overly stressed, he occasionally tends to have relapses. He started feeling terrible because Juanita didn't deserve to go through everything she was going through. He hated that she had to be a victim of his brother's occasional fiasco.

While Jerome was in the midst of his family meeting, he had his father to call Tyrone and demand his presence at the meeting. The family all agreed to have Tyrone admitted to rehab as soon as he arrived. Jerome's father immediately called the rehab center. Tyrone had been attending for years, off and on. His father notified them of Tyrone's reoccurring condition, and that they would bring him in within a few hours.

Jerome was in such a vulnerable state. He wanted to break down and cry. However, Jerome was the strong tide in the family. Before he could overcome one obstacle, it seemed as if three more stood in his way. He decided that once Kevin's going away service was over, he and Veronica were going to take a trip to an undisclosed location so no one could find them.

Kevin's service was set up for the upcoming Wednesday, which would only give Jerome two days to get everything in order. Kevin's wife, Robin, was very bitter and reluctant to assist Jerome with anything that had to do with Kevin.

She sensed that something was wrong about a year prior to everything actually happening. She had stopped having sex with Kevin over a year ago. She hadn't yet been diagnosed with HIV or AIDS. Even though she'd stopped having an intimate relationship with him well over a year ago, she was still scared that she might have a disease that may surface later.

The family concluded their meeting as Tyrone stumbled in the door, bloody and bruised. "What happened to you?" Veronica yelled out with concern.

Jerome held Veronica back from going near him. He gestured to her to end all conversation with his druggy, drunken brother. He hated the fact that Veronica had to witness the madness his family constantly had to go through. However, if she wanted to be a part of the family, she would have to learn to deal with it.

Chapter 10

*W*ednesday morning Veronica woke up next to Jerome. Her heart skipped three beats. She wasn't absolutely sure, but she didn't really know if she'd had sex with him the night before. She looked over by the wastebasket and saw empty bottles, which once contained some kind of alcoholic beverage.

She wondered if she had gotten drunk and given in to him, letting him fulfill his sexual needs and desires. If in deed she had gotten intoxicated, she had enough confidence in him to know, or at least hope, that he wouldn't have taken advantage of her while she was incoherent.

She thought she had enough self-control to prevent being in such predicament. She lifted the top sheet to smell for any kind of odor, caused by bodily secretions that may have remained and attached her to any sexual activity. She got out of bed and went to the bathroom. She sat on the toilet, wondering if she'd had sex with this man. Although he was her man, she at least wanted their first time to be a memorable one.

Jerome called her name with a cracked and groggy voice. Veronica jumped up and turned the water on in the sink, just enough to dampen her hands. Looking half way refreshed, she walked out of the bathroom to see what he wanted.

"There you are. I thought you'd left and went home." Jerome was delighted to see that she was still there with him.

"We need to get up and get going," Veronica commanded. "We have a long day ahead of us."

Jerome had no energy or enthusiasm. "I have a slight headache. I think I drank too much. Thank you for listening last night," Jerome babbled.

He explained how he had given her a few sips of his vodka before he'd started pouring out his confessions. She willingly consumed the liquor and quietly listened to him all night long, as he cried and talked about his issues. Veronica wanted to confess to Jerome, but thought it may hurt his feelings. She didn't know how to tell him that she didn't hear nor comprehend anything that was said to her last night. The truth of the matter is that Veronica had fallen fast asleep as soon as her head hit the pillows.

By 10:00 a.m. Jerome and Veronica waited patiently at his estate as all of his immediate family slowly drifted in one by one. At 11:30am, everyone who was going to attend Kevin's service was there waiting for the limo to pick them up and take them to the funeral home.

Jerome was quite surprised to see that T.J. had made it back to Atlanta in time for the service. He brought his sister, Serita, and his mother with him. Jerome introduced Veronica to Sonya, "Veronica, this is my sister-in-law, Sonya."

Sonya extended her hand to shake Veronica's. "You're Juanita's friend, right?"

Veronica was lost for words. As she took a long deep breath, her eyes crossed and her stomach suddenly felt like it was filled with lead. Veronica put on a fake smile and nodded her head.

"Yes," she said softly with embarrassment. By meeting Tyrone's wife and befriending his girlfriend, Veronica felt she was in an awkward, yet mind-boggling position. She thought it to be a bit unusual for his wife to be okay with the fact of him having a girlfriend. *"Maybe Sonya doesn't know the full story. She may think that her husband and Juanita are just business partners of some kind. God please let that be the case,"* Veronica thought and prayed.

Shortly following the service Sonya made her way over to Veronica.

"I'll be here for a few days. If I don't get a chance to bump heads with Juanita, please tell her I said hello," Sonya whispered.

"How do you know of Juanita?" Veronica asked.

"Even though I'm in Chicago, I still have children and friends here. Since Tyrone won't give me a divorce, I hired a P.I. to get proof he was cheating, so I could divorce him on adultery. Unfortunately, your girlfriend happened to be the victim of this adulterous crime. Better her than me. I've done my time with that crazy nut. I'll see you around," Sonya replied with no remorse.

Sonya and Serita had to leave directly following the memorial.

Serita was eager to see her father. She wanted nothing more than to show Tyrone what a fine, feminine young lady she had developed into. Serita wanted badly to hold a grudge against him. However, her heart wouldn't allow her to carry any animosity towards him due to her knowledge of his ignorance. She didn't hate him, but she didn't want anything to do with him at this point in her life.

Once Sonya pulled up into the rehabs parking lot, she asked Serita one last time. "Are you sure you want to do this?"

"Yes, I want him to see what he's been missing out on. He has to see that he'd given up on his family for nothing."

Serita was confident the repercussions that were set against his life were severe enough, even without her adding fuel to the fire. While Serita had her time with her father, Sonya waited in the lobby.

Serita crept up to the door knocking twice, very lightly. Tyrone ignored the knocks. He simply continued staring out the window, wishing he were on the outside. *"How can I correct the wrongs I've done to everyone in my past,"* he thought. As Serita opened the door, she felt a cold chill flow through her body, like an ice cube sliding down her spine.

"Tyrone," she whispered.

He remembered the familiar voice. The voice he thought he'd never hear again. Over the years, he had many regrets about what he'd done in the past. His pride wouldn't allow him to ask for forgiveness for him tearing his family apart.

Serita stood next to the door as Tyrone turned to look at her with widened, teary eyes.

"There are so many things I want to tell you. I don't know where to begin."

Serita purposely crossed her hands in front of her, showing off her wedding rings.

"So you're married now?" Tyrone asked with a river of emotions running inside of him.

"As a matter of fact I am…to a man," she added.

The guilt for what he had done made his flesh crawl, like it was being torn apart and turned inside out. With his arms extended, Tyrone stood up, walked over to Serita, and asked for a hug, and for her forgiveness.

Serita refused to let him touch her.

"Tyrone, I don't want your hugs now. I needed them when I was a teenager. Remember when you turned your back on me and put me out on the streets?"

"Regardless of how mad you get at me, I'm still your father. You should at least address me as dad."

"If you acted like my dad or even treated me like you were my dad, then maybe I would call you dad."

"Serita, I was young, dumb, and on drugs. I didn't know any better," Tyrone pleaded with his estranged daughter.

A part of Serita wanted to cry, but she felt as though she needed to maintain her hard-hitting image. This was the only way to let Tyrone know she was no longer the weak little girl that he once threw around and treated like the enemy.

Tyrone reached forward, in an attempt to gently take his daughter's hand and compliment her ring. Serita snatched her hand back and blurted, " You're pathetic."

She opened the door to end the visit. "Serita, do you mind if I get your number to call you so we can catch up?"

Serita looked at her father with a raging anger in her eyes. She wondered what he could possibly want to tell her after four years of a nonexistent relationship. Nothing could restore the years of desolation she'd suffered.

"If you want it bad enough, you'll find it," Serita replied remorselessly before exiting Tyrone's room.

Tyrone had been praying for the day that his daughter would come back to see him. He sat in his room, virtuously lifeless, day after day, hoping and praying that the family could actually be a family again. He sought closure with his entire family for destroying the close bond they once had. Seeing his daughter brought back the hope he'd just lost.

Veronica felt obligated to get to the hospital to inform Juanita of what was going on. She reluctantly waited for the family, who were engaged in a conversation, trying to decide on who was going to keep Kevin's ashes. Ironically, no one wanted the ashes.

Both Jerome and Robin disapproved of Kevin's secret lifestyle and held a deeply rooted grudge on him. They tried to pass the ashes off on each other. Jerome's father realized what was going on and took the urn of ashes into his possession. He despised what was happening; yet he understood the reasons behind it. He was disturbed that his son, Kevin's own father, and wife couldn't forgive him and accept his remains, even after his death.

Jerome spent time comforting and counseling his remaining children. Veronica tried to assist him in anyway possible. However, her mind was on comforting Juanita in her time of need as well. She wanted to get to the hospital as soon as possible. Jerome noticed that Veronica had gotten restless and looking suddenly agitated by something. He knew his sister-in-law probably played an enormous role in getting Veronica worked up. Jerome gathered his 'scattered' family and desperately tried to get Veronica to wherever she needed to be.

Juanita woke up trying to move her aching body. She noticed IVs taped to her arms and tubes coming from her mouth. She looked around, wondering where she was and how she got there. The last thing she remembered was being in the car with Tyrone while he lit, what appeared to be, a joint.

She eventually realized she was in a hospital room. She began to panic but couldn't scream because of the tubes in her mouth. Juanita saw Veronica coming out of the restroom and felt relieved. Veronica had been sleep for nearly two whole days from the dosages of medication and all of the blood treatments she had to go through. This was vitally needed in order to purify her blood and maintain a steady heart rate in her.

"I'm supposed to be here checking on my nephew. What am I doing laying here with all this crap attached to me?" Juanita asked pitifully. "Where's Tyrone?"

Juanita didn't realize that her stomach had been pumped and she'd been comatose for a whole day and a half. She apparently didn't remember anything after she and Tyrone left the hospital late Monday morning.

"Why are dressed like you just came from a funeral?" Juanita asked frivolously.

"I just came from Kevin's funeral. He passed on Monday," Veronica replied while holding back the tears.

"I'm so sorry to hear that. How's Jerome taking it?"

"He's taking it rather well," Veronica responded.

"Where was I? Where's my baby, Tyrone? What happened to me Veronica?"

Juanita asked a series of questions before Veronica even had time answer the first one. Veronica gave her friend a hand held mirror so she could see what she looked like. She had bruises and scratches all over her face and arms.

"Your baby Tyrone did this to you," Veronica replied with animosity.

Juanita burst into tears. She begged Veronica to tell her what happened. Veronica explained that Tyrone had drugged and beaten her up. Juanita was mad at herself for ignoring the signs of a druggy and for allowing the same thing to happen to her a second time. She vowed she would never let a man put her in that predicament again.

Juanita cried out to her best friend and jogged her memory back to a couple of years ago. This was when she spent a few months in a coma because of a domestic dispute between her and her significant other. He put her in the hospital, took everything she owned, and skipped town.

Juanita's dignity plunged to its lowest point ever. She wondered if she was really that desperate for love or if she was just extremely stupid. She felt like she carried a big "H" on her back inviting habitual druggies into her life.

Jerome and Cynthia knocked on Juanita's door. Cynthia was dressed in a cream and plum colored suit with a white carnation pinned to her jacket. She refused to dress in all black like she was ready for death. She was definitely going into remission and was anxious to resume her life.

It was clear to Jerome that Veronica needed time alone with Juanita so he could explain the mess that had been going on over the past few days. Veronica searched for ways to break the news to Juanita, as painlessly as possible, but found that there was no way to sugarcoat any of the situations. As she explained Kevin's death, Tyrone's frequent visits to rehab, and his wife's present visit to Atlanta, Juanita unburied and released her innermost degenerated emotions.

Rock and Ronnie walked along a beach in Mexico trying to resolve their issues. Ronnie hadn't felt that good since she first met Rock when she sat with him in his gazebo at his cook out. She felt like she was on top of the world again. He tried to convince her to relocate with him so they could start over fresh without drama, drugs and other plutonic friends.

Ronnie had seen sides of Rock that made her unsure in determining if she wanted to be with him long term. She loved the money. However, she also wanted to be treated like a lady at all times, the way she knew Josh would treat her. Besides, she couldn't see herself properly functioning without Nae or Monie.

Rock thought about proposing to her, but he figured it may have been too soon for her. With all the issues they had going on, he knew it would take a couple years to convince her to marry him.

After walking on the hot beach he knew she would agree to have a margarita with him. First, he wanted to take her window-shopping in town to see her reaction toward different jewels—especially engagement rings. He wanted to find a 5 carat, pink diamond ring. *"The perfect ring for the perfect woman,"* he thought. He wasn't going to get his hopes up high. He knew what the answer was going to be, but he thought he'd ask anyway.

"What do you think about us being married?"

Ronnie laughed with amusement. She truly thought he was joking.

"I'm guessing and hoping that was a rhetorical question," she replied jovially.

Rock ignored her sarcasm and directed her over to a ring he'd spotted in the next jewelry case. The platinum ring with a pink heart shaped diamond, trimmed with rubies was sparkling. She was overwhelmed with its beauty. She couldn't let Rock see her drool over the gem. She would have felt awful if he'd bought it as an engagement ring and she declined the proposal. She couldn't imagine what the repercussion would be if he spent eight thousand dollars on a ring she wasn't wearing or never planned to wear.

Rock had made up his mind that she was going to eventually be his wife, regardless of what she said at the moment. He wasn't returning to Georgia without that ring. He needed to figure out a way to buy it without her knowing it.

"This weekend I have to go to Miami. You are coming with me aren't you?"

Ronnie hadn't thought about the trip to Miami. She had bad feelings about the trip and really didn't want to go, but she didn't want to offend him, especially while she was unsure of his state of mind.

"I totally forgot. Let me think about it. I'll get back to you with an answer," Ronnie replied with sincerity.

"I told you about it a few weeks ago."

"Rock, you know I had a lot going on these past few weeks. I didn't have time to think about Miami."

"I'm sorry. I don't want to argue with you," Rock apologized understandingly.

Ronnie knew he was kissing up to her. She had the upper hand in any situation now. He knew what kind of game she was playing, but whatever it took to get back on her good side he was willing to go the extra mile to make her happy.

Ronnie put forth an effort to have an enjoyable time, but she couldn't take her mind off of her mother, Corey and Josh. She realized she was falling in love with Josh. She didn't know how to describe the feeling she had for Rock. Whatever it was, it wasn't love- maybe it was just infatuation with his body and money.

Ronnie knew this trip should've been one for relaxation. It was much needed and appreciated, but her mind was in overdrive, running like a locomotive. Her mind was on everything and everyone but Rock. Her attention span was that of a four year old; and her interest level had dropped drastically. She wanted nothing more than to go home.

The couple returned to their lavish hotel room to catch up some their rest. Rock wasn't quite ready to lie down. He decided to take a stroll down to the lobby and relax at the bar for a while. Ronnie lounged on the patio, stretched out on the lounge chair with her sunglasses and bathing suit on, enjoying the breeze from the ocean.

After two Heineken's, Rock was relaxed the way he had anticipated. Before he left to go to the room and join Ronnie, he sat listening to the rest of a Kenny G tune, playing from the overhead speakers at the bar.

A beautiful, young, and what appeared to be, a very lonely lady— an islander who had been scrutinizing him and his wad of cash since he first sat down, joined Rock.

"This is a beautiful song," the islander commented with a heavy accent, as she sat on the high bar stool with her legs crossed. With her eyes closed, she swayed from side to side, slowly trying to entice Rock. Her body was perfectly oiled and glistened from the dimmed lights of the bar. Still with her eyes closed, she opened her purse and pulled out a small fragrance bottle. She sprayed it on her neck and on the insides if her wrists, and then rubbed them together.

She put the coconut and strawberry-smelling fragrance back into her purse, opened her eyes, and extended her hand out to Rock.

"I'm Kay," the islander said softly and smiled.

"Rock," he responded as he shook her hand, blatantly uninterested.

"Is this your first time here?" she asked.

Rock wasn't in the mood for conversation, unless it was with Ronnie.

"Yeah," he reluctantly responded, as he grabbed a handful of peanuts from the bar's counter and unattractively stuffed them in his mouth, five at a time as if he had no home training.

As Ronnie enjoyed her serene surroundings, she heard an unusual ring of a phone.

Instantly, she jumped up looking for the ringing phone, which she knew had to have belonged to Rock. She took a chance on answering it, knowing that in some way or another, it was going to abruptly bring an end to her tranquil vacation.

"Hello," Ronnie said hesitantly.

"Hello? Is this Rakeem's phone?" The apparently older lady asked. Ronnie had never heard this sweet and gentle, yet subtle voice.

"Yes," Ronnie answered.

"This must be Ronnie," The lady said with confidence.

"Yes…ma'am," Ronnie was unsure of how to address the lady on the other end of the phone.

"This is Rakeem's mother. Is he available?"

"Actually, we're on a little vacation. He stepped away from the room, but I can take his phone to him and have him call you back in a few minutes."

"That would be great, but only if it's not too much trouble," Rock's mother, Ms. Wilcox, added.

Ronnie put on her stylish terrycloth robe and leather slip-on shoes, and headed down to the lobby to find Rock. From afar she spotted him at the bar with a beer in his hand, while Kay was attempting to whisper in his ear. Ronnie stood at the entrance of the bar for at least five to ten minutes. Kay put something in Rock's shirt pocket, in which Ronnie assumed was a phone number. Rock was shaking his head, "no." He reached in his pocket, pulled out the small piece of paper, and placed it on the bar's counter top.

Ronnie was pleased to see Rock attempting to turn a woman away, letting her know what kind of man he was. She watched as Kay persistently tried to come on to her man. Kay stood up behind Rock, trying to seductively give him a massage. "Why don't we go to my place so I can give you a full massage?"

Rock sat there thinking, while letting her rub his shoulders. He thought about going to get the beautiful engagement ring for Ronnie that they'd seen earlier.

"Why don't we go out for a swim tonight?" Kay asked.

Rock turned to face Kay. She was nearly nose-to-nose with him with plans to sneak a kiss from him.

"Listen beautiful, I have a woman who is crazy as hell."

"Oh, so you like crazy women? I can be crazy."

"Sweet heart, I can see that you can be a lot of things. You can definitely be sexy and attractive," Rock said in his breath taking baritone voice. "But I can see right through you to see that you can be triflin' as hell too."

Ronnie sashayed down the narrow aisle towards the couple, with an attitude and a slight touch of anger directed toward Kay. She felt like Kay was disrespecting her in her absence, but at the same time she wanted to laugh at Rock's last comment to her.

"Then where is she? Why are you here all alone?" Kay asked.

"I'm right here…why?" Ronnie replied to Kay's surprise, as she approached from behind.

"He's spoken for, so you need to walk," Ronnie said aggressively looking Kay up and down. She gave Rock his phone over her shoulder as she now faced Kay.

"Your mother called."

"Come on baby. I was just about to leave anyway," Rock commanded.

From behind, Rock wrapped his arms around Ronnie's waist and placed a gentle kiss on her neck, before they walked away together.

Before she went to work, Nae was feeling a bit nauseous, with a slight fever. She suffered from cold sweats at times and from hot flashes at others.

"It would be best if you stayed home tonight," Monie suggested.

"If I work tonight, it'll go on my last check. I'll bring home a lump some, along with tips."

"It's senseless for you to work anyway—especially since Tony makes all of that money with Rock," Monie alleged.

"I suppose you're right. Ronnie's not working and she seems to be livin' it up," Nae added.

Nae thought that if she could make it through the night at work, she'd be all right. Wednesday nights we're pretty slow, so she wouldn't have to do too much to impress her audience. Before going to work, she spent most of the evening in the bathroom, vomiting.

"It's probably just a stomach virus. It'll pass." Although Monie's stomach was too weak to deal with her sister's illness, she stayed by her side and assisted her as much as possible.

Monie drove her sister to work and waited in the audience for her to finish dancing. This was so she could take her home and doctor her until their mother got home. Nae mentioned that she would talk to the necessary people, seeing if she could perform first, so she could leave early. Even if she didn't perform first, Monie knew that Nae usually held the third or fourth spot.

Monie sat in a dark corner all alone and half frightened, drinking a Pina Colada. By the time the fourth girl went on stage, Monie start to get edgy, wondering if her sister was okay. Monie wandered around trying to either find Mike or the dressing room.

When she found the dressing room, she stumbled upon a loud crowd of young, panting and screaming women. They were all standing, hurdled over what appeared to be someone in a corner. She heard the women cheering for someone to do something, which she imagined to be totally gruesome. Monie never heard her sister's plea for help over the ruckus of the small rowdy crowd.

"Sondra, I don't think she likes that," a very young, timid and soft-spoken girl in the crowd, cried out.

"She may not like it, but I hope you will, 'cause you're next newbie." One of the bigger women bullied the young girl against the lockers, while tapping on her breast and hips.

The bully looked over at Monie and then hollered out to Sondra, notifying her of a glitch in their plan. Monie saw her sister on the floor, pinned down by four other girls, while Sondra finished performing oral sex on her.

Monie screamed for help for her sister. She ran over trying to pull Sondra away from Nae. The by-standing girls formed a barrier to keep Monie out of the circle. One of the stronger girls pushed Monie down onto the floor and walked towards her, as if she had plans to rape her.

As Monie lay almost helplessly but fearless on the floor, she spotted a half rusted pipe in the corner that was leaning against the lockers. She rolled over, grabbed the pipe, and swiftly jumped up onto her feet. She realized the pipe was a lot heavier than she anticipated, but to ensure her and her sister's safety, she had already planned to put the pipe to good use.

Monie swung the pipe uncontrollably, striking anything in its path. The crowd quickly scattered, allowing her to get to her sister. Monie struck Sondra across her back as she tried to get off of the floor.

Monie quickly pulled Nae to her feet. She struggled to get her clothing back on, so that she could help Monie fight off her harassers, until they found Mike or Rome. To their benefit, Mike came in the dressing room calling the next dancer to the stage, since she seemed to be mysteriously missing.

Mike found the dressing room in a mess with blood, hair and costumes all over the floor.

"What in the hell happened to the dressing room?!" Mike exclaimed in a rage.

He saw Nae pounding on Sondra, while Monie guarded her, daring anyone to go near her or her sister. She threatened to bash in anyone's skull that attempted to get near them, especially since she had her new found weapon in her hands.

Mike burst through the scattered and dwindled crowd to pull Nae off of Sondra.

"What is wrong you ladies? Why are you acting like cats in here?"

Mike pulled Nae to the side and asked what was wrong. He remembered the specific instructions he was given to take extra special care of Nae.

"That hoe raped me," Nae replied shocked and distraught. She couldn't believe what had just happened to her.

Before Mike got a chance to ask Sondra for her version of the story, the police walked in. The room had gotten quite empty and quiet.

The officer's first inquiry was to find out if there were any witnesses. The timid young girl, who tried to stand up for Nae, came forth confessing that she called 911. She volunteered all the information she knew. The young girl was terrified.

The girl was only seventeen, and had never seen anything like that happen right in front of her.

"Ma'am, how old are you?" The officer asked.

The seventeen-year-old girl hesitated before she answered.

"Am I going to jail?" she asked.

"No ma'am. I'm just glad you took the initiative to do the right thing. I'm sure this young lady appreciates it as well."

The young girl was a bit intimidated, but mostly overwhelmed by the tall, dark and muscular officer. His deep baritone voice pierced her soul, making her loose her power of speech. She had forgotten the reality of the situation at hand.

"Ma'am, how old did you say you were?" The officer asked a second time.

"Twenty," she replied.

"Have a seat right here. I'll be right back." The officer pointed at a bench for her to take a seat. He walked over to Nae to get a report from her.

"Ma'am, you are the victim, correct?" he asked.

Nae was leaning against the lockers, still feeling a bit nauseous. Monie stood beside her, ready to answer all of the officer's questions, whether she knew the correct answers or not.

"Yes sir," Nae finally replied after a brief study of the officer's muscular physique.

"What's your name?" He asked.

"Renae."

"And you are?" the officer asked Monie.

"I'm her sister Monica."

"I need to get a report from you. I'll make it brief so you can get to the hospital."

At 12:30a.m, the officer released Monie and Nae from his custody so they could go to the hospital. Both girls were tired, and wanted nothing more than a good night's sleep. They both were angry, frustrated and tired of dealing with hospitals.

"Nae, don't worry about anything. Once Tony finds out about Sondra, I'm sure he and the rest of the crew will put her in her place. I guarantee that by the time they finish with her, she won't try to rape anyone else," Monie assured her sick and distraught sister.

Once they reached the hospital, Monie explained Nae's situation to the nurse at the emergency room. The nurse quickly started to provide care for Nae. Monie stayed by Nae's side all morning long. By 2:00a.m., the nurse came back in Nae's room to release her.

"Well Ms. Williams, I have good news. You don't have any infections and your baby is going to be perfectly fine," The nurse reported.

"My baby!" Nae exclaimed.

The nurse dropped a bombshell that Nae knew absolutely nothing about.

"Baby?" Monie said with disbelief. "So, that explains your sickness."

"Congratulations! You're two and a half weeks," the nurse added.

During the ride home, Nae explained to Monie when her conception took place.

"Tony's really gonna have it out for Sondra when he finds out what she did…and you're pregnant too!" Monie exclaimed excitedly.

Nae didn't know how she was going to tell Veronica. "How do I tell mom something like this?" Nae asked Monie.

"You're not sixteen anymore. We're now at the childbearing age," Monie replied.

"I'm not sure I want to be with Tony long enough to raise a child."

"You don't have to be with him to raise your baby. We grew up without dad, and I think we turned out okay. Mom did a darn good job raising us alone."

Nae had so many mixed feelings about having this baby. She first thought about having an abortion. She knew that Tony would have a fit if she mentioned an abortion. She now knew that it would be beneficial to take Tony up on his offer on moving in an apartment together.

Monie tried to encourage Nae and support her decisions.

Although she and her sisters were all grown up, deep down inside, Monie was afraid of what Veronica's probable actions were going to be as well. She realized her sister's choices, which put her in such a predicament, weren't the wisest, but the damage was already done. She hoped Nae fully understood everything that was going on in her life and learn to make better decisions.

Monie felt hypocritical for telling Nae one thing and being optimistic. Within her heart she felt like Nae was really biting off more than she could chew. She was a bit bitter and having a difficult time trying to understand how her oldest sister could be so stupid and careless. If Nae had a baby, she knew it would immediately make her an instant babysitter.

The entire way home, Monie was quiet. While Nae continuously chattered about her plans of motherhood, Monie reflected on the reality of the situation.

As she drove, she thought of how incompetent her sisters could be at times. She envisioned a clear picture of her and her mother raising their children. Both Ronnie and Nae were too busy to assume the responsibilities of raising a child as a part of their daily rituals.

Chapter 11

*F*riday morning, Ronnie returned home from the get-a-way. As she headed up the stairs, she heard someone in the bathroom vomiting. She knocked on the door but received no answer. She went in her room so she could lie down peacefully. She heard a light knock on her bedroom door.

Nae walked in and curled up at the foot of Ronnie's bed. Nae began to cry as she told Ronnie about the incident with Sondra. Ronnie grabbed the phone to call Rock.

"Don't call him yet!" Nae exclaimed. "Just let me have a moment."

Nae remembered that Ronnie told her how Shonte mysteriously disappeared. She wasn't sure if she was ready to be the cause of someone's abduction. Ronnie didn't pressure her sister into telling her anything, but at the same time, she knew Nae was bothered by something that involved a man.

"Rock wants us to go to Miami with them for the weekend," Ronnie added.

Nae ignored her sister and continued talking about her issues. She mentioned that she and Tony were going to get their own apartment. She never gave a reason for her sudden decision. Ronnie didn't think it was a bad idea, and comfortably mentioned her plans of moving in with Rock.

"You better go get packed. We're leaving tonight," Ronnie announced.

"Who's leaving to go where?" Nae asked as if Ronnie never said anything to her about a trip.

It was apparent to Ronnie that her sister was in a world of her own. Ronnie figured it may have had something to do with her getting raped, especially by it being a female rapist.

"Nae, how did another female rape you?" Ronnie asked, honestly puzzled.

"She only performed oral sex on me, but it was against my will," Nae answered. She wondered how her sister could ask her a question like that, as if she didn't believe her.

"She violated me, while those other skeezers held me down!" Nae exclaimed in her own defense.

Veronica got up for work early, so she could pack her bags, with the intentions of leaving directly from work and go on a get-a-way with Jerome. As she looked through her drawers, she heard the girls conversing in Ronnie's room.

She tipped down the hallway to see what the girls were doing up so early. She lightly tapped on Ronnie's bedroom door and peeked inside.

"Did we wake you?" Ronnie asked her mother.

"No. Actually, I was up getting some things together for a much needed trip Jerome planned for us."

Veronica noticed that Nae never turned and faced her, giving direct eye contact like she normally would when her mother spoke to her. She hurried to hide her bruised legs under Ronnie's afghan.

Veronica swiftly headed over to her daughter to examine her.

"Renae, what happened to you? That Tony guy didn't do this to you, did he?"

"No. Some girls attacked me at work."

"You may need to get out of that line of work."

Veronica sat down next to the daughter, at the foot of Ronnie's bed, to first examine her face.

"Sweetie, you need to get checked out." Veronica insisted.

"Monie took me to get checked already."

Nae was scared that Monie would eventually tell Veronica about the trip to the hospital and spill the beans about her pregnancy. She knew Monie couldn't hold water, but she wasn't ready to tell anyone yet. She knew she would soon have to drill Monie and threaten her to keep her mouth shut.

"So ma, you and Jerome are getting kind of serious aren't you?" Ronnie inquired to get some of the attention off of Nae.

Veronica finally put her sarcasm on the back burner. She explained to her girls that the trials and tribulations she and Jerome had recently shared drew them closer and made the bond between them stronger.

Ronnie still knew that her relationship with Rock was soon going to be diminished, but until it was completely over, she planned to get everything she could out of it. She had finally built up enough courage to tell her mother that she was moving in with Rock.

Since this appeared to be a moment of confessions, Nae slid her confession in as well about her upcoming move with Tony. Both girls were amazed at how well Veronica took the news. They were convinced that love had taken their mother to a place she hadn't been in a while.

By 11a.m. the girls were up and revived, ready to start their day by going to the hospital to visit Corey. As Ronnie rounded up her last few miscellaneous items, the phone rang. She started not to answer it, but always feared that Veronica could possibly be in trouble.

She ran to the phone, anxiously pressing the talk button, before checking the caller ID.

"Hello?" she panted, hoping her mother wasn't in distress.

"Ronnie, I'm glad I caught you. I need you and your sisters to come over and help me do a few things before we go to Miami this evening," Rock said confidently, knowing she would come to his rescue once again.

Monie always kept her share of skeptics about Rock. She never imagined Rock needing any kind of help from her or Nae, especially knowing how they didn't get along at times. Maybe he still had had respect for her only because of the fact that he was still trying to earn cool points with Ronnie.

Ronnie pulled up to Rock's front gate and proceeded to go into the yard. Nae was impressed that Rock trusted Ronnie with his security code, but for some strange reason, Monie felt a bit weary about the whole mission and wasn't impressed at all.

Rock met the girls at the front door. He kissed Ronnie and politely greeted the other girls.

"Baby, I need you to count some money for me," Rock pleaded.

As Ronnie and her sisters counted the money with the money machines, Nae was mesmerized with the amount of money in front of her. None of the girls had ever seen that much money before at one time.

"I've already counted five thousand dollars," Monie blurted out. "I can only imagine how much they make in a year."

"Rock said he's already reached the million dollar mark a few years ago," Ronnie added.

"So how much do *you* have stashed away?" Nae asked.

Ronnie laughed it off, but never directly answered the question. She had been stashing a few hundred dollars here and there. Ronnie had a back up plan in the works.

Although she refused to let Nae in on her secret, she knew that Nae would help expedite her plan if asked. Ronnie knew that her sister was no dummy. The job at the club was only a front for all the money she had secretly gotten from Tony.

Neither of the girls had found happiness since their move from the small New Jersey town they were used to. They knew they couldn't continue living that type of lifestyle forever. The two girls kept their distance from their men, knowing that if they ever found out they had been crossed, they'd definitely be engaged in a disappearing act.

"How can you both live with the drama and negative attention that comes along with all of this money?" Monie inquired.

"There's not a lot of negative attention, but I just deal with the drama and do what I have to do for now," Ronnie added.

"For now," both Monie and Nae chimed in together and looked at each other. Monie wanted to ask if Ronnie had a Plan B, but she was skeptical about talking about it in Rock's home. There was an intercom system on the walls, which made her feel like they may have been wired to record anything that was being said in each room. In that particular room, where the money was usually counted, there was a small camera installed inside of the ceiling, centered and focused on the counting table. None of the girls had hardcore proof that they were being watched; however Monie found it impossible to shake the uncanny sentiments she had since she walked through the front door.

"What's the game plan?" Nae asked.

Ronnie just kept a peaceful smile on her face as she continued to count the money. She thought about moving to California to start fresh, with a new low-key, drama-free life in the slow lane. This would be a life where no one, except for her immediate family, would know where she resided.

"You should know by now that he's not going to let you go without a fight," Nae added.

Rock crept up the stairs, barely catching the last bit of the girl's conversation, as he eased into his cash office.

"How are you ladies coming along?" Rock asked, taking them by surprise.

Rock did a tally on all three machines. He discreetly wrote the totals on a small piece of paper and put it in his shirt pocket.

"What's the grand total?" Ronnie asked with a slight bit of reluctance.

Rock beckoned for Ronnie to step out into the hallway. He explained that he had a million dollars and fifty pounds of drugs that he had to transport to Miami. He begged her to keep his personal information confidential.

Veronica anxiously headed over Jerome's house directly from work. He waited quietly and patiently in the dining room for her to arrive. He had plans to give her a set of keys to his Lexus and the house.

After all the trials he had just overcome in his life, he still had a sweet humbleness about him. He was finally at ease. He wanted nothing more than to take his lovely companion to an isolated hide out in the Georgia Mountains.

Jerome laid Veronica across the sofa, with her head resting in his lap. He gently stroked her hair to help release the tension from her stressful day. He then sat on the edge of the sofa beside her, massaging her shoulders and lower back. He rubbed her legs and feet until she nearly fell asleep. She let out a long moan, a sigh of relief. *"I've only had this type of treatment at a day spa,"* she thought. "Thank God chivalry is not quite dead," she muttered under her breath.

He helped her to her feet and escorted her to the car to begin their journey. On the way to the mountains, the couple discussed plans of a small wedding, followed by a breathtaking honeymoon in Hawaii.

The love they shared was obvious and immeasurable. Veronica imagined her daughters standing happily at the alter with her, as she merged into a new life with the man who she felt was her soul mate.

Just as the conversation headed in the perfect direction, Jerome's cell phone rang.

"I thought we were going to leave our phones at home," Veronica said frustrated.

As Jerome grabbed for the phone out of the console, he looked at Veronica and shook his head. "Baby I swear I forgot it was in here."

He looked down at the phone and saw that Juanita was calling.

"It's Juanita. It's probably for you." He handed her the phone for her to answer it.

"Hello?" Veronica answered.

"Hey girl. I'm glad I finally found you."

"Is everything okay?" Veronica asked frantically.

Juanita explained that she wanted to visit Tyrone at the rehab center. Veronica tried hard to understand why her friend still wanted to associate herself with him; especially after everything he'd done to her. Just listening to Juanita trying to explain and plead her case in Tyrone's defense made Veronica furious. It was like having a conversation with Ronnie or Nae.

This didn't sound like the same Juanita who was always headstrong. The one who stood firm with her motto: "I'm not putting up with any man's crap." She seemed to be a totally different person since she was released from the hospital.

"Are you aware that his wife is still in town?" Veronica asked.

"Yes," Juanita replied with little concern.

"She's going to be here until he gets out of rehab. Since he's in that type of institution, she can't give him the papers until he is released."

Jerome knew the call put Veronica in a state of mind that he had planned to *quickly* get her away from. She was suddenly tense again. The tension was so thick he could cut it with a knife.

Jerome didn't know how to tell Veronica the truth about Tyrone. He knew his brother was going to get out of rehab, and continue with his same circle of lies and schemes, in which he was best known for.

He had previously tried to warn Juanita of the scandalous games his brother played. Unfortunately his charming side had already worked its magic on her, making her believe that he was some fantastic, fictional character from somebody's fairytale.

Juanita couldn't understand why everyone was infuriated with her for wanting to talk to Tyrone. No one but Jackie knew that she'd suffered a miscarriage during her stay at the hospital. At age forty, she couldn't believe she'd been so careless to get pregnant by such a monster.

She had to continue acting as if she cared about Tyrone, just long enough to talk to him face to face. She wanted to let him know about the baby that he'd poisoned. *"This would have to remain a skeleton that could never surface,"* she thought. *"What would everyone think of me if they ever found out,"* she asked herself.

Jason and Josh understood their mother suffered an emotional blow after coming from the hospital. They couldn't comprehend why her mental state was as scrambled to the degree in which it was. The boys were never told about their mother's pregnancy, and that she was forced to intake nearly fatal drugs. They were under the impression that she had been in a car accident.

Jackie sat at Corey's bedside, holding his hand, praying that God would allow him to resume his normal activities one day soon. As her eyes remained closed, she began thinking aloud about everything that her sister had been through with Tyrone, the drugs and the baby. She was unaware that Corey was able to comprehend and respond.

She felt a slight squeeze on her hand. She looked up and into his eyes, breathing uncontrollably, excited that her son was gaining full consciousness. His face was pale. The whites of his eyes were bright but glossy, and his pupils were slightly dilated. He parted his dry ashy lips to speak, but his voice was groggy from his vocal cords being inactive for so long.

Jackie had tears of joy strolling down her cheeks. "You want me to go get Jason and Josh?" she asked.

Corey slowly twisted his head, telling his mother no.

"Let me at least tell Chris," Jackie begged. But her son needed a minute alone with her. He tried his best to formulate his words properly for her to comprehend what he was saying. Unfortunately, she still had trouble understanding what her son was trying so desperately to tell her.

Jackie sprayed a small amount of water from his spray bottle in her son's mouth to moisten his dry, pasty mouth, to make talking a less complicated task for him. Once he finally started talking, he told his mother that he'd had a vision. It was of a woman going through the turmoil that she'd just finished talking about. He had no idea of who the woman was in his vision. The man in his vision was a shiester and womanizer who could never be trusted. Jackie instantly knew that the man in Corey's dream had to be Tyrone.

Jackie sat back and listened to her son as he continued telling her everything about this vision he had while he was in a coma. For a minute she didn't know what to think. Finally, she came to a conclusion that her son must have been blessed with some type of intuition while he was in a coma. Jackie and Corey sat talking and praying for at least an hour before she went to get a nurse and informed everyone that he had waken up.

While the nurses, Jason, Josh and Chris were in Corey's room indulging in triumph for him regaining consciousness, Jackie tried urgently to get in touch with Juanita to inform her of the profound vision that Corey had.

Jackie was overjoyed and convinced that her son was now telepathically gifted. She could hardly remember the last time she'd been so unbelievably happy, other than when she had given birth to him.

Veronica and Jerome finally arrived in the mountains. The isolated log cabin was small and cozy with a screened in porch, surrounded by a privacy fence, perfect for the occasion. Jerome walked in first, heading straight for the bedroom, dropping the bags in the middle of the floor. He eagerly grabbed Veronica and peeled away her clothes. He held her hand, leading her out to the Jacuzzi. After turning on the bubble jets, he swiftly disappeared back inside of the cabin. When he returned, he had two large towels along with two glasses of Champaign.

Veronica blushed and chuckled timidly. She knew he had something up his sleeve, and in his pocket. She studied the bulge in his pocket trying to decipher what it could have been.

Jerome sat on the edge of the Jacuzzi. He reached out for Veronica, helping her to get out of the water to sit with him. He held up his glass for a toast: "to my lovely companion." They took a few sips from their glasses before taking them and laying them aside. He discreetly pulled the item from his pocket.

As he swiped a few stray strands of hair from her face, he whispered softly in her ear, "Close your eyes."

She couldn't contain her excitement any longer. She burst out in laughter as she put her hands securely over her eyes. Jerome pulled out the 2 ? carat, princess cut, diamond ring. When she opened her eyes, her mouth flew open as well as she welcomed the stunning jewel. He placed it on her finger, with confidence that she would gladly accept his proposal. He asked her, "Veronica would you be my wife?"

Her eyes stretched to nearly the size of quarters. She couldn't believe what was happening to her. She stared at the ring in amazement, understanding its significance, and willing to take on the responsibilities that came along with it.

She hardly knew how to fully handle her daughters' issues. Now, she was about to take on the motherly role of three other adults. *"This was going to be challenging,"* she thought, but this type of fidelity came with the territory. She felt like Jerome may have been having similar feelings about her girls.

"Yes, I'll be your wife," she replied.

"What about our children? If I move in with you, I couldn't just kick my daughter out, especially while she's in college."

"No one said anything about kicking anyone out. You should know me better than that."

Veronica realized she'd made herself look like a fool. Jerome wondered why Monie was the only one of her daughters she'd mentioned.

"The other girls aren't in college. What are they doing?"

"They're moving in with their boyfriends," Veronica said painfully.

"I feel like I don't know what to tell them anymore. My babies are grown women now." Veronica took a brief moment to reflect on her girls' lives. She quickly snapped back into reality and started focusing on her new beginning with her soon to be husband.

Rock, Trey, Tony, Ronnie, Nae and Monie drove up to a huge extravagant home near the beach front on the boardwalk in Miami at 8 p.m. Rick, Mike and Rome trailed them in the Hummer.

"Whose house is this?" Monie asked.

"A friend of mine who's always in L.A.," Rock replied.

"Does this friend have a name?" Ronnie asked inquisitively.

"He does, but you don't need to know it right now," Rock replied sarcastically. He gave Ronnie a peck on the lips and laughed before he got out of the truck.

The guys first operation was suppose to go down at one of Miami's desolated boat yards at 11:00 that night.

Ronnie walked in the front door of the house with extreme amazement. She had never seen a home that exquisite before, other than in the movies, and Rock's of course.

"By the looks of it, I'm guessing your friend is a woman," Ronnie stated with a slight attitude, looking at Rock out of the corner of her eye.

"He's just a neat freak with a maid and interior decorator," Rock replied without actually knowing the facts of his friends' status.

"He can afford a house like this and a maid? What does he do?"

Monie blurted out once again.

Rock ignored Monie's question and began giving the girls a quick tour of parts of the house. Rock and Trey showed the girls the rooms in which they were going to stay in. They placed their bags in their designated rooms and ventured into the rest of the house in which Rock failed to show them.

"We have to go out for a few hours, but you all can go out to South Beach and go shopping or clubbing or something," Rock stated. He was only trying to keep the girls occupied so they wouldn't interfere in their plans. The guys gave the girls five hundred dollars each, before they swiftly ran out the front door of the house, jumping in the Hummer to start their mission.

Ronnie and Nae decided to stash their money and save it for their ultimate getaway.

"Why don't we pick up some pizza and a movie?" Ronnie suggested.

Rock and the rest of the guys scoped out the old boat yard for any booby traps that may have been left there by their buyers. Rock was always skeptical of everyone he dealt with on that level. He'd survived many battles and setups by deciding to explore his surroundings.

Rick, Rome and Mike set up as snipers. They were hiding out on top of the boathouses, and in broken out windows, on the top and middle floors of the building. Each sniper was armed with grenades, machine guns and shotguns. Rock, Trey and Tony were armed with grenades, and three 9mm's, each with extra magazines.

As Nae watched TV, she began to feel lightheaded and extremely nauseous. She ran to the bathroom to vomit, but fell to the floor as she made it to the toilet.

"What's wrong?" Ronnie shouted as she ran behind her sister trying to ensure that she kept her balance.

Nae knelt on the floor, holding her stomach with her head slumped over the toilet.

Monie rushed out of the kitchen, and into the bathroom when she heard all of the commotion. She nearly fell into the bathtub, as she was trying to stabilize herself on the edge.

"Did you tell him?" Monie asked Nae.

"No," Nae replied before she began crying.

"Tell who what? Will somebody tell me what the hell is going on?" Ronnie asked.

"Nae's pregnant," Monie answered.

"Nae, how could you let that happen? Now we can't go on with…" Ronnie started pacing the floor in deep thought.

"Go on with what?" Monie asked.

"Nothing," Ronnie said with frustration.

"I didn't tell him yet. I could still go to the clinic and get an abortion," Nae replied.

Nae felt awful for throwing what she thought, was a monkey wrench in Ronnie's plans.

"An abortion!" Monie exclaimed.

"Monie, won't you go watch TV or something?" Nae suggested.

"No! I'm tired of you both treating me like a baby or some sort of outcast!" Monie yelled.

Monie began to cry along with Nae, feeling very much abandoned by her sisters. She was hurt from always being isolated from everyone's plans.

"We can still do it. It just may take a little longer," Ronnie replied, trying to console her sister. Inside she was a bit furious, but she knew this wasn't the time to blast her out for being so careless. She knew Nae would crack if she received another lecture from anyone. Ronnie didn't actually know if Veronica was aware of this situation with Nae yet, but if she did, she knew the lecturing would've been on strong.

"What's the plan? I want in on it." Monie cried out as she wiped the mucus from her nose with the two squares of toilet paper she'd torn off the roll.

"Monie, we'd just planned to move, that's all," Ronnie replied knowing it was half of the truth.

"Move where? I wanna go." Monie added. "Does mom know about this?"

"About what?" Nae asked.

"This!" Monie threw out her hands gesturing towards Nae's direction. "And your plans to move?"

"Well, if she doesn't already, I'm sure you'll let her know," Ronnie replied with an attitude.

"You guys don't give me any credit." Monie added.

"Giving you credit is what got our business out in the open in the beginning…"

Ronnie threw her hands mid-way up in the air and took a long relieving sigh, grasped a breath of fresh air, and slowly released it.

"Monie, now is not the time," Ronnie replied with a new and refreshed composure.

Ronnie combatively shook her head, frustrated at Monie for starting an overabundance of unnecessary drama at the worst of times.

"Let's get her to the bedroom," Ronnie gestured to Monie.

All three girls stretched out with exhaustion across the king sized bed in Nae's designated room. They began reminiscing about growing up in Jersey, going on their first dates, kissing and having sex for the first time.

The girls tried waited patiently for the guys to return, but they fell sound asleep.

Chapter 12

*A*t 4a.m., Saturday, Rock and the fellas returned to the house where Ronnie, Nae and Monie lie sound asleep. The guys were hot and exhausted from the four hour-long drug deal and steak out.

By 8a.m., the girls were up and ready to start their day. They went to breakfast and afterwards, walked the boardwalk along side the beaches. Ronnie didn't want to spend her money on shopping. She was saving every penny so when the time came to move to California she would be able to go without borrowing anything from anyone.

Monie was quite generous with her money. She wasn't yet hip to her sister's game plan.

Today was going to be a big day for Juanita. She'd been waiting a couple of days to build up enough courage to finally face Tyrone. Her plans were to go to the rehab and tell him that she'd lost his baby, thanks to him drugging her up, resulting in having to get her stomach pumped. She also was going to tell him that she didn't want to see him anymore.

She knew that immediate family members were the only visitors allowed. Therefore, she had planned to sign in as his wife. As she looked at the visitor's log, she noticed that Jerome already had a visitor. On the line above where she was about to sign, she saw Sonya's name. Next to it, it read that she was his wife.

Anger swept through Juanita's soul like a hurricane. Part of her was a bit perturbed and confused, but another part of her was glad. She figured his wife may have come back to reclaim her good for nothing, drug addicted, womanizing husband. She even had hopes that he would move to Chicago with her.

Juanita was scorned once again. She was beginning to feel bitter, with a desire to hold grudges towards all men—something she said she'd never do again. She threw her keys on the counter top in the small window next to the visitor's log. Sitting down, Juanita took a brief moment to regroup and pull herself together. In order not to appear suspicious, she asked one of the staff members for some literature concerning the facility.

She looked up, and all of a sudden spotted Tyrone's father coming towards the glass the door. She didn't know whether to duck in the restroom, greet him, or just plain out ignore him.

It wouldn't be right to take anything out on him. *"He wasn't the one that did this to me nor is he responsible for it,"* she thought.

"Hey Mr. Ellis. How are you?" Juanita greeted and hugged the elderly man, whom at one point, she thought would've been her father-in-law.

"I'm doing pretty good sweetie, how are you?" The tall, slinky, silver haired older gentleman greeted her in return.

"Did you see Tyrone?" Mr. Ellis asked humbly.

Before Juanita could answer the question, Sonya stepped off the elevator.

"Hi dad," Sonya greeted and hugged Mr. Ellis. She looked at Juanita, as if she already knew who she was before Mr. Ellis formally introduced them.

"Hi sweetie. This is a good friend of the family. Her name is Juanita." Mr. Ellis proudly introduced the two women, having no idea of their prior knowledge of each other.

"Juanita this is Sonya. She's down here visiting us from Chicago," Mr. Ellis announced. He was trying hard not to reveal either of the women's status or relationships they held with his troubled son.

"Well ladies, it was a pleasure chatting with you both, but I need to get upstairs to my boy. You both be good." The old timer sensed tension in the air between the ladies. Mr. Ellis waived goodbye to them as he hurried to get to the elevator and avoid being caught up in the crossfire.

"So…You're a good friend of the family huh? How did that come about?" Sonya asked.

"I used to date Tyrone," Juanita replied.

"Oh really…when?"

"Listen Sonya, let's cut the bull. You know that I'm his most recent ex-girlfriend, as well as I know that you're his wife," Juanita explained.

Sonya knew about everything before Juanita explained it. She was just astonished that Juanita was so blunt and nonchalant.

"Listen, I don't know if you've come to take Tyrone back to Chicago with you, but I'm not going to be around to get hemmed up in a love triangle," Juanita stated.

"Girlfriend you need to slow down and learn the facts. The only reason I came to town was to attend my nephew's funeral, and then to get Tyrone to sign these divorce papers," Sonya explained thoroughly.

Juanita felt a bit humiliated and intimidated. Sonya was apparently all about business and was very educated. Sonya was very different from the verbal picture Tyrone had painted of her.

"I don't get it. You seem to be very business oriented. How on earth did you hook up with Tyrone?" Juanita asked.

"You're not so shabby yourself. Let's do lunch. I'll tell you all about it," Sonya replied.

Juanita was starting to get a totally different vibe than the one she'd picked up on just five minutes earlier. For a minute, she wondered if this proposed lunch date was a set up, or did this stranger who once shared the same love interest as she once did, really have some things to get off of her chest. The whole situation was taking an interesting turn. It was heading in the opposite direction in which Juanita had anticipated.

The ladies headed to a small, but cozy New Orleans style restaurant. As soon as they were seated, Sonya immediately started with her story about how she'd moved from Chicago to Atlanta during her freshman year of high school. She and Tyrone became high school sweethearts during her sophomore year. She went on to tell how domineering he was and was only interested in fulfilling his dreams.

Sonya spilled her guts to Juanita about her hurt and struggles as a teenage mother, while trying to attend junior college without any moral support from her husband. She was a full time mother, employee, and a part time student. Tyrone only attended college as a full time student.

She discreetly sobbed momentarily. Sonya then continued talking about how Tyrone often put her on the back burner to pursue the things that would only benefit him. He always left her bearing his children, forcing her to put her hopes and dreams on hold.

Sonya looked Juanita in her eyes and told her about times when Tyrone came home smelling like old sex. He was wearing scents from another woman's perfume. All of this was going on while she was in her third trimester of her pregnancy, with her fourth and youngest child, Serita.

"Tyrone never spoke of a fourth child-especially a daughter," Juanita added searching for the truth, knowing that Sonya would shortly reveal it.

"Why am I not surprised?" Sonya asked rhetorically.

Sonya shook her head with a disappointed look on her face. Deep down, Tyrone had put a life long scar on Sonya's heart. She was no longer surprised by anything anyone had to say about her soon to be ex-husband. She knew he was capable of doing and saying anything-especially when it came to trying to win a woman's heart and trust.

Sonya took a couple of sips of her apple Martini. She started explaining to Juanita about how their relationship finally came to an abrupt end and why she and her daughter moved to Chicago.

Sonya took a deep breath before actually going into the whole story. About how Tyrone reacted when he found out about their fifteen-year-old daughter being a lesbian. By age thirteen, Serita had issues with low self-esteem because her body hadn't developed like the rest of her friends. She felt like an outcast because boys teased her about looking like one of them.

Serita was a very pretty young girl. She started to appreciate compliments she'd received from other girls.

As Sonya reminisced about her tumultuous past, she appeared to be in an entirely different world. With every word being spoken with confidence, she spoke very highly of her daughter. She told the story with a smile on her face, obviously very proud of Serita.

Juanita wasn't quite sure of how to interpret Serita's character, but it wasn't her place to be the judge. To her it didn't seem like Serita woke up one morning and decided to be gay. Under the circumstances of having a dysfunctional father and shady friends, she didn't have any other alternatives.

"Could you believe that self-centered bastard wanted to put our fifteen year old baby girl out on the streets?" Sonya asked, without giving Juanita a chance to speak. "I wasn't havin' it."

Juanita was deeply consumed with the way Sonya had overcome this real life horror story. A story that had originated by someone she thought she wanted to spend the rest of her life with. Juanita was eager to hear how her new found friend had come from being a low class, part-time, some time student and mother of four, to the classy woman she evidently had become today.

Sonya excused herself from the table to go to the restroom. She needed to refresh the makeup that had been smeared and smudged by her tears. With her sassy twist and conservative style, Sonya turned the heads of men of all nationalities, shapes and sizes. Men who innocently tried to dine with their significant others were caught staring at her, as she sashayed into the restroom.

Juanita ordered another drink and sat back in her cozy booth bench, comparing her stories to the ones Sonya had just told her about. In some cases, she noticed the similarities. Juanita wondered if Sonya ever experienced any of Tyrone's drug episodes.

Sonya returned to the booth, refreshed, and ready to tell Juanita about yet another chapter in her life where she made a complete turn-around. She first finished what was left of her apple Martini, and then ordered another.

"Has he ever done drugs around you?" Juanita inquired.

Sonya explained that he'd never done drugs around her, but he'd come home high many nights. One night he beat her so badly until she was hospitalized, and later found out that she'd miscarried.

Sonya began shedding a few tears again as she told Juanita about the day she was released from the hospital after the beating. When Sonya returned home, Tyrone had put Serita out of the house. She literally had to call and visit all of Serita's friend's homes in search of her daughter.

"I told him if Serita had to leave, I was leaving too. Can you believe that sorry son of a gun put both of us out on the street?" Sonya asked. "At that moment, I knew that *family* wasn't one of his top priorities. He literally fought me to keep my boys. This wasn't gonna stop me. I moved back to Chicago with my daughter and received my master's degree. I'm now a television series producer."

"Why'd you wait so long to divorce him?" Juanita asked curiously. She knew a brilliant lady like Sonya had to have had a method to her madness. She couldn't conceive Sonya's motive as to why she remained married to him for so long.

Juanita could feel the fierce rage in Sonya's soul about to burst and eject itself.

"After all he's done to me, I couldn't see giving him one red cent. I had to wait for my children to grow up so he couldn't get child support or alimony from me."

Sonya continued to explain that she'd supported her children over the years by sending money to Tyrone's father.

The women spent over two hours talking about their unpleasant relationships with Tyrone. Juanita was astounded at how Sonya came from having absolutely nothing to having everything.

On the way to Sonya's Lexus SUV, Juanita asked, "By the way, how's Serita now?"

"She couldn't be better. As a matter of fact, she's married…to a man."

The ladies now had a special bond that couldn't be broken. Sonya insisted that Juanita take her phone number and address to keep in touch. Juanita went home with a new attitude and an abundance of confidence in which Sonya had given her.

After spending most of the day hanging out in the sun, Ronnie knew she needed to get Nae back to the house before she became dehydrated. The guys were up plotting their last and final operation, before they could take the time and enjoy their vacation.

Nae tried desperately to get Tony's attention away from all of the excitement surrounding him. Tony constantly pushed her away, making it obvious that she was annoying him, taking him away from something higher on his priority list.

Along with Nae's hormones raging, she felt like he wasn't man enough to take on the responsibility to raise a child. The thought of an abortion sounded like the route to go. Nae called Ronnie to take a walk with her outside.

Nae expressed to her sister that he wasn't the one she wanted to share this precious gift with. Ronnie had to reassure her sister that things would be all right despite the situation. Nae pondered for most of the day in search of the appropriate way to tell Tony about the baby. As Ronnie and Nae sat on the step of the beachfront house, Nae began to cry.

Ronnie was tired of seeing her sister in a state of distress. Ronnie stormed up the stairs, into the house, where the guys sat drinking beer and celebrating a successful mission from the night before.

"Tony!" Ronnie exclaimed. "My sister needs you for a moment."

"I told her I'd talk to her later!" Tony exclaimed back.

"She needs you now!" Ronnie demanded through clenched teeth.

Ronnie's nose was flaring. Her heart was beating exceedingly fast. Ronnie tried desperately to manage her composure, but If Tony didn't move instantly, she knew she would've been literally punching him as if he was another female.

"How are you gonna come in here and demand that man to do something?" Rock jumped to Tony's defense.

"You need to shut the hell up and mind your business." Ronnie snapped on Rock in front of everybody.

Rock's ego was slowly being shattered by Ronnie's defense mechanisms. He had to show his buddies that he always had the last word. Rock charged at Ronnie trying to intimidate her in front of everyone. Ronnie had no intentions of backing down from a fight.

"Who do you think you're talking to?" Rock asked fiercely as he cornered her between himself and the wall, breathing heavily down on her forehead.

"I'm talkin' to you!" Ronnie yelled back with a mighty voice from her five foot, two inch frame, and still refused to back down.

Rock felt Ronnie's heart banging against his lower torso, like it was trying to put a hole in her chest. Ronnie began getting hot from the heat emerging from Rock's body. She felt like someone had just opened the oven after baking half of a Sunday's dinner.

Trey tried talking to the couple to ease the manic tension between them. Rock kissed Ronnie on the forehead and sounded a slight bit of laughter, deliberately trying to agitate Ronnie worse than he had already.

"I'm sorry baby. What's wrong?" Rock asked.

"What's wrong!" Ronnie exclaimed. "My sister is pregnant and you all want to play around thinking everything is a damn joke."

Rock's eyes stretched big as quarters. "Nae's pregnant for real?" Rock asked with mixed feelings. He was unsure of if he should've been joyful or dismayed under the given circumstances.

Rock embraced Ronnie with hugs, kisses and apologies. Rock was ready to throw a party, still unsure of how Tony accepted the news.

"What's wrong?" Trey inquired.

"Man, Tony's about to be a father," Rock announced.

"Have you thought about the fact that she may not have wanted the world to know yet?" Monie exclaimed.

Trey looked at Monie as if she couldn't have made a more stupid comment.

"In a few months everybody's gonna know," Trey added sarcastically.

Night was starting to fall and Rock was ready to complete their final operation, before heading back to Atlanta the next day. He gathered the guys around the coffee table to map out their locations at a nearby marina. Rock sensed that this operation would be different than the last one. He was sure that shots would be fired and someone would probably end up dead.

Rock, Trey and Rick rode in Rock's escalade to the marina. Tony, Rome and Mike followed them in the Hummer. They were giving a fifteen-minute window to present the appearance to anyone on a surveillance stakeout that Rock may've been traveling without his full entourage.

Rock kept his imperceptible earpiece on, just loud enough to decipher if his entourage reported any unusual activity. Rock knew from previous operations that Sisco ran dirty operations. He stayed prepared and was constantly on the look out.

Trey sensed the deviant works of the Miami Beach drug lord who called himself Sisco. Trey attached the silencer to the end of his rifles' barrel.

"Man that wasn't in the plan. What's going on?" Rome asked.

"Something doesn't feel right." Trey responded.

Mike noticed Trey's behavior was a bit on edge. He decided it would probably be safe to add his silencer to his rifle as well. As the guys rode around the desolate port, Rome noticed a couple of guys running through the woods. He found that to be a bit strange, unless they were setting up booby traps and surveillance camps.

As the night grew later and Rock brought the deal to an end, Rome noticed an ambush was imminent. Rome focused on the guys staked out in the woods through binoculars.

"Rock, somebody's in the woods to your right. I think they're gonna to try something," Trey informed Rock through his earpiece.

As Rock swiftly walked back to the Escalade, Tony shot the guys in the woods before they fired at Rock. Mike locked his rifle's target on Sisco while Rock safely made it to the truck. As Tony and Rick were stepping in the Escalade, shots were fired from everywhere. Tony was shot in the arm as Rick sped away.

"I've been hit," Tony screamed.

"Tony's been hit! Tony's been hit! Let's get him to the hospital!" Rock yelled emotionally."

"It'll be best if we get him to the next county, just in case the police were listening to the scanners and heard about a lot of commotion." Rick panted and sped through back streets and alleyways, while trying to pay attention to Rock and Tony as well as the road.

Rick drove directly to the next county's hospital's emergency room.

"Rome, go get the girls. Tell them to pack because we're leaving tonight," Rock demanded.

Rock and Rick decided to stay at the hospital with Tony, while Rome went to get the girls. Mike took Rock's truck to the nearest car-wash to wash out the blood from the backseat.

Once Rome arrived at the house, the girls immediately became suspicious and curious as to why Rome was alone.

"Where's everyone else?" Monie inquired.

"They're waiting for us," Rome replied. "Just pack your bags. We're leaving tonight."

"Why? We're not supposed to leave until tomorrow," Ronnie added.

"Just pack your bags so we can leave now," Rome demanded.

None of the girls were around Rome often enough to know how to handle him. Ronnie figured him to be a lot like Rock. They rushed to pack their bags and jumped in the Hummer.

For the first few miles they rode in silence. Ronnie wondered if Rome was ever going to tell them what was going on, or if they were going to have to continue riding in suspense.

"Are you going to tell us what's going on or not?" Monie asked with frustration.

"Not," Rome sarcastically replied remorselessly. Rome continued to drive looking quite panic-stricken.

"Why are you gonna keep us in the dark?" Monie asked persistently. "That's not fair."

"Will somebody shut her up!?" Rome yelled.

"No, they can't shut me up! You rushed over to get us like a maniac, making us pack our bags in the middle of the damn night, haulin' ass around, taking us to who knows where in the middle of the woods. And besides, we didn't ask to come on this trip. I think the least we could get is an explanation!" Monie exclaimed with severe anger.

Rome thought about it for a moment. *"They are a part of the entourage,"* he thought.

It would only be fair to let them know what was going on.

"Everyone's at the hospital. Tony was shot," Rome broke down and confessed.

"No!" Nae screamed and burst out into tears.

It was quite obvious that Nae was emotionally stressed and overly sensitive. She'd started crying about the smallest things, whether it pertained to her or not. Ronnie remained strong throughout her sister's emotional fiasco. Although Monie tried, Ronnie was still Nae's stronghold, and yet the only one who supported and respected her left-fieldish perceptions.

"Is he okay?" Ronnie asked.

"He was hit in the arm. I don't think he's hurt too bad." Rome added.

Monie hugged and comforted Nae in the back seat, while Ronnie helped Rome navigate to the hospital. Ronnie treated the situation very delicately. She tried not to say anything that may've upset her sister worst than she was already.

"Rome, what happened?" Ronnie whispered.

"It would be better if Rock told you the whole story later," Rome replied.

Ronnie accepted his response and remained quiet for the duration of the ride. She thought about her plan to escape this uncanny lifestyle. She was unsure about Tony's status. She began silently making plans to assume the duties of the absent parent for her unborn niece or nephew.

On the way back to Atlanta, Nae and Tony rode in the backseat of the Hummer. Tony lay stretched across the seat with his head in Nae's lap, as she lightly stroked his forehead. As she continuously babbled, her story became repetitious. All she talked about was how much she didn't want her child to grow up in a drug infested and corrupt environment, in which he was living.

In the Escalade, Ronnie confessed to Rock that she was tired of living in a drug related atmosphere. She threatened to leave him upon their arrival to Atlanta. Rock refused to take heed to Ronnie's useless confessions. She pleaded her case redundantly, trying to formulate ways to make Rock understand her reasons for wanting to leave.

Rock looked over at Ronnie, figuring she was letting the fear overcome her of last night's sequence of events. Rock had a tendency to ignore Ronnie's senseless whimpers of her disappearing.

Rock grabbed her by the chin and turned her head to face him. "If you ever tried to leave me, I swear I'll kill you first," Rock threatened.

Ronnie knew that her plan had to be a solid one. The only way of escaping was to kill him first. She feared that if she succeeded in escaping, he might try to do something to her mother. Rock would do anything to gain information of her whereabouts, or arrange some other crazy occurrence to make her return halfhearted.

Rock was headed home when Ronnie suggested he take her to her mother's house.

"I need you to be with me tonight," Rock replied.

He proceeded to take her to his home, ignoring her wishes to go to Veronica's house.

"Rock, I need to be alone tonight. I need time to reflect," Ronnie said.

Rock pulled the sun visor down, pointing to the mirror, showing her own reflection. Ronnie was not at all amused with Rock's cynical sense of humor. Ronnie started to feel as if her wishes and desires were being taken as a joke to Rock. She was ready to have a man in her life that was considerate and compassionate. She no longer wanted anything to do with this appalling relationship.

Everyone stayed at Rock's house that night. While Rock attended to other, more important things than her, Ronnie attempted to leave. Before she made it to the door, she heard Rock's bold voice coming from the upstairs loft.

"Where are you going? I told you that you were going to stay here tonight."

"I forgot something in the truck." Ronnie lied, trying to make up something to justify having keys in her hand. Rock rolled his eyes, turned around, and walked in the bedroom. He sat on the edge of the bed waiting to see how long it was going to take her to get her forgotten item out of the truck. He knew she'd lied. Before he reacted to her lies, he had to wait and see what she was going to do when she didn't find any of her belongings in the truck.

Ronnie sat in the driver seat of the Mercedes for about ten minutes contemplating whether or not she should leave or stay. She thought about all the things Rock probably would've done to her if she left. She didn't want to leave her sister's behind, but she couldn't go back inside to tell them that she was trying to leave. She finally decided to stay. Before she went back inside, she had to think of something clever to say explaining her escapade.

Rock sat on the bed with his legs crossed, leaning back, resting against the headboard. He knew Ronnie contemplated leaving, but for some strange reason, he knew she'd return shortly. He sat waiting for her patiently.

Ronnie silently entered the room without conversation or an

attempt of an explanation. She avoided eye contact with Rock and began preparing for her shower.

"Did you find it?" Rock asked.

Ronnie released a sigh of frustration and ignored Rock's question.

"Did you find whatever you claimed you were looking for?" Rock asked with a slight inclination in his tone of voice.

"Yes," she snapped as she went in the bathroom, slamming the door.

Rock jumped to his feet and busted in the bathroom behind her. He slammed the door and quickly spent her half naked body around facing him, pinning her against the wall with his body. She tried to quickly recover her breath from the startling spin.

"What's wrong with you?" Rock asked.

"Nothing," Ronnie replied with an overabundance of fear. "Rock, I'm just not happy," Ronnie honestly confessed.

"Why are you so unhappy with me?" Rock asked.

"Look." Ronnie gestured at how Rock was positioned, towering over her.

"Look at how you treat me. This is intimidating," Ronnie added as her eyes began to water.

Rock hugged Ronnie, embracing her passionately, as he repeatedly kissed on her forehead, apologizing several times over.

She wished she could talk to her mother. After all the arguing and disagreements of each conversation, Ronnie found great pleasure and comfort talking to her mother. Since her mother started dating Jerome, she barely had time for any of the girls.

As Ronnie lay in the bed beside Rock, she began missing her mother more and more, even as Rock fondled her. She thought about the talks they had, and the things her mother told her about Rock. She wished she had listened.

Rock climbed on top of her, spread her legs, and began to have his way with her. Ronnie lay there lifelessly and emotionless. Rock roughly thrust his penis inside of her, as she remained lying there silently, staring at the wall.

After about two minutes of partially dry, harsh penetration, he finally realized she had absolutely no interest in any type of sexual activity with him. He removed his penis from her semi-dry womb. Rock laid behind her, finding comfort in innocently embracing her with his naked body against her warm, soft, naked skin.

Chapter 13

A few weeks before Thanksgiving, Veronica sat up in the bed alone in her quiet house with a warm cup of cocoa. She juggled two notebooks jotting plans for her holiday menu in one, and plans and ideas for her wedding in the other.

She hadn't heard from Ronnie or Nae in couple of days. Wondering if they were all right, Veronica called both of the girl's cell phones, receiving no answer on either one. She knew Monie was over Trey's house studying for midterms before the holiday break.

Ronnie and Nae had been staying at Nae's apartment for the past week. The drama of dealing with Rock and Tony had become a bit stressful for both of the girls. After a hostile argument, Tony agreed to stay at Rock's house until Nae calmed down and was ready for him to return home.

Since she hadn't been staying with him, Rock was under the impression that Ronnie was staying at Veronica's house. He called and drove by Veronica's house often to see if his Mercedes was there. He also tried calling her cell phone, but never received an answer.

It was Corey's first day home from the hospital. Juanita and Jackie were ready to celebrate. Immediately after they had arrived at Juanita's house, she called Veronica, inviting her and the girls to come over and welcome him home. Corey's only request was to see Nae. She was all he talked about during the entire ride from the hospital.

After several months of no activity and intense therapy, Juanita explained how joyful Corey was to finally come out of the hospital. He was planning to stay at Juanita's house until he fully recuperated.

Corey told his mother about the times Nae had visited him after he came out of ICU. Whenever she left the room, he reminisced of her pleasant essence and her sweet scents that always lingered. Her hearts' purity, her morals and her incredible nature made Corey realize that Nae was the woman of his dreams.

Nae waited patiently for Ronnie to come out of the gynecologist's office. When she finally came out she had quite a peculiar, but familiar look on her face. It was the same look Nae had on her face just four months ago when she found out she was pregnant. She didn't bother to ask Ronnie about the results she'd received from the doctor.

As if Nae's pregnancy wasn't enough to postpone their plans to get away from Rock and Tony once and for all. Ronnie wondered how and why this had to happen to her. She figured if they were going to make a move it would have to be soon, hopefully, before her pregnancy started to show.

The girls sat quietly in Nae's car thinking of how they were going to get themselves out of this mess.

"What'll we do now?" Ronnie asked.

"We'll have to go purchase a couple of guns," Nae replied.

To Ronnie, that idea wasn't half bad. She figured she'd probably load it and shoot herself for allowing her situation to transpire. She didn't think Nae was serious about trying to kill Tony, especially after all the homicides they'd committed and never gotten caught.

The girls headed to the pawnshop with intentions to buy two guns and ammunition. As they sat in the car, still indecisive as to whether or not they were going through with it, Ronnie began to think of the danger she'd put her unborn child in.

Nae had second thoughts about if she really wanted to kill Tony. He wasn't half as bad to her as Rock had been to Ronnie. Ronnie had been cheated on several times and often treated like she was his child instead of his woman.

On several occasions she'd been falsely accused of cheating, and received beatings from Rock like a redheaded stepchild. He was bound to get what was coming to him, whether Ronnie went through with the plan or if someone else had to do it.

Nae convinced Ronnie that if she killed Rock, her motives would be justifiable. Ronnie began to like what her sister was instigating.

Ronnie's phone vibrated as she tried to gather her thoughts.

"Hello?" she answered.

Veronica was calling to invite the girls over to Juanita's house for a small welcome home celebration for Corey. As Veronica babbled on, she finally remembered to invite them to her house for Thanksgiving dinner in two weeks.

"By the way, I already invited Rock," Veronica added.

"Why did you do that!" Ronnie exclaimed.

"I wanted everyone to be happy, so I didn't exclude anyone," Veronica explained.

"I'm not coming," Ronnie replied.

"Yes you are. How would it look to have Rock there celebrating Thanksgiving with me if you're not there?" Veronica asked.

"Ma, I'm not coming if he's going to be there!" Ronnie declared.

"Ronnie, I only did it to make you happy. What's done is done. I can't uninvited him. Tell Nae that Tony will be there as well. Corey's party starts today at five. I'll see you there," Veronica added. She quickly hung up the phone, ending the conversation that was soon going to turn into an argument.

Ronnie dropped the phone into her purse, shaking her head with unbelief. Nae stared at Ronnie and waited to hear about what her mother had to say. The message wasn't coming fast enough for Nae.

"What'd she say?" Nae inquired.

"Ms. Juanita is having a welcome home party for Corey in two hours. She also said to tell you that she'd already invited Tony to Thanksgiving dinner."

"How's *she* gonna invite Tony?" Nae asked angrily.

"It's her dinner and her house so technically she can invite anyone she wants. I won't be there," Ronnie said blatantly.

Nae started to get excited about Corey's party. This was the one moment she'd been anticipating for months. She hadn't seen him in over a month. It was about time she expressed to him her true feelings towards him. She wanted to remain honest about her pregnancy. However, the fear of rejection overwhelmed her. Nae feared he would want nothing else to do with her.

After being in seclusion for several months without any justifiable cause, Ronnie was apprehensive about facing Josh. She took a moment to reflect. "Maybe Josh still had mixed feelings about her from the encounter he and Rock had," she thought. She knew Josh's feelings were extremely strong about her; however her involvement with Rock wouldn't have allowed her to pursue anything with anyone else. Now that she was making changes in her life, which didn't include Rock, she was ready to tackle whatever came her way.

Ronnie had visions of making passionate love to Josh. However, if there were any types of sexual relations with him now, she'd feel like a cheap skeezer. In his eyes she'd probably be considered a whore. Although she wanted much more than a plutonic relationship with him, she wasn't going to let her pregnancy stop a beautiful friendship.

Ronnie called Monie's cell phone but got her voice mail. Monie had mistakenly left her phone in her purse, which was locked in Trey's truck. Ronnie then called Trey's cell phone, in an attempt to reach Monie and notify her of Corey's party. She found that Trey and Monie were at Rome's cookout.

"Monie, Ronnie needs to speak to you!" Trey shouted across the yard.

Rock's heart palpitated with anxiety from hearing Ronnie's name.

"Yo Trey, gimme' the phone," Rock yelled.

Monie looked at Rock with apprehension and snatched the phone from Trey.

"Hello?" Monie answered as she walked away from the noise of the party.

"Where are you?" Ronnie asked.

"I'm at Rome's cookout with Trey. Rock is here. He claims he'd been looking for you for the last week. Where've you and Nae been?"

Rock walked up behind Monie, hoping she would give him the phone.

"Do you want to talk to Rock?" Monie whispered.

"No! I just called to let you know that there's a welcome home party going on for Corey at Ms. Juanita's house at five."

"Okay," Monie replied.

Ronnie ended the call and told Nae to head over to Juanita's house.

"Monie, gimme' the phone before she hangs up," Rock demanded.

Monie continued to hold the phone to her ear, perpetrating as if Ronnie was still on the line. She turned around and deviously smiled at Rock.

"Okay girl, bye," Monie added fictitiously, making Rock more frustrated.

"Call her back," Rock demanded.

"She didn't wanna talk to you. If you wanna talk to her, you call her," Monie suggested, as she walked around Rock heading back to the activity.

"What did she say?" Rock yelled, asking Monie as she walked away.

Monie looked over her shoulder at Rock. "Nothing pertaining to you," as she continued walking.

Rock was hurt and missing Ronnie. He knew he'd screwed up once again. He didn't know what he had done this time to put her in a funk. He continued to hound Monie about where Ronnie was going to be, what she was doing, and with whom. Monie refused to give out any information about Corey's party, knowing Rock would try to find Juanita's house and crash the party.

At 5:30, Ronnie and Nae arrived at Juanita's house. Both of the girls were like teenagers, preparing for their first dates. Veronica met them at the door, "Where's Monie?" she asked.

"She's with Trey," Ronnie replied, as Josh ran up and hugged her.

He placed a soft, juicy, but intimate kiss on her lips.

"Excuse me," Veronica interrupted. "Could you at least wait until I leave?"

"Well hurry up and leave. Go find your man or something," Ronnie said jovially.

Ronnie and Josh both looked at Veronica and started laughing. Veronica was pleased to finally see her daughter happy. She saw the sparkles in both of their eyes. Although she had unclosed and unresolved issues with Rock, Veronica knew Ronnie was happy, and felt free when she was with Josh.

Veronica found tranquility in the young couple's reunion. This was the moment she wished and awaited for. It was exactly what she had prophetically told Monie about on their way to Atlanta. She hoped for a closer bond and longevity for the couple's relationship.

Nae found contentment in being Corey's shadow. He walked around with his stylish cane in one hand, and his other arm interlocked with hers. While accompanying him, she felt like she didn't have a care in the world. She knew that she couldn't build a stronger bond with him if she and Ronnie were going through with their plan.

She wanted to tell him about the turmoil she'd been experiencing with Tony. Somehow, she had to tell him about the baby. However, she couldn't formulate the words to let it roll off of her tongue smoothly enough. A lunch or dinner date would probably be the perfect opportunity to talk about it with him.

Jason and Jerome sat over in a secluded corner alone. Jason talked about how he was starting to miss Monie. Jerome complied, and complimented Veronica's family on being such wonderful and beautiful group of women. "You should make Monie aware of your feelings for her," Jerome advised. Jason already knew that Monie was falling for someone, and that someone wasn't him.

"Hello? Hello? Hello?" A voice from someone freshly entering the party, was coming from the front of the house.

"Sonya, I'm glad you made it," Juanita expressed her gratitude as they hugged one another.

Veronica discreetly looked at Jerome ambiguously and shrugged her shoulders. She wasn't sure what to make of this peculiar relationship suddenly formed between Sonya and Juanita.

"Hey brother-in-law," Sonya said jokingly to Jerome.

Veronica slightly tugged at Juanita's shirt signaling to meet with her in the kitchen.

Jerome stood up to hug his soon to be ex sister-in-law, while at the same time, he was studying Veronica's actions. He introduced Sonya to Jason, then to Jackie, Ronnie, Nae, and eventually to everyone else. Meanwhile, Veronica chatted with Juanita in the kitchen to find out what was going on.

"Why is your boyfriend's wife here?" Veronica asked quite perplexed.

"Ex-boyfriend," Juanita stressed, making it known that she'd cut all ties with Tyrone. "She and I had a long talk. She's cool. I'll tell you about it later," Juanita responded.

There was nothing Veronica could say or do. This was Juanita's house and it's her function. She could only respect her wishes, and be cordial to all of the other guests. Although this was an awkward situation, Veronica realized she wasn't the one who had issues with Tyrone. The only ties she had to him were the fact that she was marrying his brother.

Jackie had some jumbled feelings, similar to Veronica's concern about the questionable situation at hand. With the purpose of the gathering on her mind, Jackie didn't spend much time trying to understand her sister's affairs. She didn't care who showed up to help celebrate life on her son's behalf. She was overjoyed that Corey was home and doing well.

A couple of hours into the party, Josh and Ronnie slipped off together to be alone. Josh suggested they go to his apartment. He wanted to discuss the reasons she hadn't been giving him the time of day.

Ronnie felt like she had finally met a man who loved and cared about, her no matter what situation transpired. She was sure that she'd screwed up any chances of ever being with Josh. On the way to his apartment, she finally found enough courage to tell him that she was expecting.

Josh was overwhelmed by the news, but he couldn't throw away the feelings that had accrued over the years, and were steadily growing strong. If it meant accepting a child into his life to be with Ronnie, he was willing to step up to the plate and accept all the responsibilities and *baggage* she brought along.

The status of Ronnie's relationship with Rock was still unclear to Josh. He began to think she purposely left that portion of the story out for a reason.

"What are you going to do about Rock?" Josh inquired.

"Did my mother tell you that I was planning to move to California?" Ronnie asked, purposely ignoring Josh's inquiry about Rock. Ronnie knew full well that Veronica had no knowledge of her plans to relocate.

"No she didn't, but what kind of arrangements do you and Rock have in place?" Josh asked again.

"I just found out about the baby today," Ronnie announced.

"Did you tell Rock about it?"

"No," Ronnie said, short and snappy.

Josh thought that may've been a sign that she wasn't going to tell Rock about it any time soon. Maybe not at all.

Maybe it wouldn't be such a bad idea if she didn't tell Rock about it, Josh thought. If he adopted the baby before Rock knew anything about the pregnancy, he would legally be the baby's father, and there would be nothing Rock could do about it.

Before he suggested any of his brilliant ideas, in which he knew Ronnie would almost certainly agree with, he tried to put himself in Rock's shoes. He wondered how he would feel if she ever did that to him. He put a sudden end to that frame of mind, comparing himself to Rock.

Rock was heartless and less deserving of a woman with Ronnie's disposition. *"He shouldn't be allowed to raise another individual to grow up to be like him,"* Josh thought selfishly. He was now appreciating the values and morals he was taught by his late father, in which he felt Rock lacked.

Once they arrived at Josh's apartment, Ronnie went inside and curled up on the sofa in front of the fireplace.

"Should I start a fire?" Josh asked.

Ronnie shook her head, "no." She saw several candles on the mantle that would've been more appropriate for the occasion. Ronnie found the fire starter behind the candles, and lit three of Josh's French vanilla candles, as Josh put on some soft jazz. The couple sat on the floor in front of the sofa. They began reminiscing and laughing about the good old days during junior high school. Josh had wanted to talk to Ronnie before they were teenagers.

During the past summer when they spent time together riding his motorcycle, sitting in the park, or her mother's porch talking, Ronnie remembered how good it felt being in Josh's presence. She felt like she could trust him enough to confess everything she was planning to do.

She turned and looked into Josh's beautiful and innocent brown eyes, "Do you think I should have an abortion?"

Josh was speechless. He didn't know how to respond to such an impetuous question. He knew Ronnie didn't want to be tied to Rock for the rest of her life, but what was done was done. He wasn't sure if that would've been the right path to take. Unfortunately, there was no easy way to resolve Ronnie's problem. He assured her that whatever route she took, he would be there for her and would support her decisions.

Ronnie made an abrupt decision to have the abortion without Rock's knowledge of the pregnancy. She had enough confidence in Josh to believe that he would stick to his word.

Corey stuck to Nae like glue. She was astounded that he still had strong feelings for her as he did before the accident. Corey limped around on his stylish cane, enjoying every moment spent with his soon to be, newfound love.

At the far end of the yard, away from the commotion, the couple sat at Juanita's picnic table. Corey knew that something was bothering Nae. It was only a matter of time before she let her emotions flow like a river. Corey sat quietly. He listened and offered his shoulder for her to cry on.

Corey was shocked to hear that she was expecting a baby by

another man. Before his accident, the relationship that he and Nae were building seemed promising. As he found out that she wasn't happy and in love with Tony as she once was, a small fraction of hope lingered. Due to his injuries, he knew his chances of having a monogamous relationship with Nae were still slim. Emotionally, he hadn't fully recovered from the accident, and a baby added to his life wasn't the direction he'd planned for at least another two or three years.

What was left of the lingering hope slowly began to dwindle away as he thought about the reality of the situation. He was ready to travel and explore the world. A baby would only rain on his parade. He noticed his flow of mixed emotions about the situation. This was a whirlwind of confusion.

Corey knew that Nae's feelings for him were just as intense as his were for her. He tried to make ridiculous excuses to prohibit himself of fatherly duties that would've been expected of him if he pursued the relationship.

"Nae, I'd love to be with you, but I'm not ready for a family yet," Corey admitted.

"Neither is Tony," she thought to herself. Nae wasn't sure what her reaction should've been. As loving and caring as she presumed him to be, she was stunned at what she'd just heard. Since this wasn't his child, she could only accept and respect his honesty. She couldn't imagine hearing this a few years from now after her baby had formed a bond with him.

Rock persistently harassed Monie, trying to find Ronnie and whomever she may have been with. Monie locked herself in the bathroom to call Ronnie, advising her that Rock's behavior was irate and very scary.

Rock continuously called Ronnie's cell phone, only to find that she would repeatedly decline them. The constant rejection of his calls made Rock more furious by the minute. Rage and anger grew rapidly towards Ronnie. He threatened Monie to tell him where Ronnie was.

Monie demanded Trey to take her to Juanita's house where the rest of her family was. Trey didn't understand why all of a sudden, she was ready to leave. On the way to Juanita's house, Monie explained to Trey about Rock's irate behavior. She wasn't comfortable around him anymore.

Some of the stories she'd heard Ronnie tell Nae came to mind, about how outraged and over protective Rock was at times. She figured Ronnie may have exaggerated, or perhaps even falsified some facts, to make Rock seem a bit deranged or dangerous than he really was. After that night's episode of drama, she realized her sister was indeed telling the truth, and maybe crying out for help from this enraged character.

Trey sympathized with his companion. He knew Rock's temper would have a negative affect on Monie. However, he had no doubt that Ronnie knew how to handle Rock and put him back in his place. He remembered how Ronnie handled herself in Miami. By the end of the night, she had Rock eating out of the palms of her hand like a helpless puppy.

Monie thanked Trey for taking her over Juanita's house. As she got out of the truck, she assured him that she would call him the next day. Trey wondered why Monie was in such a rush to leave. She tried to avoid a meeting between him and Jason. Monie didn't have a hidden agenda, but just in case things didn't work out with her and Trey, she wanted to possibly keep Jason on reserve.

Monie knew she only had to tell Jason once that she was ready for a relationship with him, and he would accept the proposal with open arms. The small relationship the two had built since they reunited during the summer was innocent, but it was going to remain in the closet in case it turned out to be bigger than she anticipated.

Monie went in the house and surprised everyone. Veronica was pleased to see her. Jason was ecstatic that she showed up.

"How did you get here?" Veronica asked.

"A friend dropped me off," Monie responded, hoping her mother would end the conversation there.

"A friend," Veronica reiterated. She hoped Monie didn't get Trey to drop her off so that she could see Jason. Deep down inside, she knew that was what happened. Once again, Veronica wanted to see her soon to be lawyer, daughter, get out of a messy situation.

Monie looked at her mother with assured dignity, and began greeting everyone individually. She gave Jason a bonafide smile, indicating that her purpose for being there was clearly to see him.

Before she made it over to Jason, Monie's phone rang. It was Trey wondering why he wasn't invited in to the party. She cleverly explained that she didn't want him to miss any more of Rome's party.

"Rome's party wasn't important. I wanted to be with you," Trey proclaimed.

"Trey, I can't just invite you to someone else's party. Besides I need to spend some time with my family." Monie gave a bogus explanation hoping he'd buy it.

"I promise I'll call you tomorrow," Monie convinced Trey with her angelic voice before ending the call.

Monie made eye contact with Jason again, and sashayed in his direction. He twitched his head, gesturing for her to meet him outside on the patio. After Monie was introduced to Sonya, gave hugs and made small talk with Juanita and Jerome, she finally made it to the patio.

Jason was finally able to give Monie the hugs and kisses he'd been longing to do since she walked through the door. There, he could do it without scrutiny. He was overjoyed that she'd made it and instantly began making plans to spend the rest of the night with her.

Ronnie and Josh had been drinking Jack Daniels and Fuzzy Navels all evening. Ronnie was passed out on Josh's bed. She was sweaty and slightly sticky, dressed in one of Josh's jerseys. A sudden urge to go to the bathroom woke her up abruptly. She looked over at Josh as he slept, starring at his naked body. Before she got out of the bed she looked down on the floor beside the bed, finding her bra and panties buried under her skirt and top.

As she swung her feet out of the bed and onto the floor, she felt the room slightly spinning. She felt like she was moving in slow motion. She tiptoed into the bathroom trying not to wake Josh. As she released her urine, she felt an inconsiderable burning sensation in her vagina. She knew then that she and Josh had had sex.

She found the linen and washed up. She felt like a whore. "Just earlier today I found out that I was pregnant, and by nightfall I'm sleeping with someone else," she thought. She tipped back into the bedroom and sat on the edge of the bed. Josh rolled over, stretching out his arm around her waist, scaring her.

"I'm sorry, did I scare you?" Josh asked.

"Yeah, a little," she replied with a slight quiver in the pit of her stomach.

"Are you okay?"

"Not really," she said, still sitting on the edge of the bed.

Josh sat up on the edge of the bed beside her, forcing her to lie down and relax. He saw the worried look on her face and wondered why she wouldn't voluntarily tell him what was wrong.

"Ronnie, tell me what's wrong," Josh insisted.

"Josh, how do you expect me to feel? I feel like a hoe. I'm pregnant by Rock and just had sex with you," Ronnie explained.

"I understand your point, but you shouldn't feel like that. We have a lot of history, and it just so happened, we had a few too many drinks. Crap happens, but that doesn't make us any better or worse than we were three hours ago," Josh rebutted with an opposing explanation.

Although Ronnie felt like she had just cheated on Rock, Josh's explanation made her feel somewhat at ease. In her mind, she didn't do anything wrong. After all, Rock had been denying the fact that he had been screwing around with other women since they been together.

Ronnie snuggled up in Josh's arms. The couple lied quietly, listening to the beats of each other's hearts. Josh strongly felt in his heart that one day soon they would be inseparable.

Chapter 14

*I*t was less than a full week away from Thanksgiving. All three girls stayed at Veronica's place to help prepare for the big dinner she was having. The girls enjoyed staying at their mother's around the holidays. Every year since they were children, they would all help shop, decorate and cook.

Monie was the first to awake. She was obviously in the holiday spirit. Monie hardly ever cooked a full course meal on her own. She went downstairs and began cooking breakfast for the family. The aroma of sizzling sausage and baked bacon stirred through the house, waking Ronnie and Nae.

Ronnie spent the first fifteen minutes in the bathroom, coping with her morning sickness. While sitting on the edge of the bathtub, she suddenly felt as if she was going to fall backwards into it. She tried standing to her feet, but had to hold on to the towel bar and shower door to sustain her balance. Before going downstairs to join her sisters for breakfast, she splashed her face with cold water and gargled with mouthwash to kill the stench of vomit on her breath.

As she walked towards the table, Nae looked at Ronnie, empathizing with her sickly, hopeless looking sister.

"Is baby giving you a rough morning?" Nae asked.

Monie's eyes drastically widened, surprised at what she was hearing. She turned around with the spatula in her hand, waiting for Ronnie's response, to determine whether or not Nae was telling the truth. Out of the corner of her eye, Ronnie gave Nae an acute look. Ronnie ignored the question.

To her own surprise, Monie was shocked. She just *knew* that shortly after Nae's pregnancy, Ronnie would be sure to follow in her footsteps. She stood there, with her mouth hanging open, still waiting for Ronnie to answer Nae's question.

"What are we having for breakfast Monie?" Ronnie asked, purposely refusing to answer the question.

She placed three pancakes, a sausage patty, two bacon strips, a spoon full of eggs and a slice of toast on her plate. She poured herself a tall glass of apple juice and sat down at the table next to Nae, pretending her sisters were invisible.

"So Ronnie, *is* baby giving you a rough morning? It looks like you're eating for about two or three people," Monie commented.

"Monie, I'm hungry. We'll talk later," Ronnie replied and started eating.

Monie danced around the kitchen with the spatula still in her hand singing into it, "I'm gonna be an auntie, two times."

Monie skipped around the kitchen table hugging her sisters and singing.

"Monie, will you be quiet before you wake mom up?" Ronnie muttered with clinched teeth.

As Monie danced back to the stove to flip the last pancake, Veronica walked in the kitchen. "I'm already awake," she said catching everyone off guard. "How could anyone sleep with all this commotion going on? What's all the commotion about anyway?"

Veronica looked at Ronnie and Nae as they sat at the table eating. She walked over to the stove and grabbed a piece of bacon. She leaned against the counter top next to the stove, waiting for someone to tell her what the commotion was all about.

"What's this about you're gonna be an auntie two times?" Veronica asked. "Is Nae having twins?"

No one said anything. Veronica took a plate off the counter and fixed her breakfast. She sat at the table and blessed her food. Ronnie and Nae held their heads down, occasionally looking up at their mother as she ate peacefully.

Veronica finished chewing what was left in her mouth, took a long sigh, a few swallows of her juice, and rested her arms on the table. The girls knew a conversation was coming that was heading down a path they didn't want to go.

"So Ronnie, when's your baby due?" Veronica asked prophetically. She figured since no one wanted to volunteer any information, she'd pick them so they'd tell her involuntarily.

Ronnie wasn't sure of what to say. She felt like she was stuck between a rock and a hard place.

"Ma, Monie is just trippin. She's delirious. You can't listen to anything she says," Ronnie commented.

Veronica's motherly instincts led her to believe that something was indeed going on. Monie's imagination wasn't quite as vivid as Ronnie and Nae tried to portray. Veronica was about to let the girls know that she didn't have time for surprises, especially since she was about to live it up with her new husband.

When Monie finally sat down to eat with the rest of the family, the way Veronica wanted it, she broke the news that she and Jerome were getting married.

Monie was stunned. Ronnie wasn't surprised at all. Nae knew it was coming, but she wasn't sure when. All of the girls were happy for their mother. Veronica just hoped her pregnant daughters would be able to fit into bride maids' dresses by June. If Ronnie was going to participate in the wedding, she at least needed to know if she was pregnant or not. Without continuing to harp on the subject, and not wanting to discourage the girls, Veronica didn't prolong the conversation.

"I should be able to fit into my dress by June," Nae added without consideration for Ronnie's emotions.

Ronnie didn't say a word. She knew Nae didn't mean any harm, but she figured she could've been a little more sensitive considering her situation. Veronica detected hostility in the air stemming from Nae. Nae was suddenly overwhelmed with an attitude, feeling that Ronnie was contemplating an abortion. *"How could she do this after Ronnie knew that I made a decision months ago to have my baby,"* she thought. Nae solely based her anger upon the fact that Ronnie didn't bother to talk her out of going through with the pregnancy full term.

After finishing her meal, Ronnie gulped the remainder of her juice, and sat at the table in a rather relaxed mode. Within minutes she began to feel sick, feeling like gauze pads were in her mouth. She ran to the bathroom, just barely making it. Forced to let go of her fulfilling breakfast, Ronnie stuck her head in the rim of the toilet bowl.

Veronica heard all of the coughing and gagging and instantly knew she was expecting a baby.

"She's pregnant," Veronica said calmly.

Nae aggressively threw her silverware in her plate, stormed out of the kitchen, and went upstairs. Monie looked at Veronica with a puzzled look on her face, wondering what was going on.

"This is the time of year when we're supposed to be happy. When

I was cooking breakfast this morning, I thought we were," Monie explained.

Ronnie finished in the bathroom and went upstairs to her room to lie down, only to find Nae sitting on her bed, furious.

"Why did you encourage me to keep this baby and you're getting rid of yours?" Nae asked in a frustrated whisper, demanding an explanation.

"Don't get mad at me Ms. Thang. That was your decision! I told you I would support you regardless of what the outcome was! Did I not?" Ronnie exclaimed.

Nae finally agreed with her sister. Ronnie had never directly or indirectly given Nae any ultimatums. Nae knew she took matters into her own hands by deciding to have the baby. Rightfully, she couldn't get mad at Ronnie for having the same choices as she did. Ronnie just chose the opposite one.

"When are you going to do it?" Nae asked.

"Tomorrow," Ronnie replied.

"Tomorrow!" Nae exclaimed. "Are you crazy or have you just lost your mind? We're supposed to help mom go shopping. In two days we have to start cooking and you're not going to be well enough to participate. Mom's going to be suspicious."

"I'll hide out at your apartment for a couple of days."

"So she can question me to death? Rock is going to be here for Thanksgiving dinner. Have you told *him* yet?"

"No," Ronnie replied.

Nae sensed drama coming about. Now that their mother and Monie knew about the pregnancy, something was bound to come out at dinner. Nae questioned Ronnie repeatedly about how they were going to convince Veronica that she wasn't pregnant. Ronnie couldn't come up with a feasible answer.

Monie and Veronica sat at the table, writing out their plans for the upcoming wedding and graduation party.

"Ma, what makes you so sure that Ronnie is pregnant?" Monie asked.

"I've been there three times and I know the symptoms." Veronica responded sincerely. "You better not open your big mouth and tell anyone anything." Veronica said sternly. She knew that if she didn't nearly threaten Monie, the news would've gotten back to Rock and been all over Jersey. Veronica's intuition led her to believe that something was wrong. Her daughters had no clue that she knew what was going on.

Veronica had a reoccurring dream a few years back. It accurately showed her everything that was going on at this point in her life. She had foreseen tragedy in her dream and prayed that it wouldn't strike within her family. She became frightened, knowing that her dream was now her reality. Her dream, now obviously a vision, never revealed any names or faces, but her soul confirmed that it was surely her family that had been targeted.

She suddenly came down with a migraine headache, and felt she needed to lie back down. After taking her prescribed painkillers, Veronica laid down across her bed. The conversation her daughters had in Ronnie's room, at the other end of the hall, rang in her head quite clearly. It was as if they conversed in the room with her. "This has to be a sign from God," she deemed.

Veronica needed to let her daughters know that she was knowledgeable about what was going on in their lives. If not, she felt as if she would have to suffer major repercussions.

With her seeping breath and throbbing head, Veronica called Ronnie and Nae as loud as she could. The girls were startled, as they heard their mother calling them, with an unusual sound of distress in her voice. They rushed in her room to her rescue.

"Ma, are you alright?" Nae asked half petrified.

"Please don't talk so loud. I have a migraine headache."

Monie swiftly finished washing the breakfast dishes as she heard all of the commotion. She wasn't able to hear her mother calling her sisters, but the stampede across the floor to her mother's room made her curiosity rise. Monie crept up the stairs to see what was going on. She heard her mother telling her sisters to sit down on the bed so she could talk to them. Monie sat on the top step and leaned towards Veronica's open door, trying not to make her presence known. She was listening for *the sound,* a crucial lecture that she thought was well deserved.

Veronica began telling the girls about *the dream* she had, which was now starting to become a reality. Before getting deep into the story, she invited Monie in. Not because she had a part in the dream, as did Ronnie and Nae, but Veronica thought the discussion would be healthier as a family meeting.

Veronica scolded Ronnie about planning an abortion, especially without Rock's knowledge or consent.

"Regardless of what he's done to you, he has a right to know. He needs to know that he's about to be a father, and that you're planning to end his chances of being one, before he's given a fair chance."

She also made it known to all of the girls that it was wrong for them to entice Juanita's sons and nephew, while still maintaining a strong relationship with the *drug gang.* Once she finished explaining her vision, the girls were merely dumbfounded. Her migraine was suddenly lifted and the rain, thunder and lightning began to take charge outside. Before the girls left her bedroom, she prayed that the curse would be lifted off of her family.

"Is Rock still coming to dinner? Ronnie asked.

"I already told you that I can't un-invite him, so let's make the best of it," Veronica replied.

"I want Josh to come," Ronnie announced.

"If you want to be with Josh, you need to have Thanksgiving over to Juanita's house," Veronica said sarcastically but truthfully.

The girls returned to Ronnie's room quite astounded and partly convinced that Veronica had the phones tapped.

"It doesn't matter if the phones were tapped or not, we never talked on them. We were at your place, remember?" Ronnie reminded Nae.

After hearing Veronica's premonition, Ronnie was still planning to follow through with her plans, without Rock's consent. She vowed that after she had the abortion, she would do everything in her power to do things the right way. Veronica had put a bit of fear in her heart. *"A little fear never hurt anyone,"* she thought. Ronnie wasn't going to let that come between her and Josh's happiness.

Ronnie figured she could take matters into her own hands by inviting Josh and uninviting Rock. First, she had to call Rock and find out what his reaction was going to be like. She trembled as she dialed the number. It had been nearly two weeks since she had spoken to him.

"Hello?" he answered. He didn't recognize Veronica's number on the caller I.D.

"Hey. I was calling to let you know that my mother had a change of plans for Thanksgiving dinner," Ronnie stated.

"I talked to her yesterday. Nothing had changed," Rock replied with suspicion. "Why didn't she call me back?"

"I can't say why my mother does half the stuff she does. We had a family meeting this morning and that was the ending result."

"Okay, I'll accept that. Why haven't you returned any of my phone calls?" Rock asked, hoping to get a half way decent conversation.

"That's all I called to tell you. Goodbye," Ronnie said rudely and hung up.

Ronnie wanted to slap herself for allowing her vulnerability to emerge. Rock was determined to see and talk to Ronnie—face to face. He took it upon himself to show up unannounced, knowing that she would still be at Veronica's house until the storm passed.

Veronica and the girls enjoyed their long awaited moment together again as a family. As the rain poured fiercely, the family found great pleasure in watching a movie when the doorbell rang. Before Ronnie answered it she knew that it was probably Rock.

She opened the door and looked at Rock. He was standing there, drenched, looking quite pathetic with two bouquets of fresh flowers and a pint of Ronnie's favorite ice cream. She wondered if he'd made a special trip in the pouring rain to see her. *"Did he think it would be worth his while?"* she thought. She was grateful for the flowers, but she wasn't in the mood to deal with him.

"Do you mind if I come in for a minute? I would like to give your mother a bouquet of flowers," Rock asked.

"Rock, what are you doing here?" Ronnie asked.

"I wanted to see you. I haven't seen you in two weeks. Don't you miss me at all?"

Ronnie continued to play hard to get. She missed him as much as he missed her. Veronica heard the elevation of Ronnie's voice. She walked in the kitchen to greet Rock, and to prevent the slight quarrel from elevating into a fight.

"Hello Rock. How are you?" Veronica asked politely, trying to bring decorum back to the couple's conversation.

"These are for you," Rock said and presented the flowers to Veronica.

"Thank you very much son-in-law," Veronica replied facetiously, purposely agitating Ronnie.

Ronnie looked at her mother in disbelief of what she'd just heard. It had been nearly a year of trying to convince her mother that Rock wasn't such a bad person. Now, she was suddenly referring to him as her *son-in-law*, in which he was not about to become if it was left up to Ronnie.

"He's not your son-in-law!" Ronnie exclaimed, trying to push Rock out of the door.

"So Ms. Williams, I heard the plans for Thanksgiving dinner has changed," Rock commented, hoping he'd still be invited to the changed location if there really was one.

Veronica was stunned and lost for words. She didn't like lying for the girls, but since she was the cause of Ronnie being in this situation, she made an exception. Veronica couldn't believe Ronnie had taken it upon herself to un-invite him. She thought Ronnie was dead wrong for telling him about changes that never occurred.

She partially blamed herself for inviting him, not knowing the status of their relationship. She had to think of a cover-up fast.

"This morning the girls suggested we have dinner at my girlfriend's house." Veronica stumbled over her words, trying to get them in order, lying to cover up Ronnie's lie.

"Is this the girlfriend whose son was shot?" Rock asked to get confirmation on Josh to see if in fact he was a family friend, or if Ronnie had a hidden agenda.

"She's his aunt," Veronica added with mixed and confused feelings.

She then knew that Ronnie obviously told Rock something about Josh. She wondered if Rock was actually like the visual picture Ronnie had painted of him. It sounded as if Ronnie had mentioned something to him in which he was uncomfortable with. He was apparently trying to verify the truth through Veronica.

"I'm sorry Rock. We're just in limbo right now. Ronnie will let you know if we have dinner here for Christmas," Veronica explained.

Veronica was starting to see his insecurities. She wasn't sure if he and Ronnie would last until Christmas with all the tension in the air.

"I'm sorry to cut your visit short, but we really are having some family bonding time. You guys came and took my daughters away from me, now I hardly see them anymore," Veronica explained, clearly waiting for him to leave.

Ronnie was crushing the semi-close relationship he was trying to form with Veronica. He then realized his attempt to win Ronnie's love back, by building this relationship with her mother, was in vain. He noticed that, for some reason other than spending quality time, both women were trying to evade him.

He left the front door thinking that Ronnie was definitely seeing Josh, and Veronica may've been going along with her lies to cover up the truth. He sat in his truck for a moment, thinking that he wasn't going to let some little broke and pretty momma's boy take his woman.

As he continued to sit in the truck, he had a flashback of his childhood. One gloomy evening he went with his father to visit one of his girlfriends. After hearing a bunch of bickering back and forth, about another man that he thought was trying to invade his territory, he watched his father nearly strangle her to death. He would never forget that night. He watched helplessly as his father was hauled away in handcuffs.

He snapped out of his daze and went back to the door with a burning desire to talk to Ronnie. Before he rang the bell, he stood on the porch for a minute, to get his thoughts together. He'd already calmed down enough so he wouldn't do anything erratically that would cause him to leave in handcuffs. His intentions were to express how much he loved her and to try to persuade her to stay with him.

Of all the years Rock had played with women's minds and emotions, he was suddenly feeling the pain and the repercussions that were coming back to haunt him. He always said from the time he met her that he'd finally met his match.

Ronnie came back to the door, this time disgusted. She slung the door open, folded her arms, and shifted her weight onto one leg.

"What do you want?" Ronnie asked, slightly wiggling her neck with an attitude flaring up.

She knew he was back to beg for another chance as usual. She stood blocking the door, refusing to let him in the house. She was confident that at some point her mother would step in and intervene again. He begged her to go home with him so they could talk. She finally stepped on the porch to talk to him.

The temperature had dropped with the chilling rain. Ronnie leaned against the door, shivering with her shoulders shrugged and her arms still folded. She was snuggled tight in her sweater, trying not to let her body heat escape.

Rock took his leather coat off, threw it across her shoulders, and stood in front of her to block the cold air and mist from blowing in her face.

She had a sudden urge to tell him that she was pregnant. However, she feared he would become more infatuated with her. If this happened, she'd seriously have to kill him to get away from him. She figured she'd present the scenario as a hypothetical question.

"What would you do if I was pregnant?" she asked.

"I knew it!" he shouted. "I knew something was wrong with you. I would marry you," Rock replied sincerely and convincingly with overwhelming excitement.

"What if I didn't want to be with you anymore…at all?" Ronnie asked with fear in her heart.

"Regardless of what happens, we're always going to be together, especially if you're having my baby," Rock announced confidently. "So when's the baby due?"

"There is no baby."

"Ronnie, don't play with me…when is the baby due?" he exclaimed.

"Rock, there is no baby!"

Rock starred down into Ronnie's eyes as if he had peaked down into her soul. He pushed the door open and walked around her, pushing her aside like a paperweight. He cordially walked into the den where the rest of the family was watching TV. He asked Veronica if she had a moment to speak with him.

Veronica knew what was coming next. She followed Rock into the kitchen where the interrogation began. She didn't want to get involved. However, she knew that Rock probably had something up his sleeve, and feared for the safety of her daughter and her unborn grandchild. She convinced him to assume that she knew nothing about Ronnie being pregnant, protecting her daughter as any mother would.

Rock walked back to his truck with vengeance in his heart. He assumed that since Ronnie brilliantly made up this hypothetical scenario, as she labeled it, she in fact was pregnant and wanted to keep it from him.

"Ronnie, are you pregnant? Are you planning to have an abortion without telling him? What are you going to do if and when he finds out?" Veronica asked a series of questions before Ronnie could answer the first one.

Ronnie paused for a while before she said anything. She was ashamed to tell her mother that an abortion was in fact her exact plan. Her indestructible persona that she'd taken on was suddenly crumbling. The barrier she'd built around her heart was now melting away. She began to cry on her mother's shoulder, embracing her like she did when she was a child.

She finally told Veronica about the abortion and that it was scheduled for the next morning. Veronica tried to remain cool, but she grew furious wondering how and why her daughter would keep something like that from her. She always thought the bond in which she and her girls shared was stronger than that.

Veronica finally calmed down her frantic daughter. She assured her that she would help her get on her feet, so she can raise her child confidently, with or without Rock's help. Ronnie was unsure of how to tell her mother about her plans of settling down with Josh. However, she explained that Josh was going to take her to the appointment.

After hearing that Josh was included in Ronnie's objectionable plan of terminating her pregnancy, she couldn't allow him to be dragged along as a victim of circumstance. Rock, who was a major factor in the situation, was going to get away 'scott free' in Ronnie's set parameters, Veronica presumed.

Veronica didn't yet understand the severity of the threats in which Ronnie had been receiving from Rock. In every attempt she made, trying to break things off with him on numerous occasions, she would usually receive some sort of threat before the attempt was complete. As Nae confirmed Ronnie's stories, she explained to her mother how verbally abusive Rock was. He'd threatened to kill her and any guys he suspected she was intimately involved with. Veronica was shocked to hear these unheard of tales her girls were telling her. Ronnie used Shonte as an example of why she chose to stay with him as long as she had.

Veronica remembered hearing the story on the news about a girl who had suddenly disappeared. She was overwhelmed to find out that Rock had a hand in that messy ordeal. Veronica grabbed the phone and demanded Ronnie to give her Josh's number.

"Why do you want Josh's number?" Ronnie inquired.

Veronica's plan was to tell Josh that Ronnie wasn't going to have the abortion. She figured it would've been best if Rock and Ronnie talked, and if they ever came to an agreement about the abortion, Rock should be the one to take her.

On the way home, Rock started to think that Ronnie may have possibly been pregnant, but by another man, maybe Josh. "That's why everyone's being so secretive!" he shouted as he thought out loud.

He raced to the house to call Trey, and to find out if Monie had said anything to him about Ronnie's situation. After a brief and very disappointing conversation with Trey, learning no more than he already knew, he sat on the sofa staring at the picture of him and Ronnie on their vacation.

After he'd calmed down a bit, he called her back. Ronnie reluctantly answered the phone, knowing that he was calling to either aggravate her or to beg her to stay with him. After excusing herself from Veronica's presence, she went up to her room and decided to tell him about the situation.

Ronnie confessed that she was expecting by him, but didn't feel that they were ready to have a child. Rock appreciated the civil conversation and learned the answers to all of his lingering questions. Rock objected to the abortion and begged Ronnie to marry him.

To Ronnie, this was just another proposal he'd presented while being caught up in the moment. *"Maybe he's thinking it would at least prolong our next breakup,"* she thought. In Ronnie's ears, Rock was just babbling on about the same old stuff she was used to hearing every time he wanted to get back together. At this point, she realized she had a lot of anger built up inside of her. She needed to get some things off her chest, but she didn't want to talk to her mother or her sisters. They'd only tell her what she wanted to hear. She wanted to talk to someone like Rock's mother or his sister. She'd only conversed with them a few times, but from the few conversations she had with them, she appreciated their honesty.

Ronnie got in Rock's Mercedes and started driving. She wasn't sure exactly where Rock's mother's house was, so she rode around in a neighborhood that looked similar to the one she remembered going to with him.

She saw two females standing around a car talking. She wanted to ask them if the Wilcox residence was in the vicinity, but she feared one of the females may've been one of Rock's ex's, since it seemed to have become routine to have a run-in with one of them. As she slowly drove past the females, she recognized Rock's sister, Regina.

She pulled over to park and got of the car. Regina tried to remember Ronnie's name before Ronnie approached her, but she couldn't.

"Hey girl," Regina said playing it off. She hugged Ronnie and introduced her to her friend. "This is my girl, Carla."

"Hi Carla, I'm Ronnie."

"That's her name," Regina said under her breath.

"Are you okay? What did Rock do?" Regina asked as if she was in Ronnie's defense.

Ronnie just stood quietly as if something was on her mind, but was too ashamed to say anything in front of Carla.

"Is your mom here?" Ronnie asked Regina.

"Yeah, she's in the house," Regina replied. "Carla, I'll give you a call later." Regina nodded towards Ronnie, signaling Carla that she was going to attend to whatever Ronnie was there for, and get back with her later.

Carla got in her car and pulled off, while looking in the mirror at Ronnie and Regina.

"Was that one of Rock's ex girlfriends?" Ronnie asked.

"No. She's had a crush on Rock since we were in grammar school," Regina replied with a slight snicker.

Regina let out a long sigh, knowing there must have been some drama going on in Ronnie's life concerning Rock.

"What did he do to you?" Regina asked.

Ronnie didn't think visiting his family was a good idea anymore. She was afraid to tell his sister that she was pregnant. She was hesitant to say anything, not knowing if she'd be able to trust Regina to keep their conversation confidential.

"Did he hit you? What's wrong?" Regina asked again with genuine concern.

"I'm pregnant and I don't know how to tell him. He's accused me of being with other men. I just don't know how to deal with someone like him."

By the time Ronnie got to the front door, Ms. Wilcox greeted her with open arms. She knew Ronnie's visit was brought about because of something Rock probably had done. Ronnie tried to hold back her tears, but Regina and her mother knew that she was hurting.

"We know what Rock is capable of. We know he's done something to you or you wouldn't be here," Regina stated.

"Ms. Wilcox, I want to be out of Rock's life for good. I don't want to be affiliated with the drugs and everything that comes with it anymore," Ronnie confessed.

"Girl, have that baby and get paid for the rest of your life," Regina said trying to convince Ronnie to get everything she could from Rock.

"Regina, would you let me speak please?" Ms. Wilcox asked nicely.

"Girl, as much as he talks about you, I know he loves you to death and would give you and the baby the world. You better use that to your advantage," Regina added, after her mother asked her nicely to be quiet.

"Regina!" Ms. Wilcox said in a slightly higher but stern tone than her normal tone. "I believe Ronnie came to visit with me."

Ms. Wilcox explained to Ronnie that Rock was very persistent and regardless of what she wanted, he was going to do whatever he wanted to do. She told Ronnie that she would probably need to relocate to be completely free from Rock.

"Ms. Wilcox, I love him to death, but I don't want that kind of life for my baby and me," Ronnie blurted out.

"Sweetheart, Rock could be a dangerous person, and he's playing a very dangerous game. The drug game could be cruel enough to hurt or even kill him and everyone around him. You do whatever you have to do to survive. Just don't be the one to get killed," Ms. Wilcox advised Ronnie.

Ronnie didn't quite grasp what she was suggesting her to do. Ms. Wilcox noticed the baffled look on Ronnie's face.

"Sweetie, I hate to say so about my own child, but for everything he's done to everyone else, I know his day is coming. If you have to hurt him to save yourself and your baby, just do whatever you have to do. Just don't be the one to get killed," Ms. Wilcox said and excused herself to answer her phone.

"…especially over a domestic dispute," Regina added her corrupted opinion onto her mother's advice. "Girl, I'd have that baby and milk Rock like a cow," Regina said to get Ronnie to laugh.

As Ronnie drove back home, she thought about everything Ms. Wilcox had just told her. From that point forth, Ronnie knew she had to save herself.

Chapter 15

*I*t's 7a.m. Tuesday morning. The loud sounds of hospital intercoms, and crying babies woke Ronnie out of a sound sleep. Sitting on the edge of the bed, she realized that less than 24 hours ago, her plans were to be at a clinic getting prepped for an abortion.

Now, she wondered if she had made the right decision. She wasn't sure if in fact she made the decision on her own, if her mother made the decision for her, or if Rock had talked her into keeping the baby.

She sat there, staring out of the window, thinking of what she was going to say to Rock once she faced him again. She'd agreed to have breakfast with him that morning, however, she wasn't ready to face him that soon. Excuses of what to tell him as a cop out began to cross her mind. She knew it seemed cowardice, but being a coward was the farthest thing from her mind. A part of her wanted to grab Nae out of the bed and disappear without full preparation of their plan.

Her cell phone rang twice before she realized it was ringing. She finally answered it and was surprised to hear the voice on the other end.

"Good morning precious. I understand that your plans have changed. Does that mean that our plans have changed as well?" Josh asked.

"Good morning to you too," Ronnie replied, unsure of what to say.

Ronnie explained how her mother lectured her and Rock about having a child. She was suddenly ready to go to breakfast, but she wanted to be with Josh. Rock wasn't anywhere in her itinerary for the day. Just as she was about to ask Josh if he wanted to go to breakfast, a call came through on her other line. She hesitantly answered the phone knowing it was going to be Rock.

"Hello?" she answered in a dry tone.

"Hey baby. How do you feel?" Rock asked.

"I feel okay."

"What time are we doing breakfast?" Rock asked.

"Um…could I call you right back?" Ronnie stalled, not knowing how to tell him that she really didn't want to go with him at all.

"Oh, I'm sorry. Were you on the other line?" Rock asked inquisitively.

"Yeah," Ronnie replied without further explanation.

"It's eight something in the morning. Who are you on the phone with this early?" Rock asked with insecurity.

Rock's series of questions caught Ronnie off guard. She wasn't prepared to answer questions to an intense interrogation. "My girlfriend from Jersey called. She's headed to work. I promise I'll call you right back." Ronnie felt she explained a believable lie.

"Okay," Rock replied, satisfied with her story.

Ronnie resumed her call with Josh and apologized for the interruption. She knew her time on the phone was limited before Rock would call back.

"Let me take you to breakfast," Josh offered.

Ronnie was ready to accept, but she had to figure out another lie to tell Rock in order to get out of the breakfast date with him. Juggling two men was something that she was no stranger to, but it was getting more complicated than it used to be when she was younger. She realized Rock was no ordinary man. He was a psychopath.

"Breakfast sounds good, but let me call you right back," Ronnie finally replied.

She hung up the phone and paced her bedroom floor pondering. She knew that if she told Rock that she just wanted to stay at home, he'd want to come over. If she told him that she wasn't feeling well, he'd temporarily leave her alone, maybe even until later that afternoon. She figured it was worth a try.

Veronica stared at her big, beautiful, flawless diamond ring as she attempted to watch the assembly line from afar. She hadn't been spending as much time with Jerome as she would've liked, but she did talk to him throughout the day on a daily basis. She'd talked to him earlier that morning before she left for work. She let him know that her mother and one of her sisters' were coming to stay with her for the holiday.

She went into her office to process some paperwork, but instead, found herself scribbling her new name along side of Jerome's on pieces of stray paper. This was the same thing she did as an adolescent falling in love. Her fairly new supervisor's position was relaxed and made her job more enjoyable.

As she shuffled a few small stacks of papers around on her desk, she found a couple of transferals for several employees. Flipping through the stack, she found Juanita Robinson's file stating that she was going to be moved to a plant in Florida.

Immediately, she was distraught by the information. She paged Juanita on the overhead speaker to come to her office for a brief meeting. She didn't think Juanita would have voluntarily asked to be relocated. *"This must be a mistake,"* she thought. *She has to be here for my wedding.*

Juanita's life was turning into a tragedy. After being victimized by a lunatic, nearly losing her life, and parts of her family, she couldn't handle being alone. Juanita was used to claiming her spotlight; the one Veronica was slowly stealing from her. Now, she was beginning to feel like all she had left was a lot of love to give and no one to give it to. Her boys had their own lives, leaving her to grow older and lonely.

She was happy for Veronica, but disappointed with herself that she picked the wrong twin to fall in love with. Juanita needed a friend, sometimes more than just a friend. She used to have that in Veronica until Jerome came into her life. In addition to Jerome, Veronica suddenly started to play a major role in her girl's lives again. Juanita felt neglected, and figured her friend had no more time to spend with her anymore. Juanita always had a hard time dealing with being second in anyone's life.

Fifteen minutes later, Juanita arrived at Veronica's office.

"Did you need to see me, *BOSS*?" Juanita asked with envy in her voice.

Before anything else was said, Veronica sensed that Juanita, her *supposedly* best friend, was jealous of her. Veronica continued with the session like nothing was going on.

"Did you ask to be transferred?" Veronica asked with disappointment.

"Why? Does it even matter?" Juanita replied sarcastically.

Veronica got up from behind her desk and closed her office door. She walked back behind her desk and stood there, looking down at her best friend, who was obviously hurting emotionally and longing for

attention. Juanita slightly slouched down in her chair, becoming infor-
mal, simply ignoring Veronica's title and position.

Juanita realized she'd changed a bit, but she tended to blame her
jealous and self-centered changes on Veronica's lifestyle changes. Juanita
was starting to dislike herself and the direction in which her life heading.
This unexplainable mode was overtaking her enjoyable life that she once
had.

Veronica felt tension in the air, thick enough to be cut in half with
a sword.

"What happened between us? How did all of this tension come
about?" Veronica asked sincerely, trying hard to understand the cause of
their broken relationship.

Veronica noticed the communication wasn't as strong as it once
was. She was under the impression that Jackie's presence and Corey's
recuperation may have played a major role in Juanita's negligence to
socialize with her.

Veronica didn't know how to formulate the question properly, in
order to find out if Juanita was jealous of her. If this was true, she wondered was it because of her promotion, her upcoming wedding, or something else all together. She couldn't think of one reason why her friend
would have been envious of her. After all, *Juanita* was the socialite, with
a numerous amount of successful friends; including male friends who
had enough potential to possibly marry.

"You're supposed to be in my wedding. You can't relocate right
now!" Veronica exclaimed.

"I have to leave. I need some time away from everything…besides
I met this guy, and he is so…*ummm!*" Juanita closed her eyes, shook her
head, and moaned. She figured Veronica would fall for that.

Juanita couldn't hold water, especially if the situation was pertaining to a man. Veronica knew she would have heard about this *man* in her
friend's life by now, if in fact there really was one. Veronica was hurt,
because now she realized that Juanita had given up on their friendship
quite some time ago. She was willing to walk away from a nearly twenty
year old relationship. Veronica was still puzzled as to why Juanita felt the
way she did.

"We've been friends for so long…our kids are friends, and maybe
even lovers. Do you know what's going on with Josh and Ronnie?"
Veronica asked.

"No," Juanita said sprouting up to the edge of her chair.

Veronica explained that Josh was supposed to take Ronnie to have an abortion. Juanita didn't know Ronnie was pregnant. She looked at Veronica with amazement. She wondered why Veronica was telling her this now. She was under the impression that Ronnie may've been pregnant by Josh.

"Did my son get your daughter…Oh my God…when?" Juanita tried to form a full, sensible question. Her mind was as jumbled as gumbo. "I thought she was involved with the guy from the drug gang?" Juanita stated.

Veronica thought to herself that if Juanita had been paying more attention to her children, she would have known what was going on. She was too busy being mad at her over nothing.

Veronica dismissed Juanita to go back to work. She also suggested that they go out for drinks after work, to catch up on what was going on in each other's lives. Juanita wanted to decline the offer, but she really wanted to find out what was going on between her son and Veronica's daughter. She halfheartedly accepted the offer, and then quickly dismissed herself from Veronica's office.

Veronica watched as her sad friend walked away and returned back to work. Veronica was afraid that Juanita wasn't just walking away from her physically, but she was walking away from fifteen wonderful years of friendship, memories and laughter. She was convinced that their relationship couldn't be repaired to what it used to be.

Veronica called Jerome to tell him what happened, but suddenly got choked up. She felt like the words were balling up in her throat like bubblegum taking on a snowball effect. After shedding a few tears, and gasping for breath, she quickly regained her composure. Jerome assured her that her friendship would not end on such a sour note.

Unannounced, Rock pulled up at Veronica's house shortly after Ronnie left with Josh. Monie was on the phone with Trey when she heard the doorbell ring. She knew that whoever was at the door wasn't there to see her. She lingered around in her room, folding and putting away her clothes, procrastinating about answering the door.

When she finally answered the door, she was surprised to see that it was Rock. She thought Ronnie had just left with him. Monie was not sure if Nae was still there. She peaked out of the door, only to find that Nae's car was missing. Rock's Mercedes was parked in the garage.

"I think Ronnie went to the store to get some medicine. She wasn't feeling well at all when she woke up this morning. She looked a hot mess." Monie was lying to cover up her sister's unknown actions.

Rock invited himself in to wait for Ronnie until she returned. Monie suggested that Rock talk to Trey on her cordless phone. This was her attempt to redirect his attention until she could locate Ronnie. Frantically, she ran upstairs and called Ronnie's cell phone from her cell phone. Monie was tired of coming up with cover-ups, tangling herself up in her sister's lies and games. Ronnie's phone rang several times before she answered.

"Ronnie, where are you?" Monie whispered.

"I'm eating breakfast," Ronnie replied with her mouth partially full. "Why are you whispering?" Ronnie asked.

"Because Rock is downstairs looking for you. He said he was going to wait here until you get back." Monie continued to whisper furiously.

Ronnie's appetite vanished and was replaced by fear. She played it cool in front of Josh so he wouldn't become frightened. Monie's whisper was at its highest elevation before it turned into shouting. Rock heard her talking and figured she may've been trying to hide Ronnie upstairs. Rock ended his call with Trey and crept up the stairs, trying to find out who Monie was talking to, and what she was talking about.

Monie's intense thought process about getting her sister home, without Rock seeing her with Josh, had overtaken her ability to use common sense. She had left her bedroom door wide open, making it easier for Rock to gain access, or to stand at the top of the stairs to listen to her conversation.

"How long is it going to be before you get here?" Monie muttered though clenched teeth, looking up to find Rock standing in her bedroom door.

"Rock what are you doing up here?" Monie shouted.

"He's in your room!" Ronnie yelled.

"Yes!" Monie shouted.

Ronnie jumped up from the table and rushed out of the restaurant. Josh immediately followed her, briefly stopping at the cash register to pay for their meals. He threw the money and the bill on the cashier's desk, apologizing to the cashier, as he ran out the door trying to catch up with Ronnie.

"Ronnie what's going on? Is everything okay?"

Rock is up in Monie's bedroom yelling and screaming at her about trying to find me," Ronnie exaggerated.

Josh was under the impression that Rock was getting violent with

Monie. He became hostile and ready to come to blows with Rock for trying to hurt Monie, just to get to Ronnie.

As Josh sped to Veronica's house, he came to the conclusion that he could no longer tolerate the drama that Rock brought to his aspiring relationship with Ronnie. Either Ronnie had to let go of Rock once and for all, or she had to let him go. Although his feelings had grown extremely strong for Ronnie, her lifestyle was far more complex than he'd anticipated, and yet, he was willing to deal with.

They finally made it near Veronica's house. In front of the house about a quarter mile away, Ronnie spotted Rock's truck by the curb. As Ronnie's adrenaline rushed harder and harder, she didn't care if Rock saw her and Josh together. Her adrenaline rush was also making her braver than she'd been in years. She was ready to tell Rock that things were completely over between them and that she had plans to move on with her life with Josh.

Ronnie busted through the front door yelling out for Monie. She found Monie in the kitchen, pacing back and fourth between the refrigerator and the stove with a butcher knife in her hand, while repeating, "Don't do it. He's not worth going to jail for."

"You bastard! What did you do to my sister?" Ronnie screamed.

"If you would have kept your sick ass here you would've known," Rock replied sarcastically.

Ronnie ran over to Monie and grabbed the knife from her, hugging her. She noticed Monie's face was unusually red. Her eyes were nearly bloodshot from crying so hard. Josh walked over to Monie and Ronnie. He pried Monie from Ronnie's arms and started hugging her. He motioned for Ronnie to go talk to Rock while he attended and comforted Monie.

Rock didn't take his eyes off of Josh as he walked towards the front door.

"Is that what you left me for?" Rock yelled at Ronnie.

Rock and Josh kept eye contact. Rock stopped at the kitchen entrance before he completely left out of the kitchen.

"You want Ronnie so bad? You can have her for a minute. Just remember, she'll always be mine. That's probably your little bastard she's carrying anyway."

Rock walked backward to the front door.

"It ain't over," Rock said calmly to Ronnie, as he walked out of the door to get in his truck. Rock drove up to the end of the street to park and wait for Josh to leave.

Monie told Ronnie and Josh that Rock hadn't severely harmed her. Ronnie found small drops of blood splattered on Monie's shirt. Rock had snatched the phone from her ear, ripping her earring out, and splitting her earlobe as she tried to call Nae for help.

Monie called Trey after she'd calmed down and stopped crying. She tried vigorously to tell Trey what had happened, without having an outbreak of compelling emotions. Trey rushed over to get Monie and take her to safety.

Josh stayed with Ronnie for about an hour, until Trey and Monie left. He promised Ronnie he'd come back to get her after he finished his errands for his mother. Shortly after Trey and Monie left, Nae arrived, assuming responsibility for her sickly, drama stricken sister. Ronnie had come down with a slight fever, along with morning sickness. She begged Nae to go to the nearby store and get some medicine.

Nae's conscience convicted her for leaving her sister alone as an easy prey for Rock. She hadn't anticipated staying away for as long as she had. She'd left the night before to go home and get more clothes for the changing weather. Tony arrived at their apartment before she left. As they talked, the moment grew quite steamy and passionate, forcing Nae to stay all night.

Nae was reluctant to leave her sick sister alone after what had just happened. Ronnie convinced Nae that nothing would happen to her in the twenty minutes it would take her to go to the drug store to pick up her medicine.

Once Nae left to go to the store, Rock then realized that Ronnie was finally home alone. He walked down to the house and boldly rang the doorbell. He stood clear of the peephole hoping she would open the door to see if anyone was around. As soon as she unlocked the door, he bombarded into the house. Ronnie's temperature rose extremely high. Her mouth and throat were dry, enabling her to talk.

Rock grabbed her by the neck backing her against the wall, choking her. He felt that her temperature was higher than normal body temperature.

"So you really are sick now. Where's your little boyfriend?" Rock asked.

Ronnie gasped for air, grabbing Rock's hand trying to loosen it and pull it from around her neck. She scratched and punched him in the face. She kicked him in the groin area, only making him madder. He loosened his grip around her neck to catch his balance, allowing her to break free.

If she could just make it up the stairs to get the hammer from her mother's room, she'd be all right she thought. His hands quickly wrapped around her ankles, sending her body crashing forward onto the stairs. He drug her down the few stairs on her belly and her face, managing to grab a handful of her hair. Within seconds, she noticed she was back at square one with her back against the wall.

"Your boyfriend and your sister can't come to your rescue now. So what are you gonna do?"

He slammed her head against the wall several times. His grasp around her neck became significantly tighter, this time lifting her off of the floor. She kicked and punched trying to break free. She felt the vomit trying to emerge but had no where to go, sending most of it back down, giving her symptoms similar to acid reflux. Her face was scraped and bloodied from carpet burn. Her eyes were bloodshot; her pupils were half dilated, and began to roll to the back of her head.

He looked at her and realized that he was not only hurting her, but he was hurting or maybe even killing the child she was carrying. He noticed that he was reacting like his father would have. He was becoming someone he vowed he'd never be. He suddenly had compassion on her.

He lowered her lifeless body to the floor, laying her on the sofa, until he was able to run to the truck and get back to her to take her to the hospital. He performed enough CPR until she was able to wheeze and hiss for air on her own. Rock loaded her body into his truck and sped off towards the hospital. As he exited the subdivision, he passed Nae, but didn't bother to stop or turn around to inform her of what was going on.

Nae knew that she'd just passed Rock, however, she was confident that Ronnie wouldn't have opened the door for him to get into the house. She was sure that her sister was still there waiting for her to get back with the medicine.

Ronnie became coherent, but still wasn't able to speak very loud. She knew her life was coming to an end before nightfall, either from being ill or from Rock making her disappear like he did Shonte.

She began cramping, unlike she'd never done before. She felt fluid gushing from her vagina like it could've been her menstrual cycle. The pain she endured was much more severe than the normal pain from her cycle. She looked down at her gray sweat pants. They were saturated with heavy, thick blood.

Rock began to cry and apologize, thinking that he'd just killed his family. As he apologized, Ronnie's agonizing pain became more unbearable. He sped, running red lights, trying to get her to the nearest hospital, praying that she survived even if the baby didn't.

Nae ran in the house, finding nothing but drippings of blood on the foyer's floor. She knew that Rock had abducted and probably hurt her sister. She couldn't think of Rock's cell phone number. She nervously scrolled through the numbers in her cell phone, finding everyone's number except for Rock's. She called Tony, frantically explaining bits and pieces of the story, until she could finally affirm that she needed him to call Rock's cell phone. Hopefully, he could find out what Rock had done to her sister, and where they were.

Nae paced the floor impatiently, waiting for Tony to call her back with some valuable information. Trey called Rock's cell phone number, wondering where he may have taken Ronnie. Rock heard the phone ring, but never attempted to answer it. He tried holding Ronnie's hand. She snatched her hand back, afraid of what he might try to do next. She didn't understand how he could possibly think she would want to have anything to do with him, after he'd just tried to kill her.

Rock drove up to the emergency room's entrance blowing the horn, thinking that someone may come out to help him. He carried Ronnie into the hospital in her bloody clothes looking for a gurney to lye her on. Several nurses immediately came to Ronnie's rescue. Ronnie mumbled, "Call my sister." Another nurse gave Rock some paperwork to fill out on Ronnie's behalf.

About a half hour later, one of the nurses who assisted Ronnie came out and asked Rock if he was the baby's father. Rock held his face in the palms of his hands and began wheezing and sighing. The nurse announced that Ronnie had suffered a miscarriage. He knew that he was the cause of this mishap. He felt extreme remorse, feeling like the monster he'd said he'd never become.

Tony had given up on calling Rock after the sixth unsuccessful attempt. He finally called Nae back without any information. He felt like he needed to be there with her, to comfort her, if nothing more. Nae had failed at protecting her sister once again for the second time in one day. She called Monie to let her know that Ronnie was missing. She had to get her thoughts together and build up enough courage before she called Veronica.

Nae cried uncontrollably as she tried to explain things to Monie. Monie suggested they call all nearby hospitals to find out if she had been admitted. As Monie called several different numbers to acquire information, Rock called Trey from his cell phone.

"Rock, where are you? Monie and Nae are worried sick about Ronnie. Have you seen her?" Trey fussed at Rock for all the turmoil he was causing.

"We're here at the Austell hospital. Don't tell Monie…Ronnie had a miscarriage."

"What did you do! Rock, what did you do to her?" Trey yelled.

Monie slammed the phone down and started listening to Trey's conversation with Rock.

"Trey where are they? What did that bastard do to my sister?" Monie screamed, bursting out in tears.

Trey assisted Monie to his truck, trying to console her, while continuing to talk to Rock on his cell phone. Trey tried to get as much information from Rock as possible, but was unsuccessful due to Rock's gibberish dialog.

Trey ended the call with Rock and called Tony to inform him of what was going on. Trey gave Tony specific instructions to have Nae call Veronica, and then get Nae to the Austell hospital A.S.A.P.

Nae wasn't in any condition to talk to anyone. Once Tony arrived at Veronica's house, he found that Nae was torn to pieces. He took it upon himself to call Veronica and tell her what was going on. He broke away from Nae, finding solitude long enough to tell Veronica about Ronnie's miscarriage.

After obtaining the most essential details, Veronica immediately grabbed her keys and purse, and then headed to the hospital, forgetting about her dinner date with Juanita.

Tony finally was able to get Nae in the truck without telling her the details about Ronnie. He decided to tell her on the way to the hospital. She was speechless and began placing the blame on herself. Tony didn't want to jeopardize Nae's pregnancy by upsetting her, telling her everything that was going on.

Tony and Trey pulled into the emergency room's parking lot within minutes of each other. They helped Nae and Monie into the hospital, anxious to find and deal with Rock. The girls went into the room where Ronnie was recovering from her emergency surgery. Trey wondered the parking lot searching for Rock's truck, while Tony walked through the hospital looking for him inside.

Rock left the hospital for several different reasons. He knew that Trey and Tony would reprimand him for the horrible things that he'd done to Ronnie causing her to miscarry. He knew he'd have to answer to Veronica, Nae, and Monie. He didn't have the answers to any of their questions. He thought Veronica may've even had him arrested if he stayed around. He figured the best thing he could do was to leave until he was able to get a clear perspective on what had happened.

He headed to his mother's house to have a heart to heart conversation with her, and to release some of his anger. Rock and his mother, a strong Christian woman, often had their differences. He often ignored her, or just got up and left when she would tell him the truth about how his life. She let him know how it would be if he didn't turn to God for guidance. He was suddenly at a point where he needed guidance; but he had nowhere to go or no one else to turn to.

Having nowhere else to go, Rock headed to his mother's house. Before he could open his mouth to explain the situation to her, she could tell by his demeanor that something was terribly wrong. His mother tried to convince him to let Ronnie go her own separate way for a while. Rock was scared that he was going to lose her to Josh for good. If he did lose her forever, he couldn't place the blame on her, nor could he ever say anything bad about her. He realized he'd just lost the only woman he ever really truly loved.

He confessed to his mother that he often had dreams about his father. He told her that he was becoming more like him everyday.

"Mom, you know I adored dad so much, but I don't want to be anything like him."

"I know baby. I prayed day and night that you and Rome wouldn't grow up to be like him."

Rock's mother knew her husband was monstrous at times, but she didn't know half the things Rock had experienced with him. She knew that Rock had an enormous heart of gold, which made her question why he sometimes made derogatory comments about his father.

Veronica remained calm as she walked into the hospital looking for her daughters. She had tried to explain to all three of her daughters beforehand, about situations like this would probably occur by being affiliated with their choice of company. At least one, if not all of the guys, would eventually do something irate if the girls continued to play with their emotions. Veronica took a deep before she walked into Ronnie's recovery room, seeing what damage Rock had done to her. Veronica knew that Ronnie didn't want to have the baby, but she was certain that she didn't want to lose it because of a domestic dispute.

A few hours later Rock headed back to the hospital, hoping that everyone had calmed down. There was no justifiable explanation for his temporary insanity. He was willing to serve time in jail if that was the route Veronica chose to go.

Trey and Tony stood outside in the parking lot, giving Ronnie time to spend alone with her family. They spotted Rock's truck pull into the parking lot. They couldn't believe he'd have the audacity to show up again. They were tired of cleaning up his messes. This time he had messed with the wrong family.

Rock walked over to talk to Trey and Tony, as if he'd hadn't done anything wrong.

"What's up Trey?" Rock put his fist out to give Trey some dap. Trey looked at Rock as if he'd lost his mind. He then put his fist in Tony's direction, but received the same reaction.

"Man, I know I screwed up this time. You can't turn your backs on me now," Rock pleaded.

"Man, you almost killed that girl!" Trey yelled.

"Yeah, you almost killed her, but the baby is dead," Tony said calmly. "We're not having a part in this one. This is the family of our future wives."

"I wanna go in and see her," Rock confessed.

Trey and Tony was sure that he'd lost his natural born mind. But they played it cool as usual.

"Man, are sure you want to face Veronica right now?" Tony asked.

Rock hesitated for a while before answering. "Yeah, I can face her now," he responded.

Trey and Tony followed Rock to Ronnie's room. They were just waiting for him to receive the most crucial repercussion from Veronica. When Rock opened the door, Veronica was sitting on the bed next to Ronnie, not expecting to see Rock at all.

"Oh hell naw!" Veronica exclaimed pointing to Rock. "Rock, I need to have a talk with you." Veronica jumped off of the foot of the bed. She escorted Rock out to the parking lot with intentions to have a rational discussion with him. Veronica stared up into Rock's eyes with sincerity and began her speech.

"Rock, once upon a time Ronnie loved you unconditionally. I told her a number of times that it wouldn't work between you because of the negative things *you* were involved with. I knew this day would come. She doesn't love you anymore. You need to accept it and move on with your life. If I see you around my home again, you *will* be arrested *and* charged with attempted murder. Is that clear?" Veronica said sternly.

"Ms. Williams, I was really hurt when I caught Ronnie and Josh together. She broke a date with me to be with him! I don't want her messing with him while she's pregnant with my baby."

"Did you catch them screwing around or something?" Veronica asked.

"No, but I know how men are."

Veronica laughed and let out a long sigh. "Thank God that all men aren't like you. She doesn't love you anymore Rock. You'll just have to get over it. Get over *her*, you'll be okay."

Rock wasn't intimidated by Veronica's threats or convinced by her sarcastic sympathy for him. He had police and judges on his side that he'd been paying off for years to keep him out of trouble. Veronica's speech only tempted him more to see Ronnie against her will. He had acquired an obsession for her. He was adamant about having her all to himself. He knew he would've been considered a loser if he gave her up to Josh without a fight.

Veronica walked back into the hospital to tend to her daughter. Ronnie was sure that she had to get out of Atlanta soon, before he killed her. She knew that he wasn't going to back down as easily as everyone thought. Trey and Tony knew it as well, but trying to convince Veronica would be damn near a waste of time and breath.

The doctor came into Ronnie's room and reported that she'd have to stay over night so they could prevent any internal bleeding that may reoccur. Veronica didn't feel safe with that option. She felt like Rock would be able to come in at any time during the night to hurt her again.

Ronnie became frightened, wondering what else could possibly go wrong. She asked Monie if she and Trey could stay over night, in case Rock tried some of his devious tricks, like bringing her flowers, candy or ice cream, just to get into the room. Ronnie was confident that Trey knew how to handle Rock at any of his underhanded games.

Juanita called Veronica's cell phone several times to let her know that Josh told her what was going on. Within a half hour, Juanita and Josh walked though Ronnie's room door. Veronica had forgotten about their dinner date. She began apologizing for not calling or showing up. Josh had explained Ronnie's tragic mishap to his mother.

Juanita couldn't forget how supportive Veronica and the girls were when her family was going through their tribulations. She couldn't give up on her friend that easily. Juanita realized how close she and Veronica really were.

Veronica felt a strenuous burden lifted off of her shoulders. She felt like Rock may have been planning to do something crazy, so she had to make a plan as well. She excused herself to go outside and call Jerome to pick her up from the hospital. She gave Monie her copy of Jerome's car keys, so she and Trey could stay until morning and drive his car home. Rock doesn't know Jerome's car. Just in case he wants to scan the parking lot to find any of our cars, he won't find them, Veronica thought.

Before she re-entered the room, she sat in the waiting area for a minute. For a moment, she reflected on how strangely her life was slowly coming together. She wasn't thrilled about her daughter initially being pregnant, but being pregnant by Rock made matters that much worse. She hated the fact that Ronnie miscarried. However, this lessened the chances of Rock being around her family for the rest of their lives, for the sake of the baby. She also realized that her best friend would still be there for her when she needed her.

Rock slowly drove around the hospital's parking lot for hours, searching for either Veronica's car or Tony and Trey's trucks. He'd passed Jerome's car several times, thinking that the Williams family had left Ronnie all alone. He underestimated Veronica, thinking that she was too old school to mastermind such a plan as she did.

As the night grew later Veronica, Juanita, Nae and Tony left Monie and Trey in Ronnie's hospital room. Around midnight Trey went down to the snack bar to get some late night snacks, when he felt like he was being followed. He acquired a weird suspicion that Rock would try to come see Ronnie when he thought everyone was gone. At the end of the hall, where Ronnie's room was, he stopped at the nurse's station and asked the nurse if she'd seen a man of Rock's description, wondering around by Ronnie's room.

The young, timid nurse said he'd walked through the hallway a few minutes prior to Trey approaching her. Trey knew that Rock was up to his old tricks. He knew then that Rock had probably manipulated the young girl, making her believe some unheard of lies, so he could continue to lurk around the hospital all night.

As Trey headed back to Ronnie's room, he stopped around the corner from the nurse's station. He heard Rock's voice. He peaked around the corner, watching as Rock stood at the nurse's station, talking to the young naive nurse, while stroking her hair, giving her compliments, working his charm trying to gain her trust. As the young nurse blushed and retained Rock's attention on her voluptuous breast, Trey snuck up beside Rock and scared him nearly to death.

"What's up man?" Trey asked and put his arm around Rock's neck, purposely breaking up his romantic rhapsody. "You must be here to check on your girl."

"Oh yeah ma'am, by the way this is my cousin; the one I'd asked you if you'd seen."

The nurse smiled and rushed back behind her desk. Trey attempted to escort Rock out of the hospital.

"Man what did you do that for?" Rock asked, trying to maintain his Casanova status with the nurse, using her to enable him to gain access to Ronnie's room.

"What are you doing here? You know that Veronica could have you arrested if she knew you were here?"

"But she doesn't know I'm here, unless you're planning to tell her."

"Man, you're my cousin and I love you to death, but I can't allow you to tear this family apart," Trey confessed.

Rock was convinced that Veronica had brainwashed Trey into believing that he was the cause of their family falling apart. He was feeling like Trey had turned his back on him over a woman, something they vowed to never let happen.

"You're letting a woman come between us?" Rock asked with disappointment.

Rock failed to realize that Monie was an ordinary woman to Trey. He had paid her tuition for her last year of school, and planned to marry her when she graduated. To have her family torn apart would affect him as much as it would Monie.

Trey convinced Rock that he needed go home and relax. He

needed some time to get his mind together. Rock begged Trey to let him see Ronnie and apologize to her before he left. Trey kept his promise to Veronica that he wouldn't let anything happen to Ronnie throughout the night. Trey continually pushed Rock towards the door, encouraging him to go home, and not do anything else he might regret later.

Monie woke up and noticed that Trey wasn't next to her on the small, uncomfortable sofa that the hospital provided for her to sleep on. She looked under the bathroom door to see if the light was on. She realized Trey wasn't in the room with her at all. She quietly opened the door, trying not to wake Ronnie. She went down to the nurse's station and asked the young nurse if she'd seen the guy that came out of Ronnie's room.

The nurse explained that she saw him with a tall, bald and handsome guy who claimed to be his cousin. Monie knew then that Rock was on the prowl. The nurse told Monie that the two guys seemed to be cordial. Monie started to wonder if Trey was aware of, or had a part of Rock's devious plan to do something else to her sister.

She crept back in Ronnie's room, trying not to disturb her. Ronnie was already awake, looking around to see if any of Monie's belongings were left in the room, trying to determine whether or not she had left for the night.

"I thought you were gone," Ronnie said, scaring Monie nearly to death.

Monie's mind was playing tricks on her, telling her that Trey was there only to keep an eye on Ronnie for Rock. Monie and Ronnie talked for a while until Trey came back into the room.

"Where have you been? I've been looking all over for you," Monie asked.

"I needed some fresh air so I took a walk," Trey replied.

Monie knew Trey was lying. "Where have you been Trey?" Monie asked again, growing more furious.

Trey asked Monie nicely to meet with him in the hallway. Monie refused to cooperate with Trey's wishes. She continued sitting on the sofa, ignoring him.

"Monie, I need to talk to you in the hallway!" Trey said firmly.

She reluctantly went into the hallway to talk to him. He didn't want to upset Ronnie by telling her, while they were in the room that Rock had been to the hospital. She didn't think he would tell her about it at all. She figured if he was included in Rock's plan, he would not have confessed so easily. She suddenly became humble and was willing to listen.

Monie walked back into Ronnie's room humble and meek trying not to upset her sister.

"Trey, what is going on?" Ronnie asked.

"Nothing," he responded rather quickly.

Ronnie was no dummy. She knew something was going on. She looked at Monie, knowing that she was itching to tell her. Monie told her that Rock had been there. Ronnie was in denial. If Rock had really been there, she knew he would have caused a scene, especially if he wasn't able to see her. However, she was able to lie down contentedly for the rest of the night, knowing that Trey was there to protect her.

Chapter 16

On Thanksgiving eve, Veronica's mother, Cicely, and her sister, Patrice, flew down to visit from New Jersey for the holidays. Monie left Trey at the hospital around 6 a.m. She had promised her mother that she'd ride with Nae to pick up her aunt and grandmother from Hartsfield-Jackson airport. Veronica and Jerome went to pick Ronnie and Trey up from the hospital.

Nae parked next to the curb by the baggage claim area. She sat in the car, restlessly, while Monie danced and sang the last few bars of her favorite Alicia Keys song that was playing on the radio. After the song went off, Monie turned towards Nae and said, "I hope Rock didn't go to the hospital to do anything to Ronnie last night."

"Would you get out so nana and aunt Trice won't have to look for us?" Nae demanded.

Monie knew her sister was uptight about everything that was going on with Ronnie, their mother getting married, all while dealing with her own pregnancy. Monie got out of the car and went inside of the airport to baggage claim. She studied the arrival screens trying to find out which belt their bags would be coming in on. Coming from behind her she heard two voices yelling, "Monica." As she turned around, her Aunt Patrice was waddling towards her, struggling with several large bags, as if she and her mother were moving to Atlanta.

Monie was almost tackled to the floor by her grandmother's hugs and kisses, as she tried to take some of the heavy luggage away from her.

"We haven't seen you in nearly a year, and all you can greet us with is an old dry hello. You better give your nana a hug," Cicely panted, trying to fuss at Monie, as she struggled with her bags.

Monie escorted her aunt and grandmother to the car and loaded their bags in the trunk. Cicely got in the front seat trying to hug Nae, nearly smothering her with her oversized coat. Nae gasped for air, fighting to get her head out of the headlock her grandmother had inadvertently put her into. Monie took her fancy cell phone out of her purse. She waited until her grandmother started to get personal, and into everyone's business, before she lured her attention to the phone.

Cicely was a very talkative, retired school principal, now with an attention span of a three year old. Although she was loud and very nosey, she was a very sweet, elderly lady, in her mid sixties. In a discreet manner, she always tried to compare Veronica's girls to Patrice's children. They had attended college faithfully, but never soared for any extremely high goals in life. They found contentment with making thirty to thirty five grand a year in exchange for all their years in school.

"So, what kind of work do you do Renae?" Cicely asked. Patrice and Veronica were the closest of four siblings. Patrice knew about all of the girls' situations, but Veronica never mentioned anything to Cicely. Patrice looked at Monie as if she needed to do something to alter Cicely's attention, and take the spotlight off of Nae.

"Nana, check this out…" Monie butted in, pretending she didn't know that her grandmother was talking to Nae. She scooted up to the edge of the seat, showing her grandmother her new cell phone.

"I have to program your phone number in here so I can call you more often," Monie said as she handed Cicely the phone.

"Ooh baby, I don't have my glasses on. Can I just tell you the number and let you type it in?" Cicely asked. "So where's your mother?"

Cicely's full attention was directed to Monie's new little gadget. She then waited on either of the girls to answer her question about Veronica. Nae looked in the rear view mirror at Monie, as if to say thanks for getting the spotlight off of her.

During the whole ride to Veronica's house, Cicely talked about the flight and everything that was going on in South Jersey. She asked questions about everyone's business, swiftly moving on to the next conversation, before she received any answers. She waited impatiently for someone to chime in to help her talk about someone else.

Around 8 a.m., as Jerome warmed up the truck preparing to go to the hospital, his curiosity led him to find different types of guns, behind and under the seats, as well as in the glove compartment. He knew then that all of Veronica's girls were dating drug dealers. The situation in which Ronnie was in was now put into perspective.

To Jerome, Trey didn't appear to be affiliated with a gang or drugs. He was surprised that as positive as Monie seemed to be, she would be dating someone who was into so many negative things. He eventually would question Veronica about it, but this was not the time or the place.

Jerome and Veronica walked into the hospital under the assumption that everything had gone smoothly throughout the night. Monie and Trey was glad to see Veronica and Jerome there to relieve them. Trey didn't mention the fact that Rock had been to the hospital during the night. Although he knew Rock was wrong for what he'd done, that didn't change the fact that they were biologically connected. Their frames of mind, even throughout childhood, always lead them to believe that blood was thicker than water. He knew that if Veronica pressed charges against him, he'd be the one to get him out of jail. He didn't want anyone to think he was playing the game on both sides. It was a catch twenty-two; he knew Monie would eventually be blood.

Although Trey didn't go near his Lexus, Jerome was still jittery about riding around without checking the car for bullets, shells or shell casings. Jerome was waiting for his car to warm up. He checked the interior for any incriminating evidence. In case Trey and some of his buddies decided to go joyriding the previous night, Jerome ensured that nothing could have possibly attached him to any kind of crime.

Ronnie was released from the hospital at 9 a.m. She stood up from her wheelchair to get into Jerome's car. Across the parking lot, she thought she saw Rock sitting in his truck. For some reason or another, she was horrified to say anything about Rock around Jerome. He was the only man in her life she ever felt confident enough to consider as a father figure.

Ronnie figured she may have been paranoid, or maybe even a bit delusional from the medicine. She didn't think Rock would go as far as disrespecting an older, distinguished gentleman like Jerome just to get to her. She stretched out in the back of Jerome's spacious and luxurious Lexus and enjoyed the ride home.

Jerome drove with extreme caution trying not to hurt Ronnie in the back seat. He parked in Veronica's garage, and helped Ronnie out of the car, as if she were crippled. Ronnie made it into the house just minutes before Nae pulled up with their talkative grandmother.

Veronica made it clear to Ronnie that they weren't going to tell

Cicely about the miscarriage until she returned to New Jersey. She knew that Ronnie wouldn't get any rest if Cicely knew about everything while she was there.

"Ooh my, Veronica has out done herself with this house. Do you girls still live here with her?" Cicely asked.

"I do," Monie blurted out. "Ronnie and Nae have their own apartment."

The black Mercedes that Rock had given Ronnie was parked in the yard. Cicely began with another series of questions as soon as she laid eyes on the car. Veronica has a boyfriend, doesn't she?" Cicely continued meddling. "Is that his car?" What kind of work does he do?"

"Ma, won't you find out *how* everyone is doing before you find out *what* they're doing," Patrice stated as she grew slightly agitated with her mother for always prying.

Monie wondered why her grandmother was suddenly getting caught up in who had what and how they attained it. Besides, she owned a Mercedes and a Lexus SUV.

"A Mercedes is the symbol of success," Cicely declared.

She walked through the open garage and into the house without knocking.

"Veronica," she sang as she walked through the house opening doors, giving herself a tour.

In the den, Veronica set Ronnie up with a warm, cozy spot on the sofa to relax and watch TV. Veronica and Jerome walked into the kitchen to greet Cicely and Patrice.

Cicely embraced Jerome as if she'd known him for years. She pulled out a seat at the kitchen table and began to question him as if he was in an interrogation. Veronica constantly apologized for her mother's straight forwardness. Jerome was enlightened to see that Cicely was genuinely concerned about her daughters' happiness and well-being.

He was amazed at how much energy she had for her age. He laughed from time to time, enjoying the chemistry in which he and his soon to be mother-in-law shared.

Cicely saw the diamond on Veronica's finger and was tempted to inquire about the engagement. However, Patrice had just put her in her place, telling her that she needed to keep her nose out of everyone's business. To Cicely, the diamond appeared to get bigger as they immersed in their conversation. She asked Veronica if she had planned her wedding.

Cicely was ready to surpass any wedding plans Veronica may have already made.

Monie poured everyone lemonade and sat their glasses in front of them. Cicely took one sip of her freshly squeezed lemonade, got up from the table, and began touring parts of the house she hadn't already seen. Walking into the den, she found Ronnie lounging on the sofa. She ran over to hug Ronnie, wondering why she hadn't gotten off of the sofa to greet her yet. It was clear for Cicely to see that Ronnie wasn't feeling well. She didn't bother to ask her what was wrong.

Cicely opened the front door and stepped out onto the porch, enjoying the crisp air and abnormally warm climate of the south. Veronica and Patrice joined their mother on the porch, enjoying the sentiment of a family of three generations uniting.

As Veronica stood on the porch with her family, she saw Rock driving up the paralleling street, on the other side of the vacant lot, directly across from her house. She was almost certain that he was stalking the house to see if Josh would come to visit Ronnie or if she would leave home with him.

Although Ronnie's life was a real life soap opera, she was always on Josh's mind. He figured if he was fond of California, he may consider relocating with her to relieve her of all of the drama in Atlanta. He wondered how life would be with her, without Rock always lurking.

Rock circled around the neighborhood a few times before he stopped in front of Veronica's house. Veronica didn't want to make a scene in front of her mother, so she played it cool. *"Only if mom wasn't here,"* Veronica thought to herself. Rock bravely walked up the stairs and greeted everyone. He could see the disgust on Veronica's face. But the expression of pure admiration and appreciation for the sudden appearance of eye candy was written all over Cicely's face.

"Hi Ms. Williams. Is Ronnie here?"

"Where else would she be? She's in there," Veronica nodded toward the house and rolled her eyes at him as he walked inside.

"Ooh, sweetie who was that?" Cicely asked.

"Someone you wont be seeing again." Veronica assured her mother.

Jerome heard the conversation on the porch. He knew Veronica's reasoning for letting him in to see her daughter, after all the pain he'd caused her. He kept a close eye on Ronnie, refusing to let anything happen to her. If Rock disrespected her in any way, Jerome was ready to be all over him like poison ivy.

Josh was on his way to Alabama to pick up a few of his cousins for the holiday. He couldn't resist. He was overpowered by the temptation to call Ronnie. He inserted his earpiece and dialed the number as he drove down the expressway.

The phone rang. Jerome answered it with his eyes still glued on Rock.

"Hey Josh. How's everything?" Jerome sat back in the chair, crossing his legs, holding an enjoyable two minute long conversation with Josh, while continuing to watch Rock. Jerome started talking about the football games and the menu in which Veronica had prepared for Thanksgiving.

"Won't you join us for dinner?" Jerome asked with a pleasant smile on his face. "Okay", Jerome said nodding.

"Ronnie can't come to the phone right now, but I will make sure she calls you back."

Ronnie stared at Jerome trying to figure out what Josh could've possibly been saying. This was such a weird enigma that was going on with her entire family.

Out of the corner of her eyes, Veronica looked at her mother, but didn't say a word. All the things Patrice had been hearing about Rock throughout the year, she assumed from Veronica's reaction that he had to be Rock. Patrice looked at Veronica and responded, "That's Ronnie."

Veronica shook her head and turned away, looking down the street in the opposite direction. She hadn't had a chance to tell Patrice about the latest drama that Ronnie had incurred.

"Ooh honey, if I was thirty years younger I'd give Ronnie a *run* for her money."

Veronica was tired of hearing Cicely's lustful remarks about Rock. She gritted her teeth, and walked down onto the next step. Taking a deep breath, she exhaled slowly, trying not to say anything to disrespect her mother. She was getting fed up with Cicely meddling in everyone's love life and drooling over their mates.

Rock was still standing in the middle of the den looking down at Ronnie, wanting to sit down beside her and stroke her hair like he used to when they first met. He made small talk and asked repeatedly if there was anything he could do for her. He tried not to let his emotions take control over him in front of Jerome, but he knew Jerome wasn't going to take his eyes off of either of them.

Rock finally figured out that he was no longer welcome in the Williams' house. He knew Jerome was merely being treacherous. He told Ronnie he loved her and walked out the door.

"Oh sweetie, I didn't get your name. I'm Cicely, Ronnie's grandmother." Cicely extended out her arm to shake Rock's hand.

"He knows who you are ma," Veronica said with a piercing stare at Rock.

Rock said his goodbyes and quickly got off of Veronica's property.

"Um, Um, Um," Cicely moaned as if she desired Rock.

"Where's your southern hospitality? I never taught you to act ugly towards people...especially handsome men like that," Cicely fussed at Veronica.

Veronica looked at Cicely with disgust and pure anger. "You must have forgotten you raised me up North. That handsome man that you're drooling over damn near killed your granddaughter! She *just* came home from the hospital." Veronica informed her mother. She stampeded back into the house, leaving Cicely and Patrice on the porch.

"Oh Lord I didn't know...why didn't she tell me?" Cicely cried out to Patrice.

Patrice hugged her mother and tried to calm her down. Cicely was puzzled. She wondered why Veronica would let him go near Ronnie. She sat on the porch alone for nearly an hour, thinking of how she would have reacted if she were in Veronica's shoes.

As the day grew later, the temperature was drastically dropping. Veronica went out onto the porch and gave her mother a hot cup of cappuccino. She hugged her mother and apologized for getting angry with her for a situation she knew nothing about. She told her mother everything that Ronnie had been through with Rock from the time they met. Cicely wished she could have gotten that moment back.

"Had I known the circumstances, I probably would have slapped him instead of drooling over him," Cicely declared. "Ronnie must've put it on him for him to act like that," Cicely said with a smile.

Cicely and Veronica laughed and shivered as they made their way inside of the house. Cicely stood in the den looking at Ronnie as she slept, thinking of all the awful things she must've tolerated while dealing with Rock. She hoped Ronnie had learned a valuable lesson from the turmoil she'd endured.

As Juanita sat in Copeland's with Jackie, she sipped on her virgin daiquiri, reminiscing about the holidays during the times she had someone special to share them with. Jackie sipped on her third Apple Martini, watching her sister who was simply trying to pull her life back together. She had stopped wearing makeup and styling her hair. It was obvious that her self-esteem was shot to pieces.

Jackie felt bad for her struggling sister, but there was nothing more she could do for her. She started mentally planning a two-week vacation for the two of them. She figured a week in Hawaii, along with another week cruising around in Mexico, would be a great start for her sister to get back on the right track.

Juanita rambled on about broken and failed relationships. Jackie noticed that her sister was saddened by the lonely holidays, which were quickly approaching. Jackie jotted down notes concerning travel arrangements and ideas, hoping to channel Juanita's anger and frustrations toward something more constructive. She planned to make a few phone calls to a couple of her celebrity friends when she got back home to New Jersey. They could probably help her sister rebuild her self-esteem, and focus on herself instead of every John, Don and Larry with a habit.

A scrumptious 6'5," well dressed, well groomed man walked pass Juanita's table. His pleasant fragrance lingered in the air, making her curiosity rise. She scooted to the edge of the booth to visually follow his every move. His *spirit* uniquely differed from the average guy who usually caught her eye. Juanita stared, recognizing his face, yet trying to put a name with it. His name was on the tip of her tongue.

"What is his name?" Juanita asked rhetorically. "I read the article about him that showed his $15 million mansion," she thought to herself.

She took a few more sips of her daiquiri and finally interrupted her sister's moment of babble.

"Jackie, what's his name?" She pointed over to his table.

"He's an actor," Juanita pouted, wanting Jackie to help her remember his name.

"He's fine," Jackie responded. "Now he's gone."

Juanita looked around, watching as he walked out of the door alone. Jackie resumed mumbling about something in which Juanita had no clue as to what it meant. Jackie looked up again, seeing the tall, handsome man walking back into the restaurant with another distinguished gentleman, who was wearing a fashionable, tailored, pinstripe suit. She tapped Juanita's hand and pointed at the door.

She looked around, trying to be discreet, and saw him again. Her heart skipped a couple of beats. Juanita and Jackie finished their meal and walked outside to the car. There, she saw this same man again, shaking hands with his illustrious associate. This mystery man then got into his Bentley. She didn't want to be ghetto and shout at him to get his attention.

It would be embarrassing for herself and her sister for wanting an autograph, without even having the ability to recall his name. Juanita followed the man to his home, but kept driving straight ahead, passing his driveway as he turned off into it. She drove another half mile, before she turned around to pass the mansion again going in the opposite direction. She needed to get a second look at it, ensuring that it was the one she'd seen in the article.

Jackie talked about nothing of importance during the entire ride, until she realized what her sister was doing. She was amazed at who and what they had found. They watched outside the metal gate as the Bentley slowly drove up the long winding driveway.

On the way home, Jackie bobbed her head and snapped her fingers to the gospel music playing on the radio.

"Isn't his name Terry Tyler or something?" Jackie asked out of the blue.

Juanita thought long and hard, gradually slowing down until they came to a complete stop at a green light and shouted, "Yes, yes, that's his name!"

She was grateful that Jackie remembered his name. Yet, she was also frustrated at the fact that she remembered it so late, hindering her chances of getting an autograph.

They headed home to relax for the rest of the night. As Juanita sat in front of the fireplace, she had a vision of a project she wanted to do. With all of the drama she's been through, an exaggerated story of her life would be a best-selling novel. This could be a step to opening the door to a new life; one that she may enjoy living. Juanita powered up the computer and began pouring out her heart, combining her vision, to eventually create a novel.

She hoped and prayed that one day her writing would possibly reach and touch Terry. This could possibly begin to build a close nit, work-related relationship with him, which could take her life in a different direction, creating a new career. As she brainstormed, creative ideas began dancing around in her head.

As soon as Juanita started typing, Josh called. He informed her that his job was going to send him to California for two months after the holiday season was over.

He was anxious about going somewhere he'd never gone before. He wanted to ask his mother's opinion about taking Ronnie with him as his companion. He knew she wouldn't approve due to Ronnie's present situation, but his urge to be with her was still getting stronger by the day.

Josh knew, by the sound of his mother's voice, that she had finally come up with a brilliant idea; one that she was proud of and confident about. She had a different perk that he hadn't heard in years. He tried prying it out of her, but she'd already decided to keep her idea to herself until it was time for it to be published.

Chapter 17

*T*hanksgiving Day had finally arrived. Cicely, Veronica and Patrice awoke just after the sun rose. They made a small breakfast so they wouldn't spoil anyone's appetite for dinner.

Ronnie smelled the aroma of bacon and eggs flowing through the house, which was slowly lingering under her nose. She awoke, painlessly, without any after effects of her miscarriage. Her energy level had increased drastically and her appetite was hearty. After showering, she put on a sweat suit to lounge in. Ronnie felt better than she had ever felt before, she pranced around in the kitchen. The fear she had for Rock, which had been lingering around for months, had suddenly vanished. In her heart, she felt like she was ready to move forward with Josh.

Veronica knew that her old Ronnie had resurfaced. Ronnie now had a certain *glow* about her; the same one she had when she first met Rock. Ronnie ran back upstairs after grabbing a couple pieces of bacon to hold her over until breakfast was done. She called Josh, wishing him a happy Thanksgiving.

She extended an invitation to him to join them for dinner. He had already accepted Jerome's invitation, and planned to be there on time to spend the entire day with her. Josh wanted to ask her about taking a trip with him to California, but he feared rejection.

Trey and Tony were the first guests to arrive at Veronica's house. To Cicely and Patrice, they appeared to be the perfect gentlemen. As the girls helped prepare for dinner, Trey and Tony were enjoying themselves, laughing and talking to Jerome.

Juanita, Jackie, and Josh arrived shortly after Tony and Trey. Josh was pleased to see that Ronnie was active and back to her old self. Trey and Tony watched blissfully as Josh placed a French kiss upon Ronnie's lips. Josh saw the guys and thought they may have been there for Monie and Nae. He had no knowledge that they were affiliated with Rock.

Trey was thrilled that Ronnie was about to find happiness, and wouldn't have to deal with drama caused by Rock. He vowed to himself that he would not tell her secret until she was ready to reveal it.

Rock planned to take all of the guys to his mother's house for dinner. Rick arrived at Rock's house later than what they'd discussed, expecting to find Trey and Tony there waiting for him. Rock called Trey's phone several times but never received an answer. Rick called Tony, only receiving his voice mail. After several failed attempts, Rock called Nae's cell phone to find out if Tony and Trey were with her and Monie.

When Nae received the call, she wasn't sure of what to say. She looked at Tony, trying to whisper to him, that Rock was looking for him. Tony looked at his phone and saw that he had five missed calls. Nae brushed Rock off and suggested that he call Tony's phone again. She was unaware of how Tony may have told him he was going to celebrate the holiday. As Trey set his phone to vibrate, Rock called again.

"Hello?" Trey answered.

Rock questioned him as to why he and Tony weren't at his house. Trey went out on the porch to alleviate any disturbances of other guests, only closing the screen door in case Monie needed him. He tried to explain to Rock that he was spending time with Monie.

"After all I've done for you...after all we've been through together, you're gonna put our family's plans on a back burner for a female! I don't give a damn what you do to me. Mom is gonna be the one who's disappointed. This will be the first Thanksgiving in twenty years we haven't all been together as a family." Rock said, using his guilt trip tactics.

Rock was slightly disappointed, and he knew his mother would be hurt. He knew that if Trey was there, Tony was there as well. He tried to honestly see things from their perspectives. They wanted to be with their women on the holiday instead of the same old tradition. If Ronnie and Veronica had allowed *him*, he would've been there too.

"Well how's Ronnie doing?" Rock asked. He heard her in the background laughing and talking.

"She's okay," Trey responded with hesitance.

"Is that punk named Josh over there?"

"Man, I don't know. There's a lot of family here and I don't know who's who," Trey said. He had a feeling that Rock would eventually show up sometime during the day. This meant that Rock would indeed find that Josh *was* there to see Ronnie. Since he was the only one who knew how to handle Rock's mood swings, he was going to make sure that

Ronnie and Josh had a good time in each other's company. If Rock decided to show up, he'd be ready to take whatever steps necessary to calm him down. Even if it included getting busted knuckles and getting their backs dirty.

As the family and their guests gathered around the table to say the blessing over the food, they heard the loud sounds of Tupac blaring outside. Tony knew that it could only be one person being so disrespectful. As Cicely finished the prayer, the doorbell rang.

Josh was in a corner of the kitchen leaning against the wall. Ronnie was leaning back against Josh, wrapped snug in his arms, both with joyous facial expressions. Monie stood behind Veronica as she opened the door to find that it was Rock. She was stunned to see that he had enough nerve to still show his face, even after being told that other arrangements had been made. He asked if he could peak in to wish everyone a happy holiday. Veronica knew he was there to spy on Ronnie. Through all the commotion, she really didn't know where Ronnie and Josh were.

Rock stuck his head in the kitchen's doorway. Before he saw anyone else, Rock spotted Ronnie and Josh snuggled up in the corner. His heart started racing, and felt as if it had fallen to the floor. Suddenly, he started sweating and gasping for air, feeling like he was suffocating.

Ronnie looked up and into his eyes. She was shocked, but this time, not overcome by fear. Josh felt safe, knowing that he wouldn't do anything crazy in front of the entire family. Rock looked at Trey and Tony as if they'd betrayed him. Bobbing his head, he beckoned for them to meet him outside. He said his goodbyes to everyone and went outside to talk with Trey and Tony.

"What the hell is going on?" Rock asked indirectly. "Ya'll just going to sit around and watch my woman spend her holiday with some other nigga and don't even tell me about it when I call you. I thought we were better than that."

"Man, we don't have any say so about who these people invite to their house," Trey stated.

"I see what it's all about. Ya'll just choose some broads over your own blood. After all we've been through, and after all I've done for ya'll…this is how you repay me?" Rock said with frustration and disappointment, trying to retain the envy from revealing itself.

"Man, you just caused this girl to have a miscarriage and then tried to kill her. Do you expect for her and her family to respect you and welcome you with open arms? Tony responded with sincerity.

Rock looked at the two of them as he walked to his truck. There was no argumentative defense he could use in his favor. He knew that everything they were saying was the truth, but he always insisted that he would be the one to come out on top.

"Man you gotta' accept it. She's not your woman anymore," Trey yelled to Rock before he got in his truck.

Rock sped away from the house, knowing in his heart that he'd screwed up for the last time. He felt his eyes fill up with water, but there was no way he could stop the tears from streaming down his face. He headed back home feeling quite disgruntled and empty. Instead of going to his mother's house for dinner, he thought some time alone would help ease his pain. He figured if he couldn't spend his holiday with Ronnie and her family, he'd rather spend it by himself.

Not only did he lose his chances to spend with Ronnie, but he just lost his chances to spend the holidays with the only people he ever considered his friends. Rock was miserable and lonely. With all of his family and associates he'd showered with money over the years, he never thought he would ever be lonely. In his corrupted mind, he thought everyone wanted to be around him all of the time.

As he laid back in his recliner watching TV alone, he wished he'd never ordered Rick to kill Shonte. He never imagined that he and Ronnie would ever have such major issues, or that he'd be desperate enough to want anyone else, including Shonte. At some point, he knew his decision would come back to haunt him.

Rock sat alone for a few hours watching TV. He found his address book and started calling women he hadn't talked to since he and Ronnie hooked up, nearly a year ago. Most of them had had their numbers changed, or had gotten married, were out of town, or sobbing over unpaid bills. They mainly wanted to know how much money they could get from him. He found himself back at square one, the same old undesirable place he was when he first met Ronnie.

The phone rang, nearly scaring Rock to death. It was Rick, wondering why he'd never met him over his mothers' house as planned. Rock was in deep thought, and unable to focus on the contents of Rick's conversation, that he was apparently having with himself.

Rock suddenly had a brilliant idea, so he thought. He figured by scaring Josh with threats, it would get him out of Ronnie's life; at least until he was able to maneuver his way back into her life. He asked Rick for suggestions on how they could lure Josh to his brother's club within the following week.

Rock shared his perspective with Rick on how he thought Trey and Tony had betrayed him. With Rick's nonchalant attitude, Rock knew that he'd be willing to follow through with whatever plan he may have had in mind. Betrayal was the one of the top three things to have a nigga come up missing or found in the Chattahoochie River. It was the most unappreciated and disrespected rule in the drug game, and whatever Rock thought was an appropriate consequence, Rick was ready to carry it out.

He saw that the well-built fortress in which he'd created was crumbling fast. The close-nit family that he Trey and Tony had been a part of for so long, was slowly being torn apart. Rock couldn't understand how his cousins and closest childhood friends, who never once turned their backs on him before, could forfeit their oath and let a few women persuade them to break their bonds.

The phone rang again, breaking his meditation. He snatched the phone off the base and yelled, "Who is this!"

Rock's mother was on the other end. She knew that her love stricken son was furious and lonely. He wasn't used to spending major holidays without a pretty young female by his side; or at least what he thought was pretty.

"Hi sweetie. It's mom," Rock's mother responded to his harsh greeting.

Rock remained quiet, after releasing a slight sigh.

"I know you're heartbroken, but I'd appreciate it if you'd come over and have dinner with us," Rock's mother generously suggested.

"Ma, I don't even feel like driving," Rock said trying to make excuses.

"I know. That's why Rome is on his way to get you. I'll see you when you get here. Love you," His mother replied in her gentle tone.

Rock and his mother didn't see eye to eye on a lot of things, but she was the only one who always knew how to get him back on track.

Josh invited Ronnie over to his apartment after dinner was over. She was overwhelmed by his generosity, especially after seeing Rock at her mother's house earlier. Before Ronnie and Josh walked out the door, Trey pulled Ronnie aside and assured her that he and Tony would be there for her if Rock tried to do anything to hurt them.

Trey was starting to realize that he'd been brainwashed by Rock over the years. He could no longer tolerate Rock's nonsense and violent temper towards Ronnie. He saw that she was happier that night with Josh than she had been in months with Rock.

Tony and Nae left Veronica's house and decided to go to the movies. As Tony drove, he watched Nae rub on her perfectly smooth round belly. He placed his hand on top of hers and began to pray a silent prayer that God would protect him and his family.

Nae cuddled up in Tony's arms as they watched the movie. They both felt a strong bond they'd never felt before. Nae was surprised, yet pleased. Tony was spending much more quality time with her, instead of running off somewhere with Rock and deserting her and their plans. This was the first time in months they'd been together without bickering. Nae was sure that the baby had a role to play in his new attitude.

Ronnie lay stretched out on Josh's sofa staring at the TV, unaware of what she was staring at. She was off in her own little lost world. Josh studied her, as she appeared to be at peace. He wanted to talk to her about going to California with him, but he was still unsure of how to approach her with the proposition.

He wasn't sure if she was completely over Rock. He knew he would eventually have some resentment toward her, especially if she went to California with him, trying to use him as a substitute for Rock. She would probably be letting him know where she was, what she was doing, and with whom.

Ronnie continued to appear as if she was at peace, but in her mind, she was revising her plan to get rid of Rock over and over again. She thought that she'd have to exclude Nae from her plan since she and Tony had started getting along again.

"How would you like to go to California?" Josh finally asked.

Ronnie looked at Josh as if he'd just stepped off a spaceship. He knew she was in deep thought about something.

"Won't you go to California with me? We'll have a chance to enjoy each other's company in peace."

"California!" she exclaimed. "When?"

"My job is sending me there for three months, and I thought I'd extend the invitation. After everything you've been through, you need a break," Josh stated sincerely.

Ronnie was overwhelmed that he would think enough of her to want to get her away from all the madness that was going on there. It made her feel special for Josh to want to take her away from all of her drama, and keep her with him that long. She had never been with any-one who was that considerate before. She couldn't help but think that he had something up his sleeve.

"What's in it for you?" she asked.

He was surprised that she would part her lips to ask him something like that. Being outspoken was always the one thing he liked about Ron-nie, even when they were younger, along with the fact of her being such a challenge. He let the comment slide since he understood she was going through some emotional challenges.

"I get to be with the woman I've always adored," Josh responded.

Ronnie was shocked, and quite impressed by his answer. She did-n't realize he was that fond of her.

"So when are we leaving?" Ronnie asked.

"I have to leave next week, but I'll send for you in two weeks."

Ronnie started planning what she was going to do once she got there. She didn't know or care what part of California they were going to. She thought that maybe she wouldn't have to kill Rock after all. She was still going to keep that plan in mind as a backup.

Although it would have been nice to get some money from Rock to go shopping before she left, she didn't want him to think she was pushing for reconciliation. As Ronnie suggested a million things for them to do during their stay on the west coast, Josh rubbed and mas-saged her feet and calves.

Ronnie heard her phone vibrating on her purse. She ignored it and sat up, looking Josh in his big, beautiful eyes. She planted a short and soft kiss on his lips, and stared at him, wondering if they could build a promising future together.

Josh sat straight up on the sofa. Ronnie faced him, throwing her leg across his lap, straddling him. She sat on his lap wondering if he was going to kiss her or at least caress her body.

Although her body hadn't completely healed from her miscarriage, she wanted Josh like she never wanted a man before. He knew that she wasn't physically ready to have sex yet, but he was curious to know exactly how she wanted him to respond to her sexual gestures.

"What do you want me to do?" Josh asked.

"I want you to make love to me," she responded passionately.

"Ronnie I…I can't—I want to, but I can't. You're just not ready. I…I don't want to hurt you," Josh stammered over his word from being tantalized.

Ronnie could respect that. It was far more believable this time around than when Rock said those very same words. This time it was coming from a real man; a friend that she knew and trusted.

She began kissing and nibbling all over his chest and stomach. Ronnie noticed he was getting aroused and she couldn't do a thing about it except perform oral sex. She went back up and started nibbling on his ears and neck. Ronnie didn't want him to think that she just showing her gratitude, because he promised her to take her to the other side of the world. She wanted to maintain her clean image, at least until they were officially a couple.

Rock unsuccessfully attempted to call Ronnie again. He got more frustrated as her phone continuously rang.

"Sweetie, just leave her a message," Rock's mother advised him.

"All I want to do is apologize," Rock said with frustration. "She doesn't answer the phone when she sees my number."

"Have you prayed about it?" Rock's mother asked.

"Ma, don't start lecturing me about prayer!" Rock exclaimed and threw his hands up in the air.

"See, that's the reason you're in the predicament you're in now, because you don't pray," Rock's mother said calmly. She walked in the other room and started mingling with her other guests as if everything was a-okay.

Rock sat at his mother's kitchen table by himself, thinking about how much truth his mother's last statement held. Twenty minutes later he called her back into the kitchen, apologizing to her for overreacting to the truth.

"Ma, I gotta get her back," Rock said while shaking his head in disbelief, realizing that he had permanently lost the only thing that meant everything to him. He didn't know where Ronnie was. He was sure that her sisters knew where to look for her. He called Tony's cell phone to see if Nae knew where to find her. After several failed attempts trying to reach Tony, he called Trey at home. Trey's answering machine came on.

"Man, I know you're there. Pick up the phone," Rock said on the answering machine.

Trey and Monie listened to him beg on the machine and continued watching their movie.

"Man, I'm sorry for trippin' on you earlier. I know you and your girl are probably there handlin' business, but when you get this message call me right back."

Trey had never heard Rock apologize to anyone before. He knew that whatever was going on, it must have been serious. Trey picked up the phone right before Rock hung up.

"Yo, man what's going on?" Trey asked, knowing that he was probably up to his same old tricks.

Rock apologized again for the run-in they'd had earlier.

"Have you seen Monie?" Rock asked.

"Why? Is something wrong?" Trey asked.

"I was looking for Ronnie so I can apologize to her too. I want to apologize to everybody…especially Ms. Williams," Rock muttered sympathetically.

"Monie's probably at her mom's house," said Trey.

Monie started laughing. She knew that Rock was trying to hunt her sister down again.

"Man, if you could find out from her where Ronnie is, I'd really appreciate it," Rock begged.

"Here we go again. Rock! Ronnie's doin' her own thing without you man. You gotta accept it and let her go," Trey said, trying hard to explain things to Rock without losing his patients.

"You know where she is and who she's with, don't you?" Rock asked. "Tell me where she is Trey. Man we go way back…dammit we're blood. Why are you doin' this to me?" Rock continued to beg.

Rock calmed down and told Trey how dinner was at his mother's house. Several minutes later, Rock asked Trey if he'd seen Tony. He figured if he couldn't get anything out of one sister, he'd try the other one. Trey was already hip to his game.

"I haven't seen Tony since dinner. If I see him I'll tell him to give you a call." He knew that Tony had taken Nae to the movies.

Rock knew Monie was sitting near Trey. But Trey stood his ground and refused to succumb to Rock's guilt trips and pathetic state. Rock started to go over Trey's house, but didn't want to add to the drama that had gone on at the Williams'.

Veronica and Patrice cleaned the kitchen, while Cicely talked to Jerome about Veronica's childhood. Jerome was practically in tears just listening to Cicely's humorous versions of some of the things Veronica had already told him about.

Rock and Rome circled around Veronica's house while Rock built up enough courage to go in and apologize to the entire family.

"Maybe you should wait a while for things to die down before you try to talk to them," Rome suggested.

Rock thought about what Rome was saying. It was perfectly logical to him, but a part of him just wanted to see if Ronnie was inside. Rome headed away from the house as if he were leaving the subdivision.

"Where are you going?" Rock asked.

"Man, you really don't need to be around there right now," Rome stated matter of factly.

"So now you're telling me what I should and shouldn't do," Rock replied angrily.

Rock was starting to feel like everyone was taking sides. However, no one seemed to be on his side. It seemed as if no one wanted to be around him anymore. He wondered why his life was suddenly turning into a nightmare. They'd missed operations because Trey and Tony were never around. He felt like Nae and Monie had the upper hand in his life. They were the ones who had turned Ronnie against him, and now they were slowly turning Trey and Tony against him too.

"What should I do about Nae and Monie?" Rock asked Rome.

"What do you mean what should you do about them?"

"They're turning my life into a total wreck."

Rome didn't understand where Rock was heading with that conversation. He hoped he wasn't talking about another disappearing act like Shonte's. There was no way possible he could make half a family disappear and get away with it. Rome hoped his brother had more sense than that. This conversation had taken a major detour, which had thrown Rome for a loop.

"If Nae and Monie weren't in the picture, Ronnie would come back to me and Trey and Tony would be a part of the family again," Rock thought aloud.

Rome knew then that his brother was definitely insane.

"If that's what you have in mind, you're on your own. How do you think we can wipe off a whole family and get away with it?" Rome asked.

"You know what Rock, you are sick! You're mentally deranged. These women haven't done a thing to you. In that sick little head of yours, you truly believe that they've taken everything away from you. You did this to yourself!" Rome screamed.

"So now you're turning against me too?" Rock asked.

Rock threw his hands in the air and remained quiet. He was so mad until he wanted to punch a hole through the windshield. When they arrived at his house, he got out of the truck, slammed the door, and stormed into the house trying to slam the heavyweight oak door in Rome's face. Rome followed behind him trying to talk some sense into Rock. He tried to make Rock understand that if he hurt Ronnie's sisters, he'd never have a chance to be with her again. And, if by chance he would get her back, she'd never be the same due to the anguish of losing her sisters.

Rock grabbed a Heineken out of the refrigerator and sat down in his recliner, partially reclined. Rome was making perfect sense. Of course, Rock didn't want Rome to know that he was taking heed to what he was saying. He didn't it want to seem as though he was getting soft.

The phone rang interrupting their moment. Rock looked at it, not wanting to answer it. By the forth ring he thought it may have been Ronnie. He quickly picked it up, just before the answering machine got it.

"Hello…hello…Ronnie? Dammit say something."

The person on the other end hung up on him.

Rock sat up coming out of his partially reclined position huddling over, resting his elbows on his knees, and swishing the beer around in his mouth while staring at the floor.

"I don't know what to do." Rock sobbed as he released a tear that slid down the backside of his hand.

When they were in the truck, Rome knew that his brother was hurt and confused, and just talking out of anger. Rome didn't know exactly what to tell him. He sat on the sofa, adjacent to where Rock sat in the recliner, and assured him that things would be all right.

Chapter 18

*R*onnie woke up around mid morning feeling refreshed. She found a rose on the nightstand that Josh had left for her. A note attached to it saying that she needed to be ready for dinner around four. Getting out of bed, Ronnie opened the French doors and greeted the fresh, crisp air with a smile. She stepped out onto the balcony and looked around. The different scenery that California had to offer was impressive.

Ronnie watched as people swam and surfed on the beach below. She had only been there for three days, but had already fallen in love with the west coast. The atmosphere was totally different from what she was used to. Closing her eyes, she listened to the roaring echoes from the splashing waves. The slight mist blowing off the ocean, and the coolness of her satin pajamas caressing her skin, was enjoyable.

She went back inside and called room service. Ronnie ordered the hotel's recommended deluxe breakfast, which was nearly enough for two people. She went back onto the balcony and called Nae from her cell phone.

Nae was ecstatic to hear from her sister. Nae told Ronnie about how Rock had been disturbing her and Jerome by calling Veronica's house late at night. He continued harassing her and Monie, trying to get them to tell him where Ronnie was. Ronnie had changed her cell phone number just hours before she left for California, so Rock couldn't call and harass her everyday.

A knock came at the door.

"Room service," a young man announced.

The young man's voice sounded identical to Rock's. Ronnie pulled her robe together, tying it a little tighter. She cracked the door and peeped outside. There stood a tall, brown skinned, bald and slender man that indeed looked almost identical to Rock. Ronnie couldn't help but stare at the man.

She skeptically signaled for the man to come in and picked up the phone to tell Nae she'd call her back. The man pulled the tray into Ronnie's room, letting her know he'd be her server for the majority of her stay.

Ronnie searched her purse for a tip. She finally found two dollars.

"What did you say your name was?" Ronnie asked.

"Xavier," the young guy replied with a heavy French accent. He smirked as he headed for the door. Before opening the door, he turned around and reached for her hand. She could tell that he had an instant crush on her. To her it was like déjà vu.

"What is your name madam?" he asked.

"Oh I'm sorry. I'm Ronnie," she replied as she hesitantly put her hand in his. He kissed her hand and made it clear that he would be back quite often to check on her and refresh the mini-bar.

"I'm not supposed to ask, but are you here alone?" Xavier asked.

"No," Ronnie said snappy.

"Are you here on business or pleasure?"

"A little of both," Ronnie said with a half of a smile and gestured that she was ready for him to leave.

She didn't want to seem rude, but she was uncomfortable being alone with him. He reminded her so much of Rock. After seeing the server, her appetite had diminished to nearly nothing. She ate the eggs and ham, and drank her juice. All she did was sit picking at the rest of the food with her fork. She felt badly for having to leave her family in Atlanta, only to be harassed by Rock, while she was out enjoying the sunny beaches of California.

Ronnie took a long, hot, steamy shower before getting dressed and taking a stroll. While walking down the street, she spotted a sign that read, "Talent Agent Wanted".

Her curiosity wouldn't allow her to walk away and ignore the sign. She eased up the jarring stairs in the narrow stairwell and opened the glass door. The sound of the delayed buzzer on the creaky door made her feel jumpy. She walked into a mid sized lobby seeing only four empty desks and a couple of stray chairs. Patiently, she waited for someone to come out of the back of the office to assist her, as she sat in one of the lonely chairs.

The phones were ringing continuously ringing off the hook. No one came to the front of the office to answer them. She heard voices coming from a room in the back of the office and slowly started walking down a short and wide hallway.

A young lady, appearing to be in her mid twenties, came rushing out one of the three open office doors. The two women startled each other as they nearly ran head-on into one another.

"Oh hello. May I help you?" the young lady asked.

You could tell that she was definitely overworked. She had at least twenty-five well-sized files that she was struggling with, trying to carry to her front desk. Ronnie caught a few them as they started to slide off the top of the stack.

"Oh, thank you so much," the lady said. "By the way, I'm Tara," she added, while walking over to one of the empty desks. Ronnie was so overwhelmed by Tara's workload that she forgot to introduce herself. When Tara put the files down, Ronnie could see that her attire was quite fashionable and obviously expensive. After spending a year with Rock, having expensive designer clothes was right up Ronnie's alley. She hadn't quite become a "materialistic chick", but she was starting to enjoy the finer things in life.

Ronnie thought it was safe to assume that Tara was making a fortune by working for what appeared to be a nearly desolated firm. Besides all of the files, folders, and shuffled papers, Ronnie saw several pictures of Tara, with many well-known celebrities, on her desk.

"I saw the sign downstairs stating that you needed talent agents. What exactly are the required qualifications for that position?" Ronnie inquired.

Tara smiled and looked at Ronnie, as she reached for an application.

"What type of work do you do?" Tara asked.

"None," Ronnie replied insecurely, embarrassed to admit that she had never held down a real job before.

"What kind of work have you done in the past?" Tara asked.

"Maybe I should come back at another time," Ronnie said as she stood up getting ready to leave.

"Wait a minute. Don't run off so fast. Let's get the paperwork done first, and just leave the rest up to me," Tara said anxiously, hoping that Ronnie wouldn't give up so easily.

Things were starting to sound good to Ronnie. She figured Tara may have had some *pull* in the company. Tara told Ronnie she would hear from her within the next few days. Ronnie tried to figure out the nature of the work before she left, but didn't want Tara to think she was just lurking around with a hidden agenda. Although Ronnie played it cool and simulated the impression that she was okay with hearing from Tara within a few days, Ronnie left still feeling a bit intimidated.

Ronnie walked back down the long, narrow stairwell. Trying to decide what she was going to do next, she started walking down the street. She looked in the windows of several clothing stores, seeing outfits she only wished she could buy.

On the way back to the hotel room, she received a call from Josh. For some reason her heart palpitated. It felt as if she was a high school girl in love for the first time. Wearing a big, blushing smile, she talked to him all the way back to the hotel.

Ronnie watched TV and relaxed for a while. Nae called, letting her know that she needed to touch base with Rock, to calm him down. Rock had been over Veronica's house several times looking for her. He was outraged with a fierce temper, accusing Nae and Monie of turning Ronnie against him.

Ronnie got Nae to set up a three-way phone call with her and Rock on the line.

"Hello," Rock answered.

"So I heard you've been calling and harassing my family," Ronnie asked rhetorically.

"Ronnie, I've got to see. Where are you?" Rock asked.

"That's not important…" Ronnie attempted to explain her false whereabouts, but was rudely interrupted by Rock's aggression.

"I'm coming to see you right now!" Rock shouted.

"If you took the time to listen, you'd know that I'm in Canada," Ronnie said.

"Canada! What the hell are you doing in Canada?" Rock shouted.

"Vacationing," Ronnie replied sarcastically.

"With who?" Rock asked.

"That's none of your business!" Ronnie exclaimed.

"What part of Canada are you in?" Rock asked with a pleasant tone, in which Ronnie and Nae both knew was phony.

"That's none of your business either," Ronnie replied. "Nae, this phone call is about to end," Ronnie replied giving Nae the cue to hang up.

Nae hung the phone up in Rock's ear and called Ronnie back to finish their conversation. Within minutes Rock called Veronica's phone again. This time he was very angry, threatening to hurt everybody if he didn't find out where Ronnie was. Nae told Rock that she was going to go to the police and press charges against him for harassment.

"I don't give a damn about you going to the police! I'll get out of trouble before you make it home. I pay their salary!" Rock boasted, slamming the phone down in Nae's ear.

Rock couldn't and wouldn't take rejection as an option. He called Trey to find out if Monie had said anything to him about Ronnie leaving for Canada. He tried to keep his temper under control. Monie didn't know that he'd already cursed Nae out. He knew she definitely wouldn't give up any information knowing about the confrontation he just had with Nae.

"Hello?" Monie answered Trey's phone.

"Monie, just the person I wanted to talk to. Have you heard from Ronnie?" Rock asked.

When Monie recognized his voice, she handed the phone to Trey, without even listening to what Rock had to say. She was afraid he would start fussing and cursing at her, or just say something flat out stupid, trying to raise her blood pressure. She was not in the mood to have an argument about her sister.

Ronnie called Nae back to find out exactly what was going on. She had an uneasy feeling that Rock would try to do something to Nae. He knew her pregnancy was causing her to be vulnerable and very sensitive to the slightest of situations.

Rock's phone rang again. He thought it may've been Ronnie trying to call back to apologize, or to tell him where she really was. "Hello…hello…Ronnie, please talk to me," Rock pleaded.

He was tired of getting hung up on. This had been going on for several weeks now. The caller ID always showed private caller or unavailable. He was almost certain that it was Ronnie calling, but she may have been too afraid to reveal her whereabouts.

Nae was crying on the phone, while trying to talk to Ronnie. Ronnie thought that it would be a good idea to get Veronica's phone number changed. However, on the other hand, her mother wasn't able to change her residence that easily. She knew Rock would still stalk the house.

Nae finally got her self together, suggesting they call Monie and let her in on Ronnie's secret. Nae set up a three-way call with Monie, who was already frustrated with Rock because he had been trying to hunt her down as well. Ronnie tried to advise both of her sister's to stay close to Trey and Tony because she knew that Rock was ready to strike again and explode like dynamite.

With talk that Rock was on the prowl, Nae became paranoid, walking though the house, peeping out of windows as if she was being watched. Just in case Rock decided to come over and enforce his threats, she turned the TV down and put her shoes on. She would then be able to run out the back door, and over the neighbor's house, if necessary.

She heard the garage door going up, that nearly scared Nae to death. Veronica and Jerome were just getting home from the jewelry store. Veronica was excited about her upcoming wedding. She walked in the house to show Nae their new ring set. However, she noticed that Nae was obviously frightened about something. Nae faked a smile and told Veronica that she'd talked to Ronnie.

"Has Rock been around here harassing you?" asked Jerome.

"He hasn't been here yet, but I have a feeling he's on his way. He's been calling here and he's been calling Trey's house, trying to harass Monie. This morning Ronnie told him she was in Canada," Nae confessed.

"Good thinking," thought Veronica.

"That cowardice bastard always preys on a woman when she's down and at her weakest point!" Jerome exclaimed.

"I think it'll be a good idea if we got a restraining order against him and get the phone number changed," Veronica suggested.

Nae thought that it was ironic that her mother said the same exact thing Ronnie suggested. Although, she didn't think any of that would help, she knew that if Rock wanted to get something done, he would.

"Rock pays the police to keep him out of trouble," Nae said.

Veronica and Jerome looked at each other, and then at Nae.

"Do you know that for sure?" Jerome asked.

"Yes. He told me about it. You also have to realize, I do date his former best friend," Nae commented truthfully.

"That's it! I'm moving you in with me," Jerome demanded to

Veronica. "We're going to sell this house."

As Jerome tried to console Veronica and Nae, the doorbell rang. Veronica looked out the window to try and identify who was at the door. She and Nae automatically thought it was Rock.

Jerome answered the door, finding that it was Tony. Tony came in and had a heart to heart talk with the family. He warned them that Rock would more than likely do something stupid. He suggested that Ronnie stay hidden wherever she was.

Jerome had his skepticism about whose side Tony and Trey were on. Veronica had already developed trust in Trey, especially since he had given her Monie's tuition money. However, she still had a slight doubt in Tony, but was willing to listen to what he had to say.

"Ronnie is in Canada right now," Veronica claimed.

She looked at Nae as if she wanted Nae to keep Ronnie's real location disclosed. Nae was aware of her mother's uncertainty of Tony, but she couldn't contradict her mother's story, risking the chance of her sister's life being endangered.

Ronnie waited patiently for Josh to get off of work and make it back to the hotel. She was wearing a short-sleeve, fitted dress with lace around the cleavage, and platinum and rubies accessories.

Josh finally arrived an hour later than he said he would. Ronnie was barefoot sitting on the balcony, still in her beautiful dress, and slightly tipsy from the wine she'd been sipping on for the past two hours.

He walked onto the balcony greeting her with a half dozen fresh cut, red and yellow roses. Disappointment was written all over her face. She hoped this wouldn't turn into another disastrous relationship, like the one she'd just gotten out of with Rock. She looked down at her watch.

"Four o'clock huh," Ronnie said cynically, taking one long last sip of her wine, to finish it off.

Josh begged and pleaded with her to forgive him for being late. He was too embarrassed to admit that he had gotten lost on one of California's busiest expressways. He knew she probably wouldn't be willing to believe that excuse. Of all the times he'd been to California, he was still unfamiliar with that particular city.

It seemed to Josh that there was more to her attitude than what she was telling him.

"I promise I'll make it up to you," Josh said sincerely.

"I've heard that a million times," Ronnie said nonchalantly referring to Rock's past broken promises.

"The attitude she was carrying was very unlike her," Josh thought. He took her glass, picked up the half empty wine bottle from off of the floor, and put it in the fridge. This was to ensure that she wouldn't get anymore. He knew her too well, to settle for her nonchalant attitude and lack of an explanation. He sat her on the couch and looked her directly in her eyes.

"Ronnie, what's wrong? Have you spoken to your family?" Josh asked.

Ronnie shed a tear and tried to discreetly wipe it away before he noticed it. She was ashamed and disgusted at herself. Josh placed his hand under her chin to turn her head to face him. Holding her head down, Ronnie shed another tear that dropped onto Josh's hand. She and Rock's drama had followed her all the way across to the other side of the world.

"I'm just feeling a little homesick," Ronnie claimed as she looked into Josh's seductive eyes.

Josh knew she was still withholding the entire truth from him. This was not her first time being away from home. He remembered when she stayed on *two-week* vacations at a time. He looked at her with an expression of obvious disbelief. She finally broke down and told him what was going on.

"Rock is still constantly harassing my family."

Josh had already guessed that Rock had something to do with her unhappiness. He wanted to go on like nothing was wrong, but remembered that Juanita did tell him that this situation would arise. He couldn't be mad at Ronnie, regardless how hard he tried. He could only be mad at himself for not listening.

Josh was scared to ask her if she wanted to go back to Atlanta, thinking she might want to go back and reunite with Rock. He had to take his chances, though. It would only be right to ask if she wanted to go check on her family. He sat silently for a moment, thinking of all the reasons she would want to go back. He finally built up enough courage to ask.

Trying to prepare himself for the worse possible answer, he asked "Are you ready to go back home?"

"No! And leave all of this?" she replied.

He was able to breathe again. Walking to the room to change into her lounge clothes, she told him about the conversation with Nae. While she continuously walked in and out of the closet, he struggled to understand what she was saying. Finally, she went back out into the sitting room, to sit and talk with him, instead of at him. He was relieved to see that she had gotten comfortable and ready to wind down and relax.

Several times, she swiftly changed the subject, before he could attempt to say a word. She babbled on about how her day went, and about the fact she may have a job lined up. When he heard about a job, he was confident she was willing to stay there and start a new life with him. He instantly began a mental plan on how things were going to be.

Since she had no reason or desire to go back to Atlanta, Josh thought that all the strings that were attached between her and Rock would automatically be detached.

"…And I think she's going to make the three of us her brides maids."

Josh heard and focused on the last part of Ronnie's babble. This put an immediate halt on his mental planning. He was completely dumbfounded, looking up at her with total ambiguity. She looked back at him as if he'd just fallen from an unknown planet.

"Your mother didn't tell you?"

"Tell me what?" Josh asked. He apologized for slipping into a zone instead of paying attention to her. She explained to him, again, why they were going to have to go back to Atlanta.

"We're going to be in my mother's wedding. Your mother was supposed to ask you if you would be one of Jerome's groomsmen. I'm assuming she didn't ask you. I'm sorry. You weren't supposed to find out about it like this," Ronnie explained.

"When is the wedding?"

"I think its sometime in June."

"So you're saying I'm supposed to be in a wedding that I know absolutely nothing about, and you can't even tell me when it's going down."

Ronnie winced in the corner of the couch, *"yes,"* she whispered.

Josh got the phone and sat it on the table in front of Ronnie. "Call your mother," he said. He turned around and walked out of the room. By the time Ronnie had dialed the number, and waited for someone to pick up at Veronica's house, Josh picked up the other phone.

"Hello," Veronica answered.

Ronnie was puzzled and speechless, wondering why Josh wanted to call her mother.

"Hey ma," Ronnie said with awe.

"Hey, Ms. Williams. This is Josh," he said, continuing to make small talk. Ronnie was still wondering what the purpose was for the call. Josh asked Veronica to call his mother on three-way so he could get an understanding of what he was supposed to do and when.

Ronnie sensed a bit of frustration from Josh. She had never saw him like that before. She didn't understand why he was making such a big deal out of something so small. This was an event in which he should be honored to do.

After listening to his perception of the circumstances, Ronnie then understood where Josh's anger was stemming from. Ronnie, Veronica and Juanita then realized the dangerous situation Ronnie could be faced with if she returned.

Veronica left Josh's participation as an option, but demanded that Ronnie was going to be in her wedding.

"If Ronnie sneaks back in town, Rock doesn't necessarily have to know she's here," Juanita added.

Ronnie knew that there wasn't anything that went on in Atlanta that Rock didn't know about, but she kept her opinion to herself. She suggested that her mother should have the wedding in Jersey.

"You're forgetting that Jerome's family is a part of this too," Veronica said with a slight bit of hostility.

"I didn't forget but…" Ronnie tried to plead her case, but was rudely interrupted by Veronica.

"The wedding is going to be in May in Atlanta," Veronica demanded.

Both Ronnie and Josh knew that their argument was imperative, but everyone refused to listen. After they hung up the phones, Ronnie and Josh discussed their parents' irrational and selfish decisions.

"I don't understand…your mother is usually looking out for your best interest. What's so different about this time?" Josh asked.

Ronnie thought the decisions they made were extremely unfair. At the same time, this was her mother's day, and whatever she said was going to be final.

On his way home, Tony stopped by Veronica's house to pick up

Nae. He sat in the den with Veronica, Jerome and Nae for a minute before they left.

"Where have you been?" Nae asked Tony. "You were supposed to be here over an hour ago."

"I rode with Rome to take Rock to the airport," Tony replied.

"Where's he going?" Jerome asked.

"He said he was going to Canada," Tony replied as he thought about the conversation they all had earlier.

Everyone knew he was making an attempt to hunt Ronnie down. Veronica took a moment to reflect on everything Josh and Ronnie was just trying to tell her. She figured that by the time she was due to get married, Rock would have forgotten all about Ronnie and moved on with his life.

Tony tried to speak up on Ronnie's behalf, letting Veronica know that Rock was not giving up on getting Ronnie back.

"Did anyone tell him what part of Canada Ronnie was in?" Tony asked indirectly.

"No," Veronica replied. She paused for a while trying to convert her thoughts into words before losing her entire train of thought. "The wedding is six months away. You think he's still going to be stalking her by then?" Veronica asked.

Tony shook his head, yes, letting Veronica know that Rock wasn't going to give up until he got Ronnie back, or until someone was hurt or dead. Veronica heard what Tony was saying, but never took heed to the frankness of it. She was in denial. She was going to take her chances on having her daughter come to the wedding, regardless of what anyone had to say about it.

"My father and my children could get to New Jersey if they need to," Jerome added trying to suggest ideas to ensure Ronnie's safety.

Veronica began second guessing her plans to marry in Atlanta. Jerome realized she didn't want to alter her plans, but her daughter's life was possibly at stake.

"Is Rock really that dangerous? Did he really have something to do with Shonte's disappearance?" Veronica asked Tony. She started wondering if they really needed to be scared enough to make other arrangements.

Tony told Veronica the truth. "Rock made a call and set out a hit on Shonte's life, so he and Ronnie could be alone together without her drama."

Veronica and Jerome were appalled to know that they'd welcomed a murderer into their home.

"Oh my God. Did Ronnie know about that?" Veronica asked.

Tony shrugged his shoulders indicating that he didn't know. Veronica picked up the phone to call Ronnie. She had to get confirmation that Shonte's disappearance was no accident. It was done by Rock, intentionally, because he wanted to be with her.

Nae put her hand towards the phone, telling her mother that they shouldn't dwell on Shonte. They needed to focus on not allowing Rock to do the same thing to Ronnie.

After Nae and Tony left, Jerome and Veronica spent most of the night packing Veronica's clothes and dishes, preparing to move her into his house. He was planning to call the real estate agent the very next day and put Veronica's house on the market.

Chapter 19

*F*or hours, Rock sat at home alone in his recliner, thinking of ways to find Ronnie.

He knew that Trey and Tony's relationships with Nae and Monie had grown to a level that an enormous amount of trust had developed among them. He had to figure out a way to manipulate their intelligence and their integrity, to work in his favor to make finding the love of his life easier.

He called Rick to help him develop a plan to get information from at least one of them. As soon as he and Rock hung up, Rick headed over to Rock's house. Rock was planning to tell Trey and Tony about an 'unknown operation'. He sat back in his chair, trying to smooth out the kinks in his plan. The vicious voice in his head was very convincing. *"Make Tony believe that there are bundles of money to be made in this particular operation. Ensure Tony of the security of his growing family",* the voice said." Once Tony was convinced, Rock would then lure Trey into coming back into their circle.

Rock's phone rang breaking his concentration.

"Hello," Rock answered sounding frustrated. He read the word 'Unavailable' on the caller ID. Rock thought it might have been the same person, who he hoped was Ronnie. He'd been receiving these calls for over a month now.

The voice on the other end was deliberately nothing more than a whisper to enable him from catching the voice, "Hey Rock, I miss you. I'm coming home so I can see you again."

"Baby, I miss you so much. I've been thinking a lot lately. I swear I won't lay a finger on you or even raise my voice too loud when I talk to you," Rock confessed, under the impression he was talking to Ronnie.

"I know that by now you probably thought I'd been gone forever."

"I knew you'd probably come back to see your family from time to time."

"I just called to let you know that I'll be back soon. I can't wait to see you."

"Ronnie, I love you more than life itself," Rock replied.

"Good-bye Rock."

Shonte had been out of the hospital for over a month now. She barely survived the accident, that Rick was so confident about, which would keep her out of Rock's life forever. Since everyone thought she had been killed in the accident, Shonte figured she could come back to get the revenge that Rock very well deserved. The anger inside of her grew stronger, knowing that he tried to get rid of her to pursue his relationship with Ronnie.

On his way to Rock's house, Rick called Trey to inform him of the mysterious operation that was supposed to go down later that night.

"Trey, what's up? Rock's puttin' something together for tonight. His house. 6p.m. be there," Rick demanded.

"I told him I wasn't messin' with that stuff anymore. I'm trying to get my life together and be with Monie," Trey explained.

"He doesn't care about what you're trying to do. He wants you to be at his house at six," Rick repeated.

"To hell with Rock," Trey replied.

"To hell with him? That's the message you want me to give him?"

"I don't care what you tell him. If he needs to see me about something, tell him to call me!" Trey exclaimed and hung up on Rick.

He had finally gotten enough balls to stand up to Rock, Rick thought. Rick called Rock back to tell him what Trey said, and of course, he exaggerated the truth trying to get Rock all worked up. Rick was the biggest instigator in the entire click, always wanting to see a good fight.

Rock didn't know how to react to Trey's reactions. He knew that Trey must have been truly in love. He'd never seen him act like that before. Rock realized that he was losing his power to control his family. He couldn't let that happen. He was determined to leave the game while he was still on top.

"Man, how did he let some hoe come between us?" Rick asked Rock.

"You better watch how you talk about that *hoe*. That *hoe* just happens to be my girl's sister, and she's a very sweet person," Rock replied on Monie's behalf.

Rick was getting confused with the way Rock's emotions constantly transformed. One minute he was ready to kill someone, and the next minute he got angry over calling someone out of their name. Rick was starting to see why Ronnie often called him bi-polar. The phone conversation Rock had before Rick arrived at his house, once again gave him hope that he and Ronnie would be together again. He'd planned to keep that conversation confidential.

"Why are you so protective of Ronnie's family all of a sudden? She's not even your girl anymore," Rick added cynically.

"She will be when I get a chance to work my charm on her again. Just get your job done and get Trey and Tony over here this evening."

Rick then called Tony with the same lie. Tony was skeptical of the call, at first. Eventually, he agreed to meet with them at Rock's house as he was told.

Tony had told Nae several times before that he wasn't participating in selling drugs or weapons with Rock anymore. Now, Tony had to think of a decent lie to tell her, in order to get out of the house without an argument.

"Nae, I'm about to go take Rock to the airport," Tony said.

"Why can't Rick or Rome take him?" Nae asked, suspecting that they were up to something.

"I didn't ask him all that. He just asked if I could take him to the airport."

"You should've told him no!" Nae shouted. "Call him back and tell him that I'm having labor pains."

"No! I should only be gone for about an hour or two."

Nae knew that when he hooked up with Rock he'd be gone for several hours, and usually came back with a wad of money and a different attitude. Not that the money wasn't good, especially for their situation, but Nae had a bad feeling about this escapade. She tried quite a few times to discourage Tony from going, but he insisted that it was an innocent trip to the airport.

"Where is he going this time? Trying to find Ronnie again, huh?" she added sarcastically.

Tony knew how much heartache Rock was suffering from due to Ronnie's disappearing act. He saw that Nae obviously got a thrill from tantalizing Rock with information about her sister. She often made statements that could've been detrimental to her own life. Nevertheless, Tony tried to deal with her behavior, and be as sensitive as he knew how because of her fragile state.

"What about our quality time? You always let Rock interfere with our quality time!" she yelled.

Tony didn't bother to respond. He knew that was just another attempt to get him to stay at home with her. As he tried to walk into the kitchen to get his keys, she grabbed his arm and jumped in front of him.

"You don't hear me talking to you?"

"Nae, be for real. We've been doing nothing but spending quality time for the past month."

Nae couldn't argue with that. After all, he was telling the truth. This forced her to take a different approach at the situation. She then faked as if she was having severe stomach pain. Tony looked at her, gritting his teeth. He didn't want to believe that she was seriously in pain, but by looking at her facial expressions, he wasn't really sure.

Tony got a warm towel and sat on the sofa, allowing Nae to stretch out on her back with her head in his lap. He patted her forehead with the towel and stroked her hair, making an honest effort to ease her pain. Soon after the pampering began, she started laughing and joking with him. Tony politely got up and attempted to leave.

"So, that was your best attempt to try to get me to stay, huh?" Tony asked. He didn't appreciate her attempt to try to play him.

Nae was speechless. She begged him one last time to stay at home with her. She offered him sex. She began stripping her clothes off, and literally throwing her naked body on him. Even with her big rounded belly, she was still as sexy as she was the day he met her.

Rick called Rock back, letting him know that Trey and Tony had been informed to be at his house at six. Because of Rock's 'fickle' mind, Rick had mixed feelings about what they were getting ready to do. He thought there may have been a small operation that Rock really wanted to pull off to get more money. For the most part, he figured Rock was going to threaten them a little, hoping they would tell him where Ronnie was, or why her mother's house was for sale.

At her new job at the talent agency, Ronnie sat at her desk, talking to her boss, Tara. She was very excited and gracious to Tara, for giving her a chance to work at her first *real* job. Ronnie had never experienced independence before, or been away from her family for an extensive period of time.

After being out on her own and not depending on Veronica or Nae for anything, she felt good about going home to see her family. She explained to Tara how having a small, cozy apartment with Josh was more rejuvenating than having an expensive and lavish mansion with Rock.

Tara had been hearing bits and pieces of Ronnie's past as she walk around the office while Ronnie held phone conversations with Nae and Monie. At first Tara couldn't understand why she was willing to give up her relationship with Rock.

This image changed when Ronnie explained the beatings and cheating she'd endured while dealing with Rock. After Ronnie told her about how Rock caused her to miscarry, her perception about Rock was tarnished. Tara began to get teary eyed and immediately changed the subject.

"What time does the flight leave?" Tara asked.

"At eleven. I hadn't even started packing yet," Ronnie stated.

"Neither have I. That only gives us two hours to get everything done. After we knock this stack of files out we need to go home and pack. You and Josh meet me back here at 9:30," Tara suggested.

Tara was flying to Atlanta with Ronnie and Josh, and would then board a connecting flight, continuing to her hometown in New York.

Ronnie had been in California for nearly a month. She heard that Rock had been to Canada on several occasions looking for her, with an intense determination to find her. Regardless of Rock's demented state, Ronnie was looking forward to seeing her mother and sisters.

Ronnie wasn't used to having plenty of money of her own that wasn't either tainted or affiliated with drugs. She was relieved of not being under scrutiny, or constantly told what to do, how to do it, and when to do it.

For protection, Ronnie had bought a gun and practiced shooting at the range rather often. Since Nae still resided in Rock's vicinity, Ronnie made sure that Nae purchased at least one gun for her own protection. Although she and Tony were back together in their penthouse apartment, Ronnie didn't want her pregnant sister to be without protection during the times when Tony wasn't around.

Nae contemplated following Tony, hoping to find out where they were *really* going and what was *really* going on. She felt as though she needed Ronnie to coach her on how to go about this 'detective' work. She called Ronnie to ask her how she would have gone about handling this situation if it were her.

Ronnie was going to surprise everyone with her presence. Unfortunately, when Nae called she couldn't resist the temptation of telling her that she was scheduled to arrive in Atlanta later that evening. Nae was so excited! She called Veronica on three-way to spread the news. Her next call was to tell Tony that he needed to be home in time in order to pick Ronnie up from the airport. Pausing, she thought about it for a minute. If she told Tony, would he slip up and tell Rock about Ronnie's arrival?

Monie's curiosity started to get the best of her. She called Nae to find out if Tony had left to go conduct business with Rock. Nae couldn't wait for Monie to spit out her reason for calling. Before Monie even said, "hello", Nae had already told her about Ronnie's arrival. After Nae resumed her composure, Monie then asked if she knew what this unheard of meeting was about.

"I don't know about any meeting, but I do know that Tony left to take Rock to the airport," Nae said.

Monie informed Nae that Trey mentioned a meeting before he left. Nae began to grow furious, certain that Tony had started lying to her again.

"I think another drug deal may be going down tonight," Monie stated.

Nae stood in the middle of the bedroom floor, in denial for a few minutes, before she spoke. The bad feeling she'd had earlier when Tony first got the call was suddenly getting worse. Tony had promised her that he wouldn't have anything else to do with Rock's drug deals. She tried to keep her faith in him, but her faith was slipping rather rapidly. The situation came along exactly how it used to; starting with the lies followed by a disappearing act. She had no choice but to believe that he was up to his old tricks once again.

After Nae and Monie started trying to put pieces of the puzzle together, she started moaning and grunting, and gritting her teeth. She was having real stomach pains.

"What's wrong?" Monie yelled.

"I just had a sharp pain."

"I'm on my way over there!"

"No, Monie. I'll be okay."

"Ronnie thought she was going to be okay too," Monie replied and hung up.

By the time Monie arrived, Nae had a headache along with the pain in her stomach. Her eyes were bloodshot red and swollen from crying, mainly from being alone.

"Come on. I've got to take you to the hospital," Monie demanded.

"No! We've gotta go see what Tony and Trey are up to."

"I'm not risking going out there and something happens to you and the baby. Wasn't Ronnie's experience enough for you to open your eyes and realize that these guys are something serious?" Monie asked.

Meanwhile, Rick and Rock took Trey and Tony out to an old abandoned apartment complex in Vine City, where most of their operations took place. Trey and Tony knew something was suspicious. Things weren't explained the way they usually were. Rome was missing and they only took one vehicle. They never rode with four in one vehicle. Normally, just in case one vehicle was bum-rushed, the other one could come to their rescue. Trey noticed that Rick was a bit shifty-eyed during the entire ride.

Trey and Tony were smart enough to wear their bulletproof vests. They hadn't spoken to Rock in nearly two weeks. Now, out of the blue, he had an operation that they had never heard of or even sat down together to properly plan.

Monie helped Nae get herself together. Nae picked her cell phone up and sent a text message to Tony, stating that Ronnie was going to be home later that evening, in case he came home and couldn't find her. Nae had no plans to stay home that night. She was either going to stay with Veronica, or stay at Trey's house with Monie. After she sent the text message, she went in the room and packed an overnight bag.

Once they arrived at the apartment complex, Trey and Tony tried to get out of the truck, but realized the safety locks were on. Rock and Rick got out of the truck; let them out, and pushed them to the back of the truck. Rock questioned both of them about Ronnie's whereabouts.

"How the hell are we supposed to know?" Trey asked.

"Because ya'll are dating her sisters," Rock responded with an over-abundance of aggression.

"Yeah exactly. We date *her sisters*. Since you keep referring to her as your girl, you should know where she is," Trey said fearlessly.

"I'm sure you probably have seen some odd numbers on your phone. You never questioned that? Or maybe ya'll just don't keep your girls in check," Rock replied, looking over at Rick laughing cynically.

"We don't keep our girls in check. *Our girls* are at the house. Where's your girl, or the one that you're claiming to be your girl," Trey asked putting Rock back in his place.

"For real man, you need to let it go 'cause she obviously don't give a damn about you," Tony added. "And then, why you gonna come and harass us about her. Hell, we ain't screwin' her!"

"Neither is he," Trey said jokingly, caring less about their current circumstances.

Rock pulled his gun out and put it up to Tony's chin.

"Nigga, we go all the way back to age thirteen. Am I supposed to be scared of you all of a sudden?" Tony asked courageously as Rock held the barrel of the gun firmly against his chin.

"Yeah, we go all the way back to age thirteen, and now you're damn near thirty and you gonna let a female come between us!" Rock yelled angrily.

Rick stood back listening to Tony and Rock's conversation. He knew Rock was going about the whole situation the wrong way. He stepped back, giving Tony and Trey some slack.

"Man, Tony's right. We ain't gettin' no younger. We've been doin' this for almost fifteen years. It's time for some of us to settle down and have families of our own. They're not responsible for your failed relationships…none of us are," said Rick, speaking up to Rock, voicing his opinion for the first time.

Rock's nose flared as he starred at Rick, thinking that this was the wrong time for Rick to get a backbone and start taking sides.

"So, you're all of a sudden taking sides?" Rock asked.

"I've been taking your side for all of these years. I'm finally tired of being on the wrong side," Rick answered remorselessly.

Everyone looked at Rick, surprised that he'd finally stood up to Rock. The attention was now off of Trey and Tony and focused on Rick. The ratio was now three to one.

Rock was left alone to fight his own battle. Rick walked off, got in the truck and started the engine. Trey and Tony opened the truck door. While they were attempting to get in with Rick, Rock started waving his hands in the air, hollering for everybody to get out. He walked around the truck, trying to gather everyone together to talk. His plan was being shot to hell right before his eyes.

"Wait, wait, wait…wait a damn minute. Something just went terribly wrong!" Rock yelled.

"Man, get your sick ass in this truck so we can go home!" Trey yelled.

Rock got in the truck, realizing what the ratio was. If he kept acting silly, there stood a chance that all of them would turn on him. They all knew he was on the borderline of having a mental problem.

"Man, I'm sorry. I don't know what came over me. I just want my girl back," Rock apologized as he sobbed. "If any of you knew where Ronnie was would you tell me?"

Trey looked at Tony and showed him the text message from Nae on his phone.

They knew then that Ronnie was going to be in town that night. Tony knew that she'd been in California for the past month. However, he portrayed, even to Nae and Veronica, as if he didn't know anything. He promised himself that he would let their family secret remain just that, for Ronnie's sake.

"We thought she was in Canada. If she's not in Canada, why did you make all those trips up there?" Trey asked, revealing that Rock was a bigger fool than he would ever admit to being.

"What part of Canada is she in?" Rick asked.

"I'm not sure," Rock replied, feeling quite dumb.

"You went all the way to Canada and don't even know what part she's in?" Rick asked with a slight chuckle.

Rock didn't appreciate all of their sly remarks regarding his mishap. He didn't know how to justify his ineffective trips. He was embarrassed because he had solely gone by 'hear say', which was obviously inaccurate information. This was the first time Rock had made a fool of himself in front of everyone.

Meanwhile, Nae and Monie went to pick Ronnie and Josh up from the airport. Veronica and Juanita set up a get-together for them at

Jerome's house. Juanita was nearly finished with her book. She decided to include a celebration for her accomplishment as well, and invited her publisher to attend the party to meet her boys.

Juanita was developing some strong emotions for her publisher, Raymond, and was ready to form a realistic relationship with him. She was just getting over the drama with Tyrone and was ready for the attention of a man again.

Monie called Trey on the way to the airport, informing him that Ronnie was coming home, and that there was going to be a get-together over Jerome's.

"She is?" Trey replied, which got Rock's attention.

"What time? I don't know where Jerome lives," Trey unconsciously conversed.

Whatever was going on, Rock knew that it was going on over Jerome's house. Rock pretended like he didn't hear the conversation.

"Let's go out and get a few beers," Rock suggested.

Next, Tony's phone rang. Nae was giving him the same message as Monie had just given Trey.

"I already know. I'll ride with Trey," Tony responded, suspicious that Rock may have been listening.

"What's goin' on?" Rock inquired, hoping that one of them would tell him what was really going on.

"Nothing's going on. Monie and Nae just want us to hurry up and get back to them. Trey said cleverly.

Rock knew something was going on. Once they left his house, he'd already made his mind up to follow them. He had a feeling that Ronnie may have been lurking around, but of course, he wasn't going to ask. Besides, no one was going to tell him the truth. When they made it back to Rock's house, Rick and Rock noticed how anxious Trey and Tony were to leave.

On the way to Trey's house, he realized a vehicle had been following him from the time they'd left Rock's house. He made a few crazy turns, almost ending up in an unfamiliar area. He ran a couple of red lights, to see if he was just being paranoid, or if the vehicle was actually following them. He stopped at the grocery store to pick up a few things to take with him to the party. The suspicious vehicle stopped at the store and parked at the other end of the parking lot.

Trey called Veronica and informed her of what was going on, and then went into the store. He told her to drive to the back of the store and pick him and Tony up. Rock sat in the parking lot, patiently waiting for them to come out of the store, and continue on with their journey.

Rock thinks he's so much smarter than everyone else, Trey thought to himself.

Shortly before they arrived at Jerome's house Rock called Tony, acting as if he'd forgotten to apologize for the way he acted.

"So, where are you headed?" Rock inquired.

"I'm taking a ride with Nae," Tony explained.

"Where's Trey?" Rock pried.

"He's probably somewhere with Monie." Tony had a feasible lie for each of Rock's questions.

Rock gave up for the night. He didn't have a clue as to which way he needed to go to get to Jerome's house. He figured that if Ronnie were in town, she would surface within the next few days. Even if finding her meant putting a tracking device on one of her sister's cars, he was going to use that as a last resort. He was confident that she was as eager to see him, as he was to see her.

Rock wasn't aware that he was being followed around town, just as he followed Trey and Tony.

Everyone had made it to Jerome's house except for Josh and the girls. Jerome's children were there waiting to reacquaint with their soon to be siblings. Jason and Corey were there waiting for the chance to see Monie and Nae again, unaware that Trey and Tony were going to be there.

The girls had finally arrived. Monie and Nae hadn't told Ronnie about the get-together. She walked in the house, amazed at how her mother was still able to pull things off directly under her nose. She was proud of Monie for keeping a surprise, for once in her life. Ronnie was glad to see that her mother and Juanita had patched things up.

This was the official house party that Ronnie always wanted but never had. The music was moderately loud making it merely impossible to hear. Rock called Trey's phone once more trying to pry information out of him about Ronnie.

Trey felt the vibration on his side, and tried to get to a secluded room to talk peacefully.

"Hello?" Trey answered.

"You must've decided to go to the club," Rock said, hoping the truth would come out.

Rock heard Veronica in the background calling Ronnie's name, trying to gain her attention.

"Ronnie. Monie. Come and meet Juanita's publisher!" Veronica yelled across the room.

"Was that somebody in your background calling Ronnie?" Rock asked with heightened emotions.

"No," Trey said as he found his way to the door and stepped outside of the house.

"Trey, I heard them call her twice. It sounded like Ms. Williams. She even called Monie. Trey, if you're lying to me I swear I'll kill you!"

Trey's forehead started beading with perspiration. He spoke up to Rock earlier that night, while he had a gun under his chin, but suddenly Rock was nowhere near and he became nervous.

"Trey, could I get your help with something for a minute?" Veronica asked.

Rock begged Trey to tell him where he was.

"I'll call back," Trey responded. He ended the call and turned his phone off.

As Trey tried to find Veronica, he passed Tony and tried telling him to turn his phone off. He motioned to Tony that he would talk to him later, after he finished helping Veronica unload a few cases of beer from her trunk that she had forgotten earlier. However, Tony wasn't able to hear him or understand his pitiful sign language. A few minutes later Tony's phone vibrated. Before he looked down at it, he already knew it was Rock trying to figure out where he and Trey had gone.

Rock drove by Veronica's house to see if a number was posted on the 'For Sale' sign. The agents' number was the only one listed. He tried to remember Monie or Nae's numbers, but they were at his house across town. He didn't know Jerome's last name so he could look it up in the phone book.

Rock was becoming emotionally distressed and miserable. He was usually the mastermind under any imaginable circumstance. For some reason or another, when it came to Ronnie, his mind went blank. At last, he called his mother, hoping she would call Trey and find out what was going on and where he was. After he'd explained the situation, his mother refused because of the immorality of his reasons. Even Rock's ability to misuse people for getting anything he wanted was slacking.

Ronnie pranced around the party, mingling with her family, that she missed dearly. Without the stress caused by Rock, she felt like she was in a whole new world.

Trey's phone vibrated again. This time it was Rock's mother.

"Hey auntie. What's going on?"

Rock's mother didn't know what to say.

"Rock called me again sounding like he was about to go postal. He said that you and Tony deserted him again, and you won't even tell him where you are. What's the real story behind your discrepancies? It sounds like either that girl or those drugs has got his head all messed up."

Trey told his aunt how Rock had been acting toward Ronnie. He and Tony were just taking precautions to prevent Ronnie from being in the same predicament as Shonte.

Rock's mother didn't know he was as corrupt as everyone presumed him to be. Rock usually told his mother a one-sided story, giving her the impression as if the world, and now all of his friends, were against him.

Rock's curiosity had gotten the best of him. He tried to disguise himself by driving his Jaguar. He went back to the store where Trey had parked his truck, and sat in the parking lot waiting for him to come back. He knew that Trey wouldn't expect him to be in his car, which usually sat in the garage.

He sat for a couple of hours, as the night grew later, watching the parking lot get emptier. Rock thought that Nae would bring him to get the car in the morning. As empty as the parking lot had gotten, he would have been in plain view. He suddenly had an urge to go home and think of a plan for the following day. All of a sudden, he saw headlights stopping next to Trey's truck. He started his car and waited for a few more seconds, until he saw Trey getting out of Nae's car.

He saw two other heads remain in Nae's car after he and Tony got out. He looked closer, and realized that there were two other females with Nae. For a moment he thought it may've been Veronica, but at 1:00a.m. Rock figured Veronica would have been cleaning up from the party or already in bed. Without headlights, he speeded his Jaguar around the darkened parking lot, heading for the two vehicles.

Before anyone realized that Rock was in the parking lot, he had maneuvered his car in front of them. With his headlights already shining on them, it was difficult for Nae to get out.

Ronnie had finally got caught. Rock got out, walked up to Nae's car, leaving his engine on and the driver door open. She tried hiding her face as she blocked the lights that were shining so brightly through the windshield of Nae's car. Rock opened the door, gently grabbed her by the hand, extending it, forcing her to get out.

"Why are you running from me?" Rock asked. He was happy to see her and didn't want to seem too aggressive.

Ronnie didn't know what to say or do. All of the confidence she had when she saw him during Thanksgiving had disappeared. "I just needed to get away," she replied while trying to keep her fear from being revealed.

Nae and Monie looked at Trey and Tony as if they had set them up. Tony threw his hands up, gesturing that he didn't know where Rock came from. Tony tipped back over to Nae's car and leaned over into her window to talk to her.

"I swear I didn't know he was here," Tony confessed. "I wouldn't have let Ronnie come if I would've known."

"Well, you need to do something to get his attention so I can get her out of here," Nae demanded.

"When you leave here, go straight to Jerome's house," Tony said discreetly.

Tony walked around the back of Nae's car towards Rock trying to get his attention. Rock stood a few feet away from Nae's car with his back towards his car talking to Ronnie. He stopped talking to Ronnie and looked up at Tony to study his objective. While Rock was facing the store and Tony, he never noticed that Trey had disappeared.

"Ya'll were partying with Ronnie all night and wouldn't tell me where you were. What kind of family is that?" Rock asked rhetorically.

Trey tried to get into the Jaguar to get the keys so that Ronnie and Nae would be able to get away. Rock grabbed Ronnie's hand harder and pulled her closer to him. Tony stopped in his tracks and tried to negotiate with Rock.

"Ronnie had a long day. Let her go and we'll all hook up tomorrow," Tony proposed.

"You need to get back in the truck and go wherever you were about to go," Rock suggested.

As Trey took a few more steps towards the Jaguar, Rock pulled his gun out and cocked it. He acted as if he was ready to shoot Tony, probably for his lack of cooperation and withholding information concerning Ronnie. Tony shook his head, threw his hands up and then let them drop freely to his side.

"So we're doing this again?" Tony asked, referring to the incident they'd had in Vine City.

"This time I swear on that unborn baby of yours that I will use it," Rock said convincingly nodding at the gun.

Ronnie tried to wiggle her hand out of Rock's hand as he pulled her harder away from Nae's car and towards the passenger side of his car. Tony continued talking to Rock, becoming a decoy for Trey to do whatever he was trying to do with the Jaguar. Tony shifted his eyes a few times in Trey's direction trying to figure out exactly what he was doing. Rock and Ronnie walked backwards getting further away from Nae's car and Tony.

"Man, it's too early in the morning for this foolishness. She's moved on with her life, now it's time for you to do the same," Tony said as he prayed under his breath for Rock's cooperation.

Trey pulled his gun out and snuck up to the Jaguar and turned the engine off. Rock turned around, now with his gun pointed in Trey's direction. Ronnie broke away in the midst of all the action.

Tony pulled his gun out while Rock's back was toward him. He helped Ronnie over to Nae's car and covered her as she got in.

"Give me my damn keys!" Rock shouted at Trey.

Rock turned around, now staring down the barrel of Tony's gun. In a much calmer manner, he attempted to plead with Tony to convince Trey into giving him his keys. He then realized he had two guns pointed at him, but didn't have Ronnie. He failed to realize that he was dealing with men who had performed operations with him and knew how he'd react in certain situations.

By the time Rock realized what was going on, Nae was turning into the street heading to Jerome's. He stood there looking at his cousin and best friend wondering why they'd betrayed him.

"Put your gun down and then we'll talk," Trey said.

Rock put his gun on the ground.

"Put all of 'em down," Tony added, knowing Rock always kept at least one or more backup guns. Rock put his guns on the ground and furiously paced back and forth between his car and Trey's truck, in disbelief that all of his efforts to find Ronnie were in vain.

Rock was embarrassed more so than frustrated. "Why didn't ya'll tell me where you were?" he asked.

"Why? So you could've come over there to act stupid?" Trey asked.

Trey threw Rock's keys over to him and walked toward his truck.

"I see that nothing's changed," Ronnie panted as she rubbed her sore hands together from Rock's ungentle tugs.

Monie sat in the back seat pouting. "I thought he'd gotten rid of that Jag," she asked rhetorically. "Where did he come from? He had to have been in the parking lot somewhere watching Trey's truck." She was starting to think like the lawyer she was training to become.

Ronnie and Nae shrugged their shoulders.

"I wonder if he knows where Jerome lives," Monie thought aloud.

Veronica and Jerome were finishing up the last few dishes, when she saw headlights coming up the driveway. She was sure Ronnie was going to stay at Nae's or with Monie over Trey's house. This way they could stay up late and be as loud as they wanted to, while they caught up on each other's drama.

Ronnie walked in first. Her eyes were glossy and her face was red and semi chapped. Veronica knew that something was wrong. She figured the girls may have run into trouble.

"What's wrong?" Jerome asked.

"It's cold…" Ronnie said, shivering.

Jerome knew that her heavy leather coat trimmed with fur was warm enough to keep her from trembling, especially in fifty something degree weather. He knew it was more to the story than what she was telling. They knew Monie would tell the story in its entirety.

Monie walked in next with Ronnie's luggage. Nae shortly followed with the lightest bag.

"Ma, can you believe Rock was waiting for us in the parking lot to drop Trey and Tony off?" Monie offered.

"How did he know you were here?" Jerome asked.

Ronnie wasn't able to speak. She just shook her head. Tony called Nae on her cell phone.

"Ya'll make it back to Jerome's okay?" Tony asked.

"Yes, but how did Rock know that Trey's truck was at the store," Nae asked suspiciously.

"He must have followed me…it's been a crazy night…I'll have to tell you about it when you come home," Tony confessed. "Nae, I'm sorry. I should've listened to you when you said not to go with Rock and Rick."

"Rick was there too? Why was he there? Why couldn't he have taken him to the damn airport!" Nae shouted before Tony could say anything. She then realized she was in front of her mother and Jerome, and covered her mouth as if she'd just made a mistake.

"It wasn't a run to the airport. Like I said, I'll tell you about it when you get home."

"I'm staying over here all night," Nae told Tony and then looked up at Jerome. "If that's alright with you?" as if she had been previously invited.

Tony knew he was jeopardizing his relationship again with the stupid things he did. He felt like the whole Williams family was going to blame him and Trey for Rock's stupid actions. He lied across the bed thinking about how he could've made the day go in a totally different direction. If only he had listened to Nae, maybe Ronnie wouldn't have gotten in that predicament. He felt like he'd let Nae down once again.

Chapter 20

*F*riday, the day after Christmas, Jerome awoke first and decided that a breakfast outing would be the ideal thing for his new family. The girls made it through Christmas without a drop of drama. "This causes for a celebration," Jerome thought.

He woke everyone up by 9a.m. to begin their day. He wanted the day to be a fun-filled day for the entire family. His children and Veronica's girls were getting along perfectly together. He'd planned to take pictures and rent movies, which would set the mood for some bonding time between two, soon to be joined, families.

After breakfast, Jerome asked Ronnie, Monie and his daughters, Cynthia and Sabrina, to ride with him to the movie rental store and pick up some movies. Veronica and the rest of the family headed home. As they headed to Jerome's house, Veronica's real estate agent called her on her cell phone to inform her that someone was interested in her house.

"Veronica, how are you? Listen, I have a handsome young man who would love to see the inside of your home." The agent ranted on, refusing to let Veronica accept or decline the offer. "Are you available to stop by and assist me in showing the home?"

"Sure. I could be there in twenty minutes," Veronica said once she finally got a chance to respond.

"The young man says he already knows you," the agent said. "I'll see you in a few minutes."

Veronica was so excited about the offer that she didn't realize the agent said that the young man already knew her. Veronica took a detour so she could stop by the house and meet the potential buyer.

Veronica pulled up to her house and parked behind a hunter green Jaguar.

"The buyer must have some money," Veronica stated jovially and laughed along with Nae.

Veronica said a brief prayer before she stepped out of the car. "Oh Lord, let this be the perfect person for my house."

She and Nae walked toward the garage. Nae heard a very familiar, male voice. Before she approached him, Nae grabbed her mother's arm, pulling her back, and pointing in the direction in which the voice was coming from.

"That's Rock's voice," Nae whispered into her mother's ear.

Veronica listened carefully as the man continued talking to the agent. Her eyes stretched to nearly the size of quarters. She stared into Nae's eyes, wondering what to do next. Nae turned around and headed back toward the car. Veronica stood indecisively, somewhat in limbo, wondering if she should follow Nae, or follow through with her commitment. Once Nae had walked half way down the driveway, she turned and looked back. Rock and the agent were walking out of the house, into the garage and greeted Veronica.

"Veronica!" the agent yelled. "I'm glad you could make it. I didn't know you would be here so soon. I didn't hear you drive up," the agent said swiftly.

"How are you Barbara? I can't stay long. I just wanted to show up and assist you in any way possible," Veronica said trying to get away from Rock as quickly as possible.

"Veronica, this is Mr. Wilcox. He said the two of you already knew each other. He wanted to know if he would be able to contact you directly in case he had any other questions."

"No…that's inappropriate and unacceptable. If you *need* anything Mr. Wilcox, Barbara is the point of contact," stated Veronica, trying to remain as professional as she could under the circumstances.

Barbara cordially smiled, but wondered what type of relationship they had in order for Veronica to react in such a surly way. Veronica was suddenly in a rush to conclude their meeting and excuse herself.

Veronica started walking away from Barbara and Rock. Barbara excused herself and trotted down the driveway to catch up with Veronica.

"Are you okay? Did I do something to offend you? If I did, I'm terribly sorry," Barbara emphasized.

"No, it's not you at all. He knows I can't stand him. He's trying to use this situation to get to my daughter. They kinda had this love-hate relationship going on, more hate than love from my daughter's perspective, if you know what I mean," Veronica explained.

"Do you not want me to do business with him?" Barbara asked. "I can cut him off right now. It's your call."

"I don't care to do business with him, but if he wants the house and he has the money, so be it. I will put my personal feelings aside to conduct business *only* with him."

It was just a process that allowed Rock to go through the motions of seeing the house.

Veronica knew that at one point Rock was there more than she was. He probably knew the layout of the house better than she and all three of her daughters. She was disgusted at the thought of Rock trying to play her like a fool.

Barbara felt as if she was in the middle of something that had gone sour. She wasn't sure how to approach Rock when she went back up the driveway to talk with him. She knew he wasn't Veronica's first choice of buyers to sell her home to. Barbara had acquired a friendship with Veronica and wanted to make sure that she kept her best interest at heart. However, she also knew that Rock's financial status would allow him to buy the house, therefore, she started thinking of ways to create loopholes that would disqualify him in other aspects.

Veronica got in the car and let out a sigh of disgust.

"Who is he?" Sabrina asked.

"You don't want to know," Nae responded.

"I think I already know. He looks a lot like someone I used to date in high school. Is his name Will?"

"No, his name is Rakeem," Nae replied.

"Yeah, Rakeem Wilcox. Everyone called him Will back then," Sabrina explained.

Veronica and Nae's curiosity grew tremendously. They had to find out what she knew about Rock. First, they wanted to find out everything she'd gone through before they revealed the fact that he recently dated Ronnie and nearly killed her.

"What happened between you two?" Nae asked.

"I found out that he was crazy and I left him alone."

"How long were you involved?" Veronica inquired.

"About eight months. Then I found out that he was sleeping with my friend Tee Tee. I heard they supposedly had a child together. I never believed he fathered that little boy," Sabrina muttered.

Veronica couldn't believe her ears. Nae had heard about the little boy ever since Ronnie started dealing with Rock. Nae couldn't believe how closely all of them were connected.

"Is he laying the pipe that good? How does he make every woman he messes with fall so deeply in love with him? It must be some kind of fake charm he throws at them. Ronnie is going through some drama with him now," Veronica said while getting more furious by the moment.

"I heard about all the drama she was going through, but everyone was calling him Rock. I never knew him by Rock," Sabrina added.

Sabrina's memory had just been triggered. At the party, she had remembered Trey's face from somewhere, but just couldn't figure out where. She didn't want to get too close to him because she knew he was with Monie. It was now all coming back to her slowly.

Veronica remained in deep thought the entire way home. As they drove up into the driveway, Veronica asked Sabrina if Jerome knew about her relationship with Rock.

Sabrina told her that her father found out about the relationship after it was over. Rock had just begun selling drugs at that time, so she never introduced them. She knew her father wouldn't have approved of her dating him.

Veronica was fuming, but she could not let that spoil her day. Jerome had gone the extra mile to make the day a *stress free* day for everyone. She refused to let his efforts be in vain.

Veronica and Nae walked into the house as if nothing was bothering them. However, she couldn't fool Jerome. He knew immediately that something was wrong. He told the girls to start the movie while he went into the kitchen to start the popcorn. Jerome discreetly grabbed Veronica by the hand and snuck into his office, which was in a room adjacent to the kitchen.

He closed the door and sat her in his cozy computer chair. Jerome told her to close her eyes, as he briefly massaged her shoulders, enabling her to relax. He went around to the front of her and stooped down, looking up at her.

"Honey, what's wrong?" he asked.

She didn't think it was her place to tell him about Rock and Sabrina. However, she felt she would have been totally wrong if she didn't tell him about Rock's phony attempt to buy her house. Her mind was playing tricks on her. She took a deep breath and began telling him what had happened.

"Rock wants to buy your house?" Jerome asked suspiciously.

"He claimed he did," she replied, confused.

"This is just another trick to get to Ronnie," Jerome added.

She opened her mouth to tell him about Sabrina, but nothing came out. "Why even bother…that was over ten years ago," Veronica thought. He couldn't get mad about it now anyway. It's now considered spilled milk. Besides, she didn't want to rain on his parade.

"Is there anything else you want to tell me?" Jerome asked.

Veronica snapped back into the conversation. She'd missed half of the words Jerome was saying while conducting her thought process.

Jerome repeated himself. "You *can* talk to me about anything."

Before they headed out to watch the movies with the girls, she stood up and hugged Jerome.

"Did you know that Sabrina was once involved with Rock?" she asked, taking advantage of the offer he had just given her.

"Involved? What do you mean, involved? My Sabrina, with Rock-where'd you come up with that foolishness?"

"It's not foolishness. That's what she told me. She even knew his full name."

"Honey, I'm not calling you a liar but…that's nonsense."

"She said back in the day when they were in school, they called him Will."

He remembered the name as clearly as if it was yesterday. His eyes stretched and his bottom lip dropped almost to the floor. He thought about the days when his children were in school. He'd always hear his son, Kevin, talking about Wilcox.

He gently grabbed Veronica by the arm, stopping her before she walked out the door. "What's Rock's real name?" he asked.

"Rakeem Wilcox," she answered.

"Well I'll be damned."

"Oh, *now* you remember," Veronica said sarcastically while sashaying out of the office door into the kitchen, looking back at him out of the corner of her eye.

"I don't think he was that crazy back then. If he hurt her, she never told me about it," Jerome stated as he followed behind Veronica like a lost and hungry puppy.

Jerome continued following Veronica, and the popcorn, as it left trails of a heavenly aroma throughout the house. He sat on the sofa next to Veronica, propped his feet up on the table, and placed his arm around her.

"So Sabrina, I hear that you and Ronnie have something in common," Jerome said buoyantly.

Sabrina gave Veronica a sharp, piercing look that would've cut her, if looks could cut. She then turned her piercing stare towards Ronnie, and then back towards her father.

"Daddy, not now. Can't we all just watch the movie?" Sabrina asked.

"Oh yeah. Go ahead and watch the movie. I'll just talk to Ronnie about how similar your tastes are in men," Jerome said jovially.

"Jerome!" Veronica shouted. "This is not a game and it's certainly not funny."

"I'm sorry. I just had to put it out there. We're all family now. That's something they both should know about."

"Ronnie, what my father is trying to say is that both of us have dated Will at some point or another, or Rock, or *whatever* his name is now!" Sabrina shouted. She got up and grabbed her purse as if she was about to leave.

"Sabrina! Sweetie calm down before you get yourself all worked up," Jerome pleaded.

He jumped up and tried assisting her to sit back down.

"Daddy, stop treating me like I'm handicapped!" she yelled.

"I'm not treating you like you're handicapped, but since you want to act like a child, I'm treating you like my child."

Ronnie felt like she was the cause of this riot outbreak among the family. She excused herself. "I need to start packing for my flight in the morning," she said.

Ronnie went upstairs to call the airlines and get her flight changed. She wanted to get back to California as soon as possible, and leave the bickering in Atlanta.

Shortly afterwards, Veronica went upstairs to lure Ronnie back down to be with the rest of the family. Veronica heard Ronnie talking on the phone.

"I'm tired of being here with the perfect Brady family. You can stay as long as you want, but I'm trying to leave tomorrow," Ronnie confessed to Josh. "Your family is acting strange too?"

Veronica didn't want to eavesdrop, but she was already disturbed by what she was hearing.

"Your mom's publisher is moving in with her?" Ronnie asked.

Veronica knew then that she was talking to Josh. Veronica tapped on the door asking Ronnie if she could come in the room with her. She beckoned for her mother to come in, and subsequently ended the conversation with Josh by hanging up. Veronica didn't hear when Ronnie asked Josh to get the reservations changed for the next day.

"Sweetie, I thought you were going to be here for a few more days," Veronica said innocently.

"No…I wanted to stay longer, but we have to get back by tomorrow," Ronnie said.

"If *I* pay to get the reservations changed, would you stay?" Veronica suggested.

Veronica sensed that Ronnie wasn't thrilled or comfortable with being around Jerome's daughters. Veronica tried to reach out to her lost daughter and find out what was wrong with her.

Ronnie loved Jerome dearly, but she felt awkward by bringing him into her situation with Rock. In Ronnie's mind, this only adding fuel to the flames by knowing that Jerome already dealt with him before. Although there was nothing she could've done, Ronnie felt strange having a stepsister who made love to the same man she did.

"Did Rock put Sabrina through all the stuff he's put me through?" Ronnie asked her mother.

Veronica didn't know what to say. She shook her head and tried hugging Ronnie. She noticed that in a strange way, Ronnie kept pulling away from her. She didn't want to say anything to offend Ronnie, but her patience was wearing thin with her reoccurring attitude. She tried to be as considerate as she could to Ronnie's new transitions, but the task was becoming more difficult by the minute.

"Ronnie, what is going on with you?" Veronica asked again.

"I told you—nothing is going on. I'm okay."

Deep down inside her heart, Ronnie was still plotting on how to get rid of Rock. There was a void inside of her that would not be filled—not until Rock was completely out of her life. She subconsciously knew that Rock was the reason she never fully committed to Josh. As much as she tried to deny it, Rock still had a piece of her heart.

Ronnie heard Monie's phone ring downstairs. For a moment there was dead silence, and then Jerome's voice blared out "What's he doing calling your phone?"

Veronica listened closely to find out who he was talking to. She and Ronnie crept downstairs to get a better understanding the situation. Ronnie knew that Rock must have called Monie's phone. By the time Veronica reached the bottom of the stairs, she found Jerome giving Monie and Nae a lecture.

"When are you girls gonna learn? The only thing you have to do is get your numbers changed. If Trey and Tony love you as much as they claim, they'll look out for your safety and protect you from Rock."

Josh was packing his bags in preparation to leave.

"Why are you leaving so soon?" Juanita asked.

"I have to get back to California," Josh replied without looking up at his mother.

Jason stood in Josh's bedroom doorway listening to the conversation between his mother and brother. He knew something was bothering Josh. It was *obviously* more than what he was telling their mother.

Juanita asked Jason to talk to Josh. Hopefully, he could convince him to stay longer. She hugged Josh and then left the room. Jason closed the door and asked his brother what was wrong.

"Why is mom letting this stranger move in with her? Didn't she learn her lesson from Tyrone?" Josh asked.

"I guess not," Jason replied. "If dating all of Atlanta is going to make her happy, let her go for it. She can't tell us what to do in *our homes*, so don't try to tell her what to do in hers."

There was a knock on Josh's bedroom door. Before the boys could respond, Raymond opened the door.

"Hey guys, I'm ordering pizza. What kind do you eat?" Raymond asked.

Josh and Jason looked at each other as if they had been violated.

"We're not hungry," Jason said.

"Oh come on guys. We can eat pizza and get to know each other a little better," Raymond suggested.

"Man, we're not…" Jason tried to reiterate the fact they weren't hungry, when Josh cut him off in mid-sentence.

"It doesn't matter. We'll eat whatever you order," Josh chimed in, trying to keep the peace.

"Okay, I'm sorry if I offended you." Raymond apologized and closed the door.

"Man, ease up a little. He's just trying to be nice," Jason explained.

"I have a bad feeling about him. Have you read anything he's published?" Josh asked.

"No I haven't. I'm about to head over to see Ronnie for a minute. Do you wanna ride so you can see Monie?" Josh said teasing his brother.

Josh tossed the keys back and forth from one hand to the other as he walked down the stairs. They walked passed the sofa where their mother was tightly cuddled under Raymond's arm.

"You guys are leaving already? You *know* you can't leave before you sit down and have lunch with Raymond and me," Juanita begged.

She got up and followed them into the kitchen. She pulled out a chair from the kitchen table and sat down, waiting for them to start a decent conversation with her.

Jason grabbed an individual size juice out of the refrigerator. He stared back at his mother, as he opened it and gulped most of it down at once.

"Don't leave," Juanita begged.

"We'll be right back, and besides, you seem pretty occupied without us. So, we're going to leave you and dude here to handle your business," Josh stated.

"The name's Raymond," Raymond said at the end of Josh's statement, as he walked into the kitchen. Josh and Jason looked at Raymond, and then at their mother, and turned and walked away from both of them.

Juanita stared out of the kitchen window as her boys drove out of the driveway.

"I've never seen them act like that before," Juanita said.

"Maybe they've never seen you so in love before with such a guy," Raymond added.

Juanita thought that remark was a bit arrogant. She liked Raymond very much, but she wasn't at all in love with him. She felt the tension between him and her boys and figured she may've been overreacting.

From that one incident alone, Juanita knew that she would have to start nipping things in the bud right away before he got carried away, thinking that he was the master of her domain.

"Sweetheart, I am not in love with you."

Raymond looked at her as if she'd cursed his mother.

"Maybe I'm the confused one, but I thought that's what you moaned last night," Raymond said sarcastically.

"I may have moaned that I loved the things you do to me. I do care about you, but I'm not in love," Juanita said.

Raymond nodded his head, walked back into the den, and continued to watch TV, leaving her in the kitchen alone. She also walked back into the den and sat next to him, waiting for him to say something else. He never said a word or even put his arm back around her. He just sat there, watching TV until the pizza arrived.

Juanita started second-guessing her decision about attempting to have a relationship with Raymond. She knew that if they had any type of partnership, it could only be a business related one. A personal or intimate relationship with Raymond would only be a waste of time, feeling that it would be unsuccessful from the beginning.

She told herself several times that if she could tolerate him just long enough to get the book published and distributed, she would leave him alone for good.

"Nita. You have any cash on you to pay the pizza man?" Raymond asked. "My wallet is upstairs."

"I could run and get it for you," Juanita suggested.

"No, we don't want to keep him waiting. I'm sure he has other deliveries to make."

Juanita had a twenty-dollar bill in her pocket that Jason had given her for the juice that she'd bought for him earlier. She reluctantly gave the pizza deliveryman the twenty-dollar bill, and then a two-dollar tip, after receiving the change.

Juanita placed the pizza on the table, and turned around nearly bumping into Raymond, as he tried to place two plates on the table. He gave her a quick peck on the cheek and told her that he'd give the money back to her later.

"What's wrong sweetheart?" Raymond asked. "Why aren't you eating?"

"I'm going to wait for my boys to get back. I want to have lunch with my son. I haven't seen him in over a month."

"Your son isn't too anxious to have lunch with you."

Juanita looked at him out of the corner of her eye, and rolled them sarcastically. She went upstairs to get away from him for a while. Her curiosity led her to pick up his wallet, and look in it, just to see if he *really* had any money at all. She counted a thousand dollars in hundred dollar bills and over six hundred dollars in fifties. She wondered, *"Why did he ask if he could stay here with me until he was able to get an apart-*

ment of his own. I understand his apartment was burned down in a fire, but he has plenty of money."

She heard Raymond trying to slowly creep up the stairs. Juanita figured he may have been trying to catch her in the act of doing something she had no business doing. Acting as if she was looking for something in the closet, Juanita put his wallet back on the dresser. He gently opened the door and asked, "Can you find it?"

Juanita looked up into the mirror and saw Raymond standing in the doorway, with his arms crossed, looking at her. She looked back down into the *decoy box* that she'd found in her closet, deliberately ignoring him, hoping that he'd get the hint and go back downstairs.

He came in the room and sat on the bed, watching her every move. She closed the box and put it back in the corner of the closet. As she walked passed him to go into the computer room, she looked directly in his eyes. Just when Juanita booted the computer to play solitaire, she felt a draft from the door opening. He stood behind her, telling her which moves to make.

Juanita became annoyed with his presence. She asked for the twenty dollars that she had spent for the pizza, to go get gas in her car.

"Oh, baby I have to go to the bank to get some money. I promise I'll give it to you as soon as I get it. Have one of your boys to get your gas," Raymond replied.

She didn't know why she thought he was a different breed of man. He seemed to be a businessman, but she suddenly didn't know what kind of business he was running. She was sure that he had money, but he seemed to be inconsiderably stingy.

"You should be working on your story," Raymond said.

Juanita remained quiet, playing her game of solitaire, thinking of ways to get this *con artist* out of her house. Raymond's cell phone vibrated loudly. He perpetrated like he wasn't interested in the call. He looked at the number and walked into the hallway to talk.

Juanita noticed he talked in a rather unusual and discreet manner. The computer chair squeaked as she leaned back, resting her head on the back of the chair, trying to listen to what he was saying. He walked closer toward the stairs, getting as far away from Juanita as he could, without actually going downstairs.

"I told you I'm with a client. I'll give you a call when I get finished," Raymond whispered, as Juanita heard him.

He came back into the room as if nothing had happened. He tried to rub Juanita's shoulders to help her relax. She jumped up and headed downstairs. He followed her, purposely agitating her.

"I'm going to get some gas!" she yelled.

"Why don't you let those one of those grown boys of yours go and get it? You baby them too much. They're grown men. Let them act like grown men."

Juanita had taken all that she could stand from him, especially talking about her grown sons.

"Do you have a problem with my boys? You're just as grown as they are, so why can't you take your grown ass to the gas station to get my gas. That's the least you can do!" she exclaimed. "Obviously someone's been babying you, but I *refuse* to keep it going."

"You don't have to get so feisty. I'll go get the damn gas if you want me to, but all you had to do was ask," Raymond responded.

He picked up his car keys off of the table and put them in his pocket, before grabbing her keys. *"What kind of man would leave a woman stranded,"* she thought.

"You're just gonna leave me without any transportation?" she asked.

"Your boys should be back shortly," Raymond stated as he walked out the door.

"Damn, I sure know how to pick 'em," Juanita said under her breath.

An hour and a half later, Josh and Jason arrived back at Juanita's house.

"Ma, I thought you were gone. Where's your car?" Jason asked while snacking on some chips. He put a bag of bulky hardware on the table and continued his conversation with his mother. Josh and Jason had bought some new locks for their mother's house, with intentions of putting Raymond out, once they got back.

"Raymond went to fill it up the car with gas, almost two hours ago," she explained.

"Have you tried to call his cell phone?" Josh asked.

"No," she replied, letting out a sigh of frustration and anger.

Raymond already knew he had Juanita's car entirely too long and hadn't been close to a gas station.

"Ray, just one more time before you go back to work," his wife moaned. "I swear I haven't been intimate with anyone since we separated. I look forward for your visits to see the children so we can…you know. I miss you, won't you come back home?"

Raymond didn't believe a word she said. He looked at her as though she needed to be admitted to the insane asylum. During the ten years of dating and two years of marriage, she may have been faithful for one of those years. He only stayed with her for the sake of the children. At times, he even regretted ever marrying her.

"Your infidelity is what led to our separation. You should've known that you were going to miss me before you started sleeping with…whatever his name is," Raymond replied to his wife, Desiree, trying to remember her adulterer's name.

He tried walking out of the bedroom door, but she threw and caressed her body against him repeatedly, trying to seduce him.

"Desiree, I told you I had to go!" Raymond yelled.

He grabbed her by the arms and threw her across the room onto the bed. He stormed towards the door and remembered Juanita's keys were still in the bedroom. He didn't want to go back in bedroom, but he had no choice. When he slung the door bedroom open, Desiree had the keys dangling from her finger.

"I guess you may need these huh? Who do they belong to?" Desiree asked deviously.

Raymond walked over to Desiree, slowly and calmly, until he was standing directly over her.

"Until you get your shit together don't question mine," Raymond said calmly and snatched the key ring from around her finger. He then walked out of the house. He looked at his watch and realized he'd been gone for over two hours. He knew Juanita was going to have a fit, but it was nothing he hadn't handled before. He was confident he had everything under control.

On the way to the gas station, Raymond made a couple of stops. He went to see a few of his friends on the street corner near his house.

Juanita sat at the table, too angry to eat or even talk to her boys. She picked up the phone and dialed Raymond's cell phone number. After five attempts, she still didn't receive an answer. Juanita didn't want her sons to see her perform immaturely. However, she honestly felt like throwing bricks through Raymond's car windows, while stomping the roof in. The sad part is Juanita know she couldn't blame anyone but herself.

Jason tried to warn her about Raymond several times, but Juanita refused to listen. She was furious and embarrassed. She didn't want her boys to see that she'd made yet another bad decision about men. She didn't want them to think she was whore. As children, they weren't able to comprehend what was going on. They didn't see all of the company she kept while they were asleep.

However, they were now old enough to understand what had been going on throughout the years since their father died. She could no longer disguise her promiscuity. Even though Juanita wanted to maintain her classy image, everything seemed as if it were slowly falling apart.

Josh and Jason knew their mother suffered from loneliness, and maybe even depression. They could see that she found it difficult to find one true love. They starred at her, as Juanita sat at the table in a daze.

Juanita looked back over her life and realized her mistakes. She'd gotten into many relationships for all of the wrong reasons. She thought about the hearts that she had broken over the years, and now hoped and prayed that she would never have to suffer the same pain that she caused.

Josh looked out the kitchen window and saw Raymond coming up the driveway in Juanita's car. He began briefly pacing the floor, mumbling something under his breath. He knew he couldn't afford to get locked up in Atlanta for doing something stupid. Besides, he still had to make it back to work in California in a few days.

As soon as Raymond walked in the house, Juanita looked up at him. She tried to contain herself, but the irate behavior overpowered her body, mind, and sense of speech.

"I've never known anyone to take three hours to go get some damn gas! Where have you been in my car!?" Juanita inquired.

She took a few steps towards him and took a few tactful whiffs of his clothing. A burnt, unpleasant odor that was unfamiliar to her penetrated her nose. It smelled like a woman's perfume, mixed with marijuana mixed with something else. She didn't know what to make of the awful smell that Raymond had brought back with him.

"Ma, he's been smokin' weed," Jason said.

"Yeah, after he left his other woman," Josh added.

"Nita, you need to control your boys. You're gonna let 'em talk to me like that? Raymond asked.

"Yeah…they're right. I want to hear what kind of lies you have lined up to justify where you've been, what you've been doing, and with whom," Juanita said sternly.

"I stopped by to see my kids. You get a chance to see your boys whenever you want to, and you're not gonna stop me from seeing mine. While I was there my brother in law, I mean my ex brother in law, came by with a joint. So, I smoked a little bit with him," Raymond tried to explain, half incoherently.

"Man, you've gotta go. My mom doesn't deserve to go through this again. You need to go and get your stuff so you can leave," Josh told Raymond.

"You don't even live in the state of Georgia anymore, so how can you say what needs to happen here. This is your mom's house, not yours. If she wants me to leave she'll ask me," Raymond slurred. "Ain't that right baby?" Looking for Juanita to defend him and agree with him.

"Raymond, I'd like to end our publishing contract now and I'd like for you to leave," Juanita said politely.

"Come on baby, don't let these boys brainwash you and turn you against me. They don't have nobody, and they don't want you to have nobody. You said that I could stay here. Where am I supposed to go?"

"That's not my problem. You're a grown man. Go back to your baby's mama, or wife, or whatever she is to you," Juanita replied nonchalantly.

Raymond stormed upstairs to get his already partially packed bags. Juanita crept in the room to make sure he didn't take anything that didn't belong to him. Josh and Jason watched from the hallway to ensure that he didn't to anything to hurt their mother.

He put one of his bags on his shoulder and reached in his pocket with his other hand. He pulled out some money and threw it on the bed. Picking up the rest of his bags, he looked Juanita
directly in the eyes as he walked past her. Although she was curious, she didn't bother to ask what the money was for.

Juanita, Jason and Josh all followed him down the stairs one by one, just *waiting* for him to turn around to say something to Juanita.

"What's the money for?" Juanita finally asked once he made it to the car.

Raymond looked at her as if he had some animosity towards her. "I'm a man of my word…read your contract."

Jason and Josh stood in the garage, while Juanita stood in the middle of the driveway as they watched Raymond drive away. She closed her eyes, taking a couple of deep breaths. Juanita had to force herself to maintain her composure, long enough to turn around and face her boys.

Tightly folding her arms across her chest, she asked herself, "How could you allow them to see you fail at another relationship?" She put her head down, swiftly walking between the boys, and went into the house. By the time she made it to the stairs, she was tired. It felt as if the energy she had just minutes ago had fled from her body all at once.

She stood at the bottom of the stairs, for a brief moment, before proceeding. She was trying to understand why Raymond left the money on the bed, without an explanation. What casualties she should expect to follow.

Juanita sat on the edge of the bed and opened the nightstand drawer. She unfolded the contract that she and Raymond signed. As she read the contract, she saw the part that stated he would have to pay her $500 if he failed to fulfill his end of the agreement.

She grabbed the money and unfolded it. "Five crisp hundred dollar bills," she whispered. *"At least I got something out of this failed relationship,"* she said to herself. With disbelief, Juanita held the money in her hands and went downstairs to show the boys.

Josh was working on the front door while Jason worked on the back door. Juanita was wondering what they were doing. They had already started taking the doorknobs off to change the locks.

Juanita smiled as she watched her boys work very diligently at trying to keep her safe. She was proud that she'd raised such distinguished gentlemen. Shaking her head and thinking to herself, *"If I never find another lover, I'll always have two perfect men in my life."*

Chapter 21

*V*eronica was excited that she was able to pick up her maid of honor and bride maids' dresses. She only had two months left to get everything in tact before the wedding. One of her biggest concerns was Nae's pregnancy. Her due date was very close to the wedding. Veronica wasn't sure what size Nae was going to be when she marched down the isle with her. She would just have to get Nae's dress at a later time.

Veronica and Juanita talked and laughed over an early morning breakfast. It was just like they used to do years ago when they first met. They walked through the mall, window-shopping and exchanging home décor ideas before they picked up the dresses.

As they walked into the bridal store, Veronica's phone rang. She hesitated before answering, thinking that it may have been Jerome wanting her to run some errands for him. She was enjoying her girls' day out. On this day she was selfish; refusing to do anything other than spend her last few days with her best friend, as a single woman. Finally, on the last ring, she decided to answer the phone.

"Hello?" she answered.

"Ma, Nae's having contractions! What do I do!?" Monie asked.

"Where's Tony?" Veronica asked hysterically.

"He's somewhere with Trey!" Monie responded.

"Call Tony and tell him to meet you at the hospital," Veronica advised her obviously confused daughter.

Monie called both Trey and Tony's cell phones, but couldn't reach either one of them. She packed a hospital bag for Nae, while assisting her in walking around the apartment to try and help ease the pains of the contractions. Monie started feeling nauseous, knowing that she didn't have the stomach to assist in any type of medical situation.

While she sat on the sofa coping with excruciating pain, Nae rushed Monie to finish packing her bag. Monie was in the bedroom trying to remember everything Nae told her to pack. Nae attempted to call Tony once more.

As she walked to the door carrying Nae's overnight bag, two purses and the baby's car seat, Monie struggled to keep her balance. She looked back and noticed the seat and inseam of Nae's maternity pants were slightly wet. She quickly found a bath towel to spread on the sofa and told Nae to sit on it while she packed everything into the car.

Monie had more responsibility on her hands than she was willing to handle alone. She knew her sister was depending on her for everything. Monie wished Ronnie were there to help her through this tough situation. *"I need to call Ronnie as soon as I get Nae to the hospital,"* she thought.

Nae's water had broken while Monie was loading the car, leaving her pants saturated. When Monie walked through the door to help Nae get to the car, she noticed drops of, what she thought, was urine and blood on the floor. It was exactly in the spots where Nae tried to make it to the door on her own.

"Do you have to go to the bathroom before we leave?" Monie asked sincerely.

"No. I just need to get to the hospital before this baby comes!" Nae yelled as she panted, waddling to the door.

Nae understood that her sister was young, naïve, and nervous, and was only trying to help. However, she was easily agitated, due to her condition, which intensified Monie's disorientation.

Veronica and Juanita rushed to get the dresses, and then headed to meet Monie and see what the problem was. Veronica broke all of the speed limit laws trying to get to the hospital.

"This must be a false labor," Veronica thought aloud. "She isn't due for another month and a half."

Knowing the *witch* that Nae was capable of being during a time of distress, Veronica called Monie back to ensure that she was able to handle everything accordingly. She heard Nae in the background yelling at Monie about how slow she was driving. Monie's patience with Nae was getting short.

Monie was ready to snap on Nae at any minute. She knew she had to withstand more than she normally would, but it was becoming extremely overwhelming. Veronica tried talking to Monie, calmly explaining that she should try to comfort Nae as much as possible until they arrived at the hospital.

"Ma, she's fussing at me and I'm already over the speed limit," Monie explained.

Monie's mind flashed to the aggressive lawyer she was trying to become. She realized that she couldn't, under any circumstances, allow her emotional state to become a factor in showing her vulnerability.

She was suddenly too perturbed to cry, but yet too determined to let this situation get the best of her. She began to feel bitter towards Tony. He seemed to never be around when he was needed to perform his husbandly or fatherly duties, which he claimed he so *adamantly* wanted.

Monie continued to tune out Nae and listen to her mother.

"Monie, I need you to go a little faster!" Nae yelled.

"Dammit Nae. Would you shut the hell up? I'm already going seventy," Monie yelled back at her.

Nae knew that once Monie snapped like that, she needed to keep her thoughts to herself to prevent a bad situation from getting worse. Veronica was surprised as well to hear Monie go off the deep end.

"You need to get Tony on the phone instead of fussing at me!" Monie demanded.

"If he was here for you, I wouldn't have to go through all of this," Monie mumbled under her breath.

"Sweetheart, just stay cool and I'll meet you at the hospital in a little while," Veronica assured Monie.

Monie rushed Nae to the maternity ward's door and ran inside, trying to find a nurse to get Nae to a delivery room. Twenty minutes later, Veronica and Juanita showed up at the hospital. Monie was sitting in the waiting room outside of the delivery room, too exhausted to stay with Nae for the delivery.

"Has anyone found Tony yet?" Veronica asked.

Monie looked at her mother out of the corner of her eye and didn't say a word. She dug through her purse to find her cell phone to call Trey, hopefully to see if he and Tony were still together.

"Trey, where have you been? I've been trying to find you and Tony all morning," Monie explained.

"Tony's with Rock…don't…don't tell Nae," Trey stuttered.

"Don't tell Nae! She's at the hospital in labor."

"Okay, I'll let him know," Trey said emotionless.

Monie sensed that he was being quite indifferent. She heard several different men's voices in the background. "Are you alright?" she asked and waited patiently for a response.

"Where are you?" she asked again, hearing nothing but silence. The phone went to a dial tone due to bad reception.

"How did you say this plan was going down?" Tony asked Rock.

"If we leave this afternoon, we'll be in Miami by nightfall and make the drop by midnight," Rock replied as Tony, Rick and Rome listened.

They were headed to Miami for their final operation. Tony and Trey had already promised Monie and Nae that they had nothing more to do with Rock and his drug operations.

"So, what are we supposed to tell the girls?" Tony asked.

"Tell them you're going to an out of town funeral," Rick replied.

"Once we get back to Atlanta, we'll all have a half million dollars a piece and it'll all be over for good," Rock added.

The sound of that much money was overly enticing to Trey. This was especially good since he'd planned to purchase a three-carat, platinum engagement ring for Monie in a few months, as a graduation gift. After standing in the middle of the dining room floor in thought, he headed to the kitchen to announce that Nae was in labor.

After hearing this news, Rock knew that there was probably nothing he could do to get Tony to fulfill his commitment and complete this operation. Nae was always his first priority. Rock took this as an opportunity to finally find out where Jerome lived, so that the next time, finding Ronnie would be easier when she came to town. Rock strangely became the most compassionate and understanding person anyone had ever known him to be.

"Do you need me to drive you over there?" Rock asked Tony.

"No, Trey will take me," Tony replied, knowing there must have been something behind Rock's uncommonly new behavior.

"I know I've been a bit of a scrooge, but do you mind if I come and see the baby…or would it be better if I stopped by after she gets home?" Rock asked.

Tony shook his head and tried to rush out the front door.

"Is she going to be at your apartment or at Veronica's?" Rock asked, knowing that Veronica wasn't going to let her stay alone with a new baby for the first few weeks.

Nae was hooked up to a respirator and an I.V. by the time Trey and Tony arrived at the hospital. Tony was afraid to go into the room and check on her. When he finally built up enough courage, he walked in finding Veronica, Juanita and Monie standing around Nae, telling her to breathe. Nae felt uncomfortable with the mask covering nearly half of her face. She felt as though she was suffocating more so than receiving oxygen.

Nae tried fiercely to remove the mask from her face to talk to Tony. He was somewhat afraid of what Veronica's reaction was going to be since he wasn't there to take Nae to the hospital.

"Who brought her here?" Tony asked.

"I did! Where were you?" Monie asked as if she was interrogating him.

He wasn't going to confess that he'd been with Rock. He stood there quietly looking around the room.

"You were probably somewhere you had no business…like with Rock," Monie declared.

Trey beckoned for Monie to step into the hallway with him. On the way out the door, she rolled her eyes at Tony.

"Why don't you give him a break? He's already scared to death because the baby's coming early," Trey pleaded with Monie on Tony's behalf.

"Give him a break! He should've been the one getting fussed at and cursed out instead of me. He's the one who caused her to be in this condition. I was trying to help because I *just so happen* to be there, since the both of you had *mysteriously* disappeared," Monie argued, obviously still angry. "Where were you anyway?" Monie asked in a more calmed manner.

Trey had to think of something quick…something that would keep him out of the doghouse for the next week or two.

"We went to look for rings for you and Nae. He wanted to keep it a secret," Trey said.

Monie was awed. She felt guilty for all the bad things she'd said about Tony on the way to the hospital. Trey stared at her, hoping she'd buy his story. He always thought she had a sixth sense which enabled her to see right through him when he lied or did something wrong. He now had to fill Tony in on the lie he'd just told her.

Trey ignored his phone as it vibrated under his shirttail. A few minutes later, it vibrated again as she stood up and gave him a hug. If he ignored it a second time, he was sure she'd become suspicious.

He answered the phone without reading the caller ID.

"Hey man, did she have the baby yet?" Rock asked.

"No, I think she's still in labor."

Monie stood on her tiptoes trying to hear the conversation, and figure out the voice on the other end.

"Is that Rock?" Monie asked.

Trey nodded his head and put his finger up, indicating he'd be with her in a minute.

"How does he know about Nae being in labor?" Monie asked loudly and rudely.

Trey closed his flip phone and slid it back on his side, into its holder, wondering how he was going to explain that. He told Monie that Rock called while he was in route to the hospital and asked if he and Tony would be available to hook up with him later. Monie listened carefully and started putting two and two together. She figured the reason he wasn't able to talk on the phone when she called him was because they were probably with Rock.

"He just called you out of the blue?" Monie asked.

Trey was lost for words. He knew Monie was aware that there was more to the story than what he was telling her. Monie put that whole ordeal aside and focused on her family's situation. She stepped back into Nae's room for about five minutes, before she went outside to call Ronnie.

"Hello," Ronnie answered her cell phone enthusiastically.

"Ronnie, Nae's having the baby," Monie replied.

"She's having the baby already? Isn't she due in two months? Was she having complications?" Ronnie asked simultaneously, now worried.

Monie explained the situation to Ronnie, hoping she'd be able to come home within a few weeks. Ronnie's workload was overwhelmingly heavy. She knew she wouldn't be able to get to Atlanta any time soon, but she didn't want to disappoint her baby sister.

Monie then told Ronnie about how Tony and Trey had gotten reacquainted with Rock and the rest of the crew. She knew Trey had been lying, trying to cover up a lot of things involving Rock that he knew she'd disapprove of.

"Monie, are you listening to me?" Ronnie asked.

Monie had drifted into a meditating zone.

"I'll try to get there some time next month." Ronnie repeated what she'd said while Monie was in her zone. "I'll call you tonight, okay?"

Due to major complications, Nae had been in labor for about five hours. The time was now approaching 3p.m. She had finally given birth to a premature baby boy, weighing in at 3lbs. 7oz.

Nae couldn't tell the nurses the baby's name because of the high dosage of medication she was given. Monie couldn't remember the name that Nae had picked out for him. Veronica walked with the nurses and watched as they put her first grandbaby in an incubator, attaching heart monitors and respirators to the little fella.

Veronica nearly broke down in tears while staring at this precious little innocent baby, who was no bigger than her foot. *"Why did he have to go through so much within minutes after his arrival into the world,"* she thought. She didn't know how she was going to explain the child's condition to Nae. Hopefully, Nae would understand that it was just the normal procedure premature babies go through.

After about twenty minutes of staring and praying for her helpless little grandbaby, Veronica went back to the recovery room where Nae was, who also was on a respirator. Veronica shed a couple of tears, uncertain if they were tears of joy for having a grandchild, or tears of pain from watching both of them being hooked up to so many different machines.

Jerome had worked half of the day and was on his way out the door. While leaving, he bragged to a couple of friends about the newest addition to his family. "I have a new little grandson I'm about to go see," Jerome said to his boss and another friend as he ran out the door.

Once Jerome arrived at the hospital, he found Veronica with reddish, glossy eyes. He knew she'd been crying.

"What's wrong Veronica?" Jerome asked.

"Nothing," she replied.

Veronica couldn't say anything. She pointed to the nursery. Jerome walked down the hall and looked through the nursery's window. In the conjoining room where the babies who had special needs were kept, he saw 'Baby Williams" in a tiny incubator next to the wall.

He then understood why Veronica had been crying. Under the circumstances, he didn't know what to say to her. Veronica walked up and wrapped her arms around him.

"He'll be alright. He's little but he looks like a strong little guy. He's made it this far so you already know that he's a fighter," Jerome said trying to comfort Veronica, hoping that God would soon allow him to believe that what he just said was the truth.

Ronnie had incoming calls all day about an upcoming movie shoot. She didn't have time to clear her desk of photos and folders that needed to be filed. Tara was out with bronchitis, leaving Ronnie alone in the office putting her skills to the test.

By 4:30pm, Ronnie was exhausted from the calls and all of the nonstop running around she'd done throughout the day. It was quitting time, but Ronnie still had a dilemma on her hands. One of their biggest clients called for a brown skinned young lady, around Ronnie's height, weight, and age, for an upcoming movie that had been in the works for at least four months.

As she looked through the stack of pictures on her desk, Ronnie became frustrated, unable to find the specific description that was needed for the completion of this project.

She went to the restroom to splash her face with cold water, trying to cool off from the hot and humid temperatures of California. Of course, this was something she was not accustomed to. As she patted her face dry with a hand towel and opened her eyes, she stared at herself in the mirror, turning her head from one side to the other.

Ronnie briefly thought about auditioning for the part in her client's project that seemed almost impossible to fill. The idea of getting her big break in acting, from her client's misfortune, brought a smile on her face. Walking back to her desk, she recited a monologue that she'd heard from another clients' movie that had just been completed weeks ago.

Ronnie walked through the door of her candle lit apartment. The soft sounds of Kenny G's seductive melodies were playing on the stereo. A lit candle, a vase of long stem red roses with some of its petals scattered across the table, along with two plates of lasagna, and two flukes filled with wine, awaited for her to get home and unwind.

Josh hid in the candle lit bedroom, waiting for her to come in so he could take off her shoes. Once she found him with nothing on but a pair of sweat pants, her smile let him know that this was the highlight of her day. She sat on the bed and allowed him to assist in taking off her work clothes, to slip into something a little more *comfortable*.

He led her to the kitchen table and pulled out her chair. Before she picked up her silverware to cut her food, she closed her eyes to savor the taste of the sparkling wine. She looked up and into Josh's eyes before she started to eat her meal. *"This is an extremely special night, but there has to be more to it,"* she thought.

During the four-month course of their roommate-style living arrangement, she and Josh had never had sexual relations. However, for everything he'd gone through to make this night special for her, she was ready and willing to make the night special just for him. After dinner she had plans to relax and release everything she been holding back from him over the months.

She took another sip of her wine as Josh pulled out a shiny, white gold, two-carat engagement ring and sat it in the middle of the table. Ronnie almost choked as she looked at her unforeseen gift. It seemed a bit strange to receive an engagement ring from a person she'd never had sex with.

He smiled, staring at her confused facial expressions, as she accepted the ring with pleasure. She perceived Josh as a long time friend who was now a roommate. They weren't even dating, or so she thought.

"I know you're wondering where all of this is coming from?" Josh asked.

"Yes and where is it going?" She responded.

Josh figured she was completely over Rock. Now, they would be able to continue on with their lives the way they'd planned before she found out that she was pregnant by Rock. He didn't want to have sex with her for several months, thinking that he'd cause a set back in her recovery from the miscarriage.

"If you need time to think about it…"

"Time?" Ronnie cut him off in mid-sentence. "I would love to be Mrs. Ronnie Robinson," Ronnie offered.

"I've fallen in love with you," Josh said taking Ronnie by surprise.

Ronnie finally felt good knowing she had a real man, one with more on his mind than just sex. Josh began kissing her occasionally, telling her how beautiful she was. *"Is he putting on a front? Is he trying to hide the fact that he's gay?"* Ronnie started to wonder.

She didn't want to get married for all the wrong reasons. She knew that Josh had always loved her, but now it was confirmed that it was certainly unconditional love. Thinking about it for a moment, Ronnie realized that the security she always wanted in a man was in him. Her mind set was still a bit selfish, but at that point, she had nothing to lose. Unconditional love was staring her in the face, and she'd be dumb to let it get away.

After finishing her dinner, Ronnie got up from the table to go run a bath. On the way to bedroom, the phone rang.

"Ronnie, we have a nephew," Monie said calmly.

"Oh my God!" Ronnie yelled with excitement. "When did she have him?" Ronnie asked.

"This evening. He is so *adorable*, and he looks just like Tony," Monie said, still amazed that she had this tiny person to help care for until Nae fully recovered. After being the youngest for so long, Monie was thrilled that she now had someone who would look up to her.

"Aren't you excited?" Ronnie asked.

Ronnie wondered why Monie was so subtle. She thought something may have been wrong with Nae. She knew Monie wouldn't tell her something like that over the phone. Monie passed the phone to Veronica and grabbed the other phone to constitute a conference call.

"Hey mom, is everything okay?" Ronnie asked.

Ronnie forgot about her bath water. She chatted with Monie and Veronica, bragging on her ring, once she was reassured that things were okay in Atlanta.

"I didn't know you and Josh had gotten that serious already," Veronica stated, trying to pry on the sly.

Ronnie chuckled and whispered, "I didn't either."

"You are dumb as hell!" Monie shouted. "How can you not know? You didn't see the signs?" Monie said fussing at Ronnie.

"Monie, that's enough!" Veronica exclaimed while laughing to herself. Monie voiced everything she was thinking, but Veronica couldn't let Ronnie know how preposterous her story sounded.

Ronnie made arrangements with her mother and sisters to come home for a couple of weeks, in the beginning of June, to prepare for her mother's wedding. She jotted down a few dates on a notepad and left it next her bed. Her plans were to check the airfare for the available dates she had in mind.

By the time she got off of the phone, her bath water was lukewarm. Josh ran a steamy shower and invited Ronnie in to join him. He formed a thick lather and washed her back with her vanilla scented shower gel, which was followed by gentle, intimate kisses. He braced her against the shower wall and held her left leg up over his forearm.

The water ricocheted off of Josh's shoulders, sending a warm refreshing mist against Ronnie's face. His wet body softly bumped against hers as he made sweet, gentle, passionate love to her.

"This was way overdue," she thought. He does it so better than Rock.

Her heart skipped a few beats making her stutter as she tried to explain to him how much she enjoyed it.

"We must do that again...tonight," Ronnie insisted.

Josh smiled as he lay across the bed on his back with his legs crossed, wondering what Ronnie was going to do next. He didn't know how she was going to react to a night full of surprises.

He heard her whispering in the kitchen. He figured she must have called her sister's to inform them of what had just happened. He saw a notepad on the nightstand, with dates and flight arrangements on it. It was obviously her plans to go back to Atlanta for her mother's wedding he thought. For whatever reason, she never mentioned any dates to him. He didn't know if she was intentionally excluding him from her plans or trying to make an escape.

He picked up the notepad and took it into the kitchen to ask her about it. She ended her phone call and looked at him, wondering why he was acting so strange.

"When were you going to tell me about your plans to go home?" Josh asked.

"I haven't made any concrete plans yet. I have to go home in early June for the rehearsal dinner, and also to spend time with my new nephew. I'll probably stay for two weeks. Monie and I were just playing around with some dates and flights," she replied. She wondered why she was getting the third degree about going home for an event that he already knew about. Despite the *cross-examination* she'd received, she still responded with specific details about her plans.

"Just because he gave me a ring and made love to me doesn't give him the right to start questioning me," she thought. "And if my plans didn't include him, so what. All he could do is get mad," she laughed internally.

"These weren't the original dates for the wedding were they?" Josh asked.

"Yes," Ronnie replied as a few cruel thoughts danced around in the back of her mind.

"He knows that the dates hadn't changed because his silly mother, for whatever reasons, is in the wedding. After the way she deserted mom, she doesn't deserve to be in it," she thought to herself.

It was clear that Ronnie subliminally had an entirely different demeanor towards Josh, especially when it came to dating him, as opposed to being plutonic friends. She was never selfish when it came to the man she loved. Her experiences with Rock had obviously changed her outlook on a lot of things. She now understood and implemented the fact that she had to look out for herself. It was also obvious that she didn't yet have the same unconditional love for him as he had for her.

"Why don't we stay in Atlanta for a week? It would be nice to travel together," Josh suggested.

Ronnie looked at him with a blank stare. "He has the audacity to try and plan my time with my family," she thought.

"I have the time to take off at work and I plan to use. You can come back whenever you like," she added nicely.

He could see that she was getting agitated with the conversation. He shook his head with frustration and walked in the kitchen to grab a beer out of the refrigerator. She curled up on the sofa and began watching TV. Still looking at him out of the corner of her eye, he sat on the opposite end of the sofa and propped his feet up on the coffee table.

Rock, Rick, Rome and Trey arranged a party for Tony at Club Passions. The time was 10:00p.m. Tony was just leaving the hospital, heading to the apartment. His phone had been off for the past few hours while he enjoyed spending time with Nae and his new baby, Tonae.

After driving nearly a mile down the street, Tony turned his phone back on. It beeped, indicating he had messages. He looked down at the phone, reading that he'd received eight messages.

He checked four of the eight messages; all of them were letting him know about the same thing.

"Man, there's a party going on tonight. We can easily turn it into a celebration for you," Rock said on the first message.

"Yo Tone, come over to Passions when you leave the hospital. Rock has a little something lined up for you," Rome said on the second message.

Before he listened to the third message, Tony made a u-turn in the middle of the street, and headed back towards the club. He knew that the other messages would probably notify him of the same information as the first two. Of course, Tony didn't want to be out all night. He wanted to spend all of the next day at the hospital with Nae and the baby.

As soon as Tony walked in the club, the D.J. congratulated him on his new addition. Every man in the club congratulated him and bought him drinks all night. Tony felt special as he walked around the club with a celebrity's status.

Tony's phone rang. He tried to make his way to the front door and go outside to answer it. Rock and Trey held a conversation and escorted him outside, waiting for him to finish his call.

"Tony, this is Ronnie. I just called to congratulate you."

"Ronnie, what's going on?" Tony asked, unconscious that he should have been more discreet with the call.

"It sounds like you're at a party, so I'm not going to hold you on the phone. I'll see your little man when I come home in the beginning of June for mom's wedding."

"You're coming home in June?" Tony asked, unaware that Rock was absorbing the information he was leaking.

"Let me speak to her," Rock said, reaching for the phone.

"Hey Ronnie, hold on. Rock wants to speak to you," Tony slightly slurred from his consumption of alcohol.

"Rock was somewhere near you the whole time we've been talking?" Ronnie asked.

She suddenly had a 'hot flash' as if her blood had started boiling throughout her body. She was angry that Tony had let Rock know when she was coming home and her reason for being there. She knew that during the two weeks she was planning to be there, she'd eventually run into Rock. Thanks to Tony, Rock knew exactly when she was going to be in town.

Ronnie hung up as Tony was handing his cell phone to Rock. She didn't say a word to Josh, who was still sitting on the other end of the sofa. He looked at Ronnie and remained quiet, understanding that she was annoyed. She stared at the TV, squinting her eyes with a blank expression on her face, looking obviously disturbed.

Rock's cell phone rang. He jumped to answer it, thinking that Ronnie may have been calling him back. He was amazed to hear that whispering voice again. Shonte was sitting across the parking lot of the club, watching as Rock happily marched around trying to keep a strong reception signal.

"Ronnie, I missed you the last time you were here. I just heard Tony say that you were coming back in June. I'm going to make sure I see you then. I still love you with all my heart."

"I'm going to make sure I see you as well. I have a really big surprise for you," the voice whispered softly.

"What kind of surprise?" Rock asked with uncertainty.

"One that'll put you in shock. I gotta go. I'll see you soon."

Josh finally got enough nerve to ask Ronnie what was bothering her.

"Did Rock say something to upset you?" Josh asked.

"Everything I told him he said out loud," Ronnie said looking over at Josh.

"Rock was there listening to everything. He knows when I'm coming home and there's no telling what he may do to try and see me," she added.

"I thought you were finished with him," Josh said suspiciously.

"What are you implying? I *am* finished with him, but obviously he's not finished with me," Ronnie said. She stormed into the bedroom and slammed the door.

She sat on the bed wondering what it was going to take to convince Josh that she had absolutely nothing to do with Rock. Since she'd been in California, Ronnie had gotten over Rock. However, she didn't understand how she could love Josh so much, but still couldn't fully commit to him.

Josh pushed open the bedroom door to go in and talk with Ronnie. He was afraid to touch her. He eased onto the bed and pleaded with her to talk to him.

"We've had the most perfect night. I don't want the night to end with a fight," Josh begged.

Ronnie realized she may have been a bit hard on Josh, especially after all he'd done to make the night special. He lay alone in bed watching TV. Minutes later, Ronnie crawled up beside him, with sincere apologies for her rude behavior, accompanied by soft, sweet kisses. She cradled herself underneath his arm, resting her body snuggly against his, hugging him tightly until they both fell asleep.

Chapter 22

*I*t was Wednesday, just a couple of days before Veronica's wedding. Veronica and Monie sat down at the kitchen table together to discuss their big eventful weekend. Veronica just knew she planned the ideal weekend, one that would celebrate both her wedding and Monie's graduation.

Intentionally, her wedding was planned on a Friday, since Monie's ceremony was being held on Saturday. This would give everyone a day to rest on Sunday before heading back to their destinations. Veronica felt good being able to eliminate the need for her family having to make separate trips for two different occasions.

Ronnie was heading back to Atlanta later than she had anticipated, knowing she had to help her mother get everything in order. She was glad she could depend on her grandmother and Aunt Patrice to help out. They were scheduled to arrive later that evening. She was exhausted from working throughout the weekend and half of the week. Ronnie was trying to finish her work and help Tara get ahead for the following week, given the fact that she would be in Atlanta for the remainder of the week.

She tried to close her eyes and relax, but she was too excited to sleep. As she sat back in her snug seatbelt, the plane ascended into the air. Veronica had been calling her all morning, from the time Ronnie awoke until she boarded the plane.

Josh started falling asleep less than ten minutes after the plane was in the air, leaving Ronnie to carry on a one party conversation. Ronnie pulled out her notepad and started pairing the wedding party. She was supposed to march with Josh; Monie was to march with Jerome's son

Calvin; and Nae was going to march with Tony.

For a while she thought, *"I'm not sure who Juanita, Sabrina or Cynthia were going to march with."*

She knew that once she arrived in Atlanta, her mother would put her in charge of coordinating things for the wedding. Finally, she closed her eyes, still unable to fall asleep. She juggled her thoughts and ideas on how the wedding should be. She visualized she and Veronica having a double wedding. Everything in her vision was picture perfect.

The plane shook tremendously, due to heavy turbulence. Josh grabbed Ronnie's hand, ensuring her safety before his own.

"Are you okay?" he asked.

Just as everyone calmed down, the plane hit another air pocket. A few of the overhead compartments flew open causing more fear and commotion than the turbulence itself. Josh's heart pounded. He tried to keep his composure and assist an elderly couple that sat across the isle, while still making sure Ronnie was okay.

Ronnie smiled while she looked at Josh lend a hand to someone else in need. *"I have the most perfect gentleman,"* she said to herself. She adored his flattering protocol.

"May I have your attention ladies and gentlemen? This is your pilot speaking. We sincerely apologize for the heavy turbulence we've just encountered. We're now heading into the twin cities. Unfortunately, there are major thunderstorms and blinding lightning. We are now descending three thousand feet in order to avoid further appalling turbulence. We ask that you please keep your seatbelts on at all times, unless instructed otherwise by your stewardess. Thank you for your cooperation, and we'll try to make the remainder of your flight as pleasant as possible."

Ronnie was frantic. She clung to Josh like she'd never done before. Josh's faith was put to the test. It amazed him how he worried about someone else's well being before his own. That was enough confirmation for him to know that he truly loved Ronnie. He began to pray.

"Lord, I know you're listening. Please let us make it to Atlanta and back to California safely. Lord, please allow me to see the day that I may marry this beautiful queen. Lord, I thank you and I love you. In Jesus' name…Amen."

Josh felt the plane turn and slightly tilt to the side, ascending again. He looked out the window on Ronnie's side. He saw a rainbow in the sky and a hint of sunshine breaking through the hideous clouds. Josh then became a firm believer that the smallest prayer works for the biggest and scariest situations.

He rested his hand on top of Ronnie's on the armrest, trying to give her a sense of security. Ronnie was afraid to close her eyes and relax. While going through the turbulence, she'd never seen her life flash before her eyes like it had.

Veronica, Juanita and Nae went to get decorations for the reception. Veronica looked at her watch and panicked.

"Mom, are you okay?" Nae asked.

"No. Ronnie and Josh are due to arrive in forty-five minutes. There's no way we'll get this stuff and make it back to the airport to get them on time. Besides, we don't have enough room in the car for both of them and their luggage."

Nae called Monie, hoping she'd be able to run to her rescue once again. Monie was supposed to help Tony clean the guest bedrooms for the expected guests. Monie had been sitting for over an hour trying to put the final touches on planning her graduation party, which both Ronnie and Nae agreed to help plan. She was frustrated from running around, doing everything on her own, without help from anyone but Trey.

"Hello?" Monie mumbled from exhaustion.

"Monie, mom needs you to pick Ronnie and Josh up from the airport," Nae stated.

"You promised mom that you would pick Ronnie up this time," Monie reminded Nae.

"I know, but I'm with mom now and we don't have enough time or enough room in the car to get them. I promise I'll make it up to you," Nae pleaded.

"Nae, I'm tired of coming through for you with all of your broken promises and excuses!" Monie exclaimed. She slammed the phone down on its base. She grabbed her keys and purse and ran across the freshly mopped kitchen floor that Tony had just completed. When she got outside, Tony's car was blocking hers.

"Tony!" Monie called.

Tony came running out of one of the guests' bedroom that he'd just started vacuuming. "What's wrong?"

"We have to go to the airport to get Ronnie and Josh," Monie said while tugging on his arm, heading towards his truck.

Tony jumped in the driver's seat and headed out of the driveway.

"How are we supposed to get any cleaning done if we're running to the airport all day?" Tony asked.

"It's all because of your *girlfriend*," Monie said sarcastically.

Cicely, Patrice and a few of Veronica's nieces and nephews were arriving later that evening. Monie had agreed to have the house cleaned and pick them up from the airport as well.

Ronnie saw Monie with Tony and wondered what was going on. Josh and Tony loaded their bags in the back of the truck while Ronnie inquired what Monie was doing with Tony.

Monie let out a sigh if frustration at the thought of the conversation she'd had with Nae.

"It's a long story," Monie added. "Nana and Aunt Patrice are going to be here tonight."

"That's good. I'm staying over Jason's with Josh," Ronnie replied.

"Kyla, Angie and Taylor are coming with them," Monie said, expecting resentful comments from Ronnie.

Ronnie never could get over the fact that her grandmother had compared her to Angie ever since they were children. For some unknown reason, Angie was always quite jealous of Ronnie. Regardless of how she felt, Ronnie wasn't going to let that divert her attention from her mother's big day. She'd planned to enjoy every minute of her stay and celebrate with her mother.

Veronica pulled up in the driveway behind Tony, excited to see Ronnie and desperately seeking her assistance with setting everything up. Before she turned off the engine, she jumped out of the car.

"Ronnie!" she yelled as she ran towards Tony's truck with her arms extended, trying to hug her daughter.

Veronica stood back, looking at Ronnie, holding her hands from afar while discreetly checking out what kind of ring she had on and how big it was. The size of the stone let her know that Josh spent a decent amount on it.

"Impressive," Veronica said and walked over to hug Josh.

"Congratulations," she whispered in his ear.

Juanita walked up, hearing the tail end of the short conversation Veronica held with Josh.

"Congratulations on what?" Juanita asked.

"You haven't told your mother?" Veronica asked.

"No. I was going to surprise her once I got here," Josh admitted.

"Okay...surprise me. What's going on?" Juanita asked inquisitively.

Josh sighed and hesitated to answer his mother. "I asked Ronnie to marry me. We've relocated and Rock's not around to bother us anymore. We don't have anything to lose," Josh said happily.

"Isn't that wonderful?" Veronica added. "We'll really be one big happy family."

Before Juanita could say anything, Jerome was pulling into the driveway suddenly distracted her. He was cruising into the driveway with his best friend, Tim, who was following behind him in a royal blue Navigator with shinny chrome rims. Juanita's eyes widened and her knee's buckled as she tried desperately to see past the limo's tented windows.

Juanita tactfully tapped Veronica on the side of her hip trying to gain her attention. "Who's that?" she asked.

"I don't know," Veronica replied.

Josh realized his mother's attention was no longer on him. He looked at the truck and then back at his mother.

"Come on mom. Don't do this to yourself again," Josh begged.

"I didn't do anything," Juanita said. *"Yet,"* she added, with obvious intentions to get next to Jerome's friend.

Josh didn't want to see his mother humiliate herself. He beckoned for Tony to help him take the luggage into the house. He waved at Jerome, acknowledging him and looked at his mother, hoping she wasn't about to do anything stupid that may cause for him and Jason to take action again like they had done with Raymond.

She apparently didn't learn her lesson from dealing with Raymond. She was back to her old tricks again. He just shook his head and headed into the house. *"I wonder if I'm going to have to deal with her and some crack head that she's fallen in love with every time I come home,"* Josh thought.

Juanita took a step back and shielded herself behind Veronica, wiggling and tugging on her clothes, trying to make sure everything was a perfect fit for this stranger in this luxurious truck to see.

The dark-skinned, slender guy laughed and talked to Jerome about his driving skills on the way over to meet everyone.

"You drive like an old man Jerome. You used to drive like Andretti.

What happened?" Jerome's friend teased.

"Oh girl, he has a sexy voice," Juanita said.

"Ladies, this is my old military buddy, Tim." Jerome introduced Tim to everyone.

Jerome wrapped his arms around Veronica's waist and gave her a big kiss on her cheek. "This is Veronica, the bride to be. This is her best friend, Juanita, the maid of honor. You'll be walking with her. These are my daughters, Ronnie, Monie and Nae."

Tim kissed Veronica's hand and congratulated her. Ronnie took her purse off her right shoulder and held it by its strap in her left hand. So, if he wanted to kiss her hand as well, he would reach for her available hand and wouldn't see that her left ring finger was occupied, indicating that she was unavailable.

"He has a few gold teeth…but he's still kinda cute," Ronnie chuckled internally. *"I guess I don't stand a chance to at least flirt cause Ms. Thang is all over him already,"* Ronnie thought. *"He looks kind of young to be Jerome's best friend. Maybe he just ages well."*

Tim shook Juanita, Monie and Nae's hands, but he placed a gentle kiss on Ronnie's hand. He smiled at Ronnie, not showing a big portion of his gold teeth. *"He even knows how to be cordial,"* she thought.

Ronnie stood alone next to Tony's truck. She was about to join her mother and sisters. She didn't want Tim to single her out and start a conversation, while Juanita was mean mugging her. Ronnie stepped into the crowd of women to the join the conversation to find out what her mother was going to do next. She felt that Tim was staring at her. She smoothly put her head down and timidly looked back at him out of the corner of her eye, and smiled.

Ronnie saw that Juanita was suddenly looking at her differently. While everyone else was entertained with Veronica's conversation, Juanita noticed that Ronnie was blushing. Tim smiled again, cautiously blushing in accordance with Ronnie, as he stood alone, patiently waiting for Jerome to get some things out of his car.

Ronnie was conscience of what her mother was saying, while Juanita's full attention was on Tim and Ronnie's obvious connection.

"That little tramp has the nerve to flirt with Tim in my face, after just getting engaged to my son. What kind of mess is that," Juanita thought. *"I'mma show her who the real Queen B is."*

"Did Jerome leave you over there by yourself? He's so silly. He's just like his brother. I used to date his twin brother a long time ago. If you'd like, you can go inside with the other guys. Did Ronnie and Nae introduce you to their fiancés?" Juanita said, trying to make small talk, while making it known that Ronnie was engaged.

Tony and Josh came back outside and introduced themselves to Tim. Tim suggested that they hook up with Tyrone and give Jerome a bachelor party. Jerome joined the circle of men just as Tim was about to allocate his plan. Jerome knew he had something up his sleeve.

Josh wasn't thrilled about the idea of having Tyrone around his mother again, but he realized that he was the groom's brother. He decided that he would get along with everyone if only for this occasion.

The ladies went in the house and began cleaning all that Monie and Tony didn't get a chance to finish.

"So Ronnie, just how long have you and Josh been engaged?" Juanita asked.

Ronnie acted as if she didn't hear Juanita. She started to wonder if she really wanted to be in this type of relationship with Josh because of his annoying mother. Ronnie took off all of her jewelry before she started cleaning. She watched Juanita's reaction once she realized she didn't have the ring on.

"Josh spent all of that money on a ring and you don't appreciate it enough to wear it," Juanita stated.

Ronnie looked at Juanita and rolled her eyes. She didn't want to have any altercations with her because of who she was. *"She hadn't started acting like a lunatic until Tim came into the picture."*

"These younger generations of women really don't know the value of a good man." Juanita stated indirectly.

Veronica looked at Juanita, wondering why she kept making sly remarks and who she was directing them to. Ronnie had gotten fed up with Juanita's smart comments. She couldn't take anymore of them. She was just going to have to explain to Josh what happened between her and his mother.

"They have a good man at home, and still go out skinnin' and grinnin' in some other man's face," Juanita said, intentionally trying to push Ronnie's buttons.

"How would you know the value of a good man? You've never had one!" Ronnie blurted out. "If you want Tim go and get him. He was the one smiling at me!"

Juanita couldn't believe Ronnie had just snapped on her. "You were blushing and smiling back at him. I saw you," Juanita blabbed.

"What the hell is going on?" Veronica asked. She was unaware of the tension that had just developed between her daughter and her best friend.

"Ronnie and Tim were just making little gestures to each other. That's probably why she's not wearing her ring," Juanita said.

"What made you think Ronnie wanted to hook up with Tim? You were the one primping and prancing around trying to get his attention," Veronica said to Juanita. "We can't start a wedding with a lot of unnecessary tension over this little guy that neither one of you know nor really want. Both of you need to let it go and help me get hitched to my man," Veronica said, trying to find the comic relief in the situation.

"Could we all just apologize, get along, and continue planning my wedding?" Veronica asked, trying to reclaim the unison.

"Ms. Robinson, I'm really sorry. I wasn't trying to disrespect you in any way. You are not only my mother's friend, but you're my boyfriend's mother. I just want us to be able to get along," Ronnie said sincerely, asking for Juanita's forgiveness.

Juanita reluctantly accepted Ronnie's apology.

Before going to the airport, Veronica had to stop by Juanita's house and get her car to provide enough room for all of the arriving guests. Veronica tried talking to Juanita to find out why she was acting so childish over another guy. Veronica had always been blind of Juanita's problem with promiscuity. She thought her friend was classy and fun loving; at least decent.

Monie and Nae tried to understand what happened between Ronnie and Juanita. Ronnie explained to them what was going on and went outside to get some fresh air.

Within minutes, Tim, Tyrone and Tony came back to the house with Jerome. Tim got out of the truck and stayed outside to talk to Ronnie, while the other guys went inside.

"Where's Josh?" Ronnie asked.

"I see that you're pretty concerned about your man," Tim replied.

"Maybe I don't want him to see me talking to you," Ronnie said as if she truly had an interest in him.

Tim laughed. "Jerome dropped him off at his brother's house. He said to tell you he'd call you later. I guess his mom was getting on his nerves," Tim presumed. "I wouldn't leave my beautiful fiancée around a house full of men."

"You mean a house full of relatives. I guess you and Tyrone are the only single men here," Ronnie said, implying that he would be the only who would probably try to talk to her.

"I wouldn't disrespect him like that, but I would like to get to know you better, if that's alright with you," Tim responded to Ronnie's sassiness. "We're supposed to go to Club Passions tonight. Tony said that some of his people own it."

Ronnie shook her head. Tim could tell that she wasn't at all impressed with the idea of going to the club.

"I'd like to go somewhere a little quieter. I don't like a lot of commotion," Tim added.

"He sounds very intelligent. Umm…and he smells so good," she thought to herself.

"How old are you?" Ronnie asked bravely after wondering all day.

"I'm thirty."

"Well, how did you end up being close friends with Jerome? That age gap is kinda big," Ronnie replied.

Tim laughed it off and invited Ronnie to go out with him later that night, one on one after they mingle with everyone at Passions.

"They'll eventually start to miss us, don't you think?" Ronnie asked and sashayed back into the house.

As everyone sat in the family room planning for the night, Monie and Nae paid more attention to how Ronnie and Tim communicated through smiles, head nods, and their googly eye contact.

"I don't see why Ms. Juanita was going crazy over him. He looks too young for her and he definitely doesn't look like the type that would want her," Monie whispered to Nae on the sly.

"Nae, didn't you used to dance at Passions before you got pregnant?" Tyrone asked.

Nae looked at him and didn't respond. She was a bit embarrassed at first, but she overlooked his pure ignorance. "Didn't you just get out of rehab?" Nae redirected the embarrassment back to him.

Tyrone quickly changed the subject. Ronnie felt bad for Nae because she couldn't go out with the rest of the partying family.

"Maybe mom will watch the baby when she gets back," Monie stated before she headed out of the door behind everyone else. Tony knew it wouldn't be fair to go to the club while Nae stayed at home alone with the baby. After all, the baby had been with her all day.

He suggested they go to their apartment and have a movie night. Tony still hoped in the back of his mind that Veronica would baby sit for them while they go have a good time with everyone else. He also knew that Rock would be at the club and would probably make a scene. Both he and Nae sat, flipping through the channels, hoping Veronica would make it home before they got up to leave.

"Nae, you know that Rock is going to be at the club. I hope he and Ronnie don't start fighting."

Nae hoped Jerome wouldn't have to baby sit Tyrone all night so he could keep an eye on Ronnie. She called Ronnie's cell phone to warn her that Rock would probably be at the club. Ronnie didn't answer the phone. She dialed Monie's cell phone number only to find out that Monie had left her phone on the kitchen table.

"I want Ms. Ronnie to ride up front with me," Tim insisted.

Monie got in the back seat of Tim's truck. Tyrone rode with Jerome. This was the first time Tyrone had been to a club since he had come out of rehab. Jerome hoped his brother wouldn't have a relapse. He knew he'd have to keep a close eye on him all night like he was a child.

"Ty, don't get in the club and start acting crazy. I don't want to have to take you home early," Jerome said to Tyrone, being mindful of his substance abuse problem.

"So Ronnie, is it safe to assume that you live here?" Tim asked.

"No," Ronnie said without volunteering any further information.

Tim wanted to carry on a conversation with her, but he ran out of questions to ask, without getting too personal. Ronnie looked at him and smiled. She knew he was itching to say something else to her, but she continued to play hard to get.

"Is it safe to say that you used to live here in Atlanta?" Tim asked, trying to get a conversation started.

"Yes," Ronnie laughed, knowing that he was running out of small talk. "I just moved to California a few months ago," she finally admitted, relieving Tim of his curiosity. "I had a lot of drama going on and I just had to get away."

She didn't want to reveal what kind of drama she'd gone through, afraid of making him think she was a drama queen. Monie sat in the back seat as quiet as a mouse, just listening to their conversation. She wanted to comment but was afraid to say anything that may have triggered Tim to question Ronnie about her past.

"That must have been some heavy drama to make you move to the other side of the world," Tim replied.

Tim was looking for a reply in the form of an answer as to what kind of drama she was having, but Ronnie played it as if it was rhetorical.

The truck became quiet for a few seconds before they drifted into a synchronous laughter, but Ronnie never revealed what happened and with whom. She let his imagination wonder. She'd planned to tell him her situation once they left the club and went away somewhere else into seclusion.

As they pulled up into Club Passions parking lot, Ronnie began to have flashbacks of when she and Rock first started dating. She remembered all of the good times and free drinks she and Monie had when Nae worked there. She and her sisters were strictly 'hands off'. They got the respect from every guy who stepped foot in the club because they knew she dated Rock.

Jerome walked over to Tim's truck and waited until everyone was ready to go inside.

"Tim, if anyone even looks at Ronnie the wrong way, use your own discretion and take action," Jerome said, giving Tim a fair warning.

Tim started putting the pieces of the puzzle together. He figured Ronnie must have had some drama with a regular customer or an employee at the club. He wondered why Jerome would tell him to take action for a woman he barely knew. Tim went along with whatever was going on. He was just uneasy about being in the middle of this mysterious drama that no one seemed to want to let him in on.

Tim was a D.J. who had moved away from Atlanta several years ago. He had befriended most of the big timers who hung out at the big name clubs. He wasn't sure if Ronnie had any conflicts with them, but he sensed that he needed to watch his back, regardless. He didn't mind protecting a lady, who was simply a total stranger just a little over an hour ago. However, his safety was priority, especially since he didn't know who or what he was protecting her from.

Trey, Rick and Rome stood at the door as Jerome led the family into the club. As she entered the club hand holding Tim's hand, they all greeted Ronnie as if she was royalty.

"Hey stranger. Where've you been?" Rome asked Ronnie as he extended his arms to give her a hug.

"I relocated," Ronnie said.

"Yeah? So where do you live now?" Rome pried.

Ronnie had to think about where everyone had told Rock she was living. She couldn't find Monie to intervene. Monie was ahead of her and had already made it into the noise of the club. *"Damn. Am I supposed to be living in Colorado or Cleveland,"* Ronnie asked herself. *"Where the heck did Monie disappear to so fast?"*

Ronnie started laughing, to stall for time while she thought about where Nae had told her Rock went to look for her. "I'm sorry. I had a few drinks before I got here. I'm a little slow tonight," Ronnie said.

Rome looked at her as if he knew she was lying. "You're so slow you don't know where you live?" Rome asked.

"Man, give the lady a break. She's twisted," Tim added.

"Who's your friend?" Rome asked Ronnie.

"Where the heck do I live?" Canada popped into her head as if Monie had come over and whispered it in her ear.

"I live in Canada," Ronnie blurted out.

"Canada?" Tim thought. *"She just told me she lived in California."* Tim didn't say anything. He just went along with whatever lies she had to tell to get her past her situation.

"Oh, this is Tim," Ronnie said with delay.

Rome squinted and took a step closer to get a better look at Tim. "Oh, D.J. Tim! "What's up man? How's Virginia treatin' you?"

"Rome! What's up man? I still D.J. part time up there," Tim said after finally recognizing who Rome was.

Ronnie was glad the spotlight was taken off of her. She inched away trying to find Monie or Jerome. She spotted Monie in the D.J.'s booth telling the D.J. something as she pointed towards Tim and Rome. Ronnie kept her eyes on Monie as she made her way in that direction.

"Man, what are you doing with Ronnie? You know she's hands off?" Rome explained. "That's Rock's girl."

Tim was caught by surprise. He didn't know what to say or how to begin to explain the situation. He told Rome that he was only keeping an eye on her, making sure she didn't drink too much, as a favor for her soon to be stepfather.

"I'll probably leave to take her home for him within the next hour," Tim said to cover his tracks for whenever he and Ronnie left alone.

Rome had heard through the grapevine that Ronnie's mother was about to marry Jerome. He believed Tim's story to a certain degree. He kept an eye on the couple to see how friendly they really were towards each other, just until Rock was able to witness it for himself.

Rome called Rock to inform him that Ronnie was in town, and had been spotted with Tim. Rock rushed to get dressed and make it to the club before she left, hoping to catch her in the act. He wanted to see who this Tim character was, and what he was doing with Ronnie. He was also anxious to receive the surprise he thought she'd promised him.

Tim became furious, wondering why Ronnie failed to mention she'd been an item with the biggest drug lord of the south. Her ties that she held so tightly were slowly unraveling. Tim knew what kind of monster Rock could be at times. He didn't want any trouble with Rock or anyone from his crew. He was ready to be unattached to Ronnie once and for all.

Tim walked up behind Jerome. "Man, why didn't you tell me that your daughter was Rock's girl?"

"She not his girl. She broke up with him after he tried to kill her. She didn't tell you about that on the way here?"

To Tim, the story was starting to sound worse by the minute. He didn't know whether he should forget about their date all together, and let her leave with Jerome, or take her out to give her a chance to explain what kind of mess he had gotten into.

Tim shook Jerome's hand and explained his reasons for leaving. "Ronnie said she wanted to leave with me but I don't know where she is," Tim said without attempting to look for her. "These aren't the type of guys I like to deal with anymore. I'll see you in the morning," he said with intentions to go to Jerome's house to get some sleep.

Tim turned around and headed toward the door. Ronnie caught up with him as he was walking through the club, half way to the door.

"So, you're just going to leave me here? I thought we were going somewhere a little quieter," Ronnie asked as if nothing was wrong.

"Give me one good reason why I shouldn't leave you here," Tim replied bitterly while continuing to walk to the door.

"I'm sorry. I should've told you, but it wasn't the right time or the right place," Ronnie confessed and pleaded for a chance to make things right with him.

Monie was coming out of the restroom with Jerome's phone when she spotted Ronnie and Tim heading for the door. She made it to the door as soon as they walked out. Monie caught up with them on the steps of the club. She informed Ronnie that Nae and Tony were on their way to the club with their cousins from Jersey.

Ronnie wasn't at all enthused about seeing her jealous and arrogant cousins.

"Well, I'll see you all tomorrow," Ronnie said. She grabbed Tim's arm jovially and pranced down the stairs yelling back at Monie, "Have fun with your cousins."

Tim escorted Ronnie from the club. He opened the door for her to get in, and as she stepped up into Tim's truck, Ronnie saw Rock circling the parking lot in his truck. She prayed that he wouldn't come over and say or do anything to her or to Tim. Although Tim looked as if he could handle himself, she was sure of Rock's capabilities.

As Tim walked around to the driver's door, Rock pulled up on the passenger side of the truck. He sat thee, staring at Ronnie through the truck's windows, wondering if she was going to get out, or at least roll down the window to say hello.

He wasn't able to see through the limo-shaded tint on Tim's windows. However, it was obvious Rock had been watching her from the time she left Monie on the club's steps, up until the very moment she got in the truck with Tim.

Tim remained cordial, driving off, as if there was no potential confrontation. As Tim drove away, Rock shined his headlights on the back of his truck, making the Virginia license plate more visible. Rock assumed from the out of state plate that Ronnie had been lying and having her family to lie about her being in Canada, while in reality, she was staying in Virginia since she'd been gone.

Rock was too furious to go inside of the club and face anyone. He cruised around town, plotting and wondering. "Why didn't Tony or Trey ever bother to mention her arrival in town or her affair to me." He was overcome by the urge to run Tim's truck down and beat him until he was satisfied, or until Tim understood that Ronnie still belonged to him. He wanted to take Ronnie home with him, just long enough to scare her or her family into telling him where she really lived and with whom.

Tim remembered a blues club he used to go to for serenity. He parked in the back parking lot. In case any of Ronnie's friends showed up, it would be hard to spot his truck.

They found a small cozy booth with an intimate setting in a dark corner in the back of the club, lit only by the wax residue from a tiny candle. Tim ordered water. He wanted to remain coherent enough to think soundly, in case he had to come up with a quick plan to get them out of danger.

Ronnie started the conversation off with another apology. Tim was tired of hearing apologies. He was ready to hear the reasons behind her apologies. Ronnie explained her years' long love-hate relationship she had with Rock—from beginning to end.

Tim understood everything, except why Rock would want to kill Ronnie, especially if he claimed to love her as much as she said he did.

"Ronnie, that's not love. That's infatuation," Tim explained. "You are the only one he's ever let get so close to him. And now that you've hurt him, he's ready to go to the extreme to hurt you back; even if it means killing you. You did the right thing by moving. You're better off in California."

Ronnie knew that Tim was telling the truth. She finally heard what she needed to hear. She applied his advice, along with what Rock's mother had told her about not being the one to get hurt. She didn't think Rock would continue to mess with her family if she wasn't around. However, she knew that he wasn't going to let her go on with her life without suffering some kind of repercussion.

"Do you have a gun to protect yourself in case he catches you somewhere alone and tries to do something to you?" Tim asked sincerely.

He felt bad for Ronnie, but she was in too deep for him to try to help her now.

"My sister and I bought guns before I left," Ronnie admitted.

"Do you have it with you?" Tim asked.

"No."

Tim looked at her as if he wanted tell her how dumb she was for leaving it somewhere else while she went to the club, a place where Rock would definitely be on the prowl. He made it clear to her that it wasn't going to help her if she didn't have it with her.

"We need to go pick it up tonight so you can keep it with you until you go back to California," Tim suggested. "Even at the wedding," he added.

Ronnie gave him a ridiculous stare as if he was crazy for thinking that she would need a gun at her mother's wedding. She had to get in touch with Nae to find out where she had stashed the guns. She knew

Nae wouldn't have her cell phone on in the club, so she called Tony. Tony's phone rang several times before he acknowledged it.

Rome had already briefed Tony and Trey about Ronnie being seen in the club with Tim. Trey already knew that was bad news. For both of their sakes, he hoped Rock hadn't seen them together. He knew that if Rock saw them, he'd definitely make both of their vacations a memorable one, that is if they lived to talk about it.

Tony checked his phone to see who had been calling him so many times. He found Nae and went out to the parking lot, so she could return Ronnie's call, without the noise from the club drowning her out.

Nae told Ronnie that she would be able to find both guns at her apartment under the mattress. Tim and Ronnie stayed at the jazz club for a couple hours talking before heading over to Nae's place. Tim felt at ease having a better understanding of what Ronnie was dealing with and why he had to watch his back.

After sitting outside of Nae's apartment for at least fifteen minutes, Ronnie finally found the spare key. It was at the very bottom of what seemed to be her bottomless purse. Tim looked up. He was sure he had seen the same vehicle pass three times during the time it took Ronnie to find the key. Tim looked up into the air as far as he could, trying to see the top of the exclusive high-rise, penthouse-apartment building.

"Which floor does she live on?" Tim asked.

"Sixth." Ronnie smiled, noticing the tiresome and overwhelming expression on Tim's face.

"I'm glad she doesn't have to go to the twentieth floor," he thought.

"Ronnie, where have you been? I've been missing you," the security officer in the lobby asked.

After finding the weapons and four magazines, Ronnie came back to the truck. Tim assured her that two magazines per weapon would not be enough to stop Rock if he tried to hurt her. Tim guessed that neither she nor Nae knew how to shoot well enough to hit a moving target. Ronnie went back inside, only to find two more magazines to add to her worthless amount of ammo.

Ronnie was confident that Tim, Trey, Tony or Josh would be around her for the duration of her trip. She always heard Trey and Tony say that they'd never leave home without their weapons. With all of the support, from several strong men who truly cared about her, Ronnie was at now ease, thinking that it would be safe enough to let her guard down and enjoy the rest of her trip.

Chapter 23

*V*eronica's wedding day had finally arrived. Jerome's house was very chaotic. Cicely, Patrice and Angie all woke up early to cook breakfast for everyone.

"So where did you all end up going last night?" Cicely asked Angie.

"We went to some club. I heard Nae used to dance there before she had the baby. Ronnie probably did too," Angie replied as she beat the pancake batter.

"Nae sure looks good. You'd never guess she just had a baby," Patrice commented. "Did you get a chance to see Ronnie and Monie last night?"

"Yeah. Monie and I had a really nice time, but I guess Ronnie is still too hot to trot. She had already left with some guy by the time we got there," Angie stated. "I bet he looked like a hot mess," Angie muttered under her breath.

"You and your cousins need to get along," Cicely said.

"I don't have a problem with them. Ronnie just always hated me because I'm light skinned, with long hair, and always got better looking men than she did."

"The last time I was here, Ronnie had a guy so fine I would've gotten with him if I was thirty years younger. He looked better than anything I've ever seen you with," Cicely said inadvertently insulting Angie.

Angie popped her lips and began pouring the pancakes onto the griddle.

"Don't get mad sweetie. Your grandma's telling the truth. He was fine as wine. You'll probably get a chance to see him before we leave," Patrice cosigned Cicely's story. "He probably was at that club you all went to last night."

"Good morning everybody," Veronica said through a yawn as she stretched and entered the kitchen in her robe.

Veronica looked at the clock. The time was 8a.m. She picked up the phone to call Ronnie and Nae, knowing they were probably still asleep.

"Where are those girls?" Veronica asked rhetorically.

"Ronnie might still be with that guy," Angie said, shrewdly.

"What guy?" Veronica said, afraid that Angie may have been referring to Rock.

"I don't know his name," Angie said.

Veronica went upstairs and peeked in Monie's room to see if anyone was in there. Kyla was asleep on the air mattress at the foot of Monie's bed. Monie had obviously stayed at Nae's place or with Trey. Veronica started to panic.

She peeked outside to see if she saw Tim's truck. His truck was missing. Veronica figured Ronnie and Tim must have stayed at Nae's apartment. She called Nae's place again. Tony finally answered the phone.

"Tony, is Ronnie over there?" she asked.

"Yeah, she and Tim are on the pull out in the living room," Tony said, instantly calming Veronica's nerves.

Veronica let out a sigh of relief. "She slept…" catching herself before she said anything aloud that may have been incriminating about Ronnie. She stepped into the office and closed the door.

"She slept with Tim?" Veronica whispered.

"They slept next to each other all night. I don't think they messed around." Tony said, clarifying his story.

"Was Rock at the club last night?" Veronica asked.

Tony explained that he thought Ronnie and Rock had missed each other. Veronica requested to speak to Ronnie. Five minutes had gone by before Ronnie woke up. She didn't realize Tony had been trying to tell her that her mother was on the phone.

"Where is Tim?" Veronica inquired.

"He's asleep," Ronnie replied.

"What did you two do last night?" Veronica asked, hoping she wouldn't say that they had sex. "Ronnie, you're engaged now. You just can't do that," Veronica said before Ronnie got a chance to answer.

Ronnie thought her mother must have been on heavy medication.

"Ma, I will see you within the hour," Ronnie said and ended the call abruptly.

Ronnie looked under the cover to make sure she and Tim both were still partially dressed.

Tim and Ronnie arrived at Jerome's house before Tony and Nae. As they came through the front door, Jerome walked into the kitchen. He looked at Tim as if he'd done something wrong.

Angie looked at Tim, hoping he wasn't the guy that her mother and grandmother had just finished bragging about. Physically, he wasn't the kind of guy that Angie was usually attracted to, but he had a certain sex appeal that turned her on. He felt an unusual vibe from her that instantly turned him off.

Cicely fixed a plate of food for Ronnie and Tim as soon as they walked through the door. Jerome gestured for Tim to meet with him in the garage.

"Man, where'd you go with my daughter?" Jerome asked.

"You got me into this mess," Tim said.

Jerome could only laugh.

"We went somewhere to talk about her drama, and then we went over to your other daughter's house. Somebody was following us all night long," Tim added.

Jerome could only imagine that somebody being Rock. Tim explained that he advised Ronnie to carry her gun. Jerome agreed and thanked Tim for looking out for her.

Jerome didn't even know Ronnie and Nae had ever purchased guns.

The time was 11:30a.m. Juanita and Josh hadn't made it over to Jerome's house yet. Everyone was ready to load up in the limos to drive to the church. Ronnie wanted to talk to Tim, but was afraid that Josh would show up at any time.

Tony's phone rang.

"Hello," he answered.

"Tone, what's up?" Rock asked.

"I'm about to go to the wedding."

"Yeah, I want to go to the wedding too." Rock stated.

"Man that's not a good idea," Tony tried to talk discreetly.

"Man, I've got to see Ronnie today." Rock started with his foolish conversation.

"Okay. I'll get with you later," Tony said and ended the call.

"Who was that?" Nae asked.

Tony looked at Nae without saying a word.

"Please tell me that Rock's not trying to come to my mother's wedding," Nae asked.

Tony didn't respond. He shook his head, thinking of what he could do to keep Rock away from Ronnie. He knew Rock was going to do something to Ronnie for being with Tim.

Once they arrived at the church, everyone, except for Veronica and Jerome, stood outside near the limos waiting for Juanita to show. Veronica had become frantic, thinking that something had to have happened to Juanita since she hadn't called or showed yet.

Juanita, Josh and Jason saw everyone standing around outside as they drove into the church's parking lot.

"You need to watch your fiancée a little closer. Jerome's friend has been trying to talk to her since he got here. She looked like she was interested in what he had to say," Juanita told Josh as they found a vacant parking spot.

"I trust Ronnie," Josh said. "It's you that I have to watch."

"Me! Look at 'em. You see how's he's all over her. She smiling like she's so happy," Juanita said, instigating.

"She is happy. Her mother is about to get married. Something I wish mine would do," Josh said throwing his mother a hint.

Juanita was apparently getting on Josh's nerves. Jason sat in the back seat, quiet. He agreed with Josh, but didn't feel like arguing with his mother.

Juanita opened her door to get out of the car. "I'm just warning you. You better keep an eye on her so you won't get hurt," Juanita said slamming the door. She started hugging everyone on her way inside the church.

Jason and Josh stood next to their mother's car while Jason helped Josh get his cummerbund and bow tie on straight.

"What was that all about?" Jason asked.

"She likes Jerome's friend but she's trying to put it off on Ronnie. Before the dude got out of his truck mom was practically all over him. But she's telling me to watch Ronnie," Josh said, not understanding why his mother had it out for Ronnie.

Ronnie wanted to go over and say something to Josh since she hadn't seen him since they had been in Atlanta. She didn't want to look as if she was guilty about something, nor did she want Tim to know that she didn't want Josh to see them together.

She waited for Josh to come over and confront her.

"Hey babe, you ready to do this?" Josh asked, extending his arm to escort her into the church and assume their positions.

As Juanita marched down the aisle with Tim, he felt a slight tug from time to time. This was an obvious *distraction* for Tim to direct his attention to her. She felt as though this would give her the upper hand above Ronnie. Jerome's father marched Veronica down the aisle. She was beautiful. Her makeup was flawless, that was until the first tear fell as she stared at her groom who was waiting for her to unite with him at the altar.

During the ceremony, Ronnie imagined how she would like her ceremony to be. She wanted something extremely small, yet elegant. She thought about the intimacy she'd shared with Tim last night. They danced and caressed each other in the darkness, to some soft and mellow music. Ronnie felt like she had gone to paradise. He massaged her shoulders and back and held her close until they fell asleep.

Ronnie glanced over and saw Jerome flip her mother's veil and gave her a kiss. She imagined that being the kiss she wanted to give Tim last night for the wonderful night of wholesomeness.

Ronnie joined in as everyone clapped in congratulating the new couple. Juanita looked at Tim. "It's time to go get our dance on. So, are you at least going to dance with me?" Juanita asked, setting up the moment to make her move.

"I see that you're quite interested in my daughter in law," Juanita commented. She looked Tim up and down as she sashayed away, trying to draw attention to her curvaceous figure.

Tim smiled at her, hoping she'd disappear a little faster. Once she was gone, he could find Ronnie and have a word with her, before Josh reclaimed all of her time and attention. Juanita was still slowly tipping away, looking back at him as if she wanted him to join him right then. *"If she knows I'm interested in Ronnie, why won't she leave me the hell alone,"* Tim thought.

Tim took another quick glance around the church in search for Ronnie. Monie walked up to Tim. "They're looking for you. The photographer needs the whole wedding party in the lobby now," Monie said, relieving him from the thought of being stuck alone with Juanita.

He tried not to let Monie get away from him in case Juanita decided to join him for another conversation he didn't want to have. "Please don't leave me alone at the reception with that horny lady," Tim begged. "She's crazy."

The photographer must have used at least ten rolls of film. They spent about thirty minutes taking pictures. Juanita was enjoying every moment of it while standing next to Tim, continuously making passes at him.

"That's a wrap," the photographer said.

Tim rushed over and shook Jerome's hand, still trying to get away from Juanita.

"Ronnie, could you go out to the limo and get my slippers?" Veronica asked on her way down to join everyone at the reception.

Everyone went downstairs to the reception room while Ronnie went outside to the limo to gather her mother's things. Ronnie looked for the driver of the limo, assuming the car doors were locked. He apparently was at the reception with everyone else. She took a chance on opening the door, and to her surprise, they weren't locked.

"You could've invited me to the wedding," Rock said, coming from between two parked cars near the limos, scaring Ronnie nearly to death. "I guess you were too busy entertaining your new boyfriends to even give me a call huh?"

"Rock, what are you doing here?" Ronnie asked.

Ronnie patted her side, feeling for her purse. She remembered she had left her purse with Nae while she ran outside. She was glad she followed Tim's advice to bring her gun with her. If only she could get inside of the reception to get it, bringing it would not have been in vain.

Rock took a few steps towards her. She panted; trying hard not let her emotions overtake her. She was overcome by fear again, not knowing what to expect since he'd seen her with other men. Wanting to explain her innocence as opposed to whatever he may have heard about her being with Tim, her lungs just couldn't grasp enough oxygen to say anything.

"All I want to know is why you ran off to Virginia with Tim, and lied to me about it," Rock asked. "Was I not good enough for you?"

"Rock I've never been to Virginia before. How do you know Tim?"

Ronnie asked.

Ronnie didn't know where he'd gotten the idea that she'd been to Virginia.

"That's not important. Ronnie, I just want to be with you. I'm not gonna hurt you," Rock stated. "Ronnie, let me have just one more night with you before you go back to wherever you live," Rock asked sincerely, trying to lure her into saying yes. "Please. I promise I won't bother you anymore if you'll just give me one more night with you," Rock begged.

"What is it that you want from me…sex?" Ronnie asked.

"Ronnie! Your mom said to grab her purse too," Juanita yelled across the parking lot, trying to see if Tim was out there with her.

Ronnie nodded indicating that she would get the purse also. She turned around to resume her conversation with Rock but he was gone.

"Rock," Ronnie called with a whisper. "Rock, where are you?"

She looked around to see if she could see any movement. She slowly took a couple of steps back towards the church. Rock stood up next to his Jaguar and watched as she nervously reentered the church.

Ronnie joined the wedding party at the lead table as if nothing had happened. Josh looked at her, unaware that she was frantic as he held his toast glass up, nodding and smiling at her. Tim looked at her, unsure of what was wrong, but he knew something wasn't right. He couldn't clearly read her actions. Juanita stared at Tim as if she was studying him, as he tried to guess what was going on with Ronnie.

Rock cruised down the street listening to some smooth R&B, when his cell phone rang. "Hello?"

"I've been waiting to get my chance to be with you," the whispering voice said.

"You're sending mixed signals. You just said you didn't want to be with…" Rock stopped his sentence and figured out that this voice wasn't Ronnie's. He tried to keep the conversation going so he could recognize the voice.

"You just try to enjoy the rest of your mother's wedding," Rock said trying to see this female's reaction to what he was saying.

"My mother died of a heart attack when she heard that I was dead."

"Who is this?" Rock asked, still trying to re-familiarize himself with this anonymous voice.

He slammed his flip phone closed and thought, "That damn Shonte!"

He felt like a fool for thinking that he'd been talking to Ronnie. All the times he'd received that call he'd never picked up on the voice. It had just dawned on him that putting on that voice wasn't Ronnie's style.

After the dinner was over, Jerome and Veronica walked around thanking everyone for their help and support in making their day a success.

"Nae, where is my purse?" Ronnie asked.

Nae looked around, unable to find Ronnie's purse. Ronnie looked under tables, chairs and gifts trying to find her purse. Ronnie ran out of the reception area. She rushed up into the sanctuary, looking under pews and anything she thought was big enough to hide a small hand held purse.

Tim snuck upstairs to the sanctuary to find out why Ronnie was so adamant about finding whatever she was looking for.

"Ronnie, what's going on?" Tim asked.

Ronnie stopped looking for a minute to respond to Tim. "I can't find my purse."

Tim knew something was definitely going on. Her determination to find her purse was too strong to assume she was just looking for a tube of lipstick or a comb.

"Did you remember to bring your pistol?" Tim asked.

Ronnie looked at him as if she'd just seen a ghost. She hesitated to answer him.

"You must've seen Rock. Did he try to hurt you?"

Ronnie looked at Tim as if he had telepathy. He obviously was reading her mind and knew exactly what she was thinking.

"How did you know?" Ronnie asked with suspicion.

"I've never seen a woman look for something so hard, as if her life depended on it."

Ronnie wanted to cry, but she refused to shed any tears unless they were tears of joy for her mother. Tim saw that she was fighting to hold them back. He assured her that everything would be all right. He wanted to hug and kiss her pain away, but he knew that everything he did was being scrutinized and reported.

Juanita noticed that Ronnie and Tim were missing again. She asked Josh if he'd seen either one of them, trying to make an issue of their coincidental disappearance. Josh was quite tired of his mother's false accusations. Several times he tried ignoring her. He didn't want to make a scene, or disrespect her in front Veronica's other friends and family. He decided that the best thing he could do was to leave.

Josh told Veronica what was going on with his mother's paranoia and asked if she could talk to her. Josh explained the situation to Jason and told him that he was leaving. He found Ronnie near the restrooms and asked if she and his mother had any more confrontations.

Ronnie shrugged her shoulders and shook her head, gesturing that his mother was the least of her concerns. He was glad to know that Ronnie wasn't at all stressed about his mother's silly behavior.

"Ronnie, I love you. I promise I won't let my mother come between what we have," Josh confessed.

Ronnie could see that Josh was tired and stressed out.

"Are you going to be okay?" Josh asked.

Ronnie shook her head with a strong sense of confidence.

"Is Tim trying to get with you?"

"No. He knows Rock and he's just teaching me how to handle myself against him," Ronnie assured Josh.

Josh trusted Ronnie enough to believe that what she was saying was the truth. This made him comfortable knowing someone else cared enough about her to help her protect herself when he wasn't around. He kissed her and gave her a long hug. Josh didn't know why, but this hug seemed special. He didn't want to let her go. He starred into her big, brown, glossy eyes before he eventually realized that something was wrong. Something he should have noticed a long time ago. He and Ronnie shared a special bond before he said goodbye.

"I love you. Now go home and get some rest. I'll call you for Monie's party tomorrow," Ronnie said, reconfirming their date.

Josh had a strange, unjustifiable feeling, and found it hard to stop embracing her. He kissed her repeatedly before he and Jason finally left. Ronnie stood twisting her engagement ring around on her finger, cherishing their love, as she watched him walk away. She asked God to forgive her and take away all of her desires of infidelity and lust. She knew Josh was worthy of her loyalty and faithfulness.

Ronnie didn't give Rock an answer as to whether or not she would give him one night to say or do whatever he had in mind. She knew he was going to make it happen with or without her consent. She hoped that whatever Rock had in store for her wouldn't affect Josh in any way. Ronnie was just starting to understand why her mother had been trying so hard for so many years to get her to see why Josh was the perfect guy for her.

Tim walked around outside trying to find any traces of evidence, signifying that Rock was actually there or had been there. Josh saw Tim outside and decided it was time to confront him about the drama that had been going on between his mother and Ronnie.

Josh went over and greeted him respectfully.

"Are you looking for anything in particular?" Josh asked, as Tim appeared to be looking down on the ground and in between cars.

Tim didn't know what to tell him. He didn't want Josh to know that Ronnie was terrified because Rock had been there.

"I just needed some fresh air," Tim said.

Josh got straight to the point. "You know my mother is crazy about you."

"Yeah…she's beautiful," Tim sighed. He then hesitated, trying to think of something else to say about Juanita without offending Josh. "But I'm just not interested," Tim finally confessed. *"I wonder why everyone can see that except for her,"* Tim thought.

"What makes her think that you have a thing for Ronnie?" Josh asked.

"She thinks I want Ronnie?" Tim asked as if he was surprised. "She made it clear to me that Ronnie was *your* girl."

Josh could clearly see that Tim wasn't the problem. The problem lies with his mother's paranoia and vivid imagination. He still didn't understand why his mother insisted on making such a mess of things by starting rumors of Tim and Ronnie trying to kick it on the down low.

After Josh and Jason left, Tim went back inside to rejoin the party. Juanita was thrilled that Tim had finally given her the chance she'd been waiting for since he arrived on Georgia soil. They danced together continuously, one song after the other. Juanita grinded her body against his as R. Kelly played in the background.

"Do you find me unattractive?" Juanita asked.

"No. You're very beautiful," Tim replied.

"If he thinks I'm beautiful, why isn't he attracted to me?" Juanita asked herself.

"Why don't you want to hook up with me?" she asked.

Tim let her know that she was too aggressive for him. "You seem to throw yourself at men," Tim explained. "That's a turn off."

Juanita was suddenly embarrassed by the truth, in which none of the guys she'd ever dated stayed sober long enough to tell her. She appreciated Tim's honesty, but she still wanted a chance to go on a date with him before he left.

Although Tim treated her nicely and gave her the utmost respect, he wasn't interested in going on a with her. He made up an excuse as to why he couldn't go out with her after the reception. Juanita merely begged him to come over her house for a quiet evening of champagne and conversation.

Tim slowly eased off the dance floor, sneaking away from Juanita as everyone performed the electric slide. He grabbed a cold soda out of the cooler and found a cozy corner at the opposite end of the room, where he would be out of sight once Juanita finished dancing.

Ronnie, Patrice, Cicely and Angie started taking down the decorations while everyone was on the dance floor and out of the way. Angie spotted Tim, alone, in the corner. She went over to talk to him and eventually commented on the rumors in which Juanita had started about him and Ronnie.

"Why are you sitting over here all alone?" Angie asked.

"I obviously wanted to be alone," Tim thought.

"I just needed to catch my breath," Tim replied.

"I figured your new girlfriend wouldn't give you a chance to breathe," Angie said, sarcastically referring to Ronnie.

Tim looked at her as if he didn't know what she was talking about.

"So what are you insinuating?" Tim asked bluntly.

"Everyone's noticed how close you and Ronnie have become," Angie said trying to pry, thinking that Tim would reveal some juicy information to her.

"Man that rumor is old and I'm tired of hearing about it. If Ronnie and I have something going on then that's between us," Tim said with obvious aggravation.

Tim rudely got up and walked away. He had become annoyed with the interrogation about either Ronnie or Juanita. He didn't understand how Jerome was going to handle the pressure of Veronica's family always nagging and getting into their business.

"I don't know why everybody's making such a big fuss about him. He

is too arrogant," Angie thought. *"I guess he knows how to put it down. Huh, I guess Ronnie would be the one to ask about that."*

Tim was glad to see that Tyrone had started dancing with Juanita. He thought he may've been able to sneak out without anyone seeing him. He wished he had driven his own vehicle so he could leave the drama there at the church.

"Why didn't you come to visit me when I was in rehab?" Tyrone asked Juanita. "You were all I had."

"How dare you even talk to me!" Juanita exclaimed.

Tyrone gave her a heartfelt stare as if he was truly hurt about everything he had put her through. Juanita knew he was lying through his pearly white teeth, the very attribute that turned her on when she first saw him.

"I came up there to see you. That's where I met Sonya," Juanita bitterly informed him before she walked away and started looking for Tim.

Tyrone couldn't recall when Juanita met Sonya. *"That must have been disastrous,"* he thought.

"I need a cigarette," Tim thought. He strolled down the street alone, wondering how he'd caused so much turmoil within one family. *"I could see if I was Denzel or Tyler Perry, but they're going crazy over little old me,"* Tim said to himself. He was ready to get away from Atlanta for the second time around.

Everyone was exhausted as they rode in silence back to Jerome's house. The tension was thick enough to cut with a pair of scissors. Tim sat analyzing the family's actions. He noticed that most of the animosity was directed towards Ronnie, but the fingers were being pointed at him.

Tim hated to be in that type of atmosphere. He felt like if he could have ridden on the roof safely, he would've. Once again, he felt bad for Ronnie. It wasn't fair for everyone to think negatively about her for something she had no control over.

Ronnie figured it would behoove her to stay at Nae's apartment again to keep down a lot of confusion. She was tired of everyone, Juanita and Angie particularly, snickering behind her back and giving her nasty looks. She was ready to go back to California immediately after Monie's graduation.

Tim's original plans were to stay in Atlanta until Sunday night. After all of the drama that had gone on during the course of the weekend, he was leaving Sunday morning. He wanted to spend a little more time with Jerome and Ronnie, hopefully without all of the scrutiny or having to be judged for someone else's jealousy and false accusations.

Tim followed Ronnie over to Nae and Tony's place. He thought he may have been over reacting, but he was sure he had just seen what appeared to be, the same vehicle that repeatedly circled the apartment when he and Ronnie went to pick up her pistol on the previous night.

Tim looked out of the apartment window periodically to see how often the same vehicle traveled that street. The vehicle eventually parked across the street for about twenty minutes. Tim noticed the person would leave and come back, turning their headlights off before they park. The vehicle stayed parked for fifteen to thirty minute intervals at a time. He noticed something wasn't right.

"Tony, do you know whose vehicle that is?" Tim asked pointing at the suspicious vehicle.

Tony looked out of the window. He saw the vehicle Tim pointed out.

"That Mercedes," Tony asked.

"Over half the people around here drives a Mercedes," Tony replied.

Nae took the scrabble board out of the closet. She and Ronnie reminisced about playing scrabble as children. Tony's phone rang.

"Tone, what's up?" Rock asked with his intimidating baritone voice.

Tony knew that he was probably calling to find out where Ronnie was. He didn't want anyone to know he was talking to Rock. He didn't volunteer any information.

"Have you seen Ronnie?" Rock asked.

Tony went back over to the window to see if the strange vehicle was still parked. "Where are you?" Tony asked.

Rock tried to avoid answering the question.

"Let's go have a couple of drinks," Tony suggested.

Tony knew Rock had something up his sleeve. He tried to throw a monkey wrench in his plans by suggesting they go somewhere else as oppose to being at his place.

"We can have drinks tomorrow. I'm looking for Ronnie. Have you seen her?" Rock asked.

Tony didn't want to be in the middle of anything. He knew that if he said the wrong thing, Rock would definitely go ballistic. He figured out that Rock was on a stakeout outside of his apartment. Tony couldn't lie, saying he didn't know where Ronnie was, nor could he say that Tim had left to go back to Virginia. Through his palm size binoculars, Tony could see that Rock was looking directly at Tim's truck as he talked to Tony on the phone.

Rock knew Ronnie was at Tony's place with Tim. He wondered if Tony would lie for Ronnie to help her get out of this situation. Tony was tired of beating round the bush.

"Rock, what do you want? You already know where Ronnie is?"

"She's over there with Tim isn't she?" Rock asked.

"No, they just happened to be here at the same time," Tony explained.

Tony found a notepad. He wrote a note, telling Ronnie to call Jerome and Trey from her cell phone and explain what was going on. Just as Tim thought the drama had ceased, Rock came creating more drama, putting him in the middle of it, again.

Tony wanted to distract Rock by leaving with Tim, but he was afraid to leave Ronnie, Nae and his baby there alone. He knew that Rick was probably around the corner waiting for someone to leave so that he could trail them and make Rock aware of their destination.

Rock greeted the security officer in the apartment's lobby and proceeded onto the elevator, up to Tony's apartment. Surprisingly, Rock came inside with a rather cordial demeanor as if everyone were his friends. He spoke to Tim and shook his hand as if there were no hard feelings.

As Ronnie sat nervously in the bedroom trying to call Jerome and Trey, she heard Rock's voice in the other room. Her small fingers trembled as she dialed the numbers. Tony hoped Ronnie had gotten in touch with Jerome and Trey. He felt as though he was fighting a losing battle having Rock, Ronnie, and Tim all under one roof without backup to help get Rock out of his home once things began to get ugly.

"Let's get a game of spades going," Rock suggested as he grabbed a beer out of the refrigerator.

Rock leaned against the wall and watched Nae closely as she rambled through the kitchen drawers looking for a deck of cards. Rock peaked through the apartment, making sure everyone was occupied before he made an attempt to find Ronnie.

Tony was in the baby's room tending to the baby. Tim stood looking in the bathroom mirror trying to think of a plan, just in case Rock started some chaos. Rock gently sat his beer on a coaster on the coffee table and walked slowly through the apartment to Tony's room. He wanted to see if Ronnie was in there trying to hide from him.

He discreetly opened the bedroom door and found that she was on her cell phone. He snuck in the room and quietly closed the door behind him. For at least twenty seconds, Rock stood behind her before Ronnie even realized someone was in the room with her. She carefully looked over her shoulder realizing it was Rock.

"Mom, I'll call you right back," Ronnie bluffed and ended her call with Jerome.

Jerome knew Rock must have been somewhere near Ronnie for her to portray this fake conversation and end their call in the middle of it.

Ronnie's conscience told her to dial 911 and keep the phone in her hand. In case Rock attempted to kill her again, she would only have to push the send button to allow the operator to hear all of the commotion.

Ronnie stood up facing Rock, making sure she kept the bed as a barrier between them. "What are you doing here?" Ronnie asked.

"I didn't know I had to have a reason to stop over my best friend's house," Rock replied.

Ronnie stood in silence listening to Rock's smart remarks. She wondered if she should make a mad dash for the door or stand there and wait for him to make the first move. "Let's just get to the point. Now that you've finally found me and got me alone, what do you want with me?" Ronnie asked.

Rock smiled. "I wanna let you know how much I love you."

"We've already had that conversation several times," Ronnie said, knowing there was more on his agenda than what he was going to tell her.

Ronnie took a couple of steps towards the foot of the bed. Rock didn't move. He just kept his eyes on her every move. By the time she got to the foot of the bed and reached for the door, Rock took two giant steps and had her pent against the wall.

"Where are you going?" Rock asked as he breathed heavily down on Ronnie's forehead.

"You weren't saying anything, so I was going to go up front with everyone else," Ronnie said quickly, making up a lie.

"I've been through hell while waiting for you to come back," Rock said. "I've been all over Canada looking for you. I was about to take another trip to look for you until I heard that you were coming back to Atlanta. My own family lied to me to protect you. How did you brainwash them?" Rock said with hostility.

"I didn't brainwash anyone," Ronnie said as her heart raced fiercely.

"You owe me," Rock stated firmly. "After all we've been through, you still treat me like crap. When will you learn? I could've taken your life a long time ago, but I spared it. Now you come back to town and wanna prance around with all of your little boyfriends, and won't even part your lips to say hi to me."

"Rock, the first time I saw you I spoke to you," Ronnie said, not knowing what else to say.

He knew Ronnie was scared to death. *"If I could just get to my purse, I'd splatter his brains all over Nae's walls,"* Ronnie thought. Her fear had been overtaken by anger and braveness. She was ready to stand up to Rock regardless of what the outcome would've been for her.

She felt the handle of his gun pressed firmly against her stomach as he leaned against her, penning her against the wall. She wasn't sure how his gun was made, but the thought of killing him with his own gun sounded quite tempting. Ronnie acted as if she was going to caress his stomach the way she used to, with intentions of getting her hands on the gun. He grabbed her hands and braced them against the wall over top of her head and stared into her eyes.

"You still belong to me. I swear on my own life, if I ever see you with some other nigga', I will put both of you six feet under. No questions asked—no explanation necessary," Rock said convincingly.

"Yo Rock, I thought you wanted to play cards," Tony said as he burst into the room.

"Ronnie and I had some catching up to do," Rock said remorselessly, releasing her arms from his overpowering embrace.

Nae stood behind Tony, peeping through the bedroom door trying to see if her sister was okay.

"What did you do my sister?" Nae asked Rock.

"Nae!" Tony yelled, indicating that she needed to keep her comments to herself.

Rock went to the front of the apartment and grabbed his beer off of the table. He stared at Tim out of the corner of his eyes and dared him to say anything. He stormed out of the apartment door leaving it wide open, ready to rumble with anyone who may have come out after him. He got in his truck and sped off as if he had accomplished a major task.

Ronnie was too scared to go to the front of the apartment and face Tim, knowing Rock would put a hit on his life if he ever saw them together again. Ronnie sat on the bed for a moment trying to regroup. Nae stood next to her, rubbing her back, comforting her.

She knew that if she'd listened to her mother when she told her to stay away from Rock, she wouldn't be in her present situation. Ronnie had finally learned her lesson and understood that everything her mother had been telling her was for her own good. She regretted the fact that she didn't take her mother's advice and value her wisdom. If she could turn back the hands of time, she knew things would've worked out a lot differently.

Chapter 24

Monie could hardly wait for daylight. She had tossed and turned all night. Her eyes popped wide open as she lay on her back, staring at the ceiling in disbelief. She would be walking across the stage within hours with her bachelor's degree in her hand. She cuddled up close behind Trey, wrapping her arm around him, and enjoying the warmth of his body.

Trey smiled, imagining what Monie's reaction was going to be when he surprised her with his special graduation present. He continued to lie there, giving her the impression that he was still asleep.

Ronnie hadn't been able to sleep all night, thinking about everything that happened the night before. She was anxious to get the day over with, so she could get back home to California and resume her peaceful life with Josh. She hoped she would be able to avoid Rock, but she knew she may've had at least one more run in with him before leaving.

Since everyone was scheduled to leave by noon on Sunday morning, she knew they would want to hang out all night celebrating Monie's graduation, enjoying their last night together. She hoped their minds were not set on going to Club Passions again. She was starting to hate that place—with a passion.

Tim opened his eyes as daylight peaked through the mini blinds. He stared into Ronnie's big, brown innocent eyes.

"Good morning," they chimed in sync.

"How'd you sleep?" Tim asked.

"I didn't," Ronnie replied truthfully. "How was he able to sleep after all that drama?" Ronnie asked herself.

"I think I'm going to hit the road after breakfast," Tim said.

"I thought you were going to leave in the morning along with everyone else," Ronnie responded with disappointment in her voice.

Tim wanted to spend one more night with her, but he wasn't sure how much more excitement he could stand.

"Well let's go to IHOP. It's on me," Ronnie suggested.

Tim looked at her as if he was waiting for the catch.

"For all you've done for me, breakfast is the least I can do for you," Ronnie confessed.

Tim got out of bed and tipped over to the window. He stood to the side of the window and peaked out to see if Rock's vehicle was still parked on the side of the street.

He didn't see a Mercedes or an Escalade.

"What kind of vehicle does Rick drive?" Tim asked.

Ronnie jumped out of the bed and tiptoed over to the window. She stood in front of Tim to look at the vehicle he thought may have been Rick's. Ronnie's hips rubbed against Tim's leg.

Her nightshirt was short and snug around her hippy figure. She slightly leaned forward to see if any of the parked vehicles belonged to any of Rock's entourage. Tim stared at her behind with amazement.

"I slept in the same bed with all of this for two nights and didn't do anything with it. I must be losing my mind. I know it's time to get out of Atlanta before I get myself and her killed," Tim thought. "So that's why Rock is so insane."

Ronnie turned around and caught Tim staring at her booty. She pulled her shirt down as far as it would go and walked back to the bed and sat down. *"So he is interested,"* she thought. She started feeling jittery inside, thinking that she may have been able to talk him into staying another night, granting her the opportunity to make something happen.

"I'm really not comfortable being here while Rock and his boys are out lurking around. Are you sure you can't stay just one more night?" she asked, trying to get his sympathy first so she could seduce him later.

Ronnie prayed a brief prayer under her breath. *"Lord, it's me again. Please take away this burning desire to sit on this man's…"*

"Ronnie!" Nae yelled down the hallway startling Ronnie nearly to death.

Ronnie cut her prayer short and turned around to see what was wrong with her sister.

"Could you watch Tonae while I take a shower? Tony's still asleep."

Ronnie exhaled and thanked God for answering her prayer. She knew she wouldn't be able to stay in the same room with Tim much longer before she jumped all over him.

The telephone rang several times while Ronnie was feeding Tonae. On her way to get the phone, she passed the baby and his bottle to Tim.

"Hello?"

"What else does your sister need for her party?" Rock asked as if nothing ever happened.

"Why don't you call Trey's house and ask her?" Ronnie said and slammed the phone down before she realized what she'd done.

Nae was just getting out of the shower. She cracked the bathroom door and asked Ronnie who was on the phone.

"Rock," Ronnie said in her normal tone. She stood in disbelief, wondering how someone could threaten you and be so cold-hearted and then turn around hours later and be the best of friends with you?"

Ronnie, Tim, Nae and Tony sat peacefully as they ate breakfast. Tim attempted to play footsies with Ronnie, trying to make her smile. However, she had become agitated from receiving mixed signals from Tim ever since they met. She released a long sigh. She couldn't let her anger show toward him because he had been so tolerant and protective of her during his entire trip.

Once they finished breakfast, they all headed over Jerome's house. Tim wanted to say goodbye to everyone before he got on the road. Tim insisted that Ronnie ride with him. He was still eager to find out how she'd gotten herself into such situation with Rock. He also wanted to know how she really felt about him.

"So would you like to exchange numbers, or just keep this weekend as a fond memory?" Tim asked, giving Ronnie the option to keep their new friendship alive or end it there.

Ronnie broke it to him gently. She knew he wanted to keep their lines of communication open, but she knew it would be best if they didn't have any further contact.

She wanted to remain monogamous with Josh. If they would've exchanged numbers, she knew the urge inside of her would have been to fly to Virginia every weekend.

Tim said his goodbyes to everyone as they finished their breakfast in the huge eat-in kitchen. Before he walked out the door, Ronnie grabbed his hand. She led him up into Monie's room to give him one last intimate French kiss that he would *never* forget.

Ronnie and Jerome walked Tim out to his truck. Tim walked over to Ronnie and asked if she still had her pistol in her purse.

"Always," Ronnie replied as Tim climbed up in the truck, leaving their conversation a mystery to Jerome.

Ronnie leaned against the edge of the house smiling as Tim drove away. Jerome knew what her smile and her *trip* upstairs was all about.

"I asked him to keep an eye on you for me while we were out clubbing so Rock wouldn't mess with you. I guess he was one hell of a bodyguard huh?" Jerome asked jovially, assuring her in an unspoken way that their secret was safe.

Trey rented an Escalade limousine for Monie's graduation. Everyone piled into it and headed to the ceremony. Monie was excited. Veronica was overjoyed that one of her girls had completed a major accomplishment in her life.

The crowd grew quiet as the emcee prepared to call the next graduate.

"Monica L. Williams," the emcee announced.

Veronica, Ronnie and Nae all jumped up and hugged each other as Monie walked across the stage. The crowd's response indicated that she was quite popular. Jerome and Trey were taping her on their camcorders as she received her degree, doing her *stance* on stage. She moved her tassel from the right side to the left and danced her way over to the other side of the stage joining the rest of her graduating friends.

Veronica had given Juanita a spare key to go over Jerome's house and get a head start on decorating and setting up the food for the party. Jason and Josh took Jason's truck. In case their mother started getting on their nerves, they'd be able to leave at any time.

Josh fired up the grill, and then went inside to get the meat out of the refrigerator. Juanita heard a knock at the front door. She looked at her boys and wondered who would be knocking at the door if everyone knew that Jerome and Veronica were at Monie's graduation.

Jason answered the door. "Mom, Rock wants you."

"Rock?" Juanita asked. "What the heck does he want with me?"

By the time Juanita made it half way to the door, Rock had already started making his way through the house. He was carrying several grocery bags, with lots more to unload from the truck. Juanita was skeptical about letting him in Jerome's house, knowing that he was this family's worst nightmare. She thought she knew Veronica well enough to know that she wouldn't have made a deal with the devil under any circumstance. She wasn't sure what to make of Rock's generosity.

After the ceremony, Monie spent nearly an hour taking pictures with all of her friends and their families. Trey wanted to give her the surprise that would eventually change her life, but he decided to wait until later when things calmed down.

As the limo pulled up into Jerome's yard, the driver managed to maneuver between Juanita's car, Josh's SUV and Rock's SUV.

"What is he doing here?" Ronnie yelled.

She tightly clinched her purse under her arm. Jerome got out of the truck first to go in and see what was going on. He walked in the door and saw Rock unpacking bags of groceries. Juanita looked at Jerome as if she had no clue as to what was going on.

"I just wanted to make sure Monie had everything she needed for the party," Rock said subconsciously.

"Thanks," Jerome said with apprehension. "How did you find my house?"

"I followed Ronnie one night to see where she was going. She came here," Rock said, making up a feasible story.

Ronnie walked in the house slowly behind Veronica and Cicely. Josh looked at Rock with hatred in his eyes as he took a couple pans of meat out to the grill. Rock's evil eyes were glued to Ronnie's every move. Ronnie couldn't stand being within the same four walls as Rock. She walked back outside and stood next to Josh, as he carefully placed the meat on the grill.

Rock wished everyone a joyous celebration and excused himself, knowing that he wasn't welcomed to the party. His malicious ways led him outside to where Ronnie was. Standing next to Josh, Rock said to Ronnie, "If you could find it in your heart to give me another chance, I swear I'll do right by you."

Rock wanted to see what Josh's reaction was going to be.

"After you threatened to kill me last night, how could you ask for another chance?" Ronnie asked.

Trey was on his way outside to convince Rock to leave. Ronnie's words stopped him in his tracks. He couldn't believe what he'd just heard.

"Rock, what's wrong with you? You can't just show up at folk's house and threaten to kill 'em," Trey said.

"I think she misunderstood me. I told her that if I ever caught her with one of her little boyfriend's, I'd put both of them six feet under," Rock said just loud enough for Josh to hear.

"Rock, that's enough!" Trey yelled with compelling rage, trying not to hurt Rock on Jerome's property.

"You better keep an eye on her. Just like she slept with you when she was dating me, there's no telling what she may've done with 'gold teeth' while they were prancing around half naked over her sister's house last night."

Josh knew he was just trying to get under his skin. He looked at Ronnie and started to wonder. *"What are the chances of some guy with all of those gold teeth getting Ronnie's attention,"* Josh thought. *"As ignorant as Rock is, he got her attention. I guess anything is possible."*

"I'll see you around," Rock said, looking directly at Ronnie as he climbed into his SUV.

"He went over to Tony's house and threatened you last night?" Trey asked.

Ronnie shook her head. She didn't want to give any details because she didn't want Josh to ask questions about her and Tim.

"Why didn't you call me?" Trey yelled sympathetically.

Trey jumped in his truck and tried to catch up to Rock before he got too far away. Trey caught up with him at a gas station on the corner, about three blocks away. He got out of the truck, and walked over to Rock to have a heart to heart conversation with him.

Jason and Tony rambled through their CD's trying to find some appropriate and respectable music for the occasion. Jason put on an old school Keith Sweat CD, saving the newer up tempo music for when everyone got ready to dance.

Taylor came downstairs in his stylish new gear and walked into the kitchen where all of the women were sitting.

"Oh, look at my grandbaby. He's grown up to be a handsome young man," Cicely commented.

"How old are you now Taylor?" Veronica asked.

"Twenty two," he replied with a little bass in his voice. "So whose boyfriend can I hang out with tonight?" Taylor asked, looking at Ronnie, Monie and Nae, waiting for a response.

"Well it won't be mine 'cause he's gonna be tied up with me tonight," Monie said.

"We'll get Josh and Jason to hang out with you tonight," Juanita stated, volunteering her sons without their consent.

"Ronnie, can't you drop us off at that club we were at the other night? You don't have to stay in case your crazy boyfriend stalks the club again, he wouldn't be able to identify anybody's car in the parking lot," Taylor suggested.

Veronica and Jerome shook their heads, agreeing to Taylor's suggestion. Taylor grabbed his mother's hand and pulled her to the middle of the floor, making her dance with him.

Trey had made it back from the gas station. Chills ran though his body as he thought about how sick Rock had become. He no longer felt safe being around Rock. As soon as he could, he was planning to pack Monie up and move her away from Georgia. It was Monie's big day and he wasn't going to ruin it for her. He couldn't let her know that he was emotionally hurting and in a state of confusion. He took a deep breath and exhaled slowly.

He marched through the house announcing, "I have something special for Monie. Can I get everyone to follow me into the family room? Let me direct your attention to the front of the room."

He held the small ring box in his left hand, assisting Monie off of the bar stool with his right hand. He stood in front of the fireplace, holding her left hand. He bent down on one knee and said, "Monie, I would be honored if you'd be my wife."

He opened the ring box. Everyone's eyes were focused on the diamond.

Monie grabbed her mouth trying to hide her enormous smile. "Yes!" she shouted with overbearing emotions.

Everyone watched with smiles and laughter as he slid the white gold band, with a three-carat diamond on her finger.

"Now that I'm married, all of my girls are engaged to be married. How wonderful is that?" Veronica announced. "This causes for a bigger celebration!"

Veronica dug through her old school stack of CD's that Jason had put aside and found Cool and The Gang's 'Celebration'.

Juanita smiled and watched as Veronica and Monie happily danced around with their men. She had nothing but envy. She went over to the counter and sat on the bar stool next to Ronnie.

"You know...I used to wanna be you," Juanita said.

Ronnie looked at Juanita with amazement. *"This is just confirmation that she's really crazy,"* Ronnie thought.

"I know you've had your fair share of hard times with Rock, just as any relationship. You were always laced with the finest of everything...clothes, jewels, cars. You've managed to get out of that situation, and fall directly into the arms of my baby. I know he's gonna treat you right," Juanita said as she and Ronnie laughed together.

"You obviously still have it because you're still turning heads. I'm sorry for acting so childish this weekend. I was just jealous that the lil' boy with the gold teeth and fancy car wanted to talk to you instead of me," Juanita admitted. "Would you accept my apology?" she asked sincerely.

Ronnie laughed and hugged Juanita. Veronica watched the two of them as they came to their senses. She tapped Jerome, Monie and everyone else who was in her reach, showing them what was going on with Ronnie and Juanita. Veronica smiled and resumed dancing.

Everyone had finished eating. Taylor and Ronnie stole the show in the dancing contest. Then Ronnie, Nae and Monie put on a show like they were the sensuous trio, En Vogue. Everyone took pictures, laughed and got tipsy from drinking. It was a night to remember.

The time was approaching 10p.m. Ronnie was getting tired.

"Taylor, are you ready to hit the club?" Ronnie asked.

Ronnie was going to ride with Nae in Tony's truck. They were going to take Taylor, Josh and Jason to the club. Trey had a strange feeling when it came to Ronnie going anywhere near Passions. Therefore, Trey volunteered to take them to the club for her.

"No, my sister graduated today and you just proposed to her. You guys need some quality time alone," Ronnie insisted.

"Ronnie, I know Rock is going to be in the vicinity of the club," Trey said, trying to talk her out of going at all.

"When Nae drives up to the door, they'll jump out and we'll keep going." Ronnie still insisted that he spend time with Monie. She was confident that she and Nae would be all right for two minutes, just long enough to drop them off and keep going. "You or Tony can pick them up from the club whenever they call" Ronnie suggested.

Veronica started feeling knots in the bottom of her stomach. Her head throbbed with an instantaneous pain.

"Ronnie, won't you listen to him?" Veronica asked. "Won't you stay here and help us finish cleaning?" Veronica begged.

Ronnie looked at her mother. "Ma, I can handle myself." Ronnie said trying to assure her.

"Ronnie, please. Mama, tell Ronnie to stay here with us," Veronica said to Cicely, begging her to talk Ronnie.

Ronnie and Nae continued walking out the door. "We'll be back in forty minutes," Ronnie stated.

"I'll follow them to make sure nothing happens," Jerome whispered to Veronica.

"Baby, I wanna go too," Veronica pleaded.

After Veronica finally got her shoes on, Cicely gave a long speech about using caution when they approach the club.

"Ma, we have to go. They'll be at the club before we leave here," Veronica said, trying to get the short version of her mother's speech.

Shonte was going to be brave tonight. She'd tried to hook up with Rock a few days ago, but he'd hung up on her before she could ask him about it. He was so wrapped up into seeing Ronnie that no one else even mattered. Shonte was getting angrier by the minute. She stopped at his house but no one was there. She knew if he weren't at home he'd be at the club.

Trey asked Tony to ride with him to the club. He wanted to be there just in case Rock was there and wanted to start with his foolishness again. They parked across the street at the small 'mom and pop' liquor store, enabling them to see everything that went on at the club.

Nae had stopped at the store for Taylor to pick up some Black and Mild cigars. She pulled up about fifteen minutes after Trey.

The club's parking lot was too full for them to get close to the door. Nae parked across the parking lot and let everyone out of the truck.

Ronnie was going to walk inside with Taylor to talk to Rome, and to let him know to look out for her younger cousin who was from out-of-town. After taking about three steps, Ronnie turned around to get her purse out of the truck.

"You have your piece on you?" Ronnie asked, playing around with Nae.

Nae laughed it off, but she was sure that her pistol was in the compartment between her and the door.

Josh and Jason walked ahead of Ronnie and Taylor, while they talked.

"So you're twenty two, with no children and about to finish school next year. I'm proud of you," Ronnie said. She gave her cousin a hug before they entered the club.

"I told her that I would kill her if I seen her with another nigga. Why she gotta be so damn hardheaded?" Rock told Rick before he jumped out of the truck. He wasn't aware that Taylor was her first cousin. He was starting to have second thoughts about the entire situation.

Ronnie stayed in the club for almost ten minutes.

"There's Rock," Tony said. "He has Rick driving. I know he's up to something."

More than anything, Tony was worried about alerting Nae. Tony and Trey took the safeties off their guns and loaded magazines, preparing to take Rock down if he attempted to do anything to Ronnie. Rick turned the lights off, and positioned the truck perfectly for Rock to jump back in, so he could take off if anything happened.

Tony called Nae's cell phone hoping she'd answer before Ronnie stepped foot out of the club. Nae turned the radio down and picked up her purse off of the floor. Rock stood next to the truck as if he was waiting for Ronnie to come out.

Shonte was preparing to give Rock the surprise he'd been waiting for. She parked at the liquor store several cars away from Trey and Tony. She glided across the street in the dark staying clear of the streetlights. She made sure no one could see her. If she were spotted, she would definitely be unidentifiable.

Rome escorted Ronnie outside to the club's front step. They stood talking for a few minutes. Trey ended the call to Nae's phone. Trey knew that Rock wasn't going to do anything while Rome was outside with Ronnie. He told Tony to keep his eye on Rick, just in case he decided to assist Rock.

"I still consider you a part of my family," Rome said laughing, before he walked back inside the club. Ronnie was walking over to the truck, when she heard someone call her name.

Rock was walking slowly behind a few parked SUVs towards the club. He put his finger on the trigger and began to aim in Ronnie's direction. He had a quick flashback of the night his father nearly killed one of his girlfriends. He suddenly realized it wasn't worth it. He thought about how much he really loved Ronnie. If he killed her he'd never be with her again.

Ronnie looked up and shots were fired. Nae looked around frantically trying to see where the shots were coming from so she wouldn't drive directly into them.

"Ronnie, get down!" Trey yelled and emptied half a magazine from the direction he thought the shots came from.

Nae pulled off in Ronnie's direction to pick her up, but she didn't see her anymore. Ronnie's first reaction was to throw her hands up to guard her head. She spotted Rock with the gun in his hand. She pulled her gun out of her purse and returned fire in Rock's direction. Ronnie was running to the truck and suddenly fell to the ground.

Rock looked around wondering where the shots were coming from. He knelt down beside a parked car wondering what was going on.

Trey continued running and shooting in Rock's direction. Rick tried desperately to keep an eye on what was going on. He had no clue of Rock's intentions to kill Ronnie cold blooded. Tony walked up to Rick's window and held a gun to his head, making him drop his gun out of the window and onto the ground.

Trey kicked Rick's gun under the truck and shielded himself by a parked car, while he changed clips. He peaked around the front of the parked car to see what was going on. He saw Rock's head pop up between two parked cars. Rock looked around to see if anyone was standing.

Nae was heading directly for Rock, attempting to run him over with the truck. He jumped on top of a parked car, making her hit the car instead of him. Ronnie popped back up across the parking lot and tried to run to the truck again. She had gotten shot in the leg. She moaned in pain like she never had before. She didn't see anyone else standing.

Ronnie was scared to move from the car that was shielding her. With her wounded leg extended, she knelt down next to the car. She eased up to her feet, putting all of her weight on her good leg.

"Ronnie, stay there!" Nae yelled.

Nae spotted Trey trying to make his way over to her, to cover her while she tried to get in the truck.

"Ronnie, don't move!" Nae yelled again.

Ronnie stood up a little straighter, unable to hear Nae. Amazed, but glad that she could maintain her balance on one leg. Shots were fired again, scaring her to death. She fell to the ground again. She felt a burning sensation throughout her body as she eventually went numb.

Trey aimed his gun in Rock's direction. Before Trey released any shots, they heard shots coming from somewhere else. They suddenly saw Rock fall to the ground. After the shots ceased, Trey ran over to Rock's body to remove the gun from his hand. He checked for a pulse that was nonexistent. Trey gasped for air, realizing his biological cousin and best friend of nearly thirty years was dead.

Ronnie lay on the ground in a puddle of blood. She had flashbacks of the conversations she had with her mother when she and Rock first hooked up. She heard her mother's voice explaining the kinds of lessons that are learned, and the kinds that are unlearned. She had come to the realization that she'd learned her lesson too late. As she lay bleeding more intense, she also heard Ms. Wilcox's voice telling her to save herself and don't end up dead. Ronnie shed what would be her last tear.

Trey remembered he still had to find and maybe revive Ronnie.

"Ronnie!" Trey yelled.

"Come on Ronnie! Trey got you covered!" Nae yelled through the window of the truck.

Nae opened the door to get out, in attempt help find her sister.

"Ronnie!" Nae yelled again.

"Stay in the truck!" Trey yelled at Nae. "Stay in the truck!"

Trey had seen this scenario too many times to know that the outcome wasn't going to be good.

"Ronnie," Trey said, trying to hang on to a tad bit of hope.

Before Ronnie's eyes closed completely, she watched as the club was suddenly engulfed in flames. Everyone was running for safety. This was deja vu. The burning and collapsing building that she had been so afraid of in her dreams was now happening—directly in front of her very eyes.

Jason called Veronica's house to get someone to return to pick them up. He assumed that Ronnie and Nae should've been arriving back at Veronica's house any second. He, Josh and Taylor stood as spectators, watching the club as it burned. They were aware that a shooting had occurred outside before everyone was forced to evacuate, but never thought for a split second that the victim was Ronnie.

Jerome and Veronica scuffled out the door to get to the club to see what was going on.

As he got closer to the car that was shielding her, Trey saw Ronnie's feet. His emotions overtook him. With the inconsiderable amount of oxygen from his lungs, he tried to perform CPR on her several times.

"Ronnie," he said, still gasping for air.

Her eyes were barely open. The entire front of her shirt was saturated with blood as the puddle of blood underneath her streamed down the slight decline. Ronnie's body convulsed once more before she took her last breath.

"Tony! Tony!" Trey yelled. "Tony, please help me!" Trey cried.

Nae tried to jump out of the truck again. Tony and Rick knew from the sound of Trey's cry that Ronnie was dead. Rome called 911. Tony made it to his truck by the time Nae climbed out of it. He held her back from running over to see her sister's dead body.

Nae fell to the ground in shock, yelling her sisters' name repeatedly. Rick was the only one who could barely say anything.

"I swear I didn't know what was going down," Rick confessed.

Shonte calmly walked back across the street to her car. She watched all of the commotion as if she were watching her favorite team win the Super Bowl. As she saw the emergency vehicles arrive, she pulled off slowly. "Now Rock and his hoe got what they deserve. They deserve to be in hell with each other," Shonte thought aloud.

Veronica knew something was wrong. She hoped that if it was Rock and Ronnie that they had only gotten into a quarrel again. She hoped an arrest was the worst that had happened. Jerome pulled close enough to the scene enabling Veronica to hear Nae from afar calling Ronnie's name continuously. Jerome insisted that Veronica stay in the car.

A knot formed in her throat. She couldn't make it to her children fast enough. As they got closer to the action, Veronica tried to remain calm. She was in denial. She totally ignored Jerome's request and got out the car. She broke down when she saw Josh vomiting and crying uncontrollably.

"Where's Nae? Where's Ronnie? Where are my girls?" Veronica shouted.

Veronica's equilibrium was suddenly snatched from her body as she walked down the slight decline. Her chest tightened up, making it hard for her to breathe. She saw Nae first wrapped up in a blanket, covered in blood. She knew then that Ronnie was hurt.

"Ronnie!" Veronica cried out. "God no! No! No! God please let my baby be all right!" Veronica screamed. "Lord, this can not be happening! Lord, please don't let it be so!" she cried.

Veronica took small, baby steps and suddenly fainted as she saw the EMT zip the body bag and put her baby in the ambulance. The EMT feared Veronica was having a mild heart attack. They also loaded her in an unoccupied ambulance and took her to the hospital.

Jerome, Rick and Jason tried to remain strong enough to gather the family quickly and get them to the hospital. After an hour of waiting, Patrice called Veronica's cell phone, but received no answer. Patrice and Cicely knew something had gone terribly wrong.

The EMT monitored Veronica's heart rate on the way to the hospital. She was on the borderline of having a heart attack. They rushed her into the hospital and hooked her up to several IV's and a respirator.

Jason called Monie to notify her that she should come to the hospital with her grandmother and her aunt. Over the phone, he couldn't tell her what was going on. He preferred if Jerome told her.

"Man, I don't know where those shots came from. It didn't look like Rock was going to shoot anybody," Tony admitted.

"Rock didn't fire at all. His magazine was full and he still had one in the chamber. So who shot Ronnie?" Trey asked.

Tony shook his head and shrugged his shoulders. No one knew who shot who.

Trey and Tony were torn between families. Rock's mother wasn't going to be as surprised and torn apart as Veronica. For years, Rock's mother knew of the dangerous lifestyle her son had been living, and anticipated the news of his death at any given moment. Trey knew that Rock's mother would be distraught, especially not knowing who took her sons life.

Tony finally found enough courage to call and inform Ms. Wilcox that Rock had been involved in a serious accident. He wasn't going to tell her that Rock was dead. He wanted her and Regina to come to the hospital and see it themselves.

Jerome held Nae tight, trying to comfort her as much as he could. She would be scorned for life with two unbearable wounds. The lost of her sister and best friend would be the most excruciating pain she'd ever have to endure. But, she'd also have to cope with her fiancé that watched as his cousin was brutally murdered directly in front of him.

Josh had prayed for God to grant him the wish to see the day when Ronnie became his wife. Only God himself knew why that day never came. Josh sat waiting for whatever was next. He reminisced how Ronnie used to ignore him when they were younger. It took him almost ten years to get her, but only ten seconds to lose her. Josh had no desire to reside in California any longer. He was going to move back closer to Atlanta to keep an eye on his mother, who obviously needed supervision.

Once Monie, Cicely and Patrice arrived at the hospital, Jerome and Trey found it to be merely impossible to let such news roll off of their tongues. Monie felt like her whole world was coming to an abrupt end. She looked up to Ronnie more than anyone in the world. Monie cried herself into a state of dehydration.

Ms. Wilcox and Regina made it to the hospital shortly after Monie. Ms. Wilcox didn't shed a tear. She wanted to say something to Veronica, but didn't know how to approach Ronnie's grieving family. She sat with Trey and Tony, staring at Veronica, Nae and Monie from afar.

A half hour later, Ms. Wilcox went over to introduce herself to Veronica.

"Veronica, I'm Ms. Wilcox, Rock's mother. I'm terribly sorry for what happened. My condolences go out to you and your family. I'm sorry we had to meet on these terms."

Ms. Wilcox gently grabbed Veronica and hugged her. Veronica didn't understand how Ms. Wilcox seemed to be so undisturbed after finding out that her son was just killed.

"I know my timing may be off tremendously, but if you'd be willing to have a double funeral, I'd be more than willing to pay for all of the expenses," Ms. Wilcox offered.

"I'll think about it," Veronica said.

Ms. Wilcox shook her head and apologized again before turning and walking away.

There were a few doctors and nurses on duty. They all stared down the halls and through the windows of operating rooms, feeling sorry for the multitude of family members who had lost their loved one from such a violent and pointless crime.

Jerome didn't get home until 8a.m. He was exhausted. Everyone slept wherever they found space at his house. Once he woke up, his work was cut out for him. He had to call and postpone their honeymoon reservations and make funeral arrangements. From that point, he had to take a step-by-step process to nurse his new wife and stepdaughters back to good health and sanity. Although the entire family was distressed, Jerome was glad that he had Cicely and Patrice's help.

Epilogue

*T*he twin caskets were open in the front of the church for the viewing of the bodies. Everything was quiet. Veronica looked at all of the unfamiliar faces of the women who sat mourning in the church. She didn't think they were friends of Ronnie's. Most of them greeted Tony, Trey, Rick, Rome and Regina, and gave their condolences to the family.

"Who are all of these women?" Nae finally asked.

"They all are Rock's ex-girlfriends," Tony replied.

One half of the church was filled with these grieving women, young, old and in between, with their children of all different ages. Nae saw many similar features of Rock as she studied the children's faces.

Trey and Tony recognized a lot of the women who sat quietly, but he didn't approach them. They noticed the children's ages matched the time frame in which Rock had relationships with the mothers.

"Two, three...four...six, seven," Trey counted under his breath as he scanned the church, looking at the children who all shared comparable facial features. He couldn't believe his eyes. He counted nine of the children before stopping. Some of the children cried uncontrollably as if they knew and had some sort of relationship with Rock.

As the service went on, Veronica couldn't come to grips with reality. She was still in denial that her baby was dead. She walked up to the casket, rubbing Ronnie's face and stroking her hair, like she used to do while the girls were asleep when they were small children.

"Ronnie, it's time to get up. Get up sweetie. Baby, please wake up," Veronica repeated.

Jerome went to console her, trying to get her to understand that Ronnie wasn't going to get up. Veronica insisted on trying to pull Ronnie's body up to get her out of the casket.

"That bastard took my child away from me!" Veronica yelled.

She broke down, almost falling to the floor as Jerome embraced her, breaking her fall. Jerome and Tyrone tried desperately to get her out of the sanctuary and to the restroom. They had to help her regroup enough to get through the remainder of the ceremony. Patrice and Cicely followed Jerome to the restroom to help in whatever way they could.

Rome had a hard time coping with Ronnie's death, given that he was the last one to talk to her before she was gunned down. He blamed himself for not escorting her the entire way to the truck. *"I could have saved her and my brother's lives, but I was too wrapped up into my money,"* Rome thought.

Ms. Wilcox opened the obituary and read that Rock had at least twelve children whose names and ages were undisclosed. She knew Rock's skeletons were numerous, but she never imagined they'd be to that extent.

Regina knew of at least two of the children and their mothers, but when she read about twelve, she began looking around to see if she could single them out. She hated the fact that Rock never brought the children home to meet her and her mother.

She would have loved to have a relationship with them. This would let the children know that they had an aunt and grandmother. Two people who could give them unconditional love, which she knew they weren't getting from Rock.

Shortly following the service, Regina tried catching some of the mothers, whose children looked like they could be her nieces and nephews. She questioned them of their relationships with Rock, finding out that three of the women said they were once married to Rock. She talked to a lady name Jeanette, who told Regina that Rock always said that his parents lived on a tropical island in the Caribbean. Apparently, this was his reason for not taking Jeanette to meet her in-laws right away.

Regina was deeply hurt that Rock lied about his family. She then talked to another lady named D'Andrea, who had twin boys around the age of eight. They were identical to Rock when he was their age. She said Rock told her that he had to resort to dealing drugs to support himself, because his family had died in a car accident.

D'Andrea told Regina that she and Rock had the perfect life in Miami nine years earlier. D'Andrea was four months pregnant with the twins when the Feds invaded her home and took everything, including the home. She was hurt when Rock disappeared for nearly a year, leaving her with nothing but a broken heart and two children to raise on her own. She later found that he had faked his own death and moved to Mexico.

Regina remembered the time when Rock lived in Miami and Mexico. He used to talk to her and her mother often, but never mentioned a family. Regina didn't know how one person could have so many secrets, without any of them being revealed until this tragic event. She'd learned something Trey, Tony and Rick never knew.

Regina didn't know how to handle the disturbing news from the few women she'd just talked to. As they rode to the burial ground in the back of the limo, she started telling Rome and her mother about some of the things she has just heard.

"So, you finally got a chance to meet some of them?" Rome asked.

"You knew about all of these children and you kept it from us all of these years?" Ms. Wilcox asked. "I knew he had a couple of children, but he had all of us believing he'd never been married. How could you keep something like that from us?"

Rome remained quiet. He promised Rock many years ago, that he wouldn't reveal his secrets. He figured, in his own timing, Rock would let everyone know.

"Who's been taking care of all of those children for all of those years?" Ms. Wilcox asked.

"He has," Rome replied. "That's why he's been a drug lord for so long. Rock didn't want to live that kind of lifestyle anymore, but he didn't have a choice."

"He should've put that thing on lock," Regina butted in.

"Regina, would you please…" Ms. Wilcox said, trying to get a better understanding of her son's life.

"Mama, this needs to stay between us," Rome stated.

"Rome, Rock is dead now. Who is it going to hurt besides those children?" Regina asked. "You are just as guilty as Rock. It's a blessing to have grandparents and to know your grandparents…and you and Rock have taken that away from those children."

Rome remained quiet again, wondering why it was such a big deal for them to suddenly find out that Rock had children and ex-wives. Rock had been supplying their mother's with money to support them. Ms. Wilcox had so many questions, but Rome's answers weren't adding up.

After hearing about Rock's secretive life, it made it harder for Rock's mother to shed a tear, even while watching as they put his body into the ground. On the way to the limo, a man walked over and asked if he could speak with her.

Ms. Wilcox noticed that the tall, dark-haired man was highly tanned and spoke with a slight accent. He wore an exquisite Italian, pin-striped suit, accessorized with dark shades, platinum diamond-cut pinky rings, and expensive cuff links. He carried a stainless steel briefcase and wore very expensive cologne. She knew he was either a businessman or a mobster.

"Good evening ma'am. I am very sorry for your loss. My name is Antonio Delgoduez. I am an accountant for many Swiss banks. Your son was a very big client of mine. He left you as the beneficiary on all of his accounts. May we talk at your home?"

Rome was skeptical of letting this unfamiliar man come to his mother's house. Antonio's maroon and chrome Mercedes limo followed the family's limo to Ms. Wilcox's house. Rome made sure he didn't leave his mother's side.

Ms. Wilcox sat down at the kitchen table with Antonio. Rome and Regina didn't sit, but stood by the table. They wanted to make sure he didn't have any weapons in his briefcase before they sat down.

"Ms. Wilcox, your son has left you a very wealthy woman."

Antonio first showed Ms. Wilcox two mutual funds for Regina and Rome for five hundred thousand dollars apiece. He'd left several stocks and bonds, equaling over $3 million dollars. The last few mutual funds combined totaled to be $5.5 million dollars.

She was unsure of what she was going to do with all of that money. Regina's mouth fell wide open. She never knew her brother was smart enough to invest. She couldn't believe how much money Rock made off of investments alone. Regina was ready to help her mother spend some of the money, even before she received it.

Trey and Tony went to Rock's estate to clean the vault and divide the earned money between themselves, Rick and Rome. They counted the money and split it in half. They planned to give Veronica half and split their halves with the other guys.

"I don't want Veronica to think we're trying to pay her off just to make us look good," Tony said.

"Just look at as a life insurance plan," Trey replied.

They placed five hundred thousand dollars in a woman's Gucci backpack that Ronnie had left over there, and took it Veronica's house. She was pleased to have some of Ronnie's personal belongings.

The purse was Ronnie's favorite color and still had the scent of her favorite perfume on it. Veronica clinched the purse and stared at the TV, emotionless. She sat on the sofa, silently crying and grieving for hours.

Later that evening, Ms. Wilcox went to the bank to set up the mutual fund accounts in her name. On her way home, she stopped over to Veronica's house. She still wasn't sure of what to say to the Williams family. She prayed that God would make this easier for her.

She knocked on the door, but didn't get an answer. As soon as she turned to walk away, Monie answered the door.

"Hi sweetie. I know your mother is probably not in the mood for any company, but I just wanted to give this to her," Ms. Wilcox said, handing Monie a manila envelope.

"I'll make sure she gets it," Monie replied, watching Ms. Wilcox as she climbed back into her Mercedes SUV.

Monie put the envelope on the coffee table next to where her mother sat.

The sun had gone down. Veronica remained in her same position on the sofa. Jerome sat in his recliner, directly across from Veronica, to keep an eye on her. She finally started to unzip the backpack to see what was inside. She pulled out an envelope and bundles of twenty, fifty and hundred dollar bills. She opened the envelope and found a short note that Trey had written to her.

Dear Veronica,

I am truly sorry for what happened. Although Rock and Ronnie had their fair share of ups and downs in their relationship, I never foreseen anything like this happening. This was some of the money that was left inside of Rock's vault. Tony and I know that no amount of money will ever replace Ronnie or the void that is left in your heart, but we thought you deserved this. Ronnie had full access to this money, but due to unfortunate circumstances, I strongly feel that it now belongs to you.

Your son-in-law,

Trey

Veronica folded the letter and placed it and the money back in the bag. "Trey and Tony left us five hundred thousand dollars," Veronica said to Jerome.

"Damn. Those boys really had some money. I wish they would've given it to us while Ronnie was still alive," Jerome thought.

Veronica grabbed the envelope that Ms. Wilcox had left for her. She found that Ms. Wilcox had given her 2.5 million dollars. Veronica eyes bulged almost out of the sockets. Veronica gave the envelope to Jerome to make sure her vision wasn't playing tricks on her.

"Two point five million dollars!" Jerome shouted. "Baby..." Jerome was speechless. He got on his knees in front of the sofa and wrapped his arms around Veronica's waist. "This money is great, but no dollar amount is worth Ronnie's life," Jerome stated.

He finally convinced Veronica to go upstairs with him and get in the bed. He held her close, assuring her that they would make it through this ordeal. He gently stroked her hair and allowed her to cry herself to sleep peacefully.

Rick's cell phone rang. He answered, "Hello...hello?" There was complete silence.

"Hello...hello?" Rick asked again. The caller hung up, and he then heard a dial tone. The caller ID showed private caller.

The End

About the Author

Sha Rhonda Dukes is a New Jersey native. She acquired a love for Greek Mythology and creative writing during her high school years. She moved to Atlanta, Georgia in 1994, with the intent to eventually become an entertainer.

After going through a handful of failed relationships, she decided to use them as learning experiences. She would later take some of her own personal experiences along with some from her siblings and friends to turn them into a story.

After holding on to a vision for nearly ten years, Sha Rhonda suddenly became adamant about sharing her vision with the world. She asked herself how she would make it all come about. She had no connections or mentors to learn what it took to be a successful writer. After hearing that one of her childhood friends released a CD, it only inspired her even more to make it all come together.

She is deeply inspired by the awesome works of Tyler Perry. Kimberla Lawson Roby, Terri McMillan, Omar Tyree, Michael Baisden and Yolanda Rabb are a few of her favorite authors.